Praise for

holly hepburn

'Like a ray of sunshine on a cloudy day, this sparkling story
will sweep you away and leave your heart full of love'
CATHY BRAMLEY

'Irresistible love stories in gorgeous locations with
characters that feel like friends. A Holly Hepburn novel is a
heartwarming treat!'
MIRANDA DICKINSON

'Losing yourself in a Holly Hepburn book is one of life's
pleasures – they're the perfect escape'
MILLY JOHNSON

'Wholly satisfying reads – a warm glow is guaranteed
when you snuggle up with a HH book!'
HEIDI SWAIN

'Warm, witty and utterly charming . . . It left me with the
most wonderful happy glow'
CALLY TAYLOR

'A super sparkling star of a story'
ALEXANDRA BROWN

Holly Hepburn is the author of eight novels including *The Little Shop of Hidden Treasures*, *Coming Home to Brightwater Bay*, and *A Year at the Star and Sixpence*. Follow her on twitter at @HollyH_Author.

Also by Holly Hepburn

A Year at the Star and Sixpence
The Picture House by the Sea
A Year at Castle Court
Last Orders at the Star and Sixpence
Coming Home to Brightwater Bay
The Little Shop of Hidden Treasures
Escape to Darling Cove

holly hepburn

Return to Half Moon Farm

SIMON &
SCHUSTER

London · New York · Sydney · Toronto · New Delhi

First published in Great Britain by Simon & Schuster UK Ltd, 2024

1 3 5 7 9 10 8 6 4 2

Simon & Schuster UK Ltd
1st Floor
222 Gray's Inn Road
London WC1X 8HB

Simon & Schuster: Celebrating 100 Years of Publishing in 2024
Simon & Schuster
Australia,
Sydney
Simon & Schuster India,
New Delhi

www.simonandschuster.co.uk
www.simonandschuster.com.au
www.simonandschuster.co.in

A CIP catalogue record for this book is available from the British Library

Paperback ISBN: 978-1-3985-1198-9
eBook ISBN: 978-1-3985-1199-6
Audio ISBN: 978-1-3985-2508-5

Typeset in Bembo by Palimpsest Book Production Ltd, Falkirk, Stirlingshire
Printed and Bound in the UK using 100% Renewable Electricity at
CPI Group (UK) Ltd

MIX
Paper | Supporting
responsible forestry
FSC® C171272

To my Great Aunt Nancy, whose letters inspired this story.
And to Auntie Pauline, who saved them for me.

Part One

Spring Fever

Chapter One

'Are we nearly there yet?'

It was a question Daisy Moon had heard approximately every twenty minutes of the three-hour journey from Milton Keynes and she was sure she'd hear it at least once more before they reached their destination. Drawing on her dwindling supply of patience, she glanced in the rear-view mirror to meet the bored expression of her youngest son, Finn, and did her best to smile. 'Really not long now.'

A groan of impatience issued from the other side of the back seat. 'If you bothered to read the road signs, you wouldn't have to ask,' his brother, Campbell, pointed out, peering over the top of his glasses as though he was a white-haired professor rather than a ten-year-old. 'Look, that one says "Mistlethorpe – one mile". Big clue, don't you think?'

Finn rolled his eyes. 'But we're not going to Mistlethorpe. We're going to Half Moon Farm and who knows how far that is away?' He screwed his freckled face up in a mocking grin. 'Haven't seen any signs for that, have you, Big Brain?'

The conversation descended into good-natured bickering, as it usually did. Daisy returned her gaze to the road and wondered, not for the first time, how she'd managed to give birth to twins who were absolute polar opposites. Finn was a rough-and-tumble, sport-loving, permanently grubby child – his blond hair never sat flat against his head, his blue eyes rarely stayed focused on one thing for long and his clothes spontaneously developed holes, particularly on the knees. Campbell, by contrast, seemed to have been born middle-aged, despite only being six minutes older; his hair was meticulously combed against his skull, his blue-eyed gaze missed nothing behind the glasses he wore to correct a slight astigmatism and he would not be caught dead playing any kind of sport, not even on a games console. Reading was his passion, along with a somewhat intense fascination with all things historical, and he was often to be found with his nose between the pages of anything from an encyclopaedia to a rip-roaring steampunk adventure. Daisy was surprised he'd even spotted the sign for Mistlethorpe village – she'd barely seen him look up from the book nestled on his lap. But she'd been concentrating on the twisting, too-narrow country roads that were a world away from the sensible grid system of Milton Keynes, while simultaneously grappling with an odd sense of unreality at finding herself travelling along them after almost twenty years away. Then again, Campbell had been curious and excited about their new home from the moment she'd broken the news about the move so she should have known he'd be paying keen attention now they were near. Finn's reaction had been, and continued to be, noticeably less enthusiastic, which hadn't soothed Daisy's guilt. Both boys' lives were being uprooted but Finn was definitely losing the most and it didn't help one bit that she'd had no real choice. She could only hope he would come round once they arrived at Half Moon Farm, and fall in love with it the way she had all those years ago.

The sign welcoming them to Mistlethorpe appeared a few minutes later, dealing Daisy another jolt of incongruity. It was the oddest feeling – so much time had passed since she'd last seen that sign and yet it somehow felt as though she'd never been away. Her memory conjured up an image of the village green, the grass a yellow-brown carpet dotted by oak and horse chestnut trees, the church steeple poking above their lush green canopy at one end, reaching for the occasional cotton wool puff in an otherwise cloudless blue sky. A heat haze shimmered, blurring the shops that lined the high street and scorching the soil so that the scent of burnt earth hung pungent in the still, heavy air. Nothing moved save a broad-winged bird wheeling high above. And then a sudden spatter of raindrops hit the car windscreen, causing Daisy to blink as she steered into the long bend that hid the village from view. It would probably all be different now, she thought – apart from anything else, it was April, not August, and spring would undoubtedly bring a different vibe, even if the fabric of the village hadn't changed much. It was a funny trick of nostalgia that she only remembered sunshine and heat during those endless summer holidays. There must have been rainy days, times when she'd been cooped up in the farmhouse with a jigsaw puzzle or a book, but she couldn't recall them.

A plaintive meow issued from the basket on the passenger seat as a furry, marmalade paw batted at the wire door. 'Not long, Atticus,' Daisy soothed. 'Just another mile or so.'

He'd coped with the journey well, barely uttering a sound, and she assumed he'd slept for most of it. What he'd make of their new home was anyone's guess – the rolling fields and ancient hedgerows were a far cry from the neatness of his Milton Keynes domain but she felt a glum certainty he was going to embrace his inner wildcat. There wasn't much she could do about that either, apart from hope the birds and animals of Half Moon Farm were ready for their new feline overlord.

At last the car rounded the bend and Mistlethorpe bloomed before Daisy's tired eyes. It looked exactly as she remembered – the humped bridge rising to cross the River Mistle as it meandered through the village, the fork in the road where it split around the triangular green, the little row of shops dominated by the red-bricked elegance of the Dragon Inn and peeking above all that, at the furthest end of Mistle Lane, was the water mill and its gigantic wheel, perched somewhat precariously on top of its own sturdy stone bridge. Daisy felt something shift within her as she slowed the car to absorb the view, a settling in her bones that radiated a gentle warmth to every other part of her, a sense of gladness that she was here again. Some things were new: the clusters of daffodils that dotted the green, plus the bright and cheerful bunting zigzagging between the lamp posts over the lane. There were few people out and even fewer cars – hardly a surprise given it was late afternoon on a rainy Easter Monday – but the essence of the place seemed unchanged. A glance in the mirror revealed Campbell and Finn gazing around like meerkats, taking in their surroundings with undisguised curiosity.

'Holy Messi and Ronaldo, is that an actual castle?' Finn was craning his neck to the left, peering almost behind them to where the unmistakeable grey turrets of Winterbourne Castle rose above the treeline.

'It is,' Daisy said, smiling. 'It's mentioned in the Domesday Book, no less, although I think the current buildings only date back to the fourteenth century.'

'I told you there was a castle,' Campbell said, sounding simultaneously resigned and aggrieved. 'Don't you remember?'

Finn snorted. 'No. Does it have a moat and a portcullis?' His face lit up. 'Does it have those holes in the ceiling so soldiers could pour boiling oil on the heads of invaders?'

Daisy shook her head. Trust Finn to absorb only the most gruesome details from *Horrible Histories*. 'Probably,' she said. 'It used to be open to the public so maybe we can go and take a look round, once we've settled in a bit.'

Their instant, enthusiastic nods reminded Daisy, just for a

moment, that they were not always chalk and cheese. Perhaps it was something they could do before starting their new school after the Easter break was over, a way to ease them into village life, although a lot depended on what Daisy found at Half Moon Farm. Until she could gauge the extent of her mother's ill health it was probably best not to make promises she couldn't keep.

'The village shops are over there,' she said, waving a hand towards the terraced row of red-bricked buildings that lined the high street. 'There's a butcher, a baker—'

'A *Match Attax* trader?' Finn suggested hopefully, referring to his never-ending obsession with the thin packets of football cards that drained his pocket money each week.

'You'll have to wait and see,' Daisy replied, privately thinking it wouldn't be the worst thing in the world if he saved his pocket money rather than splurged it. 'But I'm sure they'll sell them in Canterbury if not here.'

Campbell's attention had been caught by the large wooden wheel of the mill, which was beginning to loom as they progressed through the village. 'Look at that monster,' he breathed, eyes widening again. 'Does it still work?'

'As far as I know,' Daisy replied. 'The mill produces organic flour so I assume they still use the river to power the wheel and grind the wheat.'

'It probably runs on electricity now,' Campbell said, pushing his glasses up his nose. 'Or maybe a combination of hydro power and electric for maximum efficiency.'

Beside him, Finn yawned. 'You are such a nerd. Who cares

how they make the stupid flour? What I want to know is whether we can swim in the river – can we, Mum? Please say yes.'

Daisy pictured the crystal-clear water of the River Mistle as it babbled beneath bridges and meandered alongside the high road. It twisted through the woodland to the south of the farm and she remembered chasing iridescent dragonflies through the shallows, her sandals crunching on the gravel bed as she splashed around. Had the water really been as pristine as she remembered or was that recollection rose-tinted too? 'It's not really deep enough, I'm afraid,' she told Finn, who slumped back into the seat. 'We'll have to find a pool instead.'

Campbell was still transfixed by the water wheel and its adjoining mill. He leaned into his brother to get a better view. 'Stay over your side,' Finn grumbled.

'But I can't see properly from there,' Campbell shot back.

Finn scowled. 'It's just a stupid old mill, on a stupid old bridge.'

'The only stupid thing I can see right now is *you*!'

'Boys,' Daisy cut in, a warning note in her voice.

'It's *him*,' Finn protested, sounding injured. 'Why is he so obsessed with old buildings, anyway? They're boring.'

Campbell launched into a spirited defence and Daisy ran a weary hand across her face. The journey had been less fraught with arguments than it could have been and she supposed it was only natural for them to be growing restless. 'Look, here's Thieves Lane,' she said, hitting the indicator and turning down the single-track road that led to Half Moon Farm. 'We're almost there.'

Now that there was less than a mile to go, Daisy turned her thoughts to the farm itself and she felt a tiny flutter of anxiety stir in her stomach as she considered what she might find. Would it still exude the quaint, old-world charm her grandparents had worked so hard to preserve? Daisy's mother hadn't necessarily shared their passion for the hop farm's heritage and history – she'd run away to Brighton at the age of sixteen, after all – but surely she wouldn't have made sweeping changes once it became her own. And then Daisy felt a frown crease her forehead, because there had been a bigger influence in Rose Moon's life than the wishes of her late parents. Daisy's stepfather was a cold man with no sentimental attachment to anything, let alone the place she'd held closest to her heart for years. He'd caused catastrophic damage to his wife's relationship with her only daughter and who knew what harm he might have wrought elsewhere? And while Daisy drew the line at wishing anyone dead, she was nevertheless relieved he was gone. She would not be returning to Half Moon Farm otherwise.

Behind her, the twins had stopped squabbling and adopted an expectant silence. Putting her worries firmly to one side, Daisy slowed the car as they approached the double gates at the entrance of the farm. 'Here we are,' she said, turning the steering wheel slowly to the left. 'Our new home.'

For a heartbeat, Daisy was nine years old again. Her gaze swept across the cobbled courtyard with its ancient wishing well to the comforting sight of the rectangular, two storey oast house that had been the very core of the farm for hundreds of years. Green boughs of wisteria crept around the closed oak door, heavy with unopened buds that would soon burst into lilac glory. At one end of the building sat two circular roundels, home to the kilns that dried the freshly harvested hops. Their red-tiled, conical roofs and white tipped cowls tilted gently in opposite directions as though drunk.

Other buildings were dotted around the yard, forming a horseshoe shape. Most had simply been barns for storage, as far as Daisy remembered, but one or two had been leased by locals and she could see now that all of them had signs advertising the businesses inside. It seemed as though Half Moon Farm was home to more than just hops these days. She was looking forward to finding out more about her new and unexpected neighbours.

'Is that where we're going to live?' Campbell asked and Daisy glanced back to see his saucer-like gaze was fixed on the rounded towers of the oast house.

'No, we're going to live with Granny in the farmhouse,' she said, and pointed to the gated road that wound to the left between the oast house and one of the barns. 'It's just through there.'

Finn was more interested in the signs attached to the barns, however. 'What's *Waggy Mammas*?' he asked, frowning. 'A restaurant?'

Daisy eyed the image of two stylized dogs leaping at each

other around the business name. 'I don't think so,' she replied. 'Maybe it's a grooming salon?'

'Brilliant,' Finn said, grinning. 'You know how Atticus feels about dogs.'

She swallowed a groan. It was fair to say the cat had enjoyed a certain reputation in their old neighbourhood, ever since he'd faced down a husky three times his size, but Daisy had always maintained he was a big softie beneath the snarl and swagger. That belief could be put to the test with a steady stream of pampered pooches on his patch.

Campbell was looking around too. '*Darling Buds* probably sells plants and *Dottie's Pots* must be plates and stuff.'

Both were good guesses, Daisy thought, although the names were big clues. 'And *Brew Crew*?' she asked.

'Beer!' Finn announced triumphantly.

'Might not be,' Campbell argued, although Daisy didn't feel his heart was really in it. 'Could be posh tea bags or . . . or . . .'

His brother gave him a pitying look as he trailed off, then fixed his gaze on the last building, which was the only one that looked as though it hadn't been open for a while. 'What's *Merry Mistletoe*?'

'I have no idea,' Daisy said, pursing her lips in puzzlement. 'Maybe it's a Christmas shop – decorations and things.'

Neither twin looked especially impressed by that prospect. 'Boring stuff, in other words,' Finn huffed and, for once, Campbell didn't disagree.

'Can we go and see the farmhouse?' he asked.

Daisy let the question hang for a moment. Now that the time had come, she was aware of a definite tug of reluctance in the pit of her stomach. It wasn't the house itself that was the problem – she could hardly wait to stand on the door-step and breathe in the familiar scent that had always soothed her spirits and assured her she'd arrived. But there would be no all-enveloping embrace from her grandmother to welcome her this time, no affectionate ruffle of her hair from her grandfather. No overenthusiastic slobbering from their Border Collie, Mitch. There would only be her mother, frail and in need of care, and the ghosts of holidays past.

'Mum?' Finn said, in an uncharacteristically subdued tone. 'Are you okay?'

Squaring her shoulders, Daisy aimed a reassuring smile into the rear-view mirror. 'I'm absolutely fine. Come on, let's go and find your grandmother.'

Chapter Two

The front door of the farmhouse remained shut as the car crunched slowly over the damp gravel to stop beside the woodshed. In years gone by the heavy wooden door would have been open long before the car ground to a halt and Daisy would have been tearing across the gravel the very second the handbrake had been applied. But this was now, Daisy reminded herself yet again, and switched the engine off.

'Now remember, Granny has been very ill,' she said, turning to address the boys in her most no-nonsense voice. 'That means you'll need to be quiet and considerate – no squabbling with each other, no thundering up and down the stairs and definitely no football in the house.'

This last instruction was aimed at Finn, who scowled. 'No fun, basically.'

Daisy hesitated, reminded all over again just how much she was asking of them. They'd never met their grandmother, had been born long after the rift between Daisy and her mother had widened into a yawning chasm, and yet her sudden heart attack meant they'd been unceremoniously uprooted and moved to a farm in the middle of nowhere. And while they were good kids, there was also no escaping the fact that they were ten years old, with all the natural exuberance that came with the age. Telling them to curb their behaviour could only pile an extra layer of resentment to this new life they hadn't wanted.

'There'll be plenty of fun, I promise,' she reassured them. 'But we need to settle in first. And that means being respectful of Granny and the house, okay?'

Campbell nodded but Finn simply glared in mutinous silence. 'Okay?' Daisy repeated, holding his baleful gaze until he looked away.

'Okay,' he muttered.

'Good,' she said and gave them an encouraging nod. 'Let's go and say hello. We can leave the unpacking until later.'

It wasn't until Daisy was out of the car that she surveyed the farmhouse with her full attention. The door still hadn't opened but that wasn't a surprise – her mother had a temporary live-in carer but they were hardly likely to throw open the door for every car that pulled into the yard. The doorway was framed by the roses her grandmother had lovingly tended for so many years. They were not tended now, Daisy noticed with a frown – the thin stems were woody and untamed, scrambling over one another on the trellis and beyond with feral haste, and there were only a handful of dead blooms drooping among the sparse greenery. Daisy wasn't much of a gardener but she knew from her neighbours' efforts that April was usually a good month for roses. It didn't appear to be the case here. Her eyes slid sideways, travelling over the red brickwork to the ground floor windows, which were grimy and unwashed. One pane – the pantry window if she remembered rightly – had a long crack from top to bottom. But upstairs had fared worse; several panes were cracked across different rooms and one window seemed to be entirely broken, with ugly jagged spikes picked out against a background of pale chipboard. Daisy felt her mouth gape as her apprehensive gaze took in the rest of the house – everywhere she looked she saw signs of neglect. And then she noticed the roof and let out an audible gasp. At the furthest end of the building, above what had been her grandmother's sewing room, there was a metre-wide abyss spoiling the neat red tiles.

Campbell had spotted it too. 'Is there meant to be a big hole in the roof?'

For a moment, Daisy couldn't speak, the lump in her throat was too solid. She shook her head and swallowed in an attempt to dislodge it. 'No.'

Finn let out an unimpressed snort as he kicked at a cluster of weeds beside his foot. 'I thought you said it was a nice house. Doesn't look great to me.'

'Let's just get inside,' Daisy said, struggling to take in the extent of the neglect. 'I'm sure your grandmother has some squash and biscuits waiting.'

Having seen the state of the building, she expected no such thing but crunched across the gravel with grim determination. The great iron doorknocker still worked, at least, although rust dribbled beneath it. Trying to ignore the peeling paintwork, Daisy brought the metal ring down in three sharp raps.

There was a momentary silence, filled only by the cawing of crows overhead, then a faint rustling on the other side of the door. Daisy put an arm around each of the boys and waited. Anxiety fluttered in her stomach. Broken windows, weeds running riot and a hole in the roof . . . How bad was the inside going to be?

The woman who opened the door was rosy-cheeked and cheerful. Her blue eyes crinkled at the edges as she peered out and a beaming smile split her face. 'Well, now, no need to ask who you are – you're the spitting image of your mum.'

Resisting the urge to smooth her frizzy hair, Daisy forced her shoulders to relax and did her best to return the other woman's smile. 'Hello. You must be Emily.'

The woman clasped her plump hands together as she surveyed them. 'I am. It's so nice to meet you after all the chats we've shared. I feel like I know you already.'

There had been a flurry of communication between Daisy and Emily over the past week. Her mother's discharge from hospital had come at the worst possible time, when Finn and Campbell's father was away on a business trip. Faced with being pulled in two opposing directions, Daisy had found a private care company based in Canterbury to provide twenty-four-hour support until she could be there herself. During the day, care was provided by Emily, and overnight by Magda – both carers seemed excellent but Daisy had communicated most with Emily, who had tried to dispel Daisy's inevitable guilt from the outset. 'Better to get help rather than try to do it all and wear yourself into a frazzle,' she'd said with a warm practicality that had helped enormously. 'Knowing your mum is being properly looked after must be a real load off your mind.'

And it had been, until the moment Daisy arrived at Half Moon Farm and saw the farmhouse. Now she knew that Emily and Magda had spent four days and three nights living in a building with a roof that was open to the elements and the realization made her cringe inside. What must they be thinking?

'It's nice to meet you too,' Daisy managed, hoping her cheeks weren't as flaming red as they felt. 'How's Mum been?'

'Not so bad today,' Emily replied. 'Magda reported a decent night and she managed a bowl of vegetable soup for lunch. But hark at me keeping you on the doorstep – come inside and see for yourself.'

Stepping backwards, she held the door wide. Daisy ushered the boys across the threshold and instinctively drew a deep breath through her nose. The hallway had always held the exotic scent of amber from the tiny muslin bags her grandmother hung among the coats on the dark wood rack to keep the moths away. Its rich warmth had mingled with the mouth-watering aroma of whatever had been baking in the kitchen and Daisy had subconsciously been expecting those scents to greet her once more. But all she smelled now was damp, with top notes of cabbage and onion. The old wooden coat rack was still there, its elegantly carved hooks now empty apart from two coats Daisy assumed belonged to her mother and Emily, but the red cushioned bench underneath the hooks had faded to a dusty pink, threadbare in places and smudged with old mud. A bare lightbulb dangled from the ceiling, revealing a colony of dust bunnies along the skirting board and making the general shabbiness impossible to miss.

Finn stopped dead at the frayed rug bunched on the stone floor and Daisy knew without seeing his face that his nose was wrinkled in disgust. 'Keep going,' she said, nudging him gently. 'We can't shut the door if you stay there.'

Muttering, he did as he was told and there was a muffled thud as Emily swung the door closed. 'Your granny is in the living room,' she said cheerily. 'I bet you can't wait to see her.'

Neither boy moved, reminding Daisy that Emily had no idea this was their first visit to Half Moon Farm, let alone the first time they'd met their grandmother. She squeezed between them. 'Why don't you follow me?'

She led them along the hallway, past the heavy oak door on the left and around the corner to the right. The air was chilly, prompting Daisy to wonder why the heating wasn't on. It might be April but the temperature had yet to reach much above 15 degrees and old stone buildings clung onto the cold of winter. There were fireplaces in the main rooms but she also remembered radiators and a vast boiler in the kitchen that whomped noisily into life whenever the hot tap was turned on. Surely that must have been replaced by now; it had been ancient even when she'd last visited.

The living room door was closed but the garbled sound of the television leached through it. For a heartbeat Daisy hesitated with her hand resting on the handle. Then, aware of the two boys waiting behind her, she pushed open the door. Immediately, she was engulfed by a wave of warmth; clearly the heating was working in this room, she thought as beads of sweat bloomed instantly on her forehead. Rose Moon sat in an armchair facing the television, wrapped in a crocheted patchwork blanket with an electric heater glowing orange beside her. An open puzzle book lay on her lap and Daisy was reassured to see she looked alert, if a long way from the picture of seventy-something health. Squaring her shoulders, she stepped into the room. 'Hello, Mum.'

'Oh, it is you. I thought it must be.'

She smiled but her voice was breathy, as though the effort of speaking cost her, and Daisy noticed the pallor of her complexion in spite of the warmth. Her grey bob was clean but lay limply against her scalp and she looked exhausted, which was hardly unexpected in someone recovering from heart surgery. And yet in spite of that, her appearance was a hundred times better than the last time Daisy had seen her.

Moving to one side, she encouraged the twins to come forward. 'Here's Finn, and Campbell. Say hello, boys.'

They did as she asked and Daisy was relieved to hear the politeness of their tones even if their voices were subdued. She knew their inquisitive gazes would have travelled the room, taking in the faded floral sofa and armchairs, the cold and unlit fireplace, the dusty, cluttered shelves and the unspeakably small television screen. Inevitably, they would be comparing it to the modern but cosy home they had left behind in Milton Keynes; Finn's expression looked particularly reproachful.

'You do right to keep your distance,' Emily said, obviously noticing neither boy had rushed towards Rose. 'Your grand-mother is susceptible to coughs and colds at the moment. There'll be plenty of time for cuddles once she's feeling better.'

Daisy kept her expression neutral. She couldn't remember the last time she'd hugged her mother. Even before the rift, they hadn't had the kind of relationship that encouraged physical contact. It hadn't always been that way, Daisy acknowledged, but even if Rose had been in perfect health now, hugs would not be on the menu.

'How are you feeling?' she asked, as much to cover the awkwardness as anything but her mother didn't seem to notice.

'Oh, not bad. I have my ups and downs but Emily has been wonderful.' Rose managed another wan smile. 'She's looked after me like I was her own mother.'

Daisy felt her cheeks flush. It was almost certainly a dig

and once again, she cringed at what Emily must be thinking but the carer simply beamed. 'All part of the service,' she said with the kind of smoothness that suggested she was well used to papering over family cracks. 'But you must be parched after that long journey. How about a nice cup of tea?'

'Lovely,' Daisy said fervently, because she had been fantasising about exactly that for at least thirty miles. 'I'll give you a hand.'

Emily waved the offer away. 'No need, I can manage. Sit yourselves down and have a natter.'

But the idea of sitting in the too-warm living room, making small talk as the TV flickered in the background, suddenly made Daisy feel claustrophobic and she longed for the spacious kitchen that had always been the heart of the house. 'Plenty of time to chat,' she said, hoping her eagerness to escape wasn't as obvious as it felt. 'I need to show the boys where the loo is, anyway. We could all do with freshening up.'

Rose gave a weary nod even as her gaze slid back to the television. 'She tires easily,' Emily confided over one shoulder as they made their way along the corridor towards the kitchen. 'You'll learn to recognize the signs but best to give her plenty of opportunities to rest.'

Daisy nodded gratefully. Now that she was here, the enormity of the task ahead was beginning to settle on her shoulders and she was glad she would have both Emily and Magda to support her, if only for a few days, as she and the boys adjusted to this new life. 'Thanks,' she said.

Emily smiled. 'Gives you a chance to catch your breath too,' she said, as though once again reading Daisy's mind. 'Now, why don't you pop to the loo and I'll get the kettle on.'

The downstairs toilet was by the back door and it was predictably chilly, although Daisy remembered it had always been cold, even in summer. She left Finn and Campbell bickering over who would go in first, with strict instructions not to go exploring afterwards, and made her way back to the kitchen, where Emily was bustling round laying a tea tray. Daisy paused in the doorway, taking in the old-fashioned pine cupboards, the solid Welsh dresser that lined the far wall, the ancient Aga and the heavy oak table in the centre of the room. Very little had changed; if she closed her eyes, she could almost believe her grandmother had stepped outside for a moment.

'I expect it's a bit overwhelming, being back here in these circumstances,' Emily said, without looking up. 'There's a lot to get your head around.'

A jumble of images flashed through Daisy's mind – the broken windows, the damaged roof, the cluttered and over-heated living room. The carer was right – there was a lot for Daisy to get to grips with and that was before she got down to the task of caring for her mother. Embarrassment crawled over her as she watched Emily warm the pot. 'I certainly wasn't expecting to find a hole in the roof,' she admitted, moving from the doorway and making for the larder in one corner. 'Or several smashed windows.'

The other woman shook her head. 'I've seen worse, believe

me. But Rose was embarrassed too – she said the roofer was waiting for dry weather and then she fell ill. You can't see it from the ground but it's all sealed off, although some rain did get in before the temporary repair could be made.'

'And the windows?' Daisy couldn't help asking, even though it wasn't in Emily's job description to know anything about the state of the building.

'I'd say they've been broken for a while,' Emily said. 'But at least they're boarded up. Someone's been helping out.'

Once again, Daisy prickled with guilt. She couldn't have known her mother was struggling with the upkeep of the house but she might have suspected. Her gaze roved the larder's wooden shelves without really taking in their contents as unease joined forces with guilt. What else was she going to discover over the coming days? 'I owe them, whoever it was,' she said, squaring her shoulders. 'I'll investigate once we're settled.'

Silence reigned for a moment, broken only by the bubbling of the kettle and the chink of cups and glasses being added to the tea tray. There was even cake – a sumptuous looking homemade lemon drizzle loaf that Daisy knew her boys would wolf down given half the chance. And then the door swung back and Finn poked his head into the kitchen, Campbell hovering at his shoulder. 'Mum, the match starts soon and the laptop is in the car,' Finn said. 'Can we go and get it?'

Daisy glanced at her watch, surprised to see it was after five o'clock. For a moment she was torn, wondering whether it was rude to allow Finn to watch football when they hadn't long arrived. But at least it would stop him commenting on the state of the house. She nodded. 'Go on, then. The key's in my coat pocket.'

Flashing her a grin, he wheeled around and vanished, Campbell hot on his heels. She'd warned both boys that there was no satellite dish at the farmhouse; the only way for Finn to keep up with the football and for Campbell to watch his beloved History channel would be through their laptops. The news had been met with grumbles but they accepted the compromise with surprisingly good grace.

'I don't suppose you know where the router is, do you?' she asked Emily as they made their way back to the living room with the laden tea tray.

The other woman nodded. 'It's in the living room. I haven't needed it much myself but Magda likes a bit of Netflix in the evenings. I think she's found the connection a bit unreliable.'

Daisy felt a quiver of foreboding and pushed it away. Perhaps it was Magda's device that was unreliable rather than the Wi-Fi. She could only hope.

Rose was sitting where they had left her, eyes closed and head resting against the back of her chair. Her chest rose and fell in shallow but even breaths. She looked peaceful in her slumber and, by unspoken agreement, Daisy and Emily moved carefully to avoid waking her. But the peace was broken moments later by the thunder of approaching feet. The door burst open and the boys bundled enthusiastically into the room. Before she could admonish her sons, Daisy saw her mother's eyelids fly open as one hand clutched at her chest. 'Oh!'

'It's okay, Mum,' Daisy said, watching her fluttering expression with some alarm. 'It's only Campbell and Finn.'

To their credit, both boys stopped. They fired chastened looks first at Daisy, then at their grandmother. 'Sorry,' Campbell mumbled and nudged Finn, who nodded.

Emily bustled over to Rose, giving her a practised once over. 'No harm done,' she said cheerfully. 'Now, who wants a slice of cake?'

Campbell's eyes lit up but Finn waggled his laptop. 'What's the Wi-Fi code?' he asked. 'Need to get this bad boy online.'

'In a minute, Finn,' Daisy replied. 'Did either of you check on Atticus? How is he?'

Campbell pulled a face. 'Loud,' he said. 'I don't think he's happy at being stuck in the car.'

Emily looked up from the tea she was pouring. 'Atticus? Who's that?'

'Our cat,' Campbell explained. 'He's enormously ginger.'

The carer's face formed an 'o' of understanding. 'That's going to make life interesting at Waggy Mamma's. I hope he likes dogs.'

'I wouldn't say he likes them,' Daisy said, grimacing. 'What is Waggy Mamma's? We guessed it might be a dog grooming salon.'

Emily shook her head. 'Not quite — it's doggy day care,' she said then caught Finn's puzzled look. 'Like a nursery but for dogs – they come and spend the day here when their owners have to work or need a break.'

Both Finn and Campbell looked interested, as though they had a hundred questions to ask, but Daisy's heart sank. A doggy day care right on their doorstep could be a problem if Atticus decided to assert himself. It wouldn't be an immediate issue – she planned to keep the cat indoors for a week or so to make sure he understood the farmhouse was home – but she could easily envision difficulties ahead. She'd have to go and speak to the owner, pre-empt the inevitable complaints about feline intimidation.

'Doggy day care,' Finn repeated. 'I wonder if they do painting and stuff, like we used to.'

Campbell sniffed dismissively. 'Don't be stupid, they can't hold paintbrushes. It'll be all agility training and ball chasing.' He grinned. 'Maybe they've got a football team – Mistlethorpe Rovers.'

His brother groaned but Rose shifted in her armchair. 'I like cats,' she said wistfully. 'They're so much cuddlier than dogs.'

There was a brief pause as Daisy considered the mass of fur, claws and sheer bloody-minded swagger that occupied the cat basket in the car. Opposite her, Campbell raised his eyebrows; cuddly was not a word strangers usually associated with Atticus, although he was a big softy at heart.

'Never mind Atticus or doggy day care,' Finn put in impatiently. 'What's the Wi-Fi password? It's nearly time for kick off.'

With an indulgent smile, Emily stopped what she was doing and navigated her way to a cluttered bookshelf in one corner. 'Here,' she said, handing a small rectangle of plastic to Finn. 'You'll find everything you need on this.'

'Thanks.' He took it eagerly and immediately began tapping at the computer, with Campbell supervising over his shoulder.

'Thank you,' Daisy said, grateful all over again for Emily's no-nonsense pragmatism. She reached for a cup and saucer. 'How would you like your tea, Mum?'

For a few minutes, calmness reigned. The boys retreated to the corner of one sofa, muttering to each other as they peered at the computer screen. Daisy served the tea while Emily handed round slices of cake, which briefly distracted Campbell and Finn. The box-like TV continued to flicker, mostly unwatched. And then there was an exclamation of disgust from the sofa, and Finn pushed the laptop away to glare at Daisy. 'It's not working properly. It keeps freezing.'

Daisy reached for the laptop and got a confused impression of a red and white blur on a green background. Then the pixelated image cleared and she saw the blobs were football players who jerked across the screen as though she was watching a stop-go animation. Fuzziness made their movements hard to pick out and she couldn't even see a ball. No wonder Finn was cross, she thought as she opened the laptop's settings panel. The game was unwatchable. The boys hovered at her shoulder, watching her efforts, but try as she might, Daisy couldn't do much to make the picture clearer. Eventually, she had to concede defeat. 'I'm sorry, Finn. I don't think the internet is fast enough to stream the match.'

His glare intensified. 'You said it would be okay. You said we'd be able to watch stuff on our laptops.'

Daisy glanced nervously at Rose, who was sipping her tea with her gaze fixed on the TV. 'I know. But we might need to look into updating the router and download speeds first.'

Finn pressed his lips together in mutiny and Campbell did not look happy either. 'Does this mean the PlayStation won't work either?'

'Not right now,' Daisy said, taking a deep breath. 'But I'll find out how to fix it as soon as I can.'

Emily clearly sensed an impending explosion, because she put her cup down and offered Daisy a brisk smile. 'Why don't you give the boys a tour of the house? I'll sit with Rose.'

It wasn't the worst idea Daisy had ever heard, although she thought perhaps in their current mood, showing the boys their room might be better than dragging them around the chilly house on a tour, where Finn would only point out every fixture and fitting that was a little tired or not quite working.

'Thank you, that sounds like a good idea,' she said. 'Come on, you two. Let's go and find your room.'

To his credit, Finn held it together until she had closed the door to the bedroom that would belong to the boys.

He stood in the centre of the room, taking in the flowery walls, the heavy floral bedspreads that covered the twin beds, and the worn but unmistakeably pink carpet. 'Now remember we can change the—' Daisy began but Finn rounded on her.

'I hate it here!' he shouted, his face suddenly a furious shade of red. 'You made us leave everything to come to this stupid, falling down house. Why couldn't we stay in Milton Keynes?' He sucked in a huge breath. 'Why couldn't we have gone to live with Dad?'

Daisy's heart thudded against her ribs as the accusations hit home. She'd known it would be hard to uproot the boys and bring them here but this was so much worse than she'd anticipated. 'Because his work means he can't look after you full time,' she said as steadily as she could. 'He couldn't be there to drop you off at school and collect you each day, or take you to training.'

'We could have gone to after school club,' Finn retorted. 'One of the other parents could have dropped me off at football.'

'And what happens when your dad has to work late?' she asked. 'Are the other boys' parents going to make sure you brush your teeth and put you into bed?'

Finn scowled. 'He wouldn't work late if he had us to look after.'

Daisy thought of all the times over the years that she'd had to cancel or change her plans because something had come up at Stuart's work, meaning he wouldn't be home to look after the boys. The flexibility of being an illustrator allowed Daisy to be there for the school run and sports clubs but somehow that had led Stuart to view her time as less important than his. Whether subconsciously or not, he'd assumed she would always drop everything to be there when he couldn't be and eventually it had been part of the reason their marriage had faltered. But she couldn't expect Finn to understand that, not when she and Stuart had done their utmost to shield the boys from the fallout of the divorce. There were times when Daisy wondered whether it was wise to remain friends with Stuart, whether their efforts to co-parent made it harder for their sons to accept that they were no longer together. This was one of those times.

She took a deep breath. 'I'm sorry this is so hard for you—'

'You're not!' Finn burst out and Daisy was horrified to see tears cascade down his rosy cheeks. 'You wanted to come here – it's your fault we've had to leave Dad and our friends and everything. I hate this place and I hate you!'

Whirling around he stormed out of the room, slamming the door so hard that dust shook loose from the wooden beams across the ceiling. Daisy stared after him in sickening disbelief, then turned her stricken gaze on Campbell. 'Is that how you feel too?'

His eyes didn't quite meet hers as he buried his hands in the pocket of his jumper. 'No. But I miss the internet and our old house. And Dad.'

Daisy pressed her lips together hard and fought the sudden

prickle of tears. The last few weeks had been a tornado – the unexpected call to say her mother had been rushed to hospital, the shock of seeing her so weak and the dawning realization that there was no one to care for her. No one but Daisy herself. She had to keep it together, she couldn't let Campbell see her cry. 'I know it's going to be hard not having Dad just around the corner but you'll still see him every other weekend, just like before. And this is a good house – when I was your age I wished more than anything that it was my home.' She let out a long sigh. 'Of course, it didn't have a hole in the roof then.'

'And the internet hadn't even been invented,' Campbell said. He got up and sat on the sagging sofa, wrapping his arms around her. 'Finn will be okay. He'll discover nature – find a tree to climb or a river to fall into – and then he'll like it here.'

Daisy tried not to shudder at the prospect of her devil-may-care son halfway up one of the towering oaks that lined the River Mistle. She hugged Campbell back, grateful for his efforts to comfort her. 'Thank you.'

'It's not like we have to put up with it forever, anyway,' Campbell went on, shrugging. 'Just a few months, you said, until Gran is better.'

That was the plan, Daisy thought, biting her lip. But now she'd seen the state of the farmhouse, she had the sinking feeling the three months she'd planned to stay wouldn't be enough. There was so much about the house that needed attention – the cracked and broken windows, the blocked fireplace, the horror of the gaping roof – all things that would take time and effort to put straight. She'd upended her whole life to come and nurse her mother back to health but from what Daisy had seen so far Half Moon Farm was in sore need of some TLC too and it broke her heart. Besides making it a fit place to live now, she owed it to her grand-parents to try her best and restore some of its former glory. That might just mean being away from Milton Keynes a little longer than she'd expected. But if that was the case, there was no help for it. She couldn't just walk away.

'No, it's not forever,' she said, offering Campbell a reas-suring smile even as she began to mentally compile a list of jobs to be done. 'And first thing tomorrow, I'm going to sort out the broadband and order some new bedding. We'll soon feel at home here.'

She injected as much confidence as she could into the words but they still sounded hollow and Daisy was filled with the sudden realization she was trying to convince herself as much as her son. However much she had loved being at Half Moon Farm in the past, it was a long way from feeling like home now. And the thought made her want to cry all over again.

Forcing back the unshed tears, she got to her feet. There was one job she couldn't postpone any longer, despite knowing it would subject her to an even more furious reaction than Finn's. 'Come on,' she said, swallowing a sigh. 'I suppose we'd better go and get Atticus.'

Chapter Three

When Daisy awoke the next morning, it took her several seconds to remember where she was. Dawn was filtering through the wooden slats at the window, etching stripes onto the white wall opposite in a way that stirred her memory even as her brain tried to make sense of them. Birds were singing outside, louder than usual, and the bedcovers felt wrong – heavy, weighing her down and making it hard to turn over against the hard mattress. The smell of the room was wrong too, slightly fusty but masked by the scent of dried flowers in a jar on the mantelpiece above the empty fireplace. None of it made sense, causing Daisy to wonder muzzily whether she was still asleep and dreaming. And then she blinked again and recollection flooded in. She was in her old room at Half Moon Farm.

A quick glance at her phone told Daisy it was just after 6.15. She sighed and stretched, pushing against the weight of the bedspread. At her feet, Atticus shifted to open a baleful eye. He'd made his displeasure at being cooped up in the car vocally known the night before, loudly yowling his unhappiness, and had only been more annoyed when Daisy had refused to let him explore the garden. He had prowled the kitchen, marmalade tail bristling with unbridled indignation and pausing only to stare meaningfully out of the window. She'd half-expected him to keep her awake but he'd settled on the bed with the kind of low rumbling growl that made her fear for her toes and been asleep a minute later. Daisy wished she could say the same of Finn, who had been every bit as miserable in their new surroundings; he'd taken much longer to settle into sleep but eventually exhaustion had got the better of his sullen resentment. She could only hope he would wake up in a better mood.

She found Magda in the kitchen, making tea for Rose. 'How did you sleep?' the younger woman asked, brushing her blonde fringe out of her eyes to smile at Daisy. 'I hope the owls didn't keep you awake.'

'Not at all,' Daisy said. 'Yesterday was a long day – I think I might have passed out before my head hit the pillow.'

Magda nodded sympathetically. 'Moving is always exhausting. But you'll be glad to know your mum had a good night. She's asked for a boiled egg for breakfast.'

Daisy checked the large wooden clock that hung on the whitewashed wall – almost seven o'clock. Finn and Campbell would be waking up soon and demanding breakfast of their own; she'd better find the Coco Pops. 'Shall I do Mum's egg?' she asked.

'Already done,' Magda said, gesturing at a covered tray on the kitchen table. 'We've got into a little routine over the past few days – I can fill you in once you're more settled.'

She exuded such a sense of quiet efficiency that Daisy thanked her lucky stars she'd ended up caring for Rose. Emily was different – older and more motherly, and perhaps a touch overbearing, although Daisy knew she was trying to help – but Magda had a calm assuredness that Daisy associated with medical nurses. She'd known Rose was in good hands long before she'd arrived but it was good to meet both carers, especially since they would be staying on for a few weeks to help Daisy look after her mother.

Atticus chose that moment to yowl loudly from his position beside Daisy's feet. Magda grinned. 'Looks like someone else wants breakfast.'

'Woe betide anyone who gets in the way of Atticus and his food bowl,' Daisy admitted with a sigh. 'Some cats are finicky eaters but this one definitely isn't.' She reached down to gather him into her arms. 'Luckily, he's also occasionally adorable. When he wants to be.'

'I'll leave you to it then,' Magda said, gathering up the tray. 'The kettle's just boiled if you fancy a cuppa.'

Once Atticus was fed, Daisy set about getting breakfast ready for the boys. She was somehow both surprised and not surprised to find some of the same crockery she remembered from her grandparents' day, although new items had been added to create a mishmash of patterns and styles. Once the table was laid she stood at the kitchen window, a mug of tea cradled between her hands, and gazed out at the unmown lawn leading to the privet hedge and jumble of the orchard beyond it. The trees reached up and out, thick with birds' nests and bushy with leaves that merged into their neighbours. At one time the orchard had been well-tended and thriving – she remembered the juiciest of apples bigger than her fists and sweet plums ripe with the taste of summer – but that had been when the farm was still producing food. She supposed it had been many years since anyone had gathered the fruit and trimmed the trees. Perhaps she should add it to her ever burgeoning to do list, although she was already beginning to feel overwhelmed by its size.

As though sensing her mood, Atticus leapt onto the work-surface beside the sink, nuzzling his ginger head against her with a purr so loud it vibrated a nearby cup. Daisy sank her fingers into his thick, soft fur and allowed the sensation to soothe her. Everything would get done in its own time, she told herself. All would be well.

There was a muffled clatter behind her and the sound of voices. Moments later, the kitchen door opened and Campbell appeared, closely followed by Finn.

'Did you know this part of England is full of World War Two defences?' Campbell demanded, waving an old-fashioned hardback book at Daisy. 'It says here that Kent was considered prime invasion territory if enemy forces ever landed in Britain and the authorities built lots of places for the Home Guard to lie in wait to ambush invaders.'

Daisy nodded. 'I did know that. There are a few buildings quite near here – we can go and take a look sometime, if you like.' She eyed the faded cover of the book, which definitely wasn't one of the ones they'd brought from Milton Keynes. 'Where did you find that?'

'It was in a box under my bed,' Campbell explained, taking a seat at the table and opening the book. 'Finn found one about football, although it's even older than this one.'

Finn held up an ancient-looking *Match of the Day* hardback, its cover showing players with bushy moustaches and perms. 'It's great,' he said enthusiastically. 'I've never even heard of most of these players.'

Daisy nodded, glad to see his fury of the night before seemed to have abated. 'I'm not surprised. What's the date on the cover – is it 1986?'

'1985,' Finn corrected happily and reached for the cereal box. 'Manchester City were rubbish and the Premier League hadn't even been invented.'

Once their bowls were filled, both boys sat engrossed in their books and the silence was broken only by the sound of determined crunching. Daisy watched them in appreciative amazement. Campbell loved books but even he rarely read at the breakfast table and Finn had no time for reading at all, outside of school. Perhaps this enforced break from the internet and on-demand sport on the TV would do them good, she mused, although she had no doubt it wouldn't be tolerated for long. Her first job that morning was to sort out the broadband connection and her second was to explore the damage to the roof, but all of that could wait until after breakfast.

'You should ask the businesses around the farmyard which broadband suppliers they use,' Magda suggested when she saw Daisy investigating the too-big, aged router that sat in one corner of the living room. 'They all need reliable connections and might be able to give you some advice.'

'Good idea,' Daisy said, peering at the back of the router. 'I think this thing has lasted longer than my marriage.'

'Tell me about it,' Magda said with a wry smile. 'I gave up trying to stream anything here and downloaded whatever I wanted to watch before I came over.'

Thinking back to Finn's mounting frustration the night before, Daisy could fully identify. 'Can't do that with the Premier League,' she replied, grimacing. 'I'll see what the neighbours have to say, anyway.'

Magda cocked her head thoughtfully. 'You should pop into Merry Mistletoe. I'm not sure the guy who runs it knows anything about broadband but he's very nice to look at and Emily says he's single.'

Daisy stared at her, taken aback. It was the kind of comment she might expect from one of her friends but not from someone she'd known for less than twenty-four hours. 'Uh . . . okay.'

If the younger woman noticed her discomfort, she didn't show it. 'If I was single, I'd be in there myself. ' She sighed in appreciation. 'A total silver fox.'

'Good to know,' Daisy said politely, although silver fox or

no, romance was the last thing on her mind. She hadn't dated at all in the nineteen months since her divorce had been finalized and she certainly wasn't looking for love in Kent.

'Then there's Effie who runs Waggy Mamma's,' Magda went on. 'They're bound to have good broadband, and Nancy at the Oast House café. She makes wonderful cakes. Emily and I have been taking turns to choose one to share – the lemon drizzle loaf we had yesterday was from the café.'

Daisy was sure the cake had been delicious but she'd barely had time to taste it before all hell had broken loose. Still, there was plenty of time to explore the café, she thought. Perhaps she would take the boys there for lunch, a little treat for them all after the upheaval of the day before. 'Thanks for the tip,' she told Magda.

The door opened and Rose came in, walking slowly but alert and a little less pallid than the day before. She hesitated when she saw Daisy, as though surprised to find her there, and then continued towards the armchair. 'Everything okay?' Magda asked.

Rose huffed out a breath as she settled into the chair. 'I think I can manage a trip to the toilet without difficulty,' she said with a definite hint of irritation.

'Of course you can,' Magda said smoothly. 'Now, what do you fancy doing this morning? There's the jigsaw you started with Emily – she'll be here later this morning but you could make a bit of progress before then?'

For a moment, Daisy wondered whether she should be the one to sit with Rose – she was her mother, after all.

But there was so much to do and Magda's job was actually to care for Rose. There would be plenty of time to repair the bridges of their relationship in the coming weeks – it didn't all have to be done on Day One and Rose was already nodding at the carer. 'I'd better go and check on the boys,' she said. 'They're far too quiet.'

In fact, Campbell and Finn were seated opposite each other across the kitchen table, engrossed in a game of Battleships which Daisy assumed was another under-the-bed treasure. True to form, Campbell was approaching the challenge of sinking his brother's fleet with methodical concentration, whereas Finn appeared to be peppering his opposition with random missiles and explosion sounds. Neither seemed interested in joining Daisy to explore the shops that surrounded the farmyard. 'I won't be long,' she said, clearing the last of the breakfast things from the table. 'Stay here and make sure Atticus doesn't escape.'

A faint drizzle had started to fall, misting the cobbles with a silvery sheen. Birds fluttered overhead, tweeting and chirruping. Daisy smiled as she pulled the hood of her coat up – wildlife aside, she'd forgotten how quiet it was here, although the farm had been busier when she'd been a regular visitor. Even so, there was no background buzz of traffic, no far-off sirens – none of the city soundtrack that she was used to. The silence was strange but soothing at the same time and she paused with her face raised to the rain for a moment, letting the droplets mist her skin and allowing her shoulders to relax as she soaked up the tranquillity. And then the moment was broken by a volley of distant barks. That would be Waggy Mamma's, she thought as she set off along the road that wound round to the main yard. Perhaps there wouldn't be much silence after all.

Pausing beside the wishing well, Daisy took stock. Brew Crew and Dottie's Pots both appeared to be closed, with no light showing behind their windows. Waggy Mamma's was most definitely open – there were several cars parked in the spaces outside, plus a cream transit van emblazoned with the same logo and website address that adorned the sign. Occasional barks rang out, much louder now that Daisy was nearer, making her wonder how many dogs were cared for. She'd have to ask when she visited.

Merry Mistletoe was dark but Darling Buds shone brightly in the misty rain and the café in the oast house most definitely looked open. Its windows glowed warm and inviting, drawing Daisy in with a sense of welcome. She'd order a takeaway latte, she decided, and check out the menu for lunch.

A small bell chimed as she pushed back the door. She stopped on the doormat, carefully wiping her feet, and gazed around. The café was every bit as inviting as she'd anticipated, bright and cheery, with clusters of wooden tables and chairs beneath the arched, wood-framed ceiling of the oast house. There were no other customers and the bell caused a petite, dark-haired woman to hurry through to the glass counter from a room behind. 'Hello,' she said, drying her hands on a tea-towel. 'What can I get for you?'

Daisy crossed the tiled floor and stood in front of the counter, gazing at the menu. 'A large vanilla latte, please,' she said after a moment's consideration. 'And two of your chocolate chip cookies.'

The woman nodded and turned to the coffee machine. 'Have you just dropped your dog off?'

Daisy supposed the café must benefit from the stream of dog owners using Waggy Mamma's. 'No, I'm here to look after my mother, Rose. I'll be staying in the farmhouse for a few months.'

The other woman stopped what she was doing and turned back to study her. 'I didn't know Rose had a daughter.'

'We lost contact,' Daisy explained awkwardly, heat rising in her cheeks. 'This is my first visit to Half Moon Farm in – well, let's just say in a very long time.'

'Ah,' the café owner said, resuming her coffee making. 'I bet a few things have changed since you were last here.'

An image of the farmhouse roof swam into Daisy's mind. 'One or two,' she admitted wryly. 'But some things are just the same.'

The woman finished making Daisy's drink and capped it with a lid. 'I can imagine,' she said with a smile as she placed the coffee on the counter. 'I'm Nancy Wilson, anyway. Welcome to the Oast House café.'

Her smile was so friendly that Daisy liked her immediately. 'Pleased to meet you. I'm Daisy.'

'Have you just arrived?' Nancy asked, sliding two of the biggest cookies into a paper bag.

'Last night,' Daisy said. 'My boys are with me, they'll be going to the village school for a few months, just until Mum's back to full strength.'

Nancy nodded slowly. 'Right. So it's a big change for them too.'

'Very much so,' Daisy replied fervently. Her gaze came to rest on a little chalkboard with the Wi-Fi details in neat clear handwriting. 'Which brings me onto something I wanted to ask you. The broadband at the farmhouse is practically unusable and I thought it might be worth asking the businesses around the farm which providers they use.'

'Of course,' Nancy said. 'We all use the same one – there's a fibre cable that runs to each business. I'm sure you could get the farmhouse connected to it – I'll give you the details.'

Daisy almost sagged with relief. Apart from anything else, she had a number of big illustration projects to deliver over the months ahead and she couldn't do that without a reliable internet connection. 'Thank you. My sons think their life support has been cut off.'

Nancy laughed. 'I bet. I don't know much about these things but it might take a bit of time to get connected. In the meantime, why don't you investigate some dongles to keep you going? Might save you some arguments while you settle in.'

It was a great idea, Daisy thought, and something she might have landed on herself, once the whirl of moving was over. 'I will,' she said gratefully.

The café owner rang up the cost of the coffee and cookies.

'I'll dig out the broadband supplier details this morning, so you can get in touch with them. Do you want to pop back in later?'

'Perfect. I was planning on bringing the boys over for lunch,' Daisy said as she tapped her card on the reader. 'I really appreciate your help.'

'No worries,' Nancy said, and gestured towards the gloomy farmyard. 'Have you met any of the others yet?'

'Not yet,' Daisy admitted. 'I'm slightly scared about the doggy day care place. I have a big ginger tom cat who thinks he's Scar – there may be trouble ahead.'

Grinning, Nancy tipped her head. 'I wouldn't worry too much. Effie is a real animal lover – she'll take it all in her stride.' She pursed her lips as though considering. 'So there's Nigel over at Brew Crew – he harvests the hops that still grow here and turns them into a really good beer.'

Daisy blinked. She'd assumed the hop plants would have died out years ago. It was a real surprise to hear they were still being harvested. 'Oh. That's amazing.'

Nancy winked. 'Do yourself a favour and never say that to Nigel's face. Unless you fancy spending two hours hearing about the trials and tribulations of running a micro-brewery, that is.'

'Got you,' Daisy said, suppressing a shudder.

'Then you've got Dottie, who runs the pottery. Very good if you're in need of some mindfulness or balm for the soul and she runs workshops for kids if you think your boys might be interested.'

Nodding, Daisy tried to absorb all the new information suddenly flowing her way. 'There's Michaela at Darling Buds – that's a florist's – and lastly, Drew at Merry Mistletoe.' Nancy leaned forwards conspiratorially. 'No love lost between those two in the early days – I think Michaela thought Drew was treading on her professional toes, what with the similarities in their businesses, but they've sorted all that out now.'

'Right,' Daisy said faintly. 'Good.'

At that moment, the bell chimed and two women entered the café, bringing with them a gust of damp air. Daisy took their arrival as her cue to go. 'I'd better leave you to your customers,' she said, gathering up her coffee and the paper bag containing the cookies. 'Thanks again for your help. I'll see you at lunch time.'

'No problem, it was great to meet you,' Nancy said, smiling. 'See you later.'

★ ★ ★

The café was surprisingly busy when Daisy brought Finn and Campbell back just after midday. Nancy waved at them as they came in and pointed them towards an empty table near the back of the room. She handed Daisy a thick envelope when she bustled over to take their order. 'You should find everything you need in there,' she said, blowing a strand of hair from her forehead. 'Now, what can I get you to eat?'

Both boys were engrossed in their phones as they ate, taking advantage of the café's free Wi-Fi to catch up on everything they had missed and for once, Daisy allowed them to eat and browse. Finn was watching the highlights of the match he'd missed the night before and Campbell was streaming an episode of his favourite history programme. Daisy took the opportunity to skim through the information Nancy had given her and made a note of the contact details for the broadband supplier. Then she pulled out her own phone and ordered three Wi-Fi dongles so that at least they would have some connection to the twenty-first century for the next few weeks.

The food was simple but delicious, just as Daisy had known it would be. Her vegetable soup was steaming hot and hearty, served with a freshly baked crusty roll that crackled when she broke into it. Finn and Campbell both chose ham, egg and chips and cleared their plates in record time, although they declared they had plenty of room for dessert. Daisy herself was tempted by a glistening cherry cheesecake on display beneath the counter's glass curves and afterwards felt too full to move.

'How about a walk around the village?' she suggested. 'We can take a closer look at the mill, explore a little bit.'

Finn rolled his eyes. 'Can't I stay here?'

'No,' Daisy said firmly. 'Apart from anything else, Nancy doesn't need you taking up all her bandwidth with endless football highlights.'

'Can we go to the castle?' Campbell asked over the top of Finn's melodramatic groans.

Daisy hesitated, thinking of the mountain of sorting and

unpacking she still had to do. 'Maybe later in the week,' she offered. 'I need to make sure it's still open to the public.'

Campbell picked up his phone. 'What's it called again? I can look now.'

'Winterbourne Castle,' Daisy said, 'but we really can't go this afternoon. There's too much to do at the farmhouse.'

With a reluctant nod of acceptance, Campbell began tapping at his screen. While he and Finn made the most of the last few minutes of Wi-Fi, Daisy made her way over to the till to pay. 'Everything okay?' Nancy asked, fanning her rosy cheeks.

'It was perfect,' Daisy said. 'Although I think you might have trouble keeping Finn and Campbell out of here – Wi-Fi and cake is a killer combination.'

Nancy laughed. 'So I see. They're welcome any time, as long as we're not too busy.'

Daisy glanced around. The worst of the rush seemed to be over but there were still a lot of customers. 'You're doing well, though. Is it just you or do you have help?'

'Oh, I have help,' Nancy said hurriedly. 'I couldn't do all this on my own. Lisa does most of the lunches and I help but my table staff phoned in sick this morning so it's been a bit hectic.'

'Then I'm even more impressed,' Daisy said. 'I had no idea you were short staffed.'

The café owner looked gratified. 'Thanks. My back will let me know later but I'm still high on panic at the moment.'

'Ouch,' Daisy said, grinning in sympathy as she paid.

'Thanks again for the broadband info. Do you mind if I hang onto it for a day or so while I get things sorted?'

'Not at all,' Nancy replied. She waggled her eyebrows. 'Gives you a reason to pop back in. It's all part of my masterplan to build a café empire.'

Daisy couldn't help laughing. 'Oh, I think we're already hooked.'

To his credit, Finn only grumbled a little when she instructed him to put his phone away and pull on his coat. He was quiet on the short drive to Mistlethorpe, gazing out of the window in resigned silence, although he perked up at the sight of the village shop. 'Maybe they'll sell Match Attax,' he said hopefully. 'Can we go in and see?'

'After our walk,' Daisy said in a firm tone. 'If you don't complain the whole way.'

They walked the length of the high street and crossed the river at one of the small, humpbacked bridges. Daisy found some twigs and suggested a game of Pooh Sticks, although it didn't take long for Finn to sink Campbell's twig with a stone and declare himself the ultimate Pooh Sticks champion. From the village green, the turrets of Winterbourne were clearly visible; Campbell had found its website and announced the castle was open Thursday to Sunday each week. 'So we can't go today but we could go on Thursday,' he finished, fixing his mother with a pleading look. 'Can we? Please say yes.'

Daisy shook her head, smiling. 'Okay, yes.'

The two of them raced off across the grass after that,

Campbell's enthusiasm for visiting the castle translating into a rare game of tag. Daisy watched them fondly for a moment, then allowed her gaze to roam around the village. Just as when she'd first driven into Mistlethorpe the day before, she felt an odd lurch at being back again. It wasn't time travel, because now she wasn't driving she could see that a lot had changed in the village, but it was still peculiarly jarring. It would pass, she supposed, once she adjusted but for now, she was enjoying rediscovering everything she had loved about Mistlethorpe – the crystal-clear water of the shallow river as it babbled over its stony bed, the ducks nestling against a clump of reeds, the much taller trees at one end of the green and the ever-present walls of Winterbourne presiding over everything. It was as close to the perfect English village as she could picture and it made her heart glad to be there once more, even if the circumstances of her return were less than happy.

They spent several long minutes gazing at the waterwheel attached to the mill. Campbell was fascinated by the mechanism, explaining in detail how it worked to grind flour. Daisy found the continuous cascade of water to be almost mesmeric; if she shut out the sound of cars trundling along the high street, she could almost imagine how the mill had been in Victorian times. And then Finn rolled his eyes and declared he had seen enough boring stuff – wasn't it time they went to the shop?

To his great delight, the village shop had the cards he wanted. He bought five packets, cradling to his chest as though they were precious. Campbell chose a magazine, the kind that made Finn yawn with exaggerated boredom, and they headed back to the car. If she was lucky, the purchases might buy her twenty minutes of peace once they got back to the farmhouse, Daisy thought.

They had parked in the slotted spaces that ran at an angle to the pavement, pulling into a space that had just been vacated by another car. Daisy had offered up a thank you to the parking gods at the time but it now meant she had to reverse out onto the not unbusy road. Carefully, she checked for traffic then began to edge the car backwards. Almost immediately, the air was split by a honking horn and the screech of brakes. With a startled gasp and a hot rush of horror, Daisy slammed on her own brakes but it was too late. There was a crunch and a bump that jolted all three of them as something crashed into the back of Daisy's car.

Chapter Four

Nausea washed over Daisy as she drew in a shallow panic-stricken breath and spun round in her seat to check the boys were okay. Both were staring at her with wide eyes, shocked but apparently unhurt. Relief sent the breath whooshing back out of her lungs as she realized they were fine. It seemed the collision hadn't been heavy enough to cause bumps or bruises but the flood of adrenaline currently sending her heart rate soaring was another thing entirely.

'Did you just hit someone?' Finn asked, his tone a mixture of reproachfulness and glee.

Daisy glanced in her rear-view mirror, ears roaring, unable to take in what had just happened. 'I think someone just hit me, actually.' Forcing herself to take several long breaths in and out, she reached for the door handle. 'Stay here.'

Her legs were unsteady as she got out and looked at the back of the car. A gleaming red Audi was now apparently attached to her bumper and its driver was also getting out.

'Brilliant,' he growled, scowling at Daisy. 'Didn't you think to look?'

Daisy flicked her gaze back to the spot where the two cars met, hoping she might see something different. 'I did. The road was clear, I'm sure it was.'

'Obviously it wasn't,' the man retorted. 'If it had been, you wouldn't have hit my car.'

His tone made Daisy's hackles rise. She placed a steadying hand on the cool undamaged paintwork of the rear passenger door and met the accusation head on. 'Or you hit mine.'

They glared at each other. Daisy was aware of a small crowd of onlookers gathering on the pavement, as well as the faces of Campbell and Finn, almost side by side as they stared out at her. Other cars had begun to queue along the high street behind the obstructing Audi. Forcing her fists to unclench, Daisy took another slow breath in and out. 'Look, why don't we let the insurance company decide whose fault it is? I don't imagine the damage is catastrophic so let's swap details, take some photos and stop blocking the road.'

For a moment he continued to glower at her as though he intended to argue further. Then, with an abrupt nod, he seemed to relent. 'Wait here,' he commanded. 'I'll pull into another space and walk back.'

His autocratic tone grated on Daisy's already frayed nerves. 'Hold on, I need to take a photograph before you move your car.' Pulling out her phone, she proceeded to capture the position of both vehicles from several different viewpoints, plus close up shots of the impact.

'If you've quite finished, David Bailey,' the man said dryly. Daisy checked the pictures had saved and nodded. 'Good. Don't go anywhere.'

The unspoken insinuation that she might drive off rankled but Daisy bit back her sarcastic reply. He climbed back into the Audi and slowly pulled backwards. There was a brief tortured squeal as the two vehicles separated once more, followed by the gentle tinkle of broken glass and Daisy saw the Audi had come off worse. Her car had a cracked bumper and a dent in the paintwork but the other car had a broken headlight and an ugly scratch on the glossy bonnet. She snapped several photographs then waved a hand to show she had finished. The Audi eased forwards and moved past her; she assumed he was aiming for an empty space several cars away. Perhaps sensing the show was over, the onlookers began to dissipate but Finn knocked on the window. 'Are you going to have a fight?' he asked when she opened the car door.

'No.'

'Because I saw this clip on YouTube where this man had an accident and started hitting the other car with a tree branch,' Finn went on avidly. 'If you're going to do that then there were some great branches on the village green.'

Daisy made a mental note to review the parental controls on his phone. 'No one is going to hit anything,' she said patiently. 'Just sit tight while I sort everything out and we'll go home.'

She closed the car door before Finn could offer any further advice and waited for Mr Audi to come back. Now that her adrenaline levels were dropping she was starting to feel stupid. She had been the one reversing out of a parking space and he had been on the road; the accident had almost certainly been her fault. But Stuart had once told her never to admit fault in an accident situation and it seemed like solid advice to follow now.

The other driver also seemed to have calmed down or perhaps he'd noticed Finn and Campbell on the back seat because his tone was noticeably less hostile when he re-joined Daisy. 'Are you all okay?' he asked. 'Was anyone hurt?'

It had been such a slow-motion crash that the question seemed ridiculous but she supposed it was good of him to check. In fact, now that he looked less angry, she realized he was actually quite attractive. Tall and blond, with a precisely trimmed beard and blue eyes that she suspected missed nothing. He was in his late forties, she guessed, judging from the fine lines that lined his forehead but it was sometimes hard to tell with men. And then she realized she hadn't answered his question and gave herself a mental shake. 'No, we're all fine. Thanks for asking.'

'Good,' he said crisply. 'That should make things simpler with the insurance.'

Another spike of annoyance punctured any tentative good feelings Daisy might have been developing. 'And there I was thinking you might actually have had the welfare of my children at heart,' she said with a thin-lipped, humourless smile. 'Let's just get this over with. My name is Daisy Moon. This is my phone number.'

She reeled off the number, watching as he tapped it into his own phone. 'If you give me your number, we can swap insurance details via text message.'

The man tipped his head in agreement. 'Fine. I'm Kit Devereaux. Are you local or a tourist?'

Daisy hesitated, wondering how wise it was to give too much information to a total stranger. Finn probably had some ghoulish tale from YouTube concerning an unwary motorist who had shared more than they needed to and met an unfortunate fate. 'We're from Milton Keynes,' she said, deciding to play it safe. 'Just visiting the area.'

None of it was a lie, exactly − her car insurance was still registered to her home in Milton Keynes, after all − but she felt her cheeks grow a little warm. She shrugged the guilt away. 'What's your number?' she asked.

He gave it to her, then bent to snap some photographs of her cracked bumper and dented paintwork. Evidently satisfied, he straightened up. 'I'll be in touch in the next day or so to confirm the vehicle details and supply my insurance information, Mrs Moon.'

Daisy managed a cool smile. 'It's Miss Moon. And I'll do likewise. I do hope we can resolve things without causing each other too much of a headache.'

He was regarding her more closely, a slight frown crinkling his forehead as he studied her. 'There's a Moon family farm not far from here. Are you related to them?'

The question was so unexpected that Daisy was wrong-footed; should she admit the family connection? What if things got nasty with the claim and he turned up at the farmhouse? He didn't seem the type but stranger things happened. 'Not as far as I know,' she said and this time she surreptitiously crossed her fingers at the outright lie. 'Well, goodbye. I hope it doesn't take too long to get your car fixed.'

He nodded and took a step backwards to give her room. 'And the same to you.'

Getting back into her car, Daisy sat for a moment with both hands gripping the steering wheel as she processed the speed with which the afternoon had deteriorated. The boys were silent in the back seat but she knew they would be studying her. Resisting the urge to shut her eyes, she turned to give them an anxious once-over. 'You're sure you are both okay?'

Trying not to feel too self-conscious, she checked and rechecked her mirrors before reversing out. She could see Kit Devereaux watching, no doubt assessing her driving skills to add meat to his claim, and she supposed she should be glad he wasn't filming her.

'That was ultimately disappointing,' Finn commented as they made their way along the road to Half Moon Farm. 'I was hoping for some shouting at least.'

Campbell nudged him sharply. 'You watch too much *Dashcam Devils*.'

Daisy glanced in the rear-view mirror. '*Dashcam Devils*? What is that?'

'It's a programme on the Golden Oldie channel,' Campbell

explained, dodging an elbow from Finn. 'They show clips of car accidents and road rage and stuff, while the presenter says, 'Things are about to get nasty' in a really gravelly, *EastEnders* voice.'

Frowning, Daisy flicked her gaze to Finn. 'It sounds horrible. No more of that, please.'

'It's not horrible, it's funny,' he objected. 'Dad watches it. They bleep out all the swearing.'

'I don't care who watches it,' Daisy said, deciding a conversation with Stuart about appropriate television choices was long overdue. 'You're not and that's that.'

Finn muttered mutinously but didn't argue. 'And besides,' Daisy went on, softening her tone a little. 'There wasn't any need to shout today. It wasn't a very nice experience but no real harm was done.'

'You looked like you wanted to shout at that man,' Campbell said, after a moment had passed. 'You looked really cross at one point.'

She took a deep breath and let it out slowly, remembering the manner in which Kit Devereaux had addressed her. 'I was annoyed,' she conceded slowly, 'but mostly at myself. Like I said, no harm done. Once the car is repaired we'll probably forget it even happened.'

But inside, she wasn't at all sure that would be the case. He had recognized her name and linked it to Half Moon Farm – that suggested he was a local himself, although his name hadn't rung any bells. Then again, it had been many years since she'd spent time in Mistlethorpe – there had probably been lots of comings and goings. But if he did live nearby, there was a chance she might see him again. The thought caused a spike of worry that she instantly squashed, reminding herself that he hadn't seemed unreasonable, just rude, callous and condescending. The accident would be handled by their respective insurance firms and even if their paths did cross in the village, there was no law that said they had to acknowledge each other. Really, it should be perfectly possible to forget she had met snotty Mr Audi at all.

★ ★ ★

They were met at the door of the farmhouse by Emily. Daisy's mood, which had been recovering during the drive from the village, suddenly plummeted as she took in the carer's wretched expression. 'What is it? Has something happened to Mum?'

Emily pressed her lips together and shook her head. 'No, she's fine. It's just — well, it's Atticus. He's escaped.'

Daisy's shoulders sagged, half in relief that her mother was well and half in trepidation. She'd known Atticus would hate being cooped up but it was a necessary evil when introducing cats to a new home. They were far more likely to get lost in the first few days, before they'd identified where home actually was. But she hadn't expected him to make a bid for freedom on their first full day at Half Moon Farm. 'What happened?' she asked, aware that the twins were listening with wide eyes. 'Did you see which way he went?'

'I didn't even see him go,' Emily said apologetically. 'One

minute he was in the kitchen while I was making a cuppa, the next he was gone. I think he must have snuck out of the door but I have no idea how.'

'Then he might still be in the house,' Daisy suggested, glancing at Campbell. 'Remember that time we thought he'd escaped and he turned up under the duvet on your bed?'

He nodded. 'We should organize a search party. Finn, you check in our bedroom. I'll look in the kitchen, in case he's doubled back.'

'I searched the living room and the other downstairs rooms,' Emily offered. 'There was no sign of him but I closed all the doors to make sure he couldn't get in.'

'Great, thank you,' Daisy said, smiling to show the other woman that she didn't hold her in the least responsible for the cat's escapology. 'If you want to sit with Mum, I'll check the other upstairs rooms. I'm sure he'll turn up.'

The house was soon filled with noise, the clatter of feet on stairs, the rattle of doors being opened and closed, the call of cajoling voices. Daisy made her way through each of the bedrooms, stopping to stand still in each room, listening for an elusive purr or a plaintive miaow. Her eyes strained for a flash of orange stripes or the reflection of light on the cat's eyes but she saw and heard nothing beyond the dated furniture and clutter of decades. Finally, she made her way to the last room, the one she knew must be beneath the damaged roof. It was almost impossible for Atticus to have found his way into this room – the door was firmly locked – but if she didn't check she would always wonder. Taking a deep breath, she turned the key in the lock and went inside.

The first thing that hit her was the smell of damp. Someone had done their best to pile the furniture and other contents of the room in the corners away from the leak but there was so much packed in there that it must have been a Herculean task. Emily had mentioned a roofer who had temporarily sealed the hole – perhaps he had piled everything up in order to gain access to the damaged section of roof. The result was a warren of teetering piles and precarious stacks. Books formed stalagmites to the ceiling, papers were deposited like geological strata that aged from top to bottom. Bookshelves and bedside tables were clifftops ever on the brink of collapse and all of it was tainted by the musty scent of mildew. Daisy didn't know where to start. Surely – *surely* – Atticus couldn't be in here.

Nevertheless, she stood as silently as she could to listen. Elsewhere in the house, she could hear the twins calling the cat's name and she did her best to block them out. 'Atticus,' she whispered, ears primed for any response. 'Are you up here?'

There was no reply, only the faint patter of rain on the roof tiles, on the plastic that protected the room from the elements. It was cold too and the light switch didn't work – she assumed that was a safety precaution, although it could easily have been a broken bulb. 'Atticus,' she mumbled again. 'Come out, you stupid animal. I've got treats.'

Once again, there was no answering mew. Sighing, Daisy

bent to flash her phone torch beneath the forest of furniture legs. When she rose, her balance was off and she reached out to clutch the nearest column – a tower of chairs. It toppled sideways, dislodging a sheaf of papers and sending cardboard boxes cascading to the ground. Everywhere Daisy looked something was falling. It felt as though she'd been transported to the centre of a life-sized domino run.

She grabbed the chairs first, stopped them from hitting the floor. The papers were a lost cause – she caught at a few but there were too many slithering through her hands. Finally, she tried to stabilize the boxes. They were mostly light – she suspected empty – but the last one to hit the ground made a resounding thud. It burst open at the top, allowing a river of yellowed cream envelopes to splash across the threadbare carpet. Cursing, Daisy stooped to gather them up, glancing at spidery scrawl across the top envelope as she did so. The black ink was faded, the postmark almost illegible, but the name and address were clear enough:

Miss V Finch
11 Thanet Lane
Mistlethorpe
Kent

Daisy stared at the envelope for a few seconds, then flipped to the next, which bore the same name and address. The postmark was clearer on this one – 3rd March 1944 – with the words *On Active Service* printed in neat capitals across the top. A purple stamp with a miniature pair of wings declared it had been passed by RAF Censor 380. A tiny huff of amazement escaped from Daisy's throat as she slid back the flap of the envelope to reveal a paper-thin lined sheet inside. With shaking fingers, she teased it out and began to read the now grey words.

984632 FL AJD
75 MTLRV
Royal Air Force

1st March

My darling Violet,

Thank you so much for the letter and photograph you sent, both of which reached me yesterday. Only three weeks after you sent them — things are looking up! Do not apologize for your spelling or handwriting — they were both perfect to my eyes and the photograph is by far my most precious possession out here, a real thing of beauty. I am not sure how you could bear to part with it but then I suppose you have the original to gaze at every single time you look in the mirror. How do you get anything done? In any case, please believe that I am counting the days until I can see you again for myself, although your photograph lifts my spirits in the meantime.

Things remain busy here. Of course I cannot tell you anything of what I am doing, or even describe what I can see from my lowly chair, but I doubt it would cheer you if I could. That said, I am in good spirits and tolerable good health. It doesn't do to complain and really, I have nothing to grumble about. So many have it worse than me and few have a sweetheart as adorable as you to keep their heart light. I keep your photograph hidden in case one of the blasted Corporals sees it and decides to steal it for his own.

I hope life in the village is treating you well. Spring must be well on her way now – I can imagine the daffo- dils and crocuses in bloom on the green. One day I will be home with your darling hand in mine and we can admire the flowers together. Until then, a man can only dream.

I await your next letter with impatience, dear Violet.

Ever yours,

V

Slowly, Daisy lowered the letter and gazed in wonder at the slew of envelopes. Did they all contain love letters to her grandmother from an unknown serviceman? Violet hadn't married him, that much Daisy did know – as a farmer, her grandfather had been excluded from active service and had never quite managed to reconcile himself with the guilt. His name had been Jack, which didn't match the initial on the letter. So whoever the mystery man was, he hadn't made good on his declaration of love once he returned from the war. And then an awful thought occurred to Daisy: perhaps he'd been unable to. Hurriedly, she rifled through the envelopes, relieved when she saw postmarks well into 1946. He hadn't been killed in service at least.

With great care, Daisy gathered the envelopes and tucked them reverently back inside the box. A quick investigation of the neighbouring boxes revealed no more letters. There could be more, further into the room, but Daisy had already had one near miss with the precariously balanced towers – she wasn't about to risk another. Tucking the box under one arm, she stepped backwards and locked the door.

At first, she had every intention of showing the letters to her mother but as she made her way along the landing doubt grew in her mind. They had belonged to Violet and must have been in the farmhouse for years, yet they'd been kept out of sight in a locked room, unread and forgotten for quite some time. But it didn't necessarily follow that Rose was ignorant of their existence. Perhaps she'd discovered them long before Daisy, and read them for herself. Perhaps she was the one who had locked them away. Might she have felt odd about reading love letters from a man other than her father? On the other hand, Rose might be entirely unaware of the letters, and Daisy wasn't sure there was enough of a rapport between them yet for her to reveal the find. Perhaps it might be better if she read them first and ensured there was nothing scandalous between the faded sheets of paper. Then she could broach the subject with her mother and see how she reacted. Decision made, Daisy side-tracked into her bedroom and placed the box under her bed.

Finn met her as she came out, reminding Daisy of her original mission. 'Any sign of Atticus?' she asked.

'No,' he said. 'But if Emily is right and he got outside, he could be anywhere.'

He stopped talking but Daisy could see the mute accusation in his eyes. This was her fault too. If they'd stayed in Milton Keynes none of this would be happening. 'He'll turn up,' she said, with a jolly confidence she didn't really feel. 'He always has before.'

Finn started to speak but just then a shout rang out from downstairs. It was Emily's voice, muffled but unmistakeably relieved. 'He's here! In the living room, under the sofa.'

Without another word, both Daisy and Finn clattered down the stairs and into the living room where Emily was on her hands and knees, peering under the flowery sofa. 'He's here,' Emily said. 'I heard a low rumble, thought it was Rose's tummy at first but then I realized it was coming from beneath the sofa. And there he was.' She straightened up and smiled at Daisy. 'I'll let you get him out, though. He looks like he wants to rip the skin from my hands.'

Daisy grinned, partly in relief. 'Oh, he always looks like that. Go and grab some ham, Finn. He'll be out faster than you can say "here, boy".'

Finn came back with his brother and a generous slice of ham. She tore off a sliver and waved it towards Atticus. A low purr broke out as he slunk out from between the sofa legs and stretched out a paw to snare the meat. Daisy let him take it and pulled off another bit. 'Thank goodness he's safe,' she said, beaming at Emily. 'I don't mind admitting I was worried.'

A tutting sounded from Rose, who had been watching the proceedings in silence. 'Oh, he's been under there all afternoon,' she said with a sniff. 'I thought you knew.'

They all stared at her for a moment. 'And you didn't think to mention this when you heard us calling for him?'

Rose shrugged. 'Everyone knows cats don't come when they're called. I thought he would come out when he was ready and look — I was right.'

It took a monumental effort of will for Daisy to rein in a sarcastic reply. Instead, she summoned up her sunniest smile. 'All's well that ends well, I suppose,' she said cheerfully and glanced at Emily. 'I don't know about you but I could do with a cup of tea.'

Emily looked down at Atticus, who was now happily eating ham from Finn and Campbell's hands. 'Absolutely,' she replied with a shudder. 'And I think perhaps a large slice of cake.'

Chapter Five

Daisy didn't mean to stay up late reading the letters she had found but there was something addictive about the secret doorway to the past that meant she couldn't put them down. They began in 1941, when the letter writer was still in England and based at various RAF camps around the country. The postmarks told Daisy where the letters had been posted, even if the writer didn't always disclose his location. Some were longer than others, the thin paper covered in writing so cramped that Daisy could scarcely read it, filled with the minutiae of service life. And some were so bland that she wondered if they were even worth writing, although she knew they would have been received with just as much joy as the longer letters. Those letters were usually stamped with the Censor's mark and Daisy surmised there wasn't much room for anything that might accidentally give away vital details of missions or detachments. Yet even the shortest letters managed to say more than the words alone could convey, conjuring up images of a lonely soldier far from home and desperate for the comfort of his old life. She could picture the breathless impatience with which young Violet had awaited each reply, and the delight she'd felt as she devoured every word. It was an unexpected glimpse the person Violet had been, long before she'd become a grandmother or even a mother, and Daisy was fascinated. Even so, by the time one o'clock in the morning rolled around, she reluctantly decided to call it a night. Apart from anything else, her eyes were gritty and sore, but she spent a long time staring at the dark ceiling once she'd put the light out, wondering who the serviceman might have been and what had become of him. She was still wondering when sleep came to claim her.

By the time Thursday arrived, Daisy had begun to feel she was making progress with her to-do list. The broadband was in hand – she'd contacted the provider and arranged for additional cable to be laid to the farmhouse. The cost had made her wince but there was no help for it – she needed to be able to get online for work and she couldn't piggyback on Nancy's Wi-Fi for that. The dongles she had ordered came on Wednesday morning and two had immediately been seized by the twins. Even Atticus seemed to be behaving himself, although Daisy often found him prowling along the kitchen windowsill, tail swishing as though he was plotting to take over the world. 'You can't go out there yet, I'm afraid,' she told him, rubbing his ears affectionately. 'A few more days at the very least.'

Thursday was also the day she had promised to take the boys to Winterbourne Castle. It had to be Thursday – they were going to spend the weekend with Stuart before starting their new school on Monday. And really, they'd been good since Finn's outburst on Monday evening. The dongles seemed to help enormously, although Daisy liked to think they were settling into their new home too.

She stopped by the café on their way to the castle to pick up some sandwiches for a packed lunch. 'Doing anything fun?' Nancy asked as they placed their orders to take away.

Finn nodded enthusiastically. 'Finding out how to kill people with boiling oil.'

Understandably, Nancy looked a little taken aback. 'We're going to the castle,' Daisy explained, grinning. 'I can't believe I've never actually been.'

'It's worth a visit,' Nancy said. 'Michaela over at Darling Buds raves about the walled gardens – says they'd rival Hever Castle in the summer months.'

Daisy pulled a suitably impressed face and then hurriedly stifled a yawn. 'Sorry. A bit of a late night.'

Nancy threw her a sympathetic look. 'Box set binge?'

Daisy pictured the stack of letters at the side of her bed and smiled. 'Something like that, yes.'

'You'll have to tell me what it is,' Nancy said as she handed over three paper bags containing their sandwiches. 'It must be good if it's keeping you awake.'

'Mmmm,' Daisy replied vaguely. 'Come on then, boys. Let's go and explore the horrors of Norman England.'

The café owner smiled as she waved them off. 'Have fun! Rather you than me.'

Daisy had opted to avoid the opening time of ten o'clock, assuming this would be when the queues to get in would be longest, but even so they arrived at exactly the same time as a coach load of tourists. She didn't really mind – standing in the queue allowed her time to admire the castle close up for the first time and she had to admit it was impressive. As often seemed to be the case with England's many castles, it had first been built as a Norman moated keep and Campbell assured her it had all the hallmarks of that period of history, including holes just past the portcullis for boiling oil and thin windows to allow archers to shoot arrows without running the risk of getting shot themselves. But the castle had evolved with each passing century; at some point a large, rounded tower with a pointed turret had been added to the side of the keep, overlooking the moat and completely at odds with the classic defensive crenelations of the older building. A smattering of water lilies across the moat softened the horror of battle even more and the overall result was a whimsical mishmash that somehow managed to be charming and magnificent at the same time. Why on earth had she never visited with her grandparents during those long summer holidays, Daisy wondered as she took in the view. She would have loved it even more as a child, she was sure, but perhaps her grandparents hadn't thought so.

'It says here there's a secret priest hole,' Campbell said, once they were past the ticket booths. He ran a finger down a page of the guide book Daisy had bought. 'And the castle was used as a hospital during both World Wars.'

'Never mind that,' Finn said impatiently. 'Is there a torture chamber?'

Campbell turned the page and nodded. 'There's a dungeon, complete with prison cells.' He pushed his glasses up his nose and turned an enthusiastic gaze on Daisy. 'I think this might be a two-day visit.'

Daisy held up her hands, laughing. 'Hold on, we're not even over the drawbridge yet. And we can't come back tomorrow – you're going to your dad's for the weekend, remember?'

'Next week, then,' Campbell suggested.

'School starts on Monday,' she said. 'But the castle is right on our doorstep. I'm sure we can manage another visit if we need one.'

Finn was already ahead of them, crossing the wooden draw-bridge and making for the iron portcullis with his head craned upwards. 'There,' he said, squinting at the vaulted stone ceiling on the other side of the entry defences. 'Those must be the oil holes. Imagine having your hair set on fire by burning oil.'

It was an image Daisy could live without. 'Urgh.'

Finn shrugged. 'If you can't stand the heat, stay out of the castle. Come on, let's find the dungeons.'

Campbell shook his head and held up the guidebook. 'It says here to start at Point One – The Green.'

'*You* can start there,' Finn said, rolling his eyes. 'I'm going to look for the secret room.'

'We'll stick together, if you don't mind,' Daisy said in a tone that brooked no argument. 'And that means following the guidebook. Don't worry, Finn, the dungeons have been here for hundreds of years. They aren't going anywhere.'

Daisy had to concede the castle displays were well done, managing to outline the bloodthirstiness of the past without glorifying it, and she found herself trying to imagine the hundreds of people who had passed along the stone corridors in centuries gone by. Soldiers, of course – she could picture them battling to repel invaders, sword fights on the spiral staircases and ramparts – but there must have been ordinary people too. Cooks and maids and people to empty the privies. In the sixteenth-century manor house, across the moat and separate from the castle, she fancied she could detect the scent of incense in the dark panelled room that housed the almost invisible priest hole. Portraits hung on the walls in gilt frames; austere, pale faces and rich clothing that told their own stories and Daisy found herself wondering about their lives too, even as she admired the skill of the artists who had captured them. It might be a long way from her style of illustration but she was left breathless by the technique.

She was drifting down a long gallery after lunch, only half-listening to the amiable bickering of the twins, when a name beneath a portrait caught her eye: *Charles Devereaux, Seventh Earl of Winterbourne, 1803–1879.* It reminded her instantly of Tuesday's accident – she'd exchanged precisely two messages with the owner of the red Audi, Kit Devereaux, swapping the necessary details with icy politeness and now the matter was in the hands of her insurers. But a surname like that wasn't common in Kent and certainly there couldn't be two families with the same name in a village the size of Mistlethorpe – there must be a connection. She moved on to the next painting, *Sophia Devereaux, Countess of Winterbourne, 1822–1891.* The line continued through the eighth, ninth and tenth Earls and their wives, with dogs and children appearing occasionally, until Daisy found herself standing in front of a portrait of the eleventh Earl, Alfred Charles Valentine Devereaux, who had died in 2001. It had evidently been painted when he was young – he was tall and straight-backed, dressed in a uniform that he clearly wore with great pride. The hair beneath the officer's cap was blond and Daisy thought there was definitely a family resemblance to a certain Audi driver, something about the piercing blue-eyed gaze and confident jut of the chiselled jaw that jolted her back to the accident on the high street. She glanced along the line of portraits again and noticed with a frown that there was no portrait of the current Earl. Her frown deepened as a horrible suspicion began to loom. Surely – *surely* – it couldn't be Kit Devereaux. But the idea grew more persuasive the longer she stared at the painting; he might not have dropped his title when they'd met but it would certainly explain the autocratic way he'd spoken to her, even if it entirely failed to excuse it. Puffing out a breath, she was suddenly glad all over again that she'd fudged the details of where she lived. The last thing she and Half Moon Farm needed was the local landed gentry turning up on the doorstep with a grudge. And that observation raised another question: how was it possible that she'd never heard the name Devereaux in connection with the village until now? Could it have something to do with the reason she'd never been to Winterbourne Castle itself, or was it simply an odd coincidence? Daisy shook her head. It had to be coincidence, didn't it? What else could it be?

Finn tugged at her arm, interrupting her muddled thoughts. 'Can we go home now? I've had enough of looking at old things.'

Checking the time, Daisy was surprised to see it was after two o'clock. 'Campbell wanted to see the jousting display at two-thirty and I wanted to take a look at the walled gardens.' Finn huffed out an exasperated sigh and she relented. 'But I suppose I could do that another day. Okay, let's go and get an ice cream. We can eat them while we watch the jousting and head home after that.'

She took a final, speculative look at the Eleventh Earl of Winterbourne and shook her suspicions away. If the man whose car she had hit was descended from the splendid family in the portraits, he hadn't been much of a gentleman.

★ ★ ★

Stuart pressed his lips together as he considered the back of Daisy's car on Friday afternoon. 'Could have been worse,' he said, tilting his head in assessment. 'When are you getting it repaired?'

Daisy pulled a face. 'A week on Monday. There's a shortage of courtesy cars, apparently.'

'At least it's still drivable, although I can understand why you didn't want to come up to Milton Keynes,' he said and glanced up at the farmhouse. 'It's nice to get the opportunity to see this place, having heard you talk about it so much. How's your mum?'

'Not too bad,' Daisy said, rubbing a hand across her forehead. 'But it's been a lot of upheaval for the boys coming here. I'm glad we have Emily and Magda to do most of her care – I'd be lost without them.'

Stuart studied her. 'You look tired. This has been hard on you too.'

Daisy thought guiltily of the letters in her room. She had been awake until almost midnight again, poring over them, drinking in the one-sided love story unfolding within their pages. She'd put them in date order, starting in 1941, and had read in sequence until she reached the letter she'd first read in the locked bedroom. The unknown serviceman had often mentioned receiving Violet's letters so Daisy knew his feelings had been reciprocated but she couldn't believe her grandmother had a soaring private passion she'd known nothing about. It felt like a movie unfolding before her eyes, a romance that burned throughout the darkness of war and perhaps faded once peace arrived, although Daisy knew there must have been many similar stories. For a moment, she considered telling Stuart about the letters, then felt a strange tug of reluctance. That same reluctance had prevented her from mentioning the letters to Rose, an almost subconscious desire to keep them to herself for just a little longer. They were her secret , a wonderful escape from the whirl of settling into life at the farm, and she wasn't ready to let anyone else in just yet. 'We're getting there,' she said. 'It'll be easier once the boys start school and I have more time to myself. The cabling for the new fibre link should be laid in the next few weeks too – maybe they'll stop grumbling about living in the Victorian era then.'

He laughed. 'That sounds like Finn. At least you'll get a break this weekend. Got anything planned?'

'Magda has the night off tonight so I'm caring for Mum on my own,' Daisy said. 'And Emily is off on Sunday – I don't think I'll be doing much apart from making sure the boys' things are ready for Monday morning.'

'I'll bring them back with plenty of time for showers and an early night,' he said, then checked his watch. 'Speaking of which, we should hit the road. I don't want to get snarled up in the Friday night traffic.'

She grimaced in sympathy. "Absolutely not. Which reminds me – no *Dashcam Devils* this weekend, please. Finn is enough of a backseat driver as it is."

The farmhouse felt empty once the twins had gone. Daisy was used to them spending every other weekend with Stuart – had often enjoyed the peacefulness without them – but that had been in Milton Keynes, when she'd had friends to see and the comfort of her own things around her. Half Moon Farm might be familiar and dear to her, but it wasn't home.

She consoled herself with a long phone call with one of her friends, allowing the news and gossip from her old life to soothe her. When she hung up, she poked her head around the door to the living room. 'I'm making tea if you'd like some?'

Emily looked up from the jigsaw she was doing with Rose. 'I'll do it. You come and sit down.'

Daisy waved the offer away. 'Seriously, you've made me more cups of tea this week than I can count. Let me make one for you.'

'Okay,' Emily said, smiling. 'I think I've nearly got the hang of this tricky bit of sky – be a shame to leave it now. But there's some chocolate fudge cake in the larder. Why don't you bring that in?'

Daisy shook her head wryly as she headed for the kitchen. Having Nancy's café on the doorstep was clearly dangerous. Before long she'd be needing some bigger jeans.

The carer insisted on preparing an evening meal for Rose before she left. 'All part of the job and I know what she'll eat,' she told Daisy. 'And I'm only on the other end of the phone if you need me tonight. It can be a bit scary looking after someone alone for the first time but your mum's in good shape, all things considered.'

The offer of support eased the anxiety Daisy hadn't even known she'd been carrying. It wasn't that she was worried something medical might go wrong, although that was a possibility. It was more that she wasn't sure what she and her mother would talk about. Daisy had sat with her from time to time since arriving at the farm, had managed superficial conversations and helped with jigsaws and crosswords, but they hadn't spent much more than an hour alone together. The thought of an entire evening spent in gut-twisting, awkward silence made Daisy feel slightly green.

In the event, it wasn't as difficult as Daisy had feared. For the most part, Rose seemed content to watch television and Daisy thought it didn't much matter who sat with her. As darkness fell, Rose occasionally dozed off and Daisy felt able to catch up on emails and dip into social media, Atticus purring on her lap. But then Rose surprised her. 'I'm grateful you came.'

Her tone was abrupt, the words clipped, and at first Daisy wondered if she'd misheard. Then Rose drew in a long, slow breath and went on. 'It can't have been easy, abandoning your life to bring the boys here at a moment's notice and god knows you had every reason to stay away.' She paused and turned her weary gaze Daisy's way. 'But I want you to know I appreciate it. In spite of . . . everything.'

By everything, she meant her marriage to Daisy's stepfather and the slow but methodical wedge he had driven between mother and daughter until they no longer spoke. That single word encompassed years of hurt and tears, self-recrimination and guilt and loneliness. But it was also in the past – Daisy had known that the moment she'd seen her mother in a hospital bed, small and frail and looking so much older than she was. In that moment all the reasons for their bitter estrangement had flown from Daisy's mind. Nothing could undo what had gone before but somehow it seemed to matter less. They were events that had happened in another life and had no power to upset her now. Above all, it had brought home how alone her mother must be. No one sat at her bedside. The only relative she had was Daisy, the daughter she'd given up for a man with one eye on Half Moon Farm. And Daisy had determined then, as she gazed in horrified pity at the woman in the white-sheeted bed, that she would not dwell on the things neither of them could change. All that mattered was the choices they made now. 'I couldn't have not come,' she said softly.

Rose sighed, her gaze fixed on the crocheted blanket on her lap. 'I made a terrible mistake all those years ago. But by the time I realized, it was too late – you were gone and even when Vince died, I didn't know how to reach out to you. I thought you must hate me.'

'I never hated you, Mum,' Daisy said, shaking her head hard. 'I just thought you didn't want me. So I left you alone, even when I knew you must be grieving.' She paused and swallowed. 'I didn't feel good about that and I feel even worse now I've seen the house. How have you been living like this?'

Her mother was silent then, her fingers fiddling with the edge of the blanket. 'I know it's a mess. Drew does his best to help but I hate asking for favours and it was easier to just pretend everything was fine, that it wasn't all falling apart.'

'Drew?' Daisy repeated, frowning. Where had she heard that name before?

'He lives in the village,' Rose said. 'Runs the mistletoe shop here.'

And then Daisy remembered. The silver fox Magda had raved about. 'Oh, yes. I haven't met him yet.'

A smile curled the edges of Rose's mouth, lifting her pallor a little. 'He's a good man – boarded up the broken windows for me and found someone to look at the roof.'

Daisy stared at her in confusion. 'But why didn't you just call in a glazier to fix the windows? If it's a question of money—'

Her mother lifted a papery hand. 'It's not that – Vince might have been a terrible human being but he knew how to hoard money.' She puffed out a long shaky breath. 'It was more that I didn't want to face the fact that I couldn't manage the house myself.' Tears appeared in the corners of her eyes. 'I thought it meant I might have to leave.'

Moisture prickled at the back of Daisy's own eyes as she understood. 'Oh, Mum.'

'Stupid, I know,' Rose said with exhausted resignation. 'I should have dealt with things right away. Ignoring a problem doesn't make it better.'

The words hung in the air, causing the old familiar guilt Daisy had carried for so many years to well up inside her once more. Why hadn't she guessed what was happening at the farm? Why hadn't she overcome her pride and come back sooner? 'We'll deal with them now,' she said, reaching across to take her mother's hand. 'I'm here and we'll fix things together.'

Rose managed a smile, although it was a tired effort. 'Thank you. I don't want you to feel responsible for me but like I said, I'm glad you came.'

Blinking back more tears, Daisy squeezed her fingers. 'And like I said, how could I not?'

Chapter Six

Daisy was standing at the kitchen sink, washing up the breakfast things, when she saw the man in the orchard. Startled, she dropped the cup she was cleaning and it fell into the hot soapy water with a splash that soaked her jumper. She let out a muffled curse and reached for a tea-towel, sponging off the damp patch before drying her hands. Minutes later she had pulled her wellies and jacket on and was picking her way across the too-long grass towards the trees.

'Excuse me,' she called as she got nearer and saw the man had a pair of long-handled cutters in his hands. 'Can I help you with something?'

He shaded his eyes against the glare of the sun with one hand, and raised the cutters in the other. 'I don't think so. Not unless you're handy with a pair of these.'

A needle of annoyance prickled at Daisy. 'What I mean to say is, what do you think you're doing?' she said, trampling through the knee-high yellow grasses to stand in front of him. 'These are private orchards, not open to the public.'

'I know,' he said, his tone patient. 'I'm the one who tends them.'

She stared at him in astonishment. From the wild and unkempt state of the branches, she'd assumed no one tended them. 'Sorry but who are you?'

He lowered the cutters to the ground and smiled. 'Drew Entwhistle – I run one of the businesses in the yard. You must be Daisy Moon.'

Of course he was Drew, Daisy thought as she took in his salt and pepper hair, his twinkling brown eyes and lightly tanned skin – now she came to really look at him, how could he be anyone else? But in her defence, no one had told her he had anything to do with the orchard. The only thing anyone had told her about him, apart from her mother's revelations about his kindness the night before, was that he was hot and she had to concede Magda had not lied. Drew *was* a silver fox. 'Nice to meet you,' she said, after a moment to gather her wits. 'But I'm afraid I still don't understand what you're doing here. Are you a gardener or a tree surgeon as well as whatever else you do?'

If he was perturbed by her question, he didn't show it. Instead, he simply raised his eyebrows. 'It's probably easier if I show you.' His gaze travelled to the top of the nearest tree. 'You see the leaves on the highest branches there? See the way they're all twisted into a ball?'

Daisy squinted upwards and nodded. 'Yes. It's a bird's nest, right? A lot of the trees in the orchard have them, which is why I was a bit surprised to discover anyone looks after them.'

'Except they're not nests,' Drew said. 'They're mistletoe. It grows on other trees, as a parasite although it doesn't cause them any harm if it's kept under control. There are some trees it prefers, like apple or hawthorn, but it will also grow on oak.'

The penny dropped, causing Daisy to gaze around her with renewed interest. 'Of course. These are all apple trees. And you harvest the mistletoe for your business.'

'I do,' Drew said, smiling. 'It's a time-honoured tradition in these parts. There's even a mistletoe market in Canterbury at Christmas.'

Daisy frowned. 'But it's April now – no one wants mistletoe in spring, do they?'

'Not many people,' Drew admitted. 'The berries don't start to appear until September, anyway, and they take a while to grow and ripen. So the rest of the year I look after the orchard and pick the apples when they come to turn into cider. I use Nigel's kit over at Brew Crew, sometimes help out with the hops too.'

It made perfect sense, Daisy had to acknowledge. She was only just starting to realize how much community spirit existed among the businesses that had grown up around Half Moon Farm in the years she'd been away and it seemed some of that spirit had extended to take in Rose and the farmhouse too. 'It sounds like I owe you an apology,' she said, impressed at Drew's use of the farm's natural resources and pleased they hadn't been allowed to go to waste. 'I admit I thought you were up to no good.'

'Not on this occasion,' he said solemnly. And then he winked.

It was so unexpected that Daisy laughed, a bright bubble of amusement that burst out of her before she could catch it. When was the last time an attractive man had winked at her? When was the last time *anyone* had winked at her?

'Well,' she said, warmth suffusing her cheeks as she realized she was staring at him. 'I should let you get on. Sorry to have interrupted.'

'I'm not sorry,' he said, shrugging. 'If you hadn't come out here to challenge me then we wouldn't have met and my day would be all the poorer for it.'

There was nothing unusual about the words, gentlemanly flattery aside, but Daisy felt the breath catch in the back of her throat nonetheless. Once again, she was wrong-footed but it wasn't an unpleasant sensation, more the impression that he'd offered an unspoken invitation to play and was waiting to see how she reacted. 'Then I'm glad I saw you,' she said. 'Especially since I need to thank you for helping my mother with the windows and the roof.'

He waved her words away. 'Oh, that was nothing. Any of the other business owners would have done the same, if they'd noticed the problems.'

Someone else probably had, Daisy thought. But only Drew had taken it upon himself to help. She owed him for that.

'Still, thank you. I know there's a lot that needs to be put right with the house. Mum said you've been in touch with a roofer but if there are any other local tradesmen you recommend then let me know.'

'I will,' Drew said, inclining his head. Reaching for the cutters at his feet once more, he aimed a speculative look Daisy's way. 'Would you like to help with the pruning? They're your trees after all.'

Ordinarily, she would have said no – she wasn't much of a gardener. But there was something about the way he looked at her and once again, she sensed there was more than just his words hanging in the air. 'Okay. You'll have to tell me what to do, though. I'm the least green-fingered person you'll ever meet.'

He nodded, as though pleased, and handed her the cutters. 'Come and stand here, under the tree,' he said, stepping back to give her room. 'See up there, where the branches are bowing under the extra weight of the mistletoe?'

She nodded, conscious of him directly behind her even though he was standing a discreet distance away. Her nose caught a hint of his aftershave, a woody mossed scent that was somehow warming and perfectly suited to what she knew of him. 'Yes.'

'The mistletoe here is well established and grows fast but we don't want it to overwhelm its host – that's no good for either of them.' Drew's voice was calm but also somehow intimate beneath the canopy of the tree. 'We need to prune it back so that the apple tree can thrive just as much as the mistletoe. If you cut here—' he broke off to point at a sinewy strand of the deep green plant, '—and here, some of the weight should fall away.'

Concentrating, Daisy did as he suggested, carefully snipping at the strands until they dropped back. Instantly, the tree branch unbowed itself and straightened, and a shower of mistletoe tumbled to the ground.

'Well done,' Drew said at Daisy's shoulder. 'I think you're a natural mistletoe farmer.'

She turned to smile at him, realized just how close he was and then suddenly, unbidden, remembered what this particular plant was usually for. 'Oh,' she squeaked, stepping hurriedly away and offering him the cutters. 'I don't know about that.'

He took the cutters and met her gaze with undisguised interest. 'Maybe an apprentice then. For now.'

The attention was suddenly all too much for Daisy. Flustered, she took refuge in her mother's illness. 'I'd better get back inside,' she said, the words tumbling out too fast. 'Mum's on her own, the carer won't be here until midday.'

Drew gave her an easy smile, which only served to make Daisy feel more rattled. 'Of course. It was nice to meet you.'

She took a surreptitiously calming breath and began to back away. 'And you. Thanks for the pruning lesson.'

'No problem,' he said. 'Any time, in fact.'

With a final wave, Daisy turned on her heel and hurried away through the overgrown grass. She didn't stop until she was back in the kitchen, the reassuringly solid oak door firm against her shoulder blades as she quietened her thudding heart and willed her flaming cheeks to cool. It wasn't that her encounter with Drew had upset her – far from it. It was more that it had been a long time since she'd felt the pull of such primeval, natural attraction. The realization both thrilled and dismayed her, because there was no doubt that a crush on one of the farm's near neighbours was pretty inconvenient, especially if she reacted like a lovesick teenager every time she was near him. Closing her eyes, Daisy forced herself to breathe. Silver fox or not, there was no way she could start anything with Drew – always supposing she hadn't completely imagined his signals. The best thing she could do was be coolly polite, and make sure she never found herself under the mistletoe with him again.

★ ★ ★

Monday morning had been a predictable scramble of lost shoes, unmatched socks and missing water bottles. Daisy had stood in the middle of the kitchen as Campbell and Finn charged around her, their unchannelled excitement and nerves almost a tangible force, and wondered how this could happen every single time. She'd laid everything out the night before, checked and double-checked their uniforms were where they should be and yet somehow, all that preparation had been undone. Somehow, she had got them into the car and through the school gates to meet the headteacher, who escorted them to their classroom. Somehow, she'd driven back home through a fog of post-adrenaline comedown. And somehow, she'd made it through the day, not only managing several rough spreads for a new picture book she was illustrating but also liaising with the farmyard's broadband provider about the upcoming works to lay the necessary cabling and speaking to the roofer about the repairs. By the time she returned to the school gates at quarter past three, she had almost forgotten the stresses of the morning. The twins appeared at the door of their classroom, neither sporting any kind of graze or bandage. Finn's trousers still had knees. Daisy let out a long slow breath of relief as she fist-bumped each of them in turn. It seemed they had survived their first day without major incident.

'So, how was it?' she asked as they made their way towards the school gates. 'Okay?'

Finn nodded enthusiastically. 'We played football at lunch time. Turns out they have a school team and they need players.'

'That's good,' Daisy replied cautiously, because she wasn't sure she was quite ready to fall back into the routine of ferrying him back and forth to training. 'How about you, Campbell?'

'I played chess,' he said. 'There's a girl called Alice who's quite good. In fact, I think she might be better than me.'

'Oh,' Daisy said, quirking her lips. Campbell had been able to beat her at chess from the age of six. 'That sounds interesting. So you both had good days.'

They nodded in unison, causing Daisy's smile to widen. 'Then I'm calling today a win. Who fancies a takeaway for supper?'

Unsurprisingly, this was met with enthusiasm too. Grinning, Daisy herded them through the gates towards the car. She glanced around to check the road was clear and then stopped dead. There in front of her was Kit Devereaux, his hand resting on the shoulder of a child around the same age as the twins. 'You,' she said, feeling her face flush scarlet.

He stared at her impassively for a moment, then his gaze slid to Campbell and Finn, taking in their uniforms, exactly the same as the one worn by the girl at his side. 'Miss Moon,' he said, one eyebrow raised as he shook his head in sardonic disbelief. 'It seems you're a little more local than you realized.'

Part Two

Summer Loving

Chapter Seven

'Kit Devereaux.' Nancy shook her head and gazed at Daisy with a mixture of pity and sympathetic amusement. 'Of all the cars in all of Mistlethorpe, you had to reverse into his.'

The two of them were sitting at a table in the dimly lit Oast House café, sipping hot chocolate and, in Daisy's case, nibbling at a sour cherry muffin. It was just after five o'clock and, like most of the businesses that surrounded the cobbled yard of Half Moon Farm, the café had closed for the day. Outside, the occasional rumble of a car could be heard, often accompanied by excited barking as dog owners came and went, collecting their pets from Waggy Mamma's doggy day care. But even the whipped cream and marshmallows on top of the hot chocolate could not lift Daisy's weary annoyance as she met Nancy's eyes. 'I know,' she said with a heartfelt sigh as she recalled Kit Devereaux's disdain at the school gates that afternoon. 'We exchanged a few text messages straight after the accident last week but I hoped I'd never have to deal with him again. I couldn't believe it when I saw him glaring at me across the playground.'

'He might be a bit tricky to avoid, since his daughter is in the same class as Campbell and Finn.' Nancy pulled a face, 'And his family owns Winterbourne Castle, not to mention most of the village.'

Daisy's heart sank. She'd known there must be a connection when she'd visited the public parts of the castle with her sons and discovered a lengthy row of Devereaux family portraits in the Long Gallery. Kit Devereaux might not have been among them but Daisy had felt sure the unusual name couldn't be coincidence. She thought back to the paintings, remembering the current Earl of Winterbourne had been missing and her spirits dipped even lower – she didn't need a portrait to summon up an image of Kit Devereaux's condescending disapproval. It was just her luck to have crashed into a member of the aristocracy, and worse still that she was going to be reminded of her mistake every school day for months to come. 'That explains his arrogance,' she said with a groan. 'Honestly, you'd think he'd caught me robbing a bank or something.'

'I imagine he was surprised,' Nancy observed mildly. 'You did tell him you lived in Milton Keynes.'

'I do live in Milton Keynes,' Daisy said, a little stung. 'Most of the time. A minor car accident doesn't mean I owe a stranger my life story, no matter how much of Mistlethorpe he apparently owns.'

Her friend raised her hands in a placatory gesture. 'Don't

shoot me. I'm just saying that I don't suppose he was expecting to bump into you again outside the school gates, that's all.'

There was a joke to be made about only having bumped into him *once* but in Daisy's current mood she knew it would come across as peevish rather than funny. And annoyingly, Nancy had a point. Daisy hadn't lied when Kit initially asked whether she was a local; her life, and that of her sons, *was* in Milton Keynes and they would be returning to it in a few months' time, once she was sure her mother was fully recovered from heart surgery. She could, however, accept that perhaps her appearance at the school gates had been something of a surprise. 'Yeah, I'm sorry,' she told Nancy, offering her friend a crooked smile. 'What with Mum and the move, together with everything that needs fixing at the farmhouse, things have been a bit stressful. It's making me tetchy.'

'Blimey, who wouldn't be with all of that to contend with?' Nancy pushed the plate with the half-eaten cherry muffin towards Daisy. 'But that's why we have cake. And don't worry about Kit – you've got off to a wobbly start but he's not bad for a posh bloke. The family have always done a lot for the village.'

Which raised another question that had been troubling Daisy – if the Devereaux family were such a presence in Mistlethorpe, why hadn't she heard the name before? She'd spent entire summers at Half Moon Farm as a child and no one had ever mentioned them, nor had there been any days out at Winterbourne Castle, although she'd known the rest of the village well. Was it strange that she couldn't recall her grandparents or her mother *ever* talking about them? Kit Devereaux had recognized the

surname Moon when Daisy had given it, and linked it to Half Moon Farm, but then she supposed that was less of a mystery, given who he was. She had no idea what an earl actually did but she supposed it made sense that he would be aware of who his neighbours were. One thing she did know, his title certainly didn't mean Daisy had to curtsey every time she saw him. In fact, her plan was to see him as little as possible. She had no doubt he felt the same way about her.

Sensing Nancy was watching her, Daisy dipped her head in diplomatic agreement. 'I'm sure you're right,' she said and reached for what was left of the muffin. 'Now, enough about arsey aristocrats, tell me how your day's been. I hope it was better than mine.'

★ ★ ★

Daisy awoke on Tuesday with an uncharacteristic sense of reluctance about the day ahead but it wasn't until she'd swung her legs out of bed and touched her feet to the chilly wooden floor that the reason for her unease crystalized. There was no denying that the thought of running into Kit Devereaux was the problem, despite her determination not to be intimidated, and she found herself wondering how early she could drop the boys off. Not early enough to avoid a meeting, she concluded with a dispirited huff. But perhaps she was fretting over nothing – she'd watched enough episodes of *The Crown* to know that men like Kit Devereaux didn't lower themselves to the school run twice a day. He'd leave that to his wife, or perhaps a nanny, neither of whom would know Daisy. There really was nothing to be anxious about.

And yet her thoughts returned to the conversation she'd had with her mother the evening before. They'd been in the cluttered living room, the television showing a quiz show that no one was paying attention to. Finn and Campbell were tucked up in bed, and Magda the carer had popped to the kitchen to make tea, so Daisy had taken the opportunity to ask Rose about the Devereaux family.

Rose had lowered her knitting and given her a sharp look. 'Good thing your grandfather isn't here. He'd make you wash your mouth out with soap for mentioning that name under his roof.'

The vehemence in her tone had caused Daisy to blink. She couldn't recall ever having heard her grandfather raise his voice, let alone threaten such a Victorian punishment, but it certainly seemed true that the Devereaux name had been unwelcome at Half Moon Farm. 'Why?' she asked. 'Did something happen?'

'I don't know,' Rose said. 'I always assumed it was something to do with money or land. The usual things men fight over.'

Money or land or love, Daisy thought but didn't say

because Rose was frowning down at her knitting. 'It only really bothered me when there was a party at the castle that I couldn't go to – we had a big argument over the Christmas Ball when I was sixteen or seventeen.'

Daisy was all too aware of the tempestuous relationship between teenage Rose and her parents – she could easily imagine missing out on a party at Winterbourne would be a flashpoint. 'What happened?' she asked.

Rose sighed. 'I went anyway. Climbed out of my bedroom window and almost caught my death yomping across the fields in the dead of winter. Tore my dress on the hawthorn hedge too.'

Daisy could picture the scene as though she'd been there. 'I bet you were still the belle of the ball.'

'Hardly,' Rose said, with a sudden snort. 'When I finally reached the castle, they wouldn't let me in. Stopped me at the drawbridge, like I was an invader.'

'What?' Daisy felt her jaw drop. 'Why?'

Her mother glanced at her. 'I wasn't on the list, they said, even though the whole of Mistlethorpe was invited. I mean, I did look like I'd been dragged through a hedge backwards so I could hardly blame them for turning me away.' Rose paused and shook her head, her blue eyes misty with remembrance. 'But it wasn't my appearance that was the problem – it was my name.'

Righteous indignation fizzed through Daisy's veins as she imagined how humiliated Rose must have been. 'What did you do?'

'What could I do?' Rose said with a resigned shrug. 'I walked home. Dad met me at the farmhouse door, arms folded and a face like thunder. I expected to get bawled out but he just looked at me and said he hoped I'd learned my lesson – the Moons and the Devereauxs don't mix.'

It was beginning to sound like a family feud, one that only made Daisy more curious about the cause. What could have inspired such animosity in her mild-mannered grandfather? 'And you really never knew why?'

'No,' Rose said. 'I'm sure I asked but that's all he would ever say. We always just kept our distance.'

The door had opened then and Magda bustled in with a tray laden with mugs and teapot, but Daisy had spent the rest of the evening burning with curiosity mingled with sympathy for teenage Rose. And while whatever had gone on in the past had nothing to do Daisy or Kit Devereaux, she'd be lying if she didn't think even less charitably of him after hearing her mother's story. It seemed that now, as then, the two families were destined not to get along. But no matter what the history, Daisy still had to run the gauntlet of taking Finn and Campbell to school. Telling herself she was overthinking the situation, she pulled on her dressing gown and went to wake the twins.

Her sense of trepidation returned full force as she walked towards the school gate. She had spotted Kit almost the moment she and the boys had left the car; there was something about the way he carried himself that made him instantly recognizable, but thankfully he'd been further ahead and couldn't have seen her. Daisy kept her eyes on him as Campbell and Finn chatted beside her, noticing how often he exchanged a greeting with other parents. At the gate, he stopped for a longer conversation with a member of school staff and Daisy was obliged to stop too, rummaging in her handbag and muttering about forgetting her phone.

'We're going to be late,' Campbell grumbled, with an anxious look at his watch.

'Just a minute,' Daisy said, casting a surreptitious glance towards the school gate. 'Okay, let's go in.'

She kept her head down as they entered the playground but kept an eye on Kit's location through her periphery vision. He was bending down, talking to his daughter, Alice. When he straightened up, his attention seemed focused on the classroom door and Daisy was sure he hadn't noticed her but it wasn't until the bell rang and the doors opened that she felt the tension in her shoulders ease a little. 'In you go,' she told the twins, knowing better than to attempt an affectionate goodbye. 'Have a good day.'

She watched them amble to the door, her gaze flicking once or twice to Kit, who was doing the same thing with Alice. A female voice interrupted Daisy's vigilance. 'He catches the eye, doesn't he?'

Blinking, she turned to see who had spoken. A short, dark-haired woman was standing beside her, her brown eyes dancing with knowing amusement. 'Sorry, I'm not sure I understand what you mean,' Daisy said, even as her cheeks grew warm with the lie.

The woman smiled. 'Oh, don't worry – half the village is in love with Kit Devereaux. It's the RAF thing for me. You can take the officer out of uniform and all that.'

Daisy wasn't quite sure how to react to the unexpected confidence, or the misguided inference that she fancied Kit, and latched onto the least significant aspect of the revelation. 'Oh, was he in the Forces?'

'Helicopter pilot,' her new friend supplied, apparently oblivious to Daisy's discomfort. 'Wing Commander, no less. And now he gives flying lessons over at Marston airport.' She sighed and glanced across the playground again. 'Who wouldn't want to be alone in a plane with him?'

Me, Daisy almost said but decided that would only prolong an increasingly awkward conversation, when what she really wanted was to escape. 'Mmmm,' she said, her tone non-committal. 'Well, I'd better get going. Nice to meet you.'

She flashed the woman a brisk smile and, without waiting for a reply, turned towards the gate. Out of the corner of her eye, she saw Kit turn too and the thought of meeting his disdainful gaze was galvanizing. Lowering her head, she hurried for the safety of her car and it wasn't until she was behind the wheel that she allowed herself to breathe. So Kit had been an RAF officer, had he? That fitted with the portraits she'd seen at Winterbourne – it was undoubtedly a family tradition – and also chimed with the authoritative air she'd disliked so much. But unlike the woman in the playground, his previous career held no appeal for Daisy – if anything, it made her all the more determined to avoid him.

She was a little surprised an earl had the time to offer flying lessons but with a bit of luck it might mean he was high in the sky for that afternoon's school run and she wouldn't have to run the gauntlet of dodging him again. Catching sight of her flushed cheeks and anxious eyes in the mirror, Daisy puffed out a sigh. She could only hope.

Chapter Eight

A cacophony of barking greeted Daisy as she drove into the circular yard of Half Moon Farm. She was gradually getting used to the occasional enthusiastic outburst from her neighbours at Waggy Mamma's but this level of noise was unusual even by their standards. But she was immediately distracted by the sight of Drew Entwhistle emerging from the doorway of Darling Buds flower shop. His arms were laden with a gardening bag overflowing with greenery and Daisy felt her stomach contract in pleasure as he glanced across and smiled. He stopped, clearly waiting for her, so she eased the car forwards until she was level with him and lowered the window. A fresh volley of barks caused her to wince.

'Something's got them excited this morning,' she said.

He nodded. 'Spring is in the air. I think they can smell the sap rising.'

Daisy knew what he meant – everywhere she looked, she could see things growing, from the sudden burst of green on bare brown branches that always caught her by surprise, to the riot of purple wisteria blossoming across the wall of the oast house. This morning, the sun had started to burn away the grey wisps of early cloud and the farmyard was bathed in its gentle warmth. Daisy couldn't help noticing the way the light danced on Drew's silver hair, creating a faint halo. Perhaps she could blame spring for the distinctly non-angelic thoughts she'd had about him since their first meeting at the weekend. Judging from the way her stomach was flip-flopping now, the instant attraction that had so startled her in the orchard showed no sign of abating. Swallowing, she dampened down the thought and gestured at the burden he carried. 'You've got your hands full there.'

'It's for the May Day celebrations on the village green,' he explained. 'Every year, I make a Jack in the Green costume for the parade, covered in foliage and flowers. It's a tradition that goes back hundreds of years, along with the maypole and Morris dancing.'

Daisy fought to keep a straight face. In her experience, Morris dancers were more blessed with enthusiasm than talent but she might have known Mistlethorpe would have a band of them, just as she should have expected the village would take its May Day celebrations seriously. 'There's a parade?' she asked.

'It starts at the mill, goes along the High Street and finishes on the green,' Drew said. 'Some of us dress up in costume, the kids ride hobby horses and then we crown the May

Queen and everyone spins themselves silly winding ribbons round the maypole.'

And now Daisy couldn't help a sceptical glance. 'A May Queen – seriously? Isn't that a bit beauty pageant?'

Drew grinned. 'They don't wear bikinis. And the crown is made of flowers, not diamonds. It's her job to welcome spring, to encourage bountiful growth for a good harvest later in the year.'

She raised her eyebrows. 'And the maypole, what does that encourage?'

'Dancing, of course,' Drew said, his face studiously inno-cent. 'What else could it be for?'

She held his gaze, which was twinkling with mirth that belied his guileless expression. 'Of course. I look forward to seeing your moves.'

His lips curved into a smile that made Daisy's insides fizz. 'And I can't wait to see yours.'

They gazed at each other for a moment, then Daisy remembered where she was. Managing a nod, she put the car into gear and rolled forward. She hadn't expected to meet anyone like Drew Entwhistle during her extended stay at Half Moon Farm and she definitely didn't want the complication of a romantic entanglement. But that didn't mean she couldn't enjoy some harmless flirtation. And as she snuck a sneaky glance at his retreating form in the rear-view mirror, she had to admit she very much enjoyed flirting with Drew.

Her good mood dissipated a little when she met Emily,

her mother's day time carer, in the hallway. 'Oh, you're back,' the rosy-cheeked woman said, sounding flustered. 'Effie just called, from Waggy Mamma's. She wants you to go and collect Atticus.'

Daisy blinked in surprise. The cat was still meant to be under house arrest following the move to the farm. 'Atticus? I thought he was asleep on my bed.'

Emily shifted awkwardly. 'Well, he was and then I might have accidentally let him out when I put the recycling in the bin. Sorry.'

'And now he's over at Waggy Mamma's, terrorizing the dogs,' Daisy groaned, remembering the torrent of barking she'd heard. 'I hope he hasn't hurt any of them.'

'Effie said he was sitting on the fence,' the carer replied. 'Looking like a feline Genghis Khan.'

Daisy sighed. Underneath his bulk and generally terrifying demeanour, her cat was a puddle of gingery love but dogs were his sworn enemy, to be conquered at all times. 'That sounds like Atticus.'

In the distance, renewed barking could be heard. 'You'd better go now before war breaks out,' Emily said. 'I'll put the kettle on, eh?'

Effie met her in the reception area. 'Thanks for coming over. He's shown no sign of coming down from the fence but the dogs are going crazy, as you can hear.'

'I'm so sorry,' Daisy said, cringing inside. 'He's not even supposed to be out and about yet.'

The other woman brushed her apology aside with an

understanding grimace. 'Don't worry, I've got a cat of my own. I know they're a law unto themselves.'

That made Daisy feel a little better but anxiety still squirmed within her as she followed Effie towards the back of the building. If she knew Atticus, he would be taking great satisfaction from having a captive audience to torment and even if she removed him now, he would be back for more as soon as he could escape from the farmhouse. But that was a problem for later: right now, she needed to get him down from the fence.

The rear of Waggy Mamma's was doggy heaven. The ground was a mixture of sandy areas and grassy sections, populated with a range of equipment that wouldn't look amiss in a children's playground. Toys and balls littered the floor, while several employees stood watching the dogs play. While most of the dogs mingled together in the main area, some were in a smaller, fenced off area beside what looked like indoor kennels. 'Those are our quieter guests,' Effie said, catching Daisy looking. 'Not all dogs like the rough and tumble vibe of the main enclosure and we've found giving them a chill out zone reduces disagreements.'

Daisy was about to reply when she saw Atticus. He had been sitting on the high wooden fence at the very back of the yard but now he stood, arching his back in an exaggerated stretch, and padded along the top of the fence. The response was immediate; the dogs who had been prowling along the base of the fence instantly broke into a succession of deafening barks. Atticus surveyed them, utterly unconcerned.

'As you can see, he's enjoying himself,' Effie said dryly. 'But all good things must come to an end. If we bring the dogs inside, do you think you can persuade him to come down?'

Daisy pulled an unopened tin of sardines from her pocket. 'I came prepared.'

'Excellent,' Effie said, grinning. 'Wait here, we'll round up the dogs.'

Twenty minutes later, hot and smelling slightly of fish, Daisy was back in the reception area with an unrepentant cat sulking in her arms. She puffed her hair from her sweaty forehead. 'Sorry again,' she said to Effie, who was regarding Atticus with an amused expression. 'I'll try to keep him out of your way.'

Effie laughed. 'Might as well try to stop the sun from shining,' she said. 'But I'll have a word with our maintenance guy, see if he can think of any safe deterrents.'

'Have you considered getting a lion?' Daisy suggested with a wry grin. But Effie's comment triggered another thought.. 'I'm looking for someone to do a bit of work at the farmhouse, actually. Do you think your maintenance guy might have time?'

Effie rummaged behind the reception desk. 'Here's his card — why don't you ask him? He lives in Mistlethorpe and does good work.'

Daisy slipped the card into her pocket. 'Thank you, that's really helpful.'

'No problem,' Effie replied cheerfully. 'Good luck with the cat herding.'

Adjusting her grip on the suddenly squirming Atticus, Daisy adopted a pained expression and made for the door. 'Thanks. I think I'm going to need it.'

* * *

It wasn't until Daisy climbed into bed that night that the sheer busyness of the day hit her. She'd spent the rest of the morning working on illustrations for a picture book, broken up by frequent hunts for Atticus to ensure he hadn't broken out again. Her agent, Phoebe, had emailed, suggesting they meet in London for lunch – ordinarily, that was something Daisy would have leapt at but days away from home were more problematic now she was living in Kent. The journey itself wasn't the issue – trains were frequent – but lunches with Phoebe were never short and she might struggle to get back for the school pick up, with no cushion of Stuart living nearby. But Phoebe had understood the difficulty and proposed lunch in Canterbury instead. After that, there had been more phone calls about the impending fibrelink installation, a call to Effie's maintenance man about the window repairs in the farmhouse and then it had been time to drive to the school to collect Campbell and Finn, a prospect that once again filled Daisy with unease, but she'd managed to loiter behind a group of other parents and fly underneath Kit's radar.

The twins had been full of their day – school dinners were apparently much better in Kent than at home in Milton Keynes – but both had been struggling to hide their yawns by eight o'clock. Finn maintained he wanted to watch that evening's football but gave in without too much complaint when Daisy had herded the pair of them upstairs. She wasn't sure if it was the fresh country air or the newness of their surroundings but both were asleep almost as soon as their heads hit the pillow, and Daisy knew she wouldn't be far behind them. She'd made her excuses around nine-thirty and slipped to bed with a mug of camomile tea, snapping a selfie to send to her friends in Milton Keynes.

How times change!

Immediately, messages began to ping in reply.

Kerry: *JEALOUS!*
Nic: *In bed with a book, is there anything better?*
Louise: *In bed with that guy from Bridgerton??*
Kerry: *Oooooh . . ..*
Nic: *Nah, give me a good book any day. Enjoy, Daisy!*

She didn't tell them it wasn't a book she was settling down with, but a box of faded love letters to her grand-mother, Violet. Daisy had no idea whether it was the family connection that drew her in, or the aching sense of everything not being said that made her greedy for more, but she found herself quite desperate for her nightly fix before bed. She'd decided not long after finding the letters that some kind of rationing was in order or she would binge on them faster than a boxset but she'd allowed herself the luxury of rereading the early letters. That second read had sucked her in even

further – revisiting the words had only deepened her fascination with the mystery serviceman whose eloquence had
her spellbound. She devoured each letter with the hope she
would find a clue to his identity but so far he remained
hidden behind his initial.

984632 FL AJD
75 MTLRV
Royal Air Force

1st May

My Dear Violet
 *Thank you for your recent letters, three of which have
arrived at the same time and give me an excuse to lock
myself away to reply. What joy! If I close my eyes, I can
almost pretend you are here, although it makes reality so
much more disappointing when I remember you are not.*
 *Please do not believe your letters are badly written or
boring! I very much enjoy your descriptions of village life –
they are a little slice of home that lift my spirits no end. I
hope Mr Barker and his bicycle have recovered their dignity
now, even if the duck pond may never be the same, and I
am sure Mrs Entwhistle will ensure the butcher's boy learns
from his mistake, which was just the silliness of youth, after
all. But oh, how I long to be in Mistlethorpe today,
admiring the twisting ribbons of the maypole on the green.
Are you wearing flowers in your hair while you dance,*

dearest Violet? You must surely have been crowned May Queen – there isn't a more dazzling girl than you in the whole of Kent, if not England. I shall dream of being your consort, a Jack in the Green who bows before your queenliness. Perhaps, when this war is over, we will make this dream come true. You are already queen of my heart.

Yours ever,

V

Frowning, Daisy lowered the almost translucent paper to the bed covers. It must be serendipity that had led her to read this particular letter after her conversation about May Day that morning but it was the mention of the surname Entwhistle that gave her the most pause. It wasn't a common name – surely the woman mentioned must be a relative of Drew, perhaps even his grandmother or great-grandmother. And had Violet been a May Queen? V had not returned home to marry her, of that Daisy was sure. Maybe he'd never returned home at all . . .

The temptation to pluck another envelope from the box was oh-so-strong but Daisy wrestled the impulse into submission. She knew, having put the letters into date order when she had first found the box, that they went into 1946 and stopped abruptly. Perhaps the fate of the serviceman would be revealed then, or perhaps she would never know. What mattered was the journey she was taking – Violet and her unknown soldier were giving Daisy a fresh perspective on a lot of things, from the woman her grandmother had been to how hard it must have been to love in such wretched circumstances. There must be heartbreak to come, for one or both of them, and Daisy was braced for tears, even as she wondered how much of the break up would be captured on the page. But she was trying not to think about that. For now, she was treasuring this unexpected chance to peer through a window into the past. It was a lovely way to wind down at the end of each day – far better than mindlessly scrolling through her phone – and she was in no hurry to reach the last of the letters. Something told her she would be quite bereft when she did.

Chapter Nine

'Can I join the school football team?'

It was a question Daisy had known was coming from the moment Finn had told her his new school had a team. Playing football had been a huge part of his life back in Milton Keynes and she knew he missed both the camaraderie of his team mates and the sheer joy of kicking a ball around. Daisy had been against finding a regular Saturday morning team to play for while they were living at Half Moon Farm in Kent but the school team could be a worthwhile compromise. Surely there wouldn't be many matches – it was almost summer, after all.

'That depends,' she told Finn on Friday afternoon as she manoeuvred the car out of its space and away from the school gates. 'When is training?'

'Tuesdays after school,' he said, leaning forward in eagerness. 'Our class teacher is the coach and he says they could definitely use someone with my ball control. There's a match coming up soon, against one of the other local schools – can I play?'

It would mean doing the school pick up twice, Daisy thought, knowing there was absolutely no chance that Campbell would be interested in joining his brother. But that wasn't an insurmountable hardship and it would help Finn feel more settled to be part of a team again. 'Okay, let me look into it. I'll speak to the school office on Monday.'

Finn shook his head impatiently. 'The coach is going to message you today. Please say yes.'

'We'll see,' Daisy said firmly and glanced in the rear-view mirror at her other son. 'How about you, Campbell? Any activities you'd like to join in with?'

He leaned forward too. 'Chess club. They meet on Wednesdays but it's a lunchtime, not after school.'

Beside him, Finn rolled his eyes. 'Boring. You only want to go because of Alice.'

Campbell's cheeks flushed. 'Huh. If anyone is obsessed with Alice, it's you. That's why you're so keen to join the football team, because *she's* their star player.'

'That's not true,' Finn fired back. 'Obviously, she plays for them but that's not why I want to join.'

'It's not why I want to go to chess club, either!'

Daisy frowned, her gaze flickering between the two of them. 'Hold on, which Alice are we talking about? The one in your class?'

Simultaneously, they nodded and Daisy's enthusiasm for both clubs took a nosedive. The Alice in Campbell and Finn's class was Kit Devereaux's daughter and she wasn't keen on anything that might bring her into closer proximity to him. It sounded like she'd get away with chess club but football was another matter entirely. She knew from experience that interacting with the other players' parents on the touchline was unavoidable. 'Oh.'

'I don't *like* her,' Finn insisted. 'Even though she lives at the castle and her dad has loads of money.'

'He might not have loads of money,' Campbell argued. 'Castles take loads of looking after and some posh people are really poor. There's a documentary called *Ruinous Ruins* on the History channel.'

Daisy was reminded of Kit's job as a flying instructor; maybe Campbell was nearer the truth than he knew, although Winterbourne was most definitely not a ruin. Nevertheless, she aimed a stern look towards the back seat. 'It's none of our business. I'm sure you wouldn't like people saying the same thing about you.'

Campbell snorted. 'Finn's already told everyone you're famous. He found one of your books in the library and boasted it was illustrated by his mum.'

So much for keeping a low profile, Daisy thought wryly. Her career wasn't a secret but she didn't go out of her way to shout about it either, especially not at her sons' school.

'She's not famous,' Finn said dismissively. 'No one's ever heard of her.'

Daisy couldn't help laughing – there was no chance of

her success going to her head while Finn and Campbell were around. 'Thanks.'

'Alice's dad is a pilot,' Campbell said. 'She says he's got his own plane.'

Jaw clenching slightly, Daisy turned onto the High Street. It was Friday afternoon and the whole weekend was stretching ahead – a weekend where she didn't need to worry about dodging Kit Devereaux at the school gates – and she was hearing just a little too much about him. 'Who wants an ice cream?' she said, in an effort to distract the boys.

It worked – both quivered to attention like a pair of meerkats. 'Me,' they chorused in perfect synchronicity.

Daisy nodded and pulled into a parking place outside Mario's café. 'Okay. There's just one rule. No football club chat, no chess club chat and definitely no—' She broke off, aware that she'd been about to demand 'no Alice chat', which would only cause one or both of her sons to ask what she had against their classmate. The realisation made her feel slightly ashamed as she corrected herself. 'No school chat. Deal?'

She held her breath, half-expecting Campbell to point out she'd actually listed three rules but the prospect of ice cream clearly overcame his pedantry. 'Deal!' came the enthusiastic reply and Daisy breathed out.

'Come on, then.'

Once they were seated and the boys were tucking into knickerbocker glories that were as big as their heads, Daisy checked her emails. Sure enough, there was one from Mr

Harris, the twins' teacher, asking whether Finn might like to join the school football team. Training was, as Finn had said, on Tuesdays after school and they had a match the week after the May Day bank holiday. Hesitating for a moment, she forwarded the email on to Stuart to get his opinion, although she already knew what he would say. His reply was swift and utterly predictable:

Let him play. What harm could it do?

None at all to her ex-husband, Daisy thought grumpily, since he was back in Milton Keynes and wouldn't have to adjust one little bit to fit in training and matches and all the other things that went with being part of a team. But she also had to concede that wasn't Stuart's fault — she'd accepted parenting would be pretty much a solo effort once she came to Kent — and he couldn't know she was trying to avoid one of the other player's parents. He was just putting Finn's happiness first, which of course was what Daisy should do, instead of hiding behind her own discomfort. With swift determination, she typed out a reply to Mr Harris and arrived at a resolution.. From Monday, she would hold her head up in the school playground and not scurry away like a frightened little mouse. It was time to stop caring what Kit Devereaux thought.

★ ★ ★

Work began on the hole in the roof on Monday afternoon and men with diggers arrived on Wednesday to start laying the fibrelink that would drag the farmhouse into the twenty-first century, at least where Wi-Fi was concerned, meaning

Daisy's productivity took a nosedive. She was glad of an excuse to escape the clattering and drone of machinery on Thursday as she set off to meet her agent for lunch. The restaurant Phoebe had chosen overlooked the River Stour and Daisy wasn't surprised to discover it boasted a Michelin star – Phoebe always seemed to know the best places – but the thing she was looking forward to the most was catching up. Phoebe's client list ranged from best-selling novelists like Merina Wilde to the world-famous photographer Logan Silk and she always had a story to tell about the latest glamorous party she'd been to. Sometimes Daisy wondered whether she truly belonged among the household names her agent trotted out as clients or friends but then she reminded herself that her own work was loved by children and had even topped a bestseller list or two. And Phoebe showed no sign of dissatisfaction; in fact her eyes were sparkling as she surveyed Daisy across the rustic wooden table. 'I've got the most gorgeous new commission for you – perfect now you've gone all *Darling Buds of May.*'

Daisy's lips quirked. 'Go on.'

Her agent leaned forwards. 'I'm sure you've read *The Secret Garden*, by Frances Hodgson Burnett?'

'Of course,' Daisy said, recalling a much-loved battered hardback book with a grubby flyleaf that had been on her grandparent's bookshelves. 'It was one of my favourites when I was growing up.'

'Mine too,' Phoebe said, smiling. 'I think I was a bit in love with Dickon. Anyway, it's the centenary of the author's death coming up and a major publisher has asked if you'd be interested in doing a fully illustrated, collector's edition to celebrate her life and work.'

Daisy didn't even have to think. Images of the neglected walled garden from the story were unfurling in her mind, the gothic pile of Misselthwaite Manor looming in the background as Mary and her friends restored its beauty and mended their own hearts in the process. Now she understood Phoebe's *Darling Buds* reference – Kent was known as the Garden of England, after all. 'I'd love to,' she said.

Phoebe beamed at her in delight. 'Great. I'll send over the brief, so you've got all the details, and then we can hammer out the contract. Think big on this one, Daisy – glorious double spreads that sing with joy. I can't think of anyone better suited to it, especially now that you're living the countryside dream.'

Again, Daisy's lips twisted in amusement; the tortured rumble of machinery and shouts of hi-vis jacketed workers were hardly the stuff of dreams but she knew what Phoebe meant. Mistlethorpe was fairly idyllic and there would certainly be no shortage of beautiful gardens in the area to visit for inspiration over the coming months. 'I'll get my thinking cap on,' she promised.

'Excellent,' Phoebe said, sitting back and reaching for her wine glass. 'Now, do you think pork belly or the trout? I can't choose.'

★ ★ ★

120

The chaos around Half Moon Farm lessened over the remainder of the week. The hole in the roof was mended, which meant Daisy no longer needed to keep such an anxious eye on the weather forecast, and the work to supply the farmhouse with a decent broadband connection was completed too. She almost cheered on Friday afternoon when she sent a large file to her publisher and watched the upload percentage speed to 100 without a hitch. It was a shame the twins were going to Stuart's for the weekend and wouldn't be able to marvel at the improvement but at least it should prevent any further grumbles when they came back.

'Anything I need to know?' Stuart asked when he arrived to collect them on Friday evening.

'Just the usual,' Daisy said as she handed over their weekend bags. 'Finn has his first match with the school team next week so I expect you'll be in goal for most of the weekend.'

He nodded, as though he'd been expecting as much. 'I've got us tickets for the MK Dons match tomorrow – they're playing at home.'

'Campbell will be delighted,' Daisy observed dryly. 'I hope you don't mind bringing them back on Sunday rather than Monday. They're weirdly excited about the May Day parade – apparently, they made masks in school.'

Stuart raised an eyebrow. 'A village parade. How jolly.'

There was something in his tone that made Daisy frown. 'I think it's quite a tradition – people really make an effort.'

'Each to their own,' he said, shrugging. 'Not sure the boys

will be happy about being dragged back from Milton Keynes for something so twee but that's your call.'

A needle of irritation prickled Daisy's composure. She and Stuart had worked hard to rebuild a friendship after their divorce but there were still times he could get under her skin. The fact that she'd had similar thoughts when she'd first heard about the Morris dancers was neither here nor there. 'I'm hardly dragging them back. A lot of the kids from school will be there and I'm hoping it will help all three of us feel more at home here.'

He was silent for a moment and she wondered whether he was going to point out that Mistlethorpe wasn't really their home. But he simply nodded. 'Point taken.' His gaze came to rest on the newly repaired roof and he shaded his eyes against the afternoon sun. 'I see you're making progress. How's your mum doing?'

'Getting stronger every day,' Daisy said, recalling the colour in her mother's cheeks and her general improvement in spirits. 'Her consultant seemed happy at the last appointment and I'm hopeful she'll be able to catch some of the celebrations on Monday, now that the risk of infection is less serious.'

Stuart eyed her curiously. 'That's good. But how are the two of you getting on? Any bridges being mended along with those windows?'

It was a perfectly reasonable question – Stuart was well aware of the fraught nature of her past relationship with her mother and he knew it hadn't been easy to put that aside when Rose had needed her, for all that the decision to return to Half Moon Farm had been made in a heartbeat. But the needle of annoyance scratched at Daisy's patience again. Perhaps she was more tired than she realized. 'Oh, you know. Little steps,' she said, taking care to keep her tone level. 'We've had some honest conversations, at least.'

'I suppose that's one good thing to come out of this,' he observed. 'As well as Campbell and Finn getting to know their grandmother.'

The words hung in the air but this time, Daisy knew the implied criticism was all in her head, an echo of the guilt she'd battled for years. She dug deep for a smile. 'Thanks.'

She was spared further questions by the arrival of the twins, clattering through the door of the farmhouse and into the yard with the usual arguments bouncing between them. 'I'm sitting in the front!'

'No, I am!'

'Actually, you're both sitting in the back,' Stuart said, opening one of the rear passenger doors. 'That way I can listen to all those ancient tunes without you being able to change the station.'

Finn groaned. 'Get ready for two hours of Not Bangers. Your taste in music is almost as bad as Mum's.'

Daisy met Stuart's gaze and this time her smile wasn't forced; a shared love of dance music had been one of the things that had brought them together. 'Enjoy,' she said.

He grinned as he ushered the twins into the car. 'Oh, I will. If they're really lucky I might introduce them to The Venga Boys.'

Chapter Ten

Over the weekend, Daisy noticed a flurry of activity around the village green. Several white marquees were erected, pastel-coloured bunting fluttered from anything above head height and signs at both ends of the High Street declared the road closed to traffic between the hours of 13:00 to 16:00 on Monday. At the Oast House café, Nancy was nowhere to be seen and Daisy discovered from the weekend staff that she was busy perfecting her entry to the cake competition, which was very hotly contested every year. There was even a Pet Show and Effie was hoping to win the top prize with her Chihuahua – Daisy had promised to leave Atticus at home.

Monday's sky was burdened with unpromising grey clouds and Daisy wondered how enthusiastic the celebrations would be if the heavens opened. But once again, the sun made short work of the clouds and the chance of rain vanished as lunchtime came and went. Despite Stuart's prediction, both Campbell and Finn were vibrating with excitement.

Participants in the parade needed to meet behind the Mill at 13:30 and Daisy delivered both boys to their teacher, who was handing out masks to a plethora of other excited children, before going to find Emily and Rose. The carer had offered to bring a wheelchair for Rose, which had caused the older woman to bristle. 'I haven't lost the use of my legs yet,' she'd asserted with a scowl, and Emily hadn't mentioned it again. When Daisy found the two women, Rose was sitting in a lime green fold up festival chair with an enormous sunhat shading her head, a half-eaten Mr Whippy in her hand and an expectant look on her face. 'I haven't watched the parade for years,' she said. 'Do they still light a bonfire at the end?'

Daisy squinted across the green to where several men were leaning stems of wood in a tall conical shape. 'It looks that way,' she said, trying to pick out if one of them was Drew. 'Either that or they're building the world's biggest witch's hat.'

By the time the parade began, a decent-sized crowd lined the High Street. Daisy hadn't really known what to expect but it was clear from the number of people that the May Day celebration had drawn in visitors from the surrounding area and beyond. 'Oh yeah,' Emily agreed when Daisy commented on the amount of unfamiliar faces, 'loads of people come to Mistlethorpe to join in the festivities. But this is nothing compared to the Scarecrow Festival in August – we get serious numbers for that.'

Daisy wasn't sure she liked the sound of that – to her,

scarecrows resembled life-sized creepy dolls – but she kept her opinions to herself for now. 'Look,' she said as the oompah band burst out a surprisingly good version of Britney's *Oops, I Did It Again*, 'there are Finn and Campbell.'

The theme of the masks seemed to be woodland creatures, although Daisy was certain Finn had opted for a gorilla. She cheered as they pranced by, accompanied by a cluster of younger children riding beautifully ornate, if tatty, hobby horses. At the very back, accompanied by a band of cheerful Morris dancers, she saw what she assumed to be Drew, although it might have been anyone underneath the extraordinary green-leaved costume. He looked exactly like a walking tree, wreathed from head to toe in greenery and reaching well over seven feet in height. Around him, several more children danced, each wearing a leafy crown. The air was filled by the jangle of bells from the Morris dancers, and the rhythmic smack of wood on wood as they hit their sticks against one another in time to the music. Daisy found herself caught up in the old-fashioned charm of the scene and cheered enthusiastically throughout, but most especially when Jack in the Green passed by. She thought she saw the figure turn her way but she couldn't be sure beneath all the leaves. As the end of the parade passed, the crowd joined it and followed to the tents and maypole on the village green. The oompah band broke into another rousing tune – Daisy was surprised to recognize it as a classic Arctic Monkeys song – and a young woman of around sixteen or seventeen was duly crowned May Queen. She beamed at the crowd, waving in a manner that was more excited than queenly, and a small group of children hurried forwards to grab a ribbon from the Maypole. Relieved to see neither Finn nor Campbell were among their number – she couldn't trust them not to try to strangle each other – Daisy nevertheless expected the ribbon-bearers to become hopelessly tangled but they ducked over and under the ribbons, weaving it around the pole until it was covered in colourful strands. The crowd broke into applause as the dancers took their bows.

'Very nice indeed,' Rose declared from her seat beside Emily. 'I remember doing that myself as a girl and having loads of fun. Who doesn't love a nice maypole?'

Daisy didn't dare look at Emily, knowing the carer would be grinning. Instead, she focused on the unaccustomed sparkle in her mother's eyes. 'I'm surprised you weren't the May Queen.'

'No fear,' Rose snorted, with such vigour that it made Daisy laugh. 'I was far too cool for that kind of nonsense. But your grandmother was, back in the day. I've got a photograph, in the house somewhere. I'll have to dig it out to show you.'

Her words caused a memory to stir, of the letter to Violet asking whether she'd been crowned May Queen. A photograph would add another piece to the puzzle. 'I'd like that,' she told Rose.

Emily leaned in. 'There's Campbell,' she said as the maypole dancers began to disperse. 'And Finn behind him.'

Daisy beamed at both of them once they got nearer. 'You two were brilliant,' she said and fixed a thoughtful gaze on Finn's mask, now pushed back on top of his head, 'although I'm not sure King Kong is traditionally part of the May Day celebrations.'

He shrugged. 'Our teacher said we could choose an animal or bird so I chose a gorilla.'

Campbell, whose owl mask was meticulously coloured and crafted, shook his head. 'I did try to tell him but he refused to listen.'

Finn showed no concern at the criticism. 'Can we get an ice cream? It was boiling in the parade – even my toes are sweating.'

Daisy squinted up at the cloudless sky, grateful that she'd thought to apply suncream to both boys before letting them join the fun. 'I don't think I want to know about your toes but an ice cream sounds like a very good idea,' she said, reaching into her bag for a ten-pound-note. 'If you could manage to bring me some change that would be great.'

Finn snatched the money in delight and ran off with Campbell in hot pursuit. 'You'll be lucky,' Emily said, watching them go. 'It's four quid for a ninety-nine these days.'

Daisy sighed in good-natured resignation, knowing the boys would get the largest possible confection for the money they had available. 'I wasn't expecting to get any money back, to be honest, but it never hurts to ask.'

She scanned the crowd, trying to keep the twins in sight

as they sped towards the ice cream van, and felt her spirits dip as she spotted Kit Devereaux. Her determination to put him out of her head had largely worked in the past week, mostly because he seemed to be avoiding her too, but she would really rather not put her newfound indifference to the test. 'I don't know about you but I could murder a coffee,' she said hurriedly, uncomfortably aware that her voice sounded too bright. 'Shall we head to the refreshments tent?'

'Good idea,' Emily said, fanning her pink cheeks. 'I don't want to complain but Mr Sun has got his hat on a little too much for my liking.'

Thankfully, Rose was keen to stretch her legs a little and the three of them made their way towards the sanctuary of the marquee. Under the creamy canvas, the space had been dotted with tables and chairs – Daisy deposited her mother and Emily at one and headed for the long trestle tables that lined one wall. Minutes later, she was back, gingerly carrying a tea tray laden with a teapot and mismatched but charming crockery. Leaving Emily to pour her mother's tea, Daisy skulked in the entrance of the tent, waiting for Campbell and Finn to reappear. Her twitchiness had nothing to do with Kit, she told herself firmly, but her heart still sank when the twins emerged from the crowd with Alice Devereaux sandwiched between them. All three were eating ice creams. Campbell waved when he spotted Daisy and they set off towards the entrance of the tent. There was no escape, Daisy realized, then reminded herself Alice had nothing to do with her father's pomposity. It wouldn't hurt to say hello.

'We bought Alice a ninety-nine,' Finn said, as soon as they were within Daisy's earshot. 'So there's no change.'

Alice smiled politely. 'Thank you, Mrs Moon.'

Her accent was surprisingly normal, Daisy thought and immediately chastized herself all over again for making yet another assumption. She drew in a breath and smiled at the girl.. 'You're welcome. And please, call me Daisy. Mrs Moon was my grandmother.'

Alice frowned. 'But your surname is Moon, isn't it? Finn showed me one of your books at school and it had your name – Daisy Moon – on the front.'

'She is called Moon,' Finn said in a lofty tone before Daisy could answer. 'Our surname is Sanderson, like our dad, but she's always been a Moon.'

Alice turned an interested gaze back to Daisy and she was struck by how blue her eyes were, exactly the same shade as her father's. 'That's very feminist of you,' she said, sounding approving. 'Why should you give up a good name just because you get married?'

'Well, quite,' Daisy said, not sure whether she should feel pleased or patronized. 'I do like my name and I was already using it on my artwork by the time I got married so I decided to stick with it.'

'Go you,' Alice said and took a big bite of her flake. 'My parents split up years ago and my mum says the name Devereaux is the only good thing she got from my dad.'

She said it so matter-of-factly that Daisy wasn't sure she'd heard correctly. And then the recognition that she *had* heard perfectly dawned on her and she felt her cheeks grow warm with second-hand indignation on the child's behalf. 'Oh,' she managed after a moment's hesitation. 'I didn't realize – I'm sorry to hear that.'

'It happened when I was a baby,' Alice said, still apparently unconcerned. 'She mostly lives in London now, and we live at the castle.'

That explained why Daisy had only ever seen Kit doing the school run, she thought as Campbell fixed her with an accusatory stare. 'How cool is that?' he said. 'Why don't we live in a castle?'

Beside him, Finn rolled his eyes. 'Because castles are terrible places to live,' he said, then glanced at Alice. 'No offence but I bet the Wi-Fi is even worse than at the farmhouse.'

Alice shrugged. 'We don't actually live in the castle, we live in the manor house behind it. But the internet is still a bit rubbish and sometimes the septic tank floods the bathrooms so the whole house smells.'

'See?' Finn demanded, rounding on Campbell in triumph.

Daisy cleared her throat, still reeling from the revelation that Kit Devereaux's life was apparently nothing like as effortless as she'd imagined. 'I'm sure the manor house is a lovely place to live,' she said. 'Apart from the septic tank.'

'It's okay,' Alice said. 'It's only happened a few times. Dad says if Uncle Hugh would part with some damned money then he could fix it in a jiffy but he's got his head stuck too far up his own arse to care.'

There was another short silence, during which Daisy saw

the twins' eyes become saucers. 'Brilliant,' Finn said, almost breathless with admiration. 'My dad says the same about—'

'So it's just you and your dad, is it, Alice?' Daisy interrupted quickly, before Finn could spill whatever indelicate phrase Stuart had inadvertently dropped within his hearing. 'At the manor house, I mean.'

'Yes,' the girl said. 'And our housekeeper, of course. And the cook, the cook's maid and the gardener. Oh, and the castle manager but I don't see her much.'

'Right,' Daisy said faintly. 'Just the seven of you, then.'

'And the stable hand,' Alice went on. 'But he lives in one of the cottages. Here's my dad now – I'm sure he'll remember the people I've forgotten about.'

Too late, Daisy looked up to see Kit Devereaux was indeed bearing down on them. 'Oh, I don't think we need to ask him—'

'Everything okay, Alice?' Kit's clipped tone instantly transported Daisy back to the afternoon of the car crash.

'Fine,' Alice said, lifting the remains of a sticky cornet to show him. 'Campbell and Finn bought me an ice cream and then I was telling Daisy Moon about the septic tank and Uncle Hugh.'

Kit blinked, then his gaze whipped towards Daisy. 'I see. How much do I owe you for the ice cream?'

Squaring her shoulders, Daisy met his eyes coolly. 'You don't need to pay me back. The boys were at the van and chose to get something for Alice.'

He frowned and she thought he was going to argue but

then he seemed to remember the three sets of young ears around them and his expression unbent a little. 'Thank you, then.'

'No problem,' she said, making an effort to soften her own body language.

He eyed her for a moment as though about to say something, then turned abruptly to Alice. 'We need to judge the cake competition now. Say goodbye to your friends.'

She gave him a mutinous look so familiar that Daisy almost laughed. But where Finn would have loudly expressed his dissatisfaction, Alice was clearly too well-bred to do the same. 'If I have to. Bye, Finn. Bye, Campbell,' she said in a suddenly subdued voice. 'See you at school.'

'Bye,' the boys replied, once again in unison.

With a curt nod to Daisy, Kit wheeled away and Alice trudged after him. 'Isn't she brilliant?' Finn said, watching them go.

Campbell snorted. 'Told you he likes her.'

But Daisy's eyes remained fixed on Alice and her father. 'I like her too,' she said, though she was also aware of something else – a recognition that reached out across the years from the child Daisy had once been. Unless she was mistaken, in spite of all her apparent privilege, Alice Devereaux was lonely. Daisy couldn't put her finger on exactly what made her think that – perhaps it was the blithe remark about her absent mother, or the thought of her rattling around a large house with only servants for company, although it seemed there was also the mysterious Uncle Hugh to throw into the mix. Daisy couldn't begin to fathom how he fitted in or why he might be responsible for fixing the septic tank. But that aside, Alice's description put Daisy in mind of Mary Lennox from *The Secret Garden*, although Alice didn't appear as unhappy and certainly had better manners than Mary. And on a deeper level, it reminded Daisy uncomfortably of herself – often alone, left to make her own entertainment, self-sufficient and composed beyond her years. Although she'd lived in a cramped, South London flat instead of a castle, she reminded herself wryly, so perhaps the comparison only went so far. She would certainly never have guessed Kit Devereaux was a single parent but it did explain his omnipresence at the school gates and Daisy was starting to wonder if she might have misjudged him. It seemed there was more to the Earl of Winterbourne than a haughty manner and a title.

★ ★ ★

The rest of the day passed in a whirl of music, laughter and far too much sugar. Emily took Rose back to Half Moon Farm mid-afternoon, encouraging Daisy to stay at the green for as long as she liked. 'You enjoy yourself,' she said with an indulgent smile. 'Let your hair down a bit.'

And Daisy did enjoy herself, although letting her hair down was probably stretching things too far. She chatted to several parents she recognized from school, including the woman who had been sighing over Kit – her name was Joy and Daisy couldn't help liking her. Finn spent a small fortune at the coconut shy, coming away with three coconuts that

Daisy had no idea what to do with. Nancy won Best in Show for her strawberry and cream layer cake, which came as no surprise whatsoever to Daisy, and Effie's Chihuahua took third place in the dog show. As the day turned to dusk, strings of fairy lights began to twinkle into life among the trees and a band took to the small stage in the centre of the green. Their set list incorporated a mixture of crowd-pleasing covers and well-known folk music, and it wasn't long before the dancing began. Daisy stayed on the edge of the crowd, sipping a cider and keeping an eye on the twins as they tore around with seemingly boundless energy. They would sleep well, at least. In fact, she might have trouble getting them up for school in the morning but she was loathe to drag them away and decided that was a problem for tomorrow.

'Give it up for Sonic Folk!'

The crowd cheered and applauded the band as they left the stage and the compère held his hands up for quiet. 'As some of you may know, the culmination of our May Day celebration is the lighting of the bonfire. That will happen at nine o'clock so there's just enough time to grab yourself a drink and join us to welcome the return of the light to our lives.'

Daisy looked around for Campbell and Finn, locating them chasing after an assorted group of children in what looked like a complicated game of tag. 'No running around once the bonfire is lit,' she warned. 'You'll need to stay near me, okay?'

Finn huffed, his cheeks rosy from exertion. 'You're no fun.'

'Neither are third-degree burns,' Daisy said but she kept her tone light. 'We'll be heading off soon afterwards – you both need showers before bed. Make sure you tell Campbell.'

The bonfire itself was impressively tall – once lit, she thought it would be visible for miles. Perhaps that had been the point, over the centuries; a series of beacons joining rural communities in the single purpose of invoking the change of the seasons, pushing back winter and welcoming spring. It was a comforting thought, the idea that traditions like this endured even when humanity's understanding of nature had evolved. Daisy's appreciation of the bonfire's magnificence only increased once it was ablaze. She hung back, watching the glow of the flickering flames lit up the faces around her, and the smell of woodsmoke whisked her back to long-ago evenings at the farmhouse with her grandparents. A fire had rarely been needed in the heady days of summer but her grandfather had often built one anyway, knowing how much the curling orange and yellow flames delighted Daisy.

'I didn't see you dancing.' The voice close to Daisy's ear made her jump and spin round to see Drew standing there, looking less otherworldly without his Jack in the Green costume.

'That's because I had no one to dance with.' She wasn't sure whether it was the half-light from the bonfire that emboldened her or the pint of cider she'd just finished but the words were out before she could stop them and she felt her cheeks grow warm. What was it about Drew that brought out the flirt in her?

He tipped his head as though considering. 'Does that mean you only dance for someone else's benefit?'

The question made Daisy pause. She'd done plenty of dancing when she'd been younger and she hadn't cared who she was with. And she'd danced with the twins, when they were small – crazy, silly dances that had made them all breathless with laughter – but then they'd grown and now she couldn't remember the last time she'd danced. Not even round the kitchen when Finn and Campbell were in bed. 'Maybe I just need a reason.'

He smiled. 'Perfect. Will you dance with me now?'

'Now?' Daisy repeated in surprise.

'Now,' Drew agreed. 'You said you needed a reason, and I'm giving you one. Surely you won't deny Jack a May Day dance.'

'But there's no music,' Daisy protested with an incredulous laugh. She glanced around them. 'And all these people.'

Drew stepped closer and took the empty cup from her hands, placing it on the ground. 'There's music, if you listen. The crackle of the wood, the sigh of the crowd. The hoot of the owl, soaring over our heads, and the squeak of the bats.' His eyes sought hers. 'Can't you hear it?'

And the strange thing was that Daisy could. All the sounds Drew had mentioned were there, somehow melding into a melody. It was not, as Finn would say, a banger but it was there, twisting through the night air. 'I can hear it,' she said, suddenly a little breathless.

His hand dropped to rest on the curve of her waist and

Daisy felt a burst of electricity that almost made her gasp. 'Then let's dance,' he said.

It seemed rude not to, Daisy thought, although she quickly scanned the area to ensure the twins weren't watching her. Satisfied they'd ignored her instructions and were nowhere near, she allowed herself to sway in time with Drew, moving to a symphony only they could hear. At first, there was a respectable distance between them but, as they swayed, the gap closed and they pressed together. At some point Daisy rested her head on Drew's shoulder, eyes closed as she enjoyed the feeling of his body against hers and rode the waves his nearness provoked. She wasn't sure how long they danced but she was disappointed when he pulled gently away. 'Thank you,' he said, stepping back but keeping hold of her hand. 'As first dances go, that was pretty amazing.'

Daisy blinked, suddenly unsteady without his support. 'You're welcome,' she said, and belatedly thought to check whether she'd made a spectacle of herself. But no one was looking their way – all eyes were on the bonfire.

Drew's mouth curved into a smile. 'I'm glad you came back to Half Moon Farm, Daisy. Very glad indeed.'

'Me too,' Daisy said impulsively and realized she meant it. She smiled at him, feeling the slow burn of anticipation start to smoulder inside her. 'Me too.'

Chapter Eleven

Rain arrived on Tuesday, the kind of relentless drizzle than somehow made everything more wet than during a heavier downpour, and hung around for Finn's football match after school on Thursday. Daisy stood with the other parents along the touchline, hands thrust in her pockets, watching the play ebb and flow. The teams were fairly evenly matched – Finn had scored an early goal but the opposition had pulled one back and scored another. The grass was slippery and Daisy was already dreading the state Finn's kit would be in by the end of the game but there was no doubt he was enjoying himself, in spite of the mud and the rain. Campbell, on the other hand, was very much not enjoying himself: Daisy had lost count of the number of times he had asked if it was full time. He wasn't the only sibling there – some younger children were entertaining themselves by kicking a ball back and forth – but Daisy knew from experience that Campbell would rather freeze than join them. Instead, he stood next to her, grumpily listening to an audiobook and sighing at regular intervals.

She was aware of Kit further along the touchline but had studiously avoided looking his way. Knowing a little more about him didn't mean she had to go crazy and make eye contact, she reasoned, but he took matters into his own hands at half time and materialized at her side, two hot drinks in his hands. He cleared his throat. 'A peace offering, Miss Moon,' he said, holding them both towards her. 'One is tea, the other is coffee but if you take sugar you're out of luck. Which would you prefer?'

She eyed him in surprise, then dropped her gaze to the cardboard cups. 'Where did you get these?'

'There's a machine in the staff room,' he said and the ghost of a smile flickered across his face. 'I pulled rank with the headteacher.'

Daisy didn't dare look at the other parents to see if they'd noticed the honour being bestowed upon her. 'Oh. I'll take the tea, thank you.'

Once his hand was free, Kit reached into his pocket and pulled out a chocolate bar. He held it out to Campbell who glanced sideways at Daisy for permission, then took it. 'Smart boy,' Kit said. 'You look like you need it.'

'Thanks,' Campbell said, instantly cheered as he tore the wrapper open.

Daisy took a sip of tea, savouring its comforting warmth. 'The team is playing well,' she said, searching for a topic of polite conversation. 'Alice is really good.'

'She is,' Kit replied, fixing his gaze on the players huddled around their teacher on the far side of the pitch. 'But Finn is making his mark too – he's a good addition to the team. I assume he played regularly where you lived previously – in Milton Keynes, wasn't it?'

For a nanosecond, Daisy bristled, assuming he was making a jibe at her half-truth after the accident. But his expression was one of well-mannered curiosity, nothing more. 'Yes,' she allowed, and debated how much more to say. But he had brought her a peace offering and so she unbent a little. 'I hadn't planned on him joining a team here, given we'll only be in Mistlethorpe a few months, but it's hard to say no when he loves playing so much.'

Kit gave a thoughtful nod. 'I know what you mean. Between training and matches, it's a big commitment.' A ragged cheer rang out as the teams jogged back to the centre of the pitch. 'So you're only here temporarily?'

'For a few months,' Daisy said and got the distinct sense Kit was waiting for more. 'My mother hasn't been well. I've come back to look after her.'

He looked at her then. 'Back? So you're a native?'

'Not exactly. I used to stay with my grandparents every summer when I was younger but I stopped coming after they died.'

It wasn't exactly a leap to work out that the farm had passed to her mother but if Kit thought there was anything odd in the abrupt end to Daisy's visits, he didn't say so. 'Ah, yes. I wasn't living at Winterbourne then but I remember my father mentioned their passing. Quite soon after one another, I believe.'

It felt slightly surreal that he would know the details of her grandparents' deaths, Daisy thought, but she supposed it came down to the landed gentry thing again: they kept abreast of what happened within their manor. 'Within a month,' she said with a sigh. 'They couldn't bear to be apart, even in death.'

She felt his gaze flick towards her. 'It was a good marriage, then? A happy one?'

A frown creased Daisy's forehead. 'They always seemed happy to me but I'm sure they had their ups and downs.' Unbidden, her thoughts strayed to the box of letters on her bedside table, and the man her grandmother had loved before her grandfather. 'There's no such thing as a perfect marriage, is there?'

On the football pitch, the match resumed. 'Absolutely not,' Kit said. 'But I'm glad they were happy. No sense in staying together if you're not.'

There was an undercurrent of something she couldn't quite identify but she supposed he was thinking about his own failed relationship. Whatever the cause, it rang true with Daisy. 'I'll drink to that,' she said, raising her cup.

He smiled as he tapped the cardboard rim against hers and for the first time Daisy understood what Joy had meant when she claimed half the village was in love with Kit Devereaux – it was like the sun coming out from behind a cloud, turning him from a po-faced grump into an affable hero. A smile like that could definitely turn heads, she thought, and took refuge in the football before he caught her staring.

They were both silent for a while as they drank their drinks, then Kit spoke again. 'Alice tells me you write books.'

'Sometimes,' Daisy replied, caught a little off guard again. 'I've written a couple of picture books but I'm more of an illustrator.'

'That sounds like an interesting career,' he said and she found herself the focus of his full attention once more. 'Did you study art at university?'

'Art college,' she said. 'I started off working in graphic design and eventually had enough of a portfolio to approach an agent. She introduced me to some publishers and I went from there.'

'Congratulations,' he said, sounding as though he meant it. 'Not everyone can make a living out of doing something they love.'

Again, something in his tone made Daisy wonder if he was talking from personal experience. 'That's true. You're a flying instructor, is that right?'

'Only part time,' he said. 'I try to keep my hand in but running Winterbourne takes up a lot of my time.'

Daisy's gaze settled on Alice, who was making a deter-mined run with the ball towards the opposition goal. 'I can imagine. Oh, great goal, Alice! Well done.'

She glanced at Kit, who hadn't cheered along with the other parents but there was no mistaking the pride on his face. 'That's two-two, isn't it?' he asked, although Daisy was sure he knew the score. 'Time for a final push to nab the winner.'

It gave Daisy a significant amount of pleasure when Finn did exactly that, a few minutes before the referee blew the final whistle. Her cheers seemed to rouse Campbell, who peered out from underneath his hood. 'Please tell me it's over now.'

'It is,' Daisy said, shaking rain drops from her face. 'Finn scored the winner.'

Campbell grunted. 'Great. He'll be unbearably smug all evening, then.'

'With good reason,' Kit said generously. He glanced at Daisy. 'Thanks for accepting my peace offering. I fear I was a total arse the first time we met.'

Daisy inclined her head. 'I had just reversed into your car.'

'Even so,' Kit said. 'I'd had a bit of a bad day and I took it out on you. I wholeheartedly apologize.'

'Apology accepted,' she said as a dripping wet Finn bounded victoriously towards them. 'Thank you for the tea.'

Kit smiled again. 'You're welcome.'

Once again, Daisy felt as though the sun had pierced the relentless greyness of the day. He really was much more charming when he wasn't acting like he had a broom shoved up his coat, she thought, but Finn derailed any further observations by exhaling loudly and dropping his bag onto the mud at her feet. 'That was awesome. Did you see my goal?' He turned his jubilant face to Kit. 'Did you see Alice's? What a combination we make – we're like Hardcastle and Simms, terrifying defences across the world.'

Daisy and Kit both laughed but Campbell puffed out a long sigh. 'I told you he'd be unbearable.'

'Let him have his moment,' Daisy said and smiled at Alice, who had jogged over to join them. 'Well played, Alice. You were amazing.'

Campbell brightened. 'Yeah, you were great. Brilliant goal.'

Beside him, Finn made a gagging motion. 'Come on,' Daisy said firmly, before the skirmish could descend into open war. 'Let's get you home. Straight in the shower again, I'm afraid.'

For once, Finn didn't complain and Daisy suspected it was Alice who was keeping him silent. She picked up his soggy bag and nodded at Kit. 'See you in the morning, I expect.'

His blue eyes crinkled at the corners. 'See you then.'

★ ★ ★

'See? Didn't I tell you he wasn't bad for a posh bloke?' Nancy nodded at Daisy across the café table on Friday morning and pushed an oat and raisin cookie towards her. 'He gave my cake Best in Show and anyone with taste that good can't be completely terrible.'

It wasn't an argument Daisy felt would stand up in a court of law but she had to concede Nancy had been right about Kit. 'I didn't realize he's a single parent.'

Her friend nodded. 'But from the sounds of things, he's better off that way. I don't know the full story but I think Alice's mum walked out when she was less than a year old. Left Kit holding the baby while trying to get his flying career off the ground after leaving the RAF.'

Daisy frowned. 'Lots of women struggle to cope with a newborn baby,' she said doubtfully, thinking back to how hard it had been when the twins were tiny. 'I don't think we should judge her without knowing the full story.'

'That's true,' Nancy allowed, breaking off a piece of cookie and crunching on it thoughtfully. 'But rumour has it she went straight to the airport, flew to Val-d'Isère for the ski season and never came back.'

Daisy pursed her lips. If that was true then it was harder to understand but plenty of absent fathers had done similar things. Was it any different because it was a mother they were discussing? Perhaps not but it had to have been hard on Kit and Alice. Not that it was any of Daisy's business, she reminded herself. 'Alice seems like a decent kid, in spite of everything,' she said. 'Finn and Campbell like her and I do too.'

Nancy fired a sly look across the table. 'Speaking of people you like, I hear you and Drew had a cosy little smooch on Monday evening.'

Immediately, Daisy felt her cheeks turn rosy red. 'What? No, we didn't. Who told you that?'

'Calm down,' Nancy said, grinning. 'I'm not your mum. I think it's nice that you're making new friends.'

Daisy fanned her face, willing the blush to subside. 'But we didn't – we weren't kissing or anything. It was just a dance, that's all.'

'A slow dance,' Nancy teased. 'When there wasn't even any music playing.'

Mortified, Daisy took refuge in her cup of tea. Had everyone seen her and Drew dancing? Was the whole village discussing it? 'There really wasn't anything in it.'

Nancy sat back. 'That's not what Drew told me. He seems to think sparks flew and I don't mean from the bonfire. He's keen.'

The trouble was, Daisy couldn't really argue – there had been a moment that felt as though it was just the two of them in the shadows beyond the leaping flames. And that was why she'd gone out of her way to avoid Drew ever since, dodging out of sight when she saw him heading to the orchard behind the farmhouse and finding something to busy herself with if she'd spotted him in the cobbled yard. She didn't have the time or the energy to start something with Drew, no matter how attractive he might be – it was better to draw a line under things before they got out of hand. 'Okay, there's a possibility I might have felt something,' she conceded at last. 'But it was just a one-off, a bit of harmless flirtation that can't go any further.'

'Because you're only here for a few months,' Nancy said, nodding her understanding.

'Exactly,' Daisy replied. 'What's the point?'

Her friend shrugged. 'I dunno. A roll in the hay with a

guy you fancy? Not everything has to be forever, Daisy. Sometimes Mr Right is simply Mr Right Now.'

The prospect of rolling in the hay with Drew was . . . well, it was something Daisy didn't want to think about with Nancy's gimlet gaze trained upon her. 'I can't. What about the twins?'

'They don't have to know,' Nancy said patiently. 'You're a hot single woman as well as a parent. Not everything you do has to be about your kids.'

The only hotness she could lay claim to was in her burning cheeks, Daisy wanted to point out. And hadn't they just been judging Alice Devereaux's mother for abandoning her daughter to pursue her own pleasures? 'I don't know—'

Nancy spread her hands encouragingly. 'Just give it some thought,' she coaxed. 'Drew's a decent enough bloke, not exactly an angel but good with his hands and that's always a promising sign. You might have the time of your life. And if you don't – well, you're leaving in a few months. Where's the harm?'

Daisy opened her mouth to object and closed it again. There was no denying she was attracted to Drew, stomach-churningly attracted in a way she didn't recall feeling since she'd been a teenager. But it wasn't as simple as just falling into bed with him. There were things she had to consider, like the strong possibility her children might find out. Even so, Nancy made it sound so simple. There was definitely part of Daisy that was tempted. 'I'll think about it,' she conceded.

'That's all I ask,' her friend said. 'And if you decide he's not for you, there's always Kit.'

'Ha ha,' Daisy said, flicking a cookie crumb across the table. 'I think there's more chance of Atticus becoming a lap cat.'

Nancy winked. 'Stranger things have happened. Kit's easy on the eye and he comes with a castle, if you know what I mean.'

'Absolutely not,' Daisy said, ignoring the less-than-subtle innuendo and adopting the same air of finality she used to close down arguments with Campbell and Finn. 'If coming back here has taught me anything, it's that the Moons and the Devereauxs still don't mix.'

Chapter Twelve

The invitation caught Daisy completely by surprise. She stood beside the kitchen table midway through Monday morning, staring down at the heavy, expensive looking square of card, and blinked to make sure she wasn't imagining the words.

The Honourable Kit Devereaux

requests the pleasure of the company of

Miss Daisy Moon

at Winterbourne Castle for a Summer Ball
7pm – Saturday 3rd June
Carriages at midnight

RSVP

Her first thought, once she'd convinced herself she wasn't dreaming, was that she had nothing to wear. Her second thought, hot on the heels of the first, was that it didn't matter because there must be some mistake, the invitation couldn't be for her – she was a *Moon*, for heaven's sake. And her third thought was that it didn't matter even if by some miracle it wasn't a mistake – she couldn't go to a party at Winterbourne Castle. Not without grievously upsetting her mother. Now that she came to think about it, she'd probably committed Moon family treason just by accepting a cup of tea from a Devereaux. And yet . . . she ran her fingertips over the ornate black print and gilt-edging – a glamorous party in a location to die for. There was a significant part of her that was tempted to say yes.

'That looks fancy,' Emily said, glancing over her shoulder with undisguised nosiness. 'Ooh, a ball at the castle. Lucky you!'

'Mmmm,' Daisy said, tucking the invitation back inside the envelope. 'It's a shame I can't go.'

Emily stared at her as though she'd just grown another head. 'Can't go? Why ever not?'

Unwilling to betray her mother's confidence by giving the real reason, Daisy said the first thing that came to mind. 'I'm busy that night.'

'Busy?' Emily sniffed. 'I'd unbusy myself for a chance to dress up and hobnob at Winterbourne Castle.'

'It's a work thing,' Daisy improvised, knowing she sounded feeble. 'In London. Very important.'

The carer stared at her for a moment more, then shrugged. 'I'm sure you know your own business. But invitations to balls don't come along every day. At least not for me.'

They didn't come along very often for Daisy, either, but she didn't say so. Instead, she recalled the pain in her mother's voice as she'd recounted the story of her own brush with a Devereaux family party all those years before. It didn't seem likely that history would repeat itself – the invitation was proof of that – but there was a very real danger that by opening up old wounds, Daisy might drive a wedge into her newly repaired relationship with Rose. And she wasn't sure that was a risk she was willing to take.

★ ★ ★

'If I didn't know better, I'd say you've been avoiding me.' It was an accusation that could have been levelled at Daisy by several people that week but on this occasion, it came from Drew. He was leaning against the well in the centre of the cobbled yard, watching her emerge from Waggy Mamma's with a surly Atticus in her arms, and she could only assume he'd been waiting for her. He didn't seem annoyed by her elusiveness – if anything, he looked amused but the words still filled Daisy with guilt. 'Sorry. Between work, the twins and a cat who seems determined to become the terror of Mistlethorpe, I've been a bit tied up.'

It wasn't a lie – she'd started rough illustrations for *The Secret Garden* commission, fitting them in between her other work and several hospital appointments with her mother. Both Finn and Campbell's social lives were starting to expand now that they had settled into school, which was also keeping her on her toes. Atticus was probably the weakest excuse

– apart from demanding food, he was almost totally self-sufficient but he was there in her arms and she wasn't about to look a gift cat in the mouth.

'What you need is some downtime,' Drew said, falling into step beside her. 'How about a stroll along the river? If we're lucky, we might even catch some water voles.'

It was on the tip of Daisy's tongue to turn the offer down but something made her pause. The river that wound through the village was a chalk bed river, with crystal clear waters that bubbled musically across its stony base and twisted out into the woodland that lay to the east of Mistlethorpe. The path through the woods had been one of her grandmother's favourite walks and even though she really didn't have the time, Daisy suddenly found herself longing to see how much it had changed in the decades since she'd last visited. 'Okay,' she told Drew, surprising herself almost as much as she surprised him. 'Let me take Atticus home and I'll meet you here in ten minutes.'

Daisy deliberately didn't allow herself the headspace to change her mind. Depositing Atticus back in the farmhouse with strict instructions to leave their neighbours alone, she pulled on her wellies, grabbed a rain jacket and hurried out of the door. The clock on the kitchen wall had told her there was still plenty of time before she was due to collect Campbell and Finn, and she was sure Drew had work of his own to take care of, but it wouldn't hurt to have an excuse to get back home.

He was waiting where she'd left him, although she saw

he'd pulled a navy-blue sweatshirt over his t-shirt. Her stomach gave a lazy somersault at the sight of him and she did her best to damp down her body's enthusiasm. It was a walk with a friend, nothing more, she told herself sternly even as she wondered whether Nancy had seen the two of them through the window of the café.

'You must know these woods already,' Drew said as they crossed over the road and climbed the stile that led to the footpath. 'I bet you practically ran wild around here when you were a kid.'

'Hardly,' Daisy laughed. 'My grandparents were really protective of me − I think they were scared I'd get lost so I never went anywhere on my own. But we often explored the paths along the Mistle so I used to know them quite well.'

He nodded. 'The river hasn't changed much. The water voles mean it's a site of scientific interest, so most of the area is protected. But most of the people who walk around here are respectful of nature.' He glanced across and flashed a knowing, almost intimate smile her way. 'I think it's going to be a real trip down memory lane for you.'

It was exactly the same smile that had got her into trouble at the bonfire. Hurriedly, she concentrated on the path beneath her boots. 'Did you grow up around here?'

'In and around Mistlethorpe,' he said. 'I went to the same school Finn and Campbell attend now, collected conkers on the village green and got into all kinds of scrapes trying to break into the castle.'

Daisy's eyes widened. 'Why would you try to break in?'

Drew grinned. 'Not into the castle itself – just into the grounds. Believe it or not, I used to be best friends with Kit Devereaux. We used to have some epic games of hide and seek in the ramparts, after the visitors had all gone home.' He sighed. 'They've upped the security since then. Not that I've tried to sneak in recently, of course.'

'I should hope not,' Daisy said, laughing. 'Are you still friends with Kit?'

Was it her imagination or did Drew's expression shift? 'Not really. We grew apart – he went to boarding school and I was at the local comprehensive. And then he joined the RAF and we lost touch completely.'

Daisy didn't know Drew well enough to be sure but she got a definite sense of things not being said. Reading between the lines, she guessed Kit's elevated status might have proved the kiss of death for the friendship long before they lost contact but perhaps that was something Drew didn't want to acknowledge. 'You didn't pick things up when he came back to live here?'

He shook his head. 'We were different people by then. Obviously, I have no idea what horrors he saw on active service but it changed him. The kind-hearted, generous boy I knew was long gone, replaced by someone hard and distant. The truth is I hardly recognized him.'

She supposed it made sense. PTSD was sadly all too common in the Armed Forces so it was quite possible, perhaps even likely, that Kit had come back damaged by his experiences. But whatever the reason for the end of Drew's friendship with him, it was clearly a wound that still rankled. 'That sounds really hard for both of you,' Daisy sympathized.

'It's his daughter I feel really sorry for,' Drew went on as though he hadn't heard. 'A mother who drops in and out of her life depending on her holiday plans and an emotionally unavailable father. If she's not in therapy already, she soon will be.'

Daisy puffed out her cheeks. While she'd be the first to admit she'd considered Kit cold and aloof after their initial meeting, his obvious love for Alice at the school football match had softened her opinion considerably. And while she'd recognised a kindred lonely spirit in Alice, she didn't seem like a child in need of therapy, just company. Yet on the other hand, Drew knew Kit much better than she ever would.

'But none of that is your problem and the last thing you need is to hear me droning on about things no one can change,' Drew said, throwing her a sheepish look. 'Sorry.'

'No problem,' Daisy said, even though she was privately starting to wonder just how many more conversations in Mistlethorpe were going to involve Kit – it seemed everyone she spoke to had something to say about the Earl of Winterbourne. Then again, perhaps it wasn't such a surprise, given he was the closest thing they had to a celebrity. And then the banks of the river came into view and she forgot all about Kit, instantly carried back in time to when she'd last been there. It felt longer than she wanted to admit but also like yesterday and she heard her grandfather's voice as clearly as if he was standing beside her now. 'Can you see the kingfisher, Daisy? Watch for the flash of blue on the far bank!'

The yearning she felt in that moment almost knocked her off her feet. She'd never really got over the loss of both her rocks in so short a time – perhaps that had been part of the reason she'd never come back to Half Moon Farm, although her mother's marriage had to take most of the credit. But as the ache in her chest subsided it felt good to stand on the bank of the river, dappled by sunlight through the leaves, and remember everything she'd loved about her grandparents.

'Look,' Drew whispered, gently intruding into her reminiscence. He pointed across the babbling water to where a small, chestnut brown mammal was perched among the longer grass on the far bank. It held a stalk of green between its paws and looked for all the world like it was just waiting for Sir David Attenborough and his camera crew.

'Oh!' Daisy exclaimed, the breath catching in her throat as she gazed at the water vole.

'And there's another,' he murmured. 'On the rocks to the left. Do you think they're a couple?'

It was impossible to know, of course, but Daisy found herself hoping they were. Perhaps they were making a nest for the family they hoped to produce. Or maybe they were the water vole equivalent of Bonnie and Clyde, about to commit a series of daring yet thrilling heists. The thought made her smile and she wished she could capture the scene on her phone to draw later. It might make the basis of a great picture book, although she suspected any movement now would send the would-be parents or partners in crime scurrying for the safety of their burrow. At the very least she could include them in her illustrations for *The Secret Garden*.

Daisy could have stayed there all day but it wasn't long before Drew touched her arm. 'Shall we leave them in peace? There's a bench about half a mile along the path – we could aim for that.'

Reluctantly, she nodded and they continued, with Drew pointing out the hawthorn trees in flower and the swathes of bluebells hidden away beyond the well-worn track. Daisy committed it all to her memory, determined to use it to enrich her work. A short while later, they reached the bench. It rested beneath the boughs of an ancient oak tree, the branches heavy with shiny new leaves that offered shaded respite to the weary. Daisy was sure the bench hadn't been there in her grandparents' day and said as much to Drew.

'No, it's only been here a few years,' he agreed and twisted to read the inscription on the metal plaque screwed to the wooden seat. '*For Enid and Bob. Bologna 1945.*'

Daisy turned to stare at the words. 'Wow. Talk about intriguing. Do you know who they were?'

'Not a clue,' Drew said. 'They sound fun, though.'

They did, Daisy thought as her imagination took flight. 'Were they spies, do you think?'

'Absolutely,' Drew agreed. 'They met in Italy during the war and fell in love, risking everything for a passion that consumed them. This bench is their one concession to the secrets they kept from their family.'

Daisy smiled, delighted he was playing along. 'Or perhaps it's a code, left here for the right person to discover.'

'Could be.' He squinted at her suspiciously. 'Are you that person?'

'No,' she admitted, 'although I wish I was. How about you?'

'Not me either.' Reaching out, Drew tucked a strand of hair behind Daisy's ear. 'You know, I don't think I've ever met anyone quite like you, Daisy Moon.'

For the second time that day, the breath caught in her throat but now it had nothing to do with her surroundings and everything to do with the man beside her. She knew he was going to kiss her several long seconds before he cupped her face with both hands and lowered his mouth to hers. The sound of the birds stilled and the babble of the river faded with the touch of his lips. Time seemed to stretch and slow but at the same time everything happened too fast for her to stop him. Not that she would have – now that he was kissing her she accepted it was something she had wanted from the moment he'd first stood behind her in the orchard, his breath warm on her cheek as he showed her how to cut the mistletoe from the apple trees. And then she gave up any attempt at coherent thought and surrendered to the surge of heat taking her body by storm. She dug her fingers into his hair, fighting the urge to press herself against him the way she had at the bonfire. It was as though she was sixteen again, drunk on her very first kiss, and she wanted it to last forever.

When they did finally break apart, it was with a tenderness that belied the passion of the moment. Drew's gaze was cloudy as he looked into her eyes, and she had the fleeting impression he saw everything she'd just felt. 'Wow,' he whispered, his voice huskier than it had been before. 'Now that's what I call a kiss.'

She smiled, already wanting to repeat the experience, but forced herself to straighten and edge along the seat a fraction. If he kissed her again, she wasn't sure what might happen. Drew picked up the unspoken message, as she'd known he would. 'No, you're right. We should be getting back.'

He stood and held out a hand, which she took and allowed him to pull her to her feet. She almost leaned into him but stopped herself just in time. He didn't let go of her hand. Instead, he twirled his long fingers around hers and they walked that way until they stood beside the stile opposite the farm once more.

'I hope you appreciate how much willpower it's taking for me not to kiss you again right now,' he said as he helped her across the wooden step.

Daisy felt a pleasurable stab of warmth in her belly at his words. 'I do,' she replied in a low voice. 'Believe me, I do.'

In a swift movement, he raised her hand to his mouth and pressed his lips to the back of her fingers. 'The next time, I might not be able to stop.'

It was all Daisy could do not pull him close there and then, in full view of Half Moon Farm. She satisfied herself with resting her free hand on his shoulder and standing on tiptoes, so that her whispered words tickled his ear. 'The next time, I might not let you stop.'

Chapter Thirteen

Nancy's face was a picture of scandalized delight as she surveyed Daisy across the table in the Green Dragon. 'You didn't!'

'Sssssshhh!' Daisy hissed, hurriedly looking round the pub to see if anyone had overheard. 'Not so loud – I don't want the entire village to know what a strumpet I am.'

Her friend's eyes danced. 'You're no such thing. But I can't believe you actually snogged him, and in the middle of the woods too.' She paused to grin. 'How very Drew. Did he have a sprig of mistletoe?'

It was early on Friday evening and the pub wasn't yet busy. Daisy had chosen a table in the corner, expecting an explosive response from Nancy when she shared her news, and her caution had been well judged. It was exactly why she hadn't confessed what had happened straight after her walk with Drew but had waited three days until Finn and

Campbell were safely in Milton Keynes; she hadn't wanted anyone else to get caught in the blast.

'He didn't need one,' she admitted, blushing a little at the memory. 'I practically jumped on him the moment we sat down.'

Nancy cackled in triumph. 'I knew you fancied him.' She leaned forward conspiratorially. 'So when are you going to do the deed?'

And now Daisy's cheeks caught fire. 'Nancy!'

'Why be coy about it?' her friend asked, undaunted. 'It's obvious you have to.'

Daisy squirmed in her seat, recalling the wanton way she'd whispered in Drew's ear. What on earth had come over her? 'I do not.'

Nancy frowned. 'Okay, maybe I phrased that badly – of course you don't have to. But you want to. Don't you?'

She could understand Nancy's confusion, Daisy thought wretchedly. For around an hour after kissing Drew, she'd been certain she wanted to take things further too. But then reality had come crashing back in and she'd remembered all the reasons it couldn't happen. And now she was right back where she'd started, except everything was worse because she kept daydreaming about how good the kiss had been. 'No,' she told Nancy. 'And yes. But I can't, for all the reasons I told you before. And I don't want to lead Drew on when it can't go anywhere.'

Across the table, Nancy took a long sip of wine. 'Firstly, Drew is a grown man – he'll cope,' she said firmly. 'And who's to say he wants it to go anywhere? I didn't want to mention this before but – well, let's just say Drew likes the thrill of the chase but isn't so good at the stuff that comes after. The general consensus in the village is that he's got commitment issues.'

Daisy sat back. 'Oh.'

'But that's not a problem for you,' Nancy continued. 'If you're looking for some no-strings fun then he's exactly what you need.'

Daisy groaned. 'You sound like a Tinder profile.'

'Fun,' Nancy repeated. 'And secondly, I hate to break it to you, Daisy, but it's going to happen whether you like it or not. Sooner or later, you're going to find yourself alone with Drew and you won't be able to keep your hands off each other and all of a sudden you've got nettle rash in unmentionable places.' She fixed Daisy with a pragmatic gaze. 'So why not accept the inevitable and keep things comfortable? Obviously the farmhouse is out of the question but he's got a very nice cottage on the other side of the village.'

Daisy wanted to cover her ears but she had to admit Nancy had a point. 'I'm not sure I like being just another notch on someone's bedpost.'

Nancy raised her eyebrows. 'So think of him as another notch on yours.' She shook her head. 'You haven't been with anyone since Stuart, have you?'

'No,' Daisy admitted, her mortification smouldering back into life.

'Then Drew is the perfect way to rediscover your va-va-voom,' her friend said kindly. 'You both have fun, no one gets hurt and you can leave Mistlethorpe with your head held high.'

'You make it seem so easy,' Daisy said, unconvinced by Nancy's blithe assertions.

'That's because it is. What do your friends in Milton Keynes think?'

She blew out her cheeks. 'Pretty much the same as you.'

'I rest my case,' Nancy said, with evident satisfaction. Draining the last of her wine, she got up to go to the bar. 'Same again?'

When she returned with two more glasses of chilled white, Daisy had laid Kit's invitation on the table. 'What's this, a way to change the subject?' Nancy asked, picking it up. Her eyes widened. 'Very nice, you've clearly made an impression, in spite of smashing into his car. What you going to wear?'

'That's not the problem,' Daisy said, pulling a face. 'Obviously, it's only a few weeks away but I haven't replied yet. I'm torn about whether or not I should go.'

Taking a deep breath, she outlined the conversation she'd had with her mother, explaining the humiliation Rose had suffered and the apparent enmity between the Moons and the Devereauxs. Nancy listened in silence, then sat back. 'That does sound crappy, although a lot of it sounds like water under the bridge. Do you want to go to the ball?'

'Maybe,' Daisy said, then sighed. 'It sounds glorious, doesn't it? Would I be a terrible person if I said yes?'

'I would,' Nancy replied, shrugging. 'The party Rose went to was decades ago, long before you were born – long before Kit was born too. Neither of you is responsible for what happened back then.'

'No, but—'

'But what?' Nancy asked, spreading her hands. 'Sure, your mum might not want you to go but if there's one thing I've learned from family feuds, it's that two wrongs don't make anything right. Do you know why your families apparently hate each other?'

Daisy shook her head. 'No.'

'Do you get the sense that Kit knows?'

This time, Daisy was more emphatic. 'Not at all. I'm not sure he even knows there is a feud.'

Nancy folded her arms. 'Then it's time to put the whole thing to bed.' She fixed Daisy with a meaningful stare. 'A bit like Drew.'

Daisy couldn't help laughing. 'Okay, I get the message. Thanks for being my agony aunt.'

Chinking her glass against Daisy's, Nancy smiled. 'No problem. What are friends for, if not to encourage you to make dubious choices?'

★ ★ ★

Daisy awoke on Saturday morning with a headache and the unpleasant suspicion she'd done something stupid the night before. There'd been several more glasses of wine that were probably ill-advised, and a vague memory of joining a group of villagers for the music quiz, but that wasn't the cause of her disquiet. Cautiously rolling over in bed, she reached for her phone and squinted at the screen. No late-night messages or phone calls, apart from one to order a taxi home from the Green Dragon just before eleven o'clock. No drunken purchases from random Instagram adverts, as far as she could tell. She lay still, trying to find the source of her discomfort, then her gaze came to rest on her handbag, lying on the floor with its contents spilling out across the bedroom floor. And suddenly she knew what she'd done. With Nancy's encouragement, she'd emailed Kit Devereaux and accepted the invitation to the ball.

Swiftly, she pulled up her Sent Emails list and scanned the wording she'd used. Thankfully, it was typo free and all made sense, even if she had signed off with a distinctly informal *Cheers!* But the knowledge that there was no backing out now rested uneasily on her conscience. What was she going to tell her mother? And then another memory surfaced, something Nancy had said later in the evening; did she have to tell her mother anything? What Rose didn't know couldn't hurt her and it wasn't as though Daisy was a teenager who had to account for her every move. But the prospect of lying by omission somehow seemed worse than an actual lie, although less awful than admitting the truth, and suddenly the whole subject was more than Daisy could cope with on an empty stomach.

'Coffee,' she croaked, forcing herself to push the covers aside and roll out of bed. Steadying herself, she grabbed a packet of painkillers and swallowed a couple with some water from a glass she'd had the sense to leave by her bed the night before. Maybe once the tablets had kicked in she'd crawl over to the café for a hangover curing fry up. She raised one hand to her thudding temple and winced. Or maybe she'd just go back to bed.

* * *

By midday, Daisy's headache had receded and she was almost feeling better. But as always when the twins were with Stuart, the house felt too quiet. Popping her head round the door of the living room, she smiled at Rose and Emily. 'Fancy lunch in Mistlethorpe?' she asked, encompassing them both. 'My treat.'

It was after one o'clock by the time Rose was ready to go out in public and the High Street was bustling. While her mother got changed, Daisy had rung around and managed to snag a cancellation at Sandrine's, a French bistro-style café that was usually fully booked. Smiling, the waitress showed the three women to their table and handed them menus. 'Today's specials are moules mariniere fresh from Whitstable this morning, and chicken Basquaise, served with creamy mashed potatoes.'

Unable to resist the garlicky lure of the mussels, Daisy chose the moules mariniere, while her mother opted for a chicken salad. Emily went for steak and frites, and Daisy was touched to see her share some of her meal with Rose. 'Got to keep your strength up,' Emily said, placing a portion of steak on

Rose's plate. 'Salad is all very well but it won't put meat on your bones, or help with that low iron count of yours.'

Rose clucked but Daisy noticed she ate the steak and ordered dessert when Emily encouraged it. Both Magda and Emily had been an absolute godsend when it came to caring for her mother and Daisy knew she was lucky to have found them. She and Rose would miss them when the time came to let them move on to a new patient but happily the time for that was still some way off. In fact, Daisy was starting to wonder if she might keep one of them on permanently once her mother was fully recovered, to set her mind at rest when she and the twins were back in Milton Keynes. But that was something for the future too. Right now, Daisy was simply glad to have their help.

'I could get used to this,' Rose said as they made their way out of Sandrine's and into the afternoon sunshine. 'Being a lady who lunches, I mean.'

Emily patted her ample stomach, contentedly. 'Me too, although my waist might not agree.'

Daisy smiled. 'Shall we take a stroll along the High Street?' she suggested. 'Walk those delicious puddings off?'

Even though Rose was much stronger than she had been a month earlier, they still took things slowly, stopping often to look in the shop windows. Daisy exchanged several greetings with parents from school, and nodded at someone she remembered chatting to in the Green Dragon the night before. 'You know more people than I do,' Rose grumbled, when Daisy was hailed with yet another friendly wave.

'It's mostly thanks to Campbell and Finn,' she replied. 'They seem to know everyone.'

Their gradual progress continued and they were just about to go into the wool shop when Daisy heard a familiar voice. 'Hello. No twins today?'

She looked over her shoulder from the doorway to see Kit studying her, Alice by his side. Anxiety prickled across Daisy's palms but her mother had continued into the shop with Emily. Relieved, Daisy stepped back onto the street and shaded her eyes against the sun. 'They're with their dad, in Milton Keynes. How are you?'

He grimaced. 'Regretting throwing a summer ball but otherwise okay. We do it every year but I always seem to forget how much work it involves.'

'I can imagine,' Daisy said, with a quick glance to make sure her mother wasn't within earshot. 'Thank you for the invitation, I'm really looking forward to it.'

'My pleasure,' he said warmly and Daisy was struck yet again by the contrast between this Kit and the one she'd first met. The circumstances had been less than ideal but she found it hard to believe how much she'd disliked him..

Afraid she might be staring, she turned her attention to Alice, who was gazing towards the green as though planning her escape. 'How about you? Are you looking forward to the ball?'

The girl shook her head. 'No.' Kit's blue eyes crinkled. 'Alice hates it when we have parties. She's not allowed to play football in the long hall.'

'Ah,' Daisy said gravely. 'Yes, Finn would feel similarly aggrieved. If we had a long hall. What will you be doing instead?'

Alice fixed her attention on the green once more. 'I'll be in London with my mum.'

Her voice was a peculiar mixture of flatness and anticipation, which Daisy thought she understood. It was the way she'd often felt as a child, when plans to do things had fallen through due to lack of money or other, less understandable reasons. Maybe Alice was worried her mother would change her mind. Beside her, Kit opened his mouth to speak then seemed to catch sight of someone further along the street. Instantly, his demeanour changed – a light went out in his eyes and his lips compressed into a thin, bloodless line. 'Time to go, Alice.'

Blinking at the sudden chill, Daisy followed his gaze and saw Drew heading their way. Kit gave her a curt nod. 'Enjoy your weekend.'

He was already turning away, drawing Alice with him, by the time Daisy had gathered her wits enough to respond. 'You too. See you on Monday, maybe.'

Several things happened at once then. Rose materialized in the door of the shop, holding two balls of almost identical lilac wool. 'Who was that you were talking too?' she asked, peering out with a frown and for a heart-stopping moment Daisy thought she had seen Kit. But her attention was caught by Drew, who was waving in their direction, and her frown was replaced with a smile. 'Oh, it's my favourite man and just in time to help me make an important decision.'

Drew smiled but his eyes were fixed upon Daisy's and despite the jumbled emotions Kit's sudden frostiness had provoked, she felt a familiar flutter of interest. 'Anything for you, Rose,' he said easily.

If Rose noticed that she only had half his attention, she didn't show it. She held up the two balls of wool for him to inspect. 'Which do you prefer – Scottish Heather or Ripe Plum.'

Daisy looked at the wool – she was no knitter but as far as she could tell there was no discernible difference between the two balls. Drew's lips twitched a fraction and she suspected he was thinking the same thing but he managed to keep a straight face. 'There's a lot to be said for Scottish Heather but, being a gardener, I've always enjoyed a nice Ripe Plum.'

There was something about the way he looked at Daisy when he spoke that made the words almost sound suggestive and she fought a ridiculous urge to giggle. She fixed her gaze on the pavement and fought to restrain her childishness.

'You're right,' Rose announced. 'Plum it is.'

She turned away and bustled back into the shop, leaving Daisy and Drew alone. 'I've been thinking about you,' he said without preamble. 'In fact, I can't stop thinking about you.'

The words caused a shiver of anticipation to run through her but she forced herself to recall Nancy's comments of the night before, that Drew was a flirt. Perhaps this was how he spoke to every woman he met, although they couldn't all be as pathetically susceptible as her – hearts would be swooning all over the village. And yet she couldn't resist being drawn in. 'I've been thinking about you too,' she admitted. 'But I'm not sure I should be.'

He raised an eyebrow. 'Oh? Why not?'

Daisy checked her mother's location before she continued. 'Honestly? I'm not sure I'm ready for – for this.' She flapped a hand and stared at the ground again. 'For anything to happen, with you and me. You know.'

'Ah.' He nodded, almost to himself. 'I get that. But the last thing I want is to make you uncomfortable, Daisy. Would you like me to back off?'

It was the perfect way out, she knew. All she had to do was say the word and Drew would leave her alone. But now that he'd made the offer, her treacherous emotions had shifted like quicksand and she didn't know what she wanted. 'I'm not . . . ' She trailed off and gave in. 'No, I don't want you to back off.'

Drew waited in silence for a moment, then placed a finger beneath her chin, gently lifting her head so that her eyes met his. 'Then I'm happy to wait, as long as it takes, until you are ready.'

She forced herself to take a breath. 'Okay.'

'And if you decide you're never going to be ready—' he shrugged and stepped back, allowing his hand to fall away. 'Well, I'll be disappointed but it's your call. No pressure.'

Right at that moment she wanted nothing more than to

close the distance between them once more but she was beginning to recognize that this was how her body reacted every time he touched her. Grateful for his understanding, she managed a smile. 'Thanks, Drew. I just didn't expect this.'

'Me either,' he replied and nodded. 'Say goodbye to your mum for me. I look forward to seeing what she knits with that wool.'

A moment later he was striding along the pavement, heading in the opposite direction to Kit and Alice. Daisy watched him walk away, willing her overheated senses to calm down before joining Rose and Emily inside the shop. She wasn't sure how but somehow, Drew's considerate reaction to her doubts seemed to have only made her want him more. Maybe Nancy had a point, she thought feverishly as she made admiring noises over her mother's purchases. Maybe to get over her attraction to Drew she was just going to have get under him.

Chapter Fourteen

Half term arrived the following week and Daisy welcomed the break from the morning scramble to get to school on time, even as she accepted the inevitable decline in her productivity. It was nice to spend some unhurried time with Campbell and Finn; she took them down to the river, where there were no water voles to be seen, and they spent a day on the beach at Margate, although both boys were more interested in the penny arcades that lined the sea front than messing about on the sand. On Wednesday evening, she drove them up to Milton Keynes and left them in Stuart's capable hands. And on Thursday, she went to Canterbury in search of something to wear that wouldn't look like a dishrag among the grandeur of Winterbourne Castle.

The trouble was she wasn't sure what she was looking for. After visiting several shops, none of which had anything she deemed suitable, she gave in and messaged Phoebe.

I need your help. What does one wear to a ball?

Her agent's reply was fast. *That depends on whose ball is it. The Earl of Winterbourne's. In an actual castle.*

Go long and glamorous, Phoebe advised. *And wear flat shoes – balls are just like publishing parties. There's a lot of standing up.*

It wasn't much help, Daisy thought as she headed up to the Eveningwear section of John Lewis, but it was better than nothing and Phoebe attended so many parties that there was no chance she would steer Daisy wrong. Eventually, she found something she thought might do – a floor-length, emerald-green satin dress that miraculously clung to the right places while somehow skimming her less flattering bits.

'Oh yes,' the assistant declared when Daisy stepped out of the changing room to get a second opinion. 'It's perfect. Gorgeous, in fact.'

Daisy eyed herself in the mirror doubtfully. 'I'm going to need shoes as well,' she said, and the other woman's eyes lit up.

'Wait here,' she said, after checking which size Daisy took.

'Flat,' Daisy called after her. 'Just make sure they're flat.'

She tried not to wince as she paid, reminding herself it would be worth it not to feel utterly like a fish out of water among all the other dazzling dresses that would undoubtedly be on display. And Emily's reaction was gratifying when Daisy came downstairs on Saturday evening. 'Oh!' she whispered, because Daisy had confided in the carer where she was going but had also sworn her to secrecy. 'You look like you belong on the red carpet.'

Instantly, Daisy was swamped by the same doubts she'd felt in the shop. 'Too much?'

Emily shook her head. 'Absolutely not. Just exactly right.'

A honk from outside told Daisy her taxi had arrived. It was now or never. 'Wish me luck,' she said, swallowing a sudden desire to dash back upstairs.

But Emily sighed. 'With a dress like that, you won't need luck. You're going to be the belle of the ball.'

'Hardly,' Daisy disagreed. 'But thank you. That makes me feel better.'

Yet by the time she reached the entrance to Winterbourne, her misgivings were back in full force. Guests had been instructed to use the formal entrance, rather than the gateway across the drawbridge that was reserved for tourists, and Daisy's nerves threatened to overwhelm her as the taxi swept up the tree lined driveway and the magnificence of the castle loomed into view. She almost told the driver to turn around when they reached the vast stone steps that led up to the ornate wooden doors but she knew it was far too late to chicken out now. A liveried doorman stepped forward to open the car door and, taking a wobbly breath, Daisy got out of the car.

Another doorman waved her up the stairs and through the doors, but she stopped dead in the splendour of the entrance hall to admire the sweeping stone staircase and the shimmering chandelier overhead. This hallway hadn't been open when she'd visited with the twins and she was immediately cowed by its grandness. She didn't belong here, no matter how much money she'd spent on her dress. But just as she was about to turn around and make a run for her departing taxi, Kit appeared, dashingly handsome in an immaculate black dinner suit and tie. If Emily's wild flattery was to be believed and Daisy was red-carpet ready, Kit might equally have stepped off the set of a Bond movie. 'Daisy,' he said and she was gratified to see him pause as he took in her appearance. 'You look – wonderful. Welcome to Winterbourne.'

'Thank you,' she said, trying to ignore the breathy nervousness in her voice.

'Would you like to freshen up at all?' he enquired. 'There's a ladies room just to our left.'

Daisy fought the urge to pat her face, suddenly convinced her carefully applied make up must be sliding off her skin. 'Do I need to? Is my mascara smudged?'

Kit smiled in reassurance. 'Not at all. You look quite perfect.' Angling his left elbow away from his body, he offered her a black-clad arm. 'Let's get you a drink. And once you've settled in, there's someone I want you to meet.'

He snagged a flute of champagne from a passing water and offered it to her. She took a gulp, then reminded herself that she absolutely should not get drunk. Not unless she wanted this party to end in even more ignominy than her mother's.

She'd been inside the Long Hall before, while visiting the castle as a paying visitor, but it still took her breath away. Perhaps it was the lit chandeliers, their crystals sparkling and reflecting the light against the opulently carved ceiling, or it might have been the riot of colourful dresses that assaulted her senses as she and Kit made their way into the room. It might even have been the hit of alcohol fizzing through her veins, or a combination of everything but she felt as though she was moving through a dream. The only thing that kept her feet on the ground was the reassuring presence of Kit at her side, anchoring her whirling senses and giving her something to hold onto.

'I'm not sure who else you'll know here,' he said, as he steered her towards the edge of the crowd. 'My brother invited several author friends, perhaps your paths have crossed professionally, or there's Nick Borrowdale, the actor. He seems to know everyone.'

Daisy felt her heart flutter with a sudden flash of unreality. She'd been to plenty of publishing parties with the great and the good, usually smattered with an unfortunate number of oily politicians and unsavoury comedians, but she didn't think she'd ever rubbed shoulders with a star of Nick Borrowdale's calibre. Of course she knew him – she'd watched him smoulder his way through any number of television shows and films – but she'd only ever seen him on the screen. *Nancy is not going to believe this*, she thought numbly as Kit guided her onwards. *I don't even believe it.*

Somehow, she managed not to faint when Kit introduced her to Nick. He flashed the smile she'd seen a thousand times. 'Good to meet you, Daisy,' he said, his Irish accent every bit as warm as it was on TV. 'So you're an illustrator?'

She nodded, subtly trying to unstick her tongue from the

roof of her mouth. 'Daisy is an award-winning artist,' Kit supplied smoothly, giving her time to regain her composure. 'She's just been commissioned to illustrate a new edition of *The Secret Garden*.'

Now Daisy had to battle not to stare at him. How did he know that, she wondered. 'That's right,' she managed.

'Such a wonderful book,' Nick said, sounding nostalgic. 'I almost played Mary's Uncle Archibald in that adaptation a few years back but blasted Colin Firth beat me to the role.'

Daisy had watched that version and thought Colin Firth perfect in the part. It would have been quite a different experience if Nick had played the role – she wasn't sure the audience was meant to fancy the pants off Uncle Archibald. 'I'm really enjoying the illustrations,' she said, surprised to discover her voice had lost some of its breathiness and was almost back to normal. 'Any excuse to visit country houses and shamelessly plagiarize their gardens.'

She was inwardly delighted when both Nick and Kit laughed. 'I'll have to show you the gardens here,' Kit said, turning to her. 'The walled garden is undergoing renovation so it's not open to the public at the moment but I'm sure you'll find some inspiration there.'

'That would be great,' she said, and a little more of her nervousness slipped away. 'Thank you.'

Nick raised a dark eyebrow. 'Watch this one,' he said, tipping his head towards Kit. 'He says he wants to show you his magnificent gladioli but actually what he means is—'

'Pay no attention to him,' Kit cut in good-naturedly, before

Nick could finish his sentence. 'He's just jealous because he doesn't have a walled garden.'

'True,' Nick replied sombrely. 'That's the reason I'm still single.'

Kit shook his head. 'No idea what my excuse is.'

Their easy banter put Daisy at ease. She looked back and forth between them. 'You poor, poor boys,' she said, her tone sorrowful. 'Not an ounce of eligibility between you.'

Nick laughed. 'I like you. Come back and talk to me some more once Kit's finished showing you off.'

Once again, Daisy felt her head spin. Had Nick Borrowdale really just said he liked her? 'I'll see what I can do,' she said, as a gentle pressure on her arm told Kit was ready to move on.

'Feeling more relaxed?' he asked with a solicitous glance.

'I am,' Daisy said, surprised to discover it was true.

'Good,' he said, sounding pleased. 'Come and meet my brother.'

It was the second time he'd mentioned his brother and it belatedly occurred to Daisy that this must be the uncle Alice had referred to. She wasn't really sure what she'd been expecting – a slightly younger version of Kit, perhaps – but it wasn't the stocky older man he approached. 'Hugh, I'd like to introduce you to Daisy Moon, children's illustrator and mother to a future footballing superstar,' Kit said. 'Daisy, this is Hugh Devereaux, the Eleventh Earl of Winterbourne, Marquess of Blisswood, Baron Malnoir and incumbent of a handful of other titles neither he nor I can remember.'

Daisy blinked, feeling as though the floor had been swept clean out from under her feet. Either the champagne had gone to her head faster than she'd realised or she'd totally misheard what Kit had said, because she was sure he'd just introduced this man as the Earl of Winterbourne and that couldn't be true because Kit was the Earl. Wasn't he? Except that Hugh was quite clearly older, although there was a striking family resemblance, and if that was true then Kit couldn't be the Earl because that wasn't how hereditary titles worked. Her head spun as she looked first at Hugh, with his greying blond hair and faded blue eyes, then at Kit, and realized she'd been wrong all this time. The invitation had given it away, if she hadn't been too stupid to pay attention – it hadn't borne the title Earl of Winterbourne but the Honourable Kit Devereaux. And now she had been staring at the two of them for so long that one or both must think she was an idiot.

'I'm very pleased to meet you, Your Grace,' she stumbled, grateful her stunned brain had managed to supply the correct address for an earl. 'Thank you for inviting me to your party.'

Hugh grunted, apparently oblivious to her confusion. 'Oh, this is Kit's party. I just pay for it. How do you do, Daisy Moon?'

'Very well,' Daisy said, trying not to think of septic tanks. Thankfully, Kit chose that moment to place a hand on the arm of a woman facing away from them. She turned, an enquiring smile on her beautiful face, and Daisy saw she was heavily pregnant. 'Allow me to introduce Countess of

Winterbourne, Cressida Devereaux, my sister-in-law. Cress, this is Daisy Moon.'

Cressida's smile widened. 'How do you do? Kit's told me so much about you.'

'Has he?' Daisy said, wrong-footed yet again.

She patted her enormous stomach. 'Darling Alice too, They say you write the most wonderful children's books and of course I'm hoping this little one will be an avid reader.'

'Oh.' Daisy felt the world right itself again. 'Yes, that makes sense.'

She sensed rather than saw Kit studying her. 'Would you like to get some fresh air? It's a little warm in here.'

'Yes, please,' Daisy said and allowed him to guide her towards the door at the far end of the hall. It wasn't until she was out in the cool night air that she realized how tightly wound her nerves had become. Kit came to a halt on a patio overlooking a landscaped garden complete with intricate topiary hedges and lowered his crooked arm, releasing her hand.

'Are you okay?' he asked, eyeing her with some concern. 'You seem a little flustered. Was it Hugh? He can be a bit intimidating but he's all right really.'

Grateful for the breeze that cooled her cheeks, Daisy shook her head. 'Yes. I mean, no,' she said, then took a breath and tried again. 'It wasn't really him. I'd misunderstood, you see – I thought you were the Earl. So it took me a minute to adjust and then I felt like an idiot, which of course I am.'

Kit's expression was suddenly understanding. 'Oh. Yes, I'm not the Earl of Winterbourne.' He gave her a self-deprecating smile. 'I'm what's commonly known as the spare. And happily to be made redundant from even that role, once my nephew puts in an appearance.'

Daisy couldn't help it. She gaped. 'So you don't own the castle?'

He shook his head. 'Not at all. I look after it for Hugh, and he lets me and Alice live in the manor house, but none of it belongs to me. Eventually, it will all go to Hugh's son.' He paused to offer another smile that was oddly tinged with something else. 'Which is all as it should be, of course, but also why it's so important for me to make a go of the flying school − I need an income in case Hugh ever decides to kick us out.'

'Is that likely?' Daisy gasped.

Kit grimaced. 'Probably not. But I like to be prepared.'

If Daisy hadn't been wearing such a ridiculous dress, she might have sat on the floor. As it was, she fanned her cheeks, shaking her head in bewilderment. 'I had no idea.'

'I'm amazed nobody told you,' he said, shaking his head. 'It's obviously not a secret.'

She thought back over the many conversations she'd had about Kit since arriving in Mistlethorpe. Had anyone ever actually referred to him as the Earl? Or had she simply put two and two together and made five? 'Oh, I'm an idiot.'

'You're not at all.' He regarded her sympathetically for a moment. 'Would you like me to show you the walled garden, since we're already out here?' He waved towards a red-bricked wall with an arched blue door in the centre.

Daisy looked down at her dress and tried not to shudder at the thought of getting mud out of the hem. 'I'm not sure I'm really dressed for it,' she said doubtfully.

'Nonsense,' Kit said. 'We'll find you a pair of wellies and you'll be good to go.'

The suggestion wasn't any more surreal than the rest of her evening so far. She gave in and laughed. 'Why not?'

Kit was as good as his word, leaving her on the patio and returning a few minutes later with a pair of glossy yellow half boots that fitted her better than the green ballet slippers she'd bought to match her dress. Producing a key from his pocket that she was sure would have ruined the line of his dinner jacket had he been carrying it before, he led her to the door. 'It's not quite a secret garden,' he said, turning the key in the lock and pushing the door back, 'but I think you'll like it.'

Carefully gathering her skirt, Daisy stepped inside and felt her mouth drop as a fairy-tale blossomed before her eyes. Bathed in the golden light of the setting sun, the garden was a labyrinth of narrow paths that wound between beds and raised boxes, each containing an explosion of every kind of flower she could imagine, all perfectly placed to create a visual delight. She took a few steps forward, the gravel crunching beneath her feet, and stopped to gaze around again in mute delight. Hollyhocks mingled with lupins, alliums danced with purple and yellow irises and, she was amused to see, the gladioli were quite magnificent. It was the stuff of dreams, a heavenly vision that she could spend hours absorbing. And once her eyes had stopped feasting, her nose was demanding her attention – the air was filled with a heady mix of rose, gardenia and a hundred other scents she couldn't immediately identify that made her feel as though she stood in the doorway of a perfume factory. 'Wow,' she said when at last she found her voice. 'I don't know where to start.'

Kit smiled. 'I know. But let me show you my very favourite part.' He set off along the path, with Daisy trailing behind, occasionally pausing to touch an exquisite bloom as though she could not believe they were real. There were signs of the refurbishment Kit had mentioned earlier – one or two beds were empty and the far end of the garden was evidently being redesigned – but there was so much to see that the blanks spaces barely registered.

Kit waited beneath a tall horse chestnut tree that was flowering in one corner, providing a canopy of wonderful pink and yellow blossom that reminded Daisy of a cocktail. 'I found this when I was a kid,' he told her when she stopped admiring the flowers long enough to reach him. 'I'm not sure even Hugh knows about it.'

Daisy frowned, because the tree was well established and most definitely too big to be a secret. But Kit reached around the back of the tree, then pulled out his phone to shine a light on the bark. 'There. Can you see it? Someone has carved their initials into the trunk.'

Craning her head, she followed his pointing finger. Sure enough, carved clumsily into the wood were two initials surrounded by a jagged but unmistakeable heart. 'V & V,' she said, running her fingers over the carving. 'Who are they?'

Kit shrugged. 'No idea. My grandfather's middle name was Valentine, would you believe, so it could have been him. But equally, it might have been someone who worked on the estate – a gardener or something who wanted to leave their mark.'

But Daisy had stopped listening. She was picturing the box of letters on her bedside table, each addressed to her grandmother, Violet. Each signed with the initial V.

V & V.

She took a long shaky breath and let it out again, all the while running the dates and possibilities through her mind. It couldn't be, could it? It couldn't.

Aware that Kit was staring at her, she took one more breath and met his gaze. 'Your grandfather. He served in the RAF like you, did he?'

"Yes, it's a family tradition. But what's that—'

'He wasn't stationed overseas during the war, was he?' she interrupted.

Kits eyebrows shot up. 'Yes, he was. In France, mostly. Why?'

Daisy closed her eyes and fought the crazy bubble of laughter trying to escape her. 'Because . . . Because I think I know who V and V are. And you're never going to believe it!'

186

Part Three

Autumn Dreams

Chapter Fifteen

The scream brought Daisy from asleep to awake in 0.5 seconds. She sat bolt upright. The room was light – a dazed glance at the bedside clock told her it was a little after nine on Sunday morning – but something was clearly very wrong. It had been a single scream, shrill and panicky, and it had come from somewhere inside the house. Finn and Campbell were at their dad's in Milton Keynes so there was only one likely source and it caused Daisy's heart to stutter.

'Mum?' she called, throwing back the bedcovers back and stumbling to the door. 'Where are you?'

Silence. 'Mum?' Daisy called again, from the top of the stairs, and this time she got a reply.

'In the kitchen.'

It hadn't been her mother's voice, but that of Emily, her carer. Taking the stairs to the ground floor too fast, Daisy hurried along the hallway and burst through the kitchen door. The scene that greeted her caused her to gasp. Rose was sitting on a wooden chair, her face pale and perspiring, eyes closed in evident distress as she fanned herself with one hand. Emily stood beside her, gripping a shoulder as though in support, but oddly she was not looking at her charge. Instead, her gaze was fixed on the floor and there was a strange trepidation about her expression. Neither woman seemed to have registered Daisy's arrival, although she'd been anything but silent. 'What's wrong?' Daisy asked, fearing the worst. 'Is it your heart?'

That got their attention. Rose's eyes fluttered open. 'No, but it should be after a shock like that.'

'Like what?' Daisy said, her gaze shooting to Emily in alarm. 'What's happened?'

The carer shuddered. 'It seems Atticus has brought us a present,' she said, her usually cheery tone subdued. 'Poor Rose stepped on it and it gave her quite a turn.'

Relief eased Daisy's jangling nerves as she took a couple of steps into the room. 'Is that all? I thought—'

'All?' Rose suddenly bristled. 'I wasn't expecting to stand on a corpse in my own kitchen.'

It was on the tip of Daisy's tongue to observe that the scream had been shrill enough to wake the dead but she bit the comment back. She'd encountered enough of her cat's gifts to know that they were often a little grisly – stepping on one would be quite unpleasant, slippers or no slippers. 'I'm sorry,' she said. 'Where's the – uh – body? I'll deal with it now.'

Emily pointed to the area in front of the kitchen sink without looking. 'Over there.'

Her evident squeamishness surprised Daisy – a practical attitude was a big part of being a carer after all. Perhaps the massacre had been particularly gruesome. But as she bent to squint at the floor she understood a little better. The victim on this occasion hadn't been a mouse or a vole. It was a frog and plenty of people weren't keen on them. 'Ah,' she said, glancing around to see what tools she had at her disposal. 'Could you just pass me that bowl, please?'

The frog lay motionless as Daisy approached. Splayed on the tiles, it looked as though it had hopped its last hop but Daisy wasn't fooled. Atticus had once dropped a clammy, limp body onto her forehead while she slept and, once she'd recovered from the horror of that rude awakening, matters had rapidly descended into a scene from an amphibian zombie movie – just when she'd decided the thing was dead, it had leapt back into life and hit her between the eyes again. This time, she was taking no chances. With a deft flick of her wrist, she upended the plastic bowl and dropped it over the frog. Scooping a piece of cardboard from the recycling pile, she slid it under the bowl, grimacing as it met resistance from the body, then swept the cardboard and the bowl up and made for the kitchen door. Emily hurried to open it for her and moments later, the whole bundle had been carefully deposited at the edge of the orchard. Daisy did not look back to see if this frog also sprang back to life – that was its business, not hers. Instead, she returned to the kitchen and shut the door. 'I'm going to need at least two cups of tea to recover from that,' she said, raising one hand to her head as adrenaline ebbed away and left her to the mercy of the previous night's champagne. 'And probably a fry up.'

Emily squared her shoulders. 'I'll get the kettle on.'

'Thanks,' Daisy said, settling at the kitchen table opposite her mother. 'I'm sorry Atticus gave you a scare. Are you okay?'

Rose sniffed. 'I will be.' She fixed Daisy with a look. 'That cat of yours is a menace. I hear he's been tormenting the dogs over at Waggy Mamma's.'

'Only from a distance,' Daisy defended. 'He sits on the fence and watches them.'

'Picking out his next victim,' Rose replied with dark certainty. 'Today it's Kermit but tomorrow it might be Mr Ainsley's Rottweiler.'

Her tone was so disapproving that for a moment Daisy wasn't sure whether Rose was being serious. She glanced at her in consternation and was relieved to see a definite twinkle in her mother's eye. 'I think we need a bigger bowl.'

Emily glanced across at them. 'That Rottweiler is the soppiest dog I've ever met – he'd probably lick Atticus to death.'

The image of the tomcat glaring balefully around, his ginger fur dripping with dog slobber, made Daisy smile. 'Let's hope it doesn't come to that.'

From the other side of the table, Rose was studying her closely. 'You look tired. Was it a late night?'

Daisy's smile slipped, because although her mother knew she had been out the night before, she hadn't been totally transparent about where she was going. Rose harboured an intense, not unreasonable dislike for the Devereaux family that stretched back decades and she was adamant that the Moons had no business mixing with them. But Daisy had found Kit Devereaux's invitation to a ball at Winterbourne Castle impossible to resist and so she had dressed up and snuck out of the farmhouse, much like Rose had once done in her youth. And she didn't regret the decision – once her initial nerves had passed, she'd had an exhilarating whirlwind of an evening – but now she felt like a teenager again, confronted by her mother about the night before. It didn't help that Emily knew exactly where she'd been. 'Fairly late,' Daisy said evasively. 'But nothing a good breakfast won't fix.'

'This should pick you up a bit,' Emily said, placing a mug of tea on the table in front of her. 'We were just going to have some poached eggs, weren't we, Rose? I can make you some too if you'd like.'

Daisy shook her head, still uneasy beneath her mother's scrutiny. 'That's kind but I think I'll pop over to the café for one of Nancy's specials.' Pausing, she looked at Rose again. 'As long as you're sure you're okay?'

She flapped a hand dismissively. 'I'm fine now and I have Emily if I need anything. Off you go.'

'Great,' Daisy said and gathered up her tea. It wasn't an escape, she told herself as she headed up the stairs to her room. She was a fully grown, forty-something woman – the mother of two boys of her own, for goodness' sake – she was perfectly capable of facing her mother's ire when she needed to. But her reasons for keeping the ball to herself had been less to do with disapproval and more to do with trying not to cause unnecessary upset. And then there was the not insignificant matter of the bombshell she'd uncovered last night at the castle, that relations had not always been frosty between the Moon and the Devereaux families. In fact, it looked very much as though love had bloomed between Kit's grandfather and Daisy's grandmother, and until she could find out more, Daisy planned to keep her discovery well away from her mother. And if that meant she had to tell a few half-truths along the way, then it couldn't be helped.

* * *

'So? How was the ball?'

Nancy's face had lit up in expectation the moment Daisy entered the Oast House café, just as she'd known it would. Unfortunately, she'd been followed inside by an influx of other customers and it had been several long minutes before the café owner materialized at Daisy's table.

'It was good,' Daisy said, hoping she sounded casual. 'The Devereauxs throw a nice party.'

Nancy waited, her pen poised over her notepad with the air of an old-school reporter anticipating a scoop. 'And?' she said, when it became clear further information was not going to be forthcoming. 'Who was there? What were they wearing? Did you snap any sneaky photos?'

Daisy couldn't help smiling. 'Loads of people were there. Nick Borrowdale, the actor. Merina Wilde, the novelist – we share an agent and I had a lovely chat with her.' She paused and fixed her friend with a steely look. 'Not to mention the Earl of Winterbourne. Why didn't you tell me that wasn't Kit?'

Nancy's forehead crinkled. 'I thought you knew,' she said, in a tone of genuine perplexity. 'As the eldest, Hugh inherited the title when their father died, although we don't see much of him these days. It never occurred to me that you thought Kit was the earl, although maybe it should have.'

'I really wish it had,' Daisy said, remembering how she'd gawped at Hugh when Kit had introduced her. 'I spent a very confusing few seconds trying to process who he was and probably looked a complete idiot.'

'Oh, I bet he's used to that reaction from peasants like us,' Nancy said cheerfully. 'But never mind him, tell me about Nick Borrowdale. Is he as gorgeous in real life as he is on the screen?'

If anything, Daisy had found the actor more attractive in person but she wasn't going to admit that on an empty stomach. 'Coffee first,' she said firmly. 'And a full English, please. You can have the rest of my meagre gossip once I've eaten.'

'Anyone would think this was a café,' Nancy grumbled good-naturedly as she turned away, leaving Daisy alone to ponder just how much more of the evening she should reveal to her friend. Part of her was aching to confide in someone, to share the secret she'd discovered in the castle's glorious walled garden, but she was still trying to get her head around the possibility herself. Inevitably, her thoughts looped back to the night before, when Kit had shown her the letters

V&V surrounded by a heart, carved into the trunk of a horse chestnut tree, and she'd known immediately who they referred to. That moment of stunned recognition had been followed by disbelief, and then the dawn of understanding as she connected the dots: she knew exactly who V and V were, even if Kit had no idea. It was a vital piece of a jigsaw puzzle Daisy hadn't realised she was solving until then.

Kit had gaped at her in astonishment when she'd announced she knew who had carved the initials. 'But how could you?' he'd said, nonplussed. 'You're not even from Mistlethorpe.'

'But my family is.'

That had given him pause. His blue eyes sharpened with interest. 'Fair point. Who do you think V and V are?'

She puffed out her cheeks as the thrill of solving the puzzle subsided. Now that it came to it, she wasn't sure she should tell him about the box of old letters she'd found in the cluttered bedroom at Half Moon Farm – love letters addressed to her grandmother, Violet, and signed with the letter V. It was almost like betraying a confidence – not only giving up her grandmother's secrets but also those of the mystery man who'd professed his love over and over again. Because if what Daisy suspected was right, then she understood why he had never signed his letters with his name. Just as she knew why Violet had eventually married another man.

'I could be wrong,' she said, hedging her bets.

'As I said, so could I. It might not be my grandfather's work. Maybe there was a Victor who loved a – a Vanessa.

196

Who knows?' Kit shrugged. 'I just like being one of the few people who knows it's even there.'

His words only fuelled Daisy's hesitancy but she couldn't shake the odd certainty her suspicions were correct. *My grandfather's middle name was Valentine,* Kit had told her, and he'd served overseas throughout the war. Perhaps it was all a coincidence. Yet she knew in her bones it was not.

'I found a box of letters at the farm,' she said after what felt like an age. 'They're addressed to my grandmother, who I believe was an apprentice gardener here at the castle for a time, before the war. Her name was Violet.'

Kit was still, regarding her intently. 'Okay.'

Daisy drew in a breath. 'The letters span the duration of the war, sent by an officer on active service in the RAF. They're beautifully written but there's clearly a difference in education level – he constantly tells Violet not to worry about spelling and grammar, for example. And he knows Mistlethorpe well; there are loads of references to the village and the people who live here.' She glanced at Kit, knowing he must be putting two and two together, just as she had done. 'The letters were signed with a V.'

Seconds ticked by. 'And you think V is for Valentine.'

'Maybe,' Daisy said, wondering what to make of his impassive expression. Was he sceptical? Intrigued? Outraged at her audacity in even making such a suggestion? She couldn't tell. 'It all fits.'

And then he laughed, a soft incredulous sound that mirrored her own surprise just moments earlier. 'I definitely did not have this on the bingo card for this evening,' he said, shaking his head. 'A below stairs fling.'

There wasn't a trace of derision in his voice, just astonishment and gentle amusement, but the words 'below stairs' still made Daisy bristle. 'A fling that went on for at least five years.'

His mouth quirked. 'Yes, that is more than a fling. A liaison, perhaps.'

Daisy resisted the urge to clench her jaw. Had he somehow forgotten this was her grandmother they were discussing? 'How about relationship? Or is that impossible with someone from *below stairs*?'

She hadn't meant for the last two words to be quite so pointed but they appeared to hit the mark because Kit glanced at her and his expression sobered. 'Not today,' he said mildly. 'Although it would still be heavily frowned upon and gossiped about. But in my grandfather's day? Yes, I'd say a relationship with someone of such significantly lower status would be quite impossible.'

Focusing resolutely on the intricate pattern of the tree trunk, Daisy counted to ten, reminding herself he hadn't read the letters. He was approaching things from a pragmatic, if horrendously snobbish, viewpoint whereas she was being swept along by the aching love story that poured from the page. And she'd watched enough *Downton Abbey* to know that he was right – upstairs–downstairs relationships were always doomed – but did he have to be so dispassionate about it? 'He loved her,' she said finally, once she was sure she wasn't going to snap. 'And while I only have one side of the story, every word he wrote suggests he was sure of her love for him.'

Kit was silent for a long moment, reaching out to trace the carving. 'If you're right, they must have both been very young,' he said eventually, his tone reflective. 'My grandfather was only 19 when war broke out.'

'Violet was 17,' Daisy said, and when she closed her eyes she could imagine the girl her grandmother had been, standing in the shelter of the horse chestnut tree, wrapped in the arms of a faintly familiar blond-haired boy on the cusp of becoming a man.

'But he was old enough to know better,' Kit went on, as though he hadn't heard Daisy. 'Perhaps the war skewed things.'

She opened and closed her mouth several times before speaking. 'I'm sure it did,' she said at length. 'I can't claim to know your grandfather but the V who wrote those letters was a long way from home, scared and lonely despite an admirable stiff upper lip. If that made him yearn for the woman he loved and dream of a future with her then I can understand that.'

Kit frowned. 'A future he could never have.'

Daisy thought she might actually punch him. 'I imagine,' she said, finally allowing her irritation to show, 'that when you're sitting in a war zone, any kind of a future seems impossible, let alone the one your family demands.'

The speed with which Kit's expression turned blank instantly made her regret the words. Of course he knew what it was like to be in a war zone, Daisy reminded herself too late. Hadn't Drew told her he'd come back from serving in the RAF a different man? 'You're right,' he said quietly.

Cursing her own thoughtlessness, Daisy took a deep breath. 'I'm sorry. I should have – I shouldn't have said anything. That carving could have been done by anyone.'

His gaze stayed fixed on the tree and Daisy got the impression he was pulling himself back from a place she couldn't see. 'No need to apologize. And for what it's worth, I think your suspicions are bang on the money.' A flicker of a smile crossed his face as he turned to her. 'You caught me on the hop, that's all. I just wanted to share this little secret with you – I didn't expect you to solve the mystery.'

The revelation that he'd wanted to show her the carving caused a little shiver to run thought Daisy. She puffed out her cheeks. 'Believe me, I didn't either. I was expecting a fancy party, some nice champagne and sore feet from pretty but impractical shoes.'

Kit glanced at her feet, clad in yellow wellington boots, and smiled. 'Maybe you should keep those on.'

'Maybe,' Daisy said as her own lips curved into a smile. 'Do you think anyone would notice?'

'Probably not,' he said. 'And even if they did, they'd all be far too polite to say anything.'

'Until afterwards,' Daisy observed dryly. 'I think I'll change back to my impractical footwear, if you don't mind.'

His gaze had been steady on hers. 'I don't mind at all.'

'Earth to Daisy.' Nancy's voice jolted Daisy back to the café. 'Coffee and water are here, food is on the way.'

Glancing down, Daisy saw there were indeed two drinks on the table, along with some neatly wrapped cutlery. 'Sorry, I was miles away. Thanks.'

'You're welcome.' The bell above the door of the café tinkled and several more customers came in. Nancy sighed. 'I think the debrief might have to wait until after the lunchtime rush, though.'

It wasn't the worst thing that could happen, Daisy thought – at least it would buy her time to work out how much of her night at the ball she wanted to share. 'The twins aren't due back until seven-ish. Why don't I pop in around closing time and fill you in?'

'Perfect,' Nancy said, flashing her a faintly distracted grin as she homed in on the newcomers. 'I can't wait to hear every juicy detail.'

★ ★ ★

'It sounds like a lovely evening,' Nancy said across the table, when Daisy finished describing the ball and its guests. 'A bit lacking in actual juiciness but I suppose everyone was on their best behaviour. And Nick Borrowdale sounds like an absolute dream.' She sighed as though dreaming about the actor was something she did often, then gave Daisy a speculative look. 'Are you glad you went?'

'Yes,' Daisy said, and hesitated, wondering how much more to spill.

The pause didn't escape Nancy's gimlet gaze. 'But?'

Daisy picked at a fleck of paint underneath her thumbnail

that had escaped her post-work scrub. She'd spent the afternoon poring over her grandmother's letters, scouring them for any confirmation that the mysterious V was indeed Kit's grandfather but there'd been nothing concrete, no tell-tale clue that would unravel his identity, and she'd been forced to accept that she only had her gut instincts to go on. As things stood, she wasn't ready to share her suspicions with anyone, even though she was longing to see the amazement on Nancy's face when she revealed all. 'Oh, nothing,' she said, aware that her friend was waiting for her to speak. 'It's just – it's a completely different world, isn't it? The aristocracy, I mean. Kit said his brother has titles he can't even remember but Kit himself almost has to depend on family charity to provide a home for Alice.' She took a long sip of tea. 'If I owned Winterbourne, I'd live there, wouldn't you?'

'I suppose it would depend on how grand my other houses were,' Nancy said sardonically, then her expression sobered. 'But I'm afraid there's a good reason Hugh doesn't spend much time around Mistlethorpe. It's something else you won't have heard about it, given you had no idea he even existed before yesterday.'

Mystified, Daisy shook her head. 'No.'

'Hugh used to live here, around ten years ago,' Nancy went on. 'This was before he was married to Cressida. When his first wife was still alive.'

The words hung in the warm, vanilla-scented air, jangling against the comforting scent of freshly baked scones. 'Ah,' Daisy said, trying to work out how old Hugh might be. He'd seemed to have some years on Kit – mid to late fifties, perhaps? Which suggested his wife had died young, or at least before her time.

'As you might have guessed, it's a tragic story. A riding accident.' Nancy's gaze flickered away to rest on a beam of sunlight scything across the café from one of the upstairs windows, snaring dust motes. 'The worst of it was Elspeth was five months' pregnant, so Hugh lost his wife and his child in one awful moment.'

Daisy's hands flew to her face as the horror of the revelation sank in. 'Oh no. The poor man.'

Her friend nodded. 'It was terrible – the whole village was in mourning. Understandably, Hugh couldn't bear to be here afterwards. Kit was out of the RAF by then and living at the manor house so I suppose it made sense for him to take over the day-to-day management of Winterbourne while his brother grieved.'

'Poor Hugh,' Daisy said, struggling to comprehend how anyone could cope with such crushing grief. 'What a devastating loss.'

Nancy leaned back in her wooden chair, hands cradling her cup. 'Kit's wife had already left by then and I think Elspeth had been a big help with Alice. Her death must have hit Kit hard too, at a time when he was already struggling.'

'I bet,' Daisy murmured, recalling Kit's sudden distance in the garden. Perhaps her barb about impossible futures had affected him in ways she hadn't understood and she was reminded all over again that you never knew what emotional burdens people were carrying.

'No one was surprised when Hugh eventually remarried,' Nancy went on. 'I mean, I suppose it's expected when you're from a family like that and have a walloping great title to pass on but I'm glad Hugh's got a second chance at happiness.'

'Mmmm,' Daisy agreed. That was something else that had come up the night before – the weight of family expectations – but she didn't tell Nancy that. 'His wife looked very well.'

'As she should,' Nancy said approvingly. 'I bet Hugh wrapped her up in cotton wool the moment she discovered she was expecting.'

Daisy remembered Cressida's easy manner, her glowing skin and radiant smile – she hadn't seemed especially smothered. But they'd spoken for mere seconds, with Hugh at their side, and when Kit and Daisy had returned from the walled garden, there had been no sign of the countess. 'Understandably.'

Nancy waved a hand. 'Oh yeah, totally understandable. Just like the whole village understands that the current Earl of Winterbourne won't ever live here again.'

Remembering her mistaken belief that Kit had been the earl, Daisy felt her cheeks heat up. 'But you have Kit instead, who seems to genuinely be part of the community.'

'That is true,' Nancy said. She eyed Daisy over the rim of her cup. 'You've changed your tune a bit. Have you decided he's not as bad as you thought?'

If she was honest, Daisy's view of Kit as the arrogant lord of the manor had begun to soften well before she discovered he wasn't actually the earl but the time she'd spent with him at the ball had made her see him in a whole new light. From his courteous welcome to his kindness in helping to ease her nerves, he'd been the perfect gentleman, even though he'd had many other guests to entertain. But it wasn't until he'd shown her the tree in the garden that Daisy had felt she'd caught a glimpse of the real Kit – the man beneath the prickly exterior and public persona. Somewhat unexpectedly, she found she liked him, in spite of wanting to punch him at times. 'I suppose I'm coming round to the idea,' she admitted.

'Good.' Her friend raised enquiring eyebrows. 'And did you manage to play Sherlock Holmes and solve the mystery of the feud between the Moons and the Devereauxs while you were hobnobbing with the great and the good?'

An image of the carved letters on the tree bloomed before Daisy's eyes. It had to be a piece of the puzzle but she had no idea how significant it might be and it was far too early to share it with Nancy. Instead, she crossed her fingers beneath the table and shook her head. 'Not really.'

'I suppose you were hardly likely to stumble across the old earl's diary spilling all the beans,' Nancy acknowledged with a rueful grin. 'But I could ask in the village, if you like. Make discreet enquiries. There's bound to be someone who remembers that far back, or who heard rumours from their grandparents.'

Given how tight-lipped her grandfather had been, Daisy wasn't sure that was true but it didn't feel like the right time to publicly open up old wounds. 'No, let's leave it for now. I get the feeling Mum knows more than she's telling and I don't want her to feel I'm going behind her back.'

'Fair point,' Nancy conceded. 'It sounds as though you and Kit have started to mend a few bridges in any case.'

Daisy thought back to the end of the ball, when Kit had thanked her for coming and assured her she was welcome to visit the garden whenever she liked. There'd been several moments when she'd thought exasperation might overwhelm her but she couldn't deny that he'd been an excellent host. 'You know,' she said slowly. 'I think perhaps we have.'

The words stayed with her long into Sunday evening, even when Finn and Campbell's boisterous return shattered the calm of the farmhouse and plunged her into the whirl of preparation for the start of the school week. It did feel as though there was a tentative friendship blossoming between her and Kit, in spite of their differences, but she couldn't help wondering whether it could survive the scandal of a love affair between Valentine and Violet. If what Daisy suspected was true, she could be about to reignite the feud between the Moons and the Devereauxs for another generation and that was the last thing she wanted. The best way to defuse the situation was to keep Kit in the loop, she decided. With a bit of luck, both families would allow the mistakes of the past to rest.

Chapter Sixteen

As June blossomed into the kind of idyllic English summer Daisy remembered from her childhood, she found herself finally settling into a routine that seemed to work for everyone. Her mother's health was improving every day, meaning she was gradually becoming more independent, and the twins were doing well at school. Finn was happy to be playing football again and Campbell had quickly become a firm favourite with their class teacher, meaning both boys bounced out of the car each morning ready for a fresh day. For Daisy's part, it was a relief that she no longer dreaded bumping into Kit at the school gates. Now when they saw each other, they smiled and nodded, occasionally stopping to exchange a few words. The twins and Alice seemed to be developing firm friendships too.

'You'll have to bring the boys to the castle,' Kit suggested one morning as they watched the three children amble towards their classroom, heads bent in tumbling conversation. 'I know Alice would enjoy some company.'

'They'd love that,' Daisy said. 'Or at least Campbell would. Finn will only be impressed if you produce the decomposing corpse of a heathen invader.'

Kit's mouth quirked. 'I'll see what I can do. It's been a while since we've been invaded – most people just pay the entrance fee.'

'Much better for everyone,' Daisy said in amusement. 'Campbell is fascinated by history but Finn says its deadly boring unless there's horribleness involved.'

'Alice can give them the tour. She knows all the most gruesome stories, I promise Finn won't be bored.' He glanced enquiringly at Daisy. 'How are the illustrations coming along? You must be finding inspiration in this glorious weather.'

It should be true, Daisy thought as she felt a familiar knot of anxiety form in the pit of her stomach. Everywhere she looked, she saw flowers in bloom; even her grandmother's roses around the door of the farmhouse had recovered from years of neglect and were now flourishing. But the pictures Daisy was creating for the anniversary edition of Frances Hodgson Burnett's *The Secret Garden* seemed to be lacking something and she wasn't sure why. Too often, she viewed her day's work with dissatisfaction – the colours were flat, the shapes one dimensional, the composition uninspired. It wasn't a problem yet – she had plenty of time to meet her deadline – but it was troubling her and no amount of roughs seemed to be resolving the problem. 'Progress is slower than I'd like,' she admitted. 'But I'll get there.'

Kit regarded her for a moment. 'Sounds like you need a visit to the castle too. The walled garden is particularly lovely at the moment – it might give you some ideas.' He paused. 'You could even do some deadheading if you like – I'm sure Athers the gardener would be glad of the help.'

A memory of the immaculately laid-out flowerbeds materialized in Daisy's head, each bursting with blooms of assorted colours and heights and textures, and suddenly she was there among them, drinking in the heady mix of perfumes in the warmth of a summer evening. Perhaps that was what she needed, she thought, reluctantly dragging herself back to the school playground. Perhaps to really capture the essence of *The Secret Garden* and do the gentle beauty of the story justice, she needed to get her hands dirty. 'I might take you up on that,' she told Kit. 'If you really think your gardener wouldn't mind.'

'He'll be thrilled,' Kit said promptly. 'Especially when I tell him your grandmother used to tend the gardens.'

Daisy cleared her throat. They hadn't spoken about the carving on the tree since the night of the ball, or what it might mean, and she was uncomfortably aware of its shadow now. But she hadn't been able to prove or disprove her suspicions, and she found herself wanting very much to accept Kit's offer, so she pushed the tree and its implications to the back of her mind. 'Then we'd love to come. We're free most evenings, apart from football training but Alice will be tied up with that too. Just let me know when works for you.'

Kit shrugged. 'The castle closes to the public at six o'clock and the public are usually gone by six-thirty. Why don't we say this Friday?'

Daisy mentally reviewed her diary, making sure it wasn't a weekend the twins were due to spend with Stuart in Milton Keynes. 'Sounds good, thank you.'

'But if you need to get the creative juices flowing earlier, let me know. You're welcome to drop by any time. The walled garden won't be open to the public for some months yet.'

She thought of the room she was using as a studio, of the stacks of discarded illustrations and paintings. 'I might just take you up on that,' she said, suddenly keen to shake off her creative torpor. 'Is this afternoon too soon?'

He laughed. 'Not at all. I'll be teaching at the flight school but I'll let Athers know to expect you. Just turn up when you're ready.'

'Great,' Daisy replied. 'I'll bring my easel and my gardening gloves. And thank you. This is very kind of you.'

Kit smiled. 'Well, I must confess I have an ulterior motive.'

'Oh?' Daisy said warily, wondering what was coming next. Was he about to demand a fee? An acknowledgement in the finished copies?

He gave her a look that was half-embarrassed, half-hopeful and wholly charming. 'It's probably a bit of an imposition but I'm rather hoping you'll sneak my favourite tree into the book somewhere.'

And just like that, Daisy's burgeoning misgivings melted away. It was the last thing she'd been expecting Kit to suggest yet somehow she wasn't surprised. The chestnut tree, with all the secrets it guarded, would fit perfectly into her illustrations. 'I can't think of anything I'd like more,' she said.

★ ★ ★

'Hello. Going on location?'

Daisy looked up from loading the car to see Drew Entwhistle watching her from a few metres away. Instantly, her stomach swooped as though she'd stepped off a cliff and she gripped the wooden leg of the easel to ground herself. It was almost two months since she'd first met him underneath the mistletoe in the farmhouse orchard and her crush on him was as strong and as inconvenient as ever. She knew he felt the same way – he'd told her so – but he'd also made it very clear that it was up to her to make the next move. In the meantime, she simply had to ride the waves of attraction that threatened to swamp her every time she saw him. 'Hello,' she said, after a moment's grappling with the usual giddy rush of adolescent hormones. 'Yes, I'm going to the spend a few hours in the castle gardens.'

'Is this for the new book?' he asked, stepping nearer to peer curiously into the boot..

She nodded. 'I'm hoping to find some inspiration.'

'Isn't it all a bit manicured?' he said, frowning. 'I thought you'd want something wilder, more natural.'

There was a faint undercurrent of disapproval behind the

words and Daisy supposed she understood why – there wasn't much love lost between him and Kit Devereaux these days, despite having once been friends. 'When Mary first finds the garden it's overgrown, so those illustrations need to capture that wildness but they gradually restore things to how it used to be, which is more formal.' She smiled. 'And of course I get to spend an afternoon surrounded by flowers, which is never a bad thing.'

The lines creasing his forehead softened. 'I couldn't agree more. But perhaps when you need inspiration for the wild garden, you'll let me show you some of my special places.'

It was a perfectly innocent offer but it still managed to cause a flutter of butterflies in Daisy's stomach and Nancy's warning of a few weeks ago rang uncomfortably in her ears: *Sooner or later, you're going to find yourself alone with Drew and you won't be able to keep your hands off each other and all of a sudden you've got nettle rash in unmentionable places . . .*

'That's very kind of you,' she managed, as heat swarmed her cheeks. 'Thank you.'

He raised an eyebrow, as though reading her thoughts. 'It's no trouble,' he said. 'There's an abandoned house a mile or so west of here that Mother Nature has done an excellent job of reclaiming. I think you'd like it.'

The last time they'd been alone under the trees, they'd shared a kiss that had almost led to more, Daisy recalled as her face grew warmer still. She would have to drag the twins along for safety. 'It sounds great,' she said. 'Campbell would love it, he's really into old buildings.'

If the suggestion of company surprised Drew, he didn't show it. Instead, he grinned. 'And Finn would hate it. I'll have to brush up on my football knowledge, keep him distracted.'

And that made Daisy grin too because Drew was about as interested in sport as Finn was in nature. 'That is a supreme sacrifice. Thank you.'

'Anything I can do to help out,' he said. 'They're both great boys, it'll be a pleasure to hang out with them. And you, of course.'

His eyes met hers and a devilish, treacherous part of her was tempted to suggest they went looking for the abandoned house right now. With an effort of will, she focused on securing her paints in the boot of the car. 'I'd better get going or I'll only have an hour before school pick up time.'

Drew smiled. 'Of course. I hope you get what you need.'

Daisy closed the boot and tried to ignore the way his eyes crinkled at the edges. 'Me too,' she said, making for the safety of the driver's door. 'See you later, maybe.'

She knew without looking that he watched her all the way out of the farmyard. Taking a deep breath, she tuned the radio into something upbeat and did her best to put Drew Entwhistle out of her mind. He was a distraction she definitely didn't need this afternoon.

★ ★ ★

Daisy wasn't sure why she had expected Athers to be old, or at the very least middle-aged and bearded. The man who met her at the grand front steps of the manor house appeared to be in his early thirties, was clean-shaven and almost cherubic, with a halo of golden curls and pink cheeks that wouldn't look out of place on a Renaissance portrait. Less angelic were his grubby clothes and mud-encrusted boots but somehow they suited him perfectly. 'Hello,' he said, crunching over the gravel and holding out a surprisingly clean hand to shake hers. 'You must be Miss Moon.'

'Call me Daisy,' she said. 'And you must be Athers.'

'I am,' he said, and glanced at the equipment she had piled on the drive. 'What can I carry for you?'

A few minutes later, he was leading her around the side of the house to the ornamental privet garden she remembered from the night of the ball. 'Famously laid out by Capability Brown,' Athers said as Daisy once again admired their precision neatness. 'Anyone who was anyone in the eighteenth century had their gardens landscaped by Brown.'

'Did he design the walled garden too?' Daisy asked but Athers shook his head.

'I believe that was Beatrice, wife of the eighth earl. It's changed a bit since her time, of course, but I like to think we've stayed true to the spirit of her design.'

The late June sun was beating down as they approached the red brick walls, making Daisy glad she'd thought to bring a sunhat. Inside the walls, the garden was even more breathtaking than it had been on her first visit. New blooms had sprung up between the flowers she thought had been there on the evening of the ball, lending their beauty and colour to the overall feast for the senses. But when Daisy looked closely, she could see areas that were in need of attention – roses that needed deadheading, tall buddleia stems that would benefit from a trim, despite being loved by bees and butterflies alike. 'It must be a full-time job, keeping these beds looking good all summer.'

He nodded. 'Luckily, I have a couple of others to help when I need it. And I'm not responsible for the castle grounds. Those guys take their life into their own hands when they mow the top of the moat.'

It wasn't something Daisy had ever considered before but now she came to think about it, how did they mow that grass without falling in? 'Very slowly,' Athers answered with a grin when she asked him. 'Now, where would you like to set up? There's some shade under the chestnut tree in the far corner, if that helps.'

It was blessedly cool beneath the canopy of thick green leaves and Daisy was grateful for the shade, even as she wondered how often her grandmother had done exactly the same thing many years earlier. Athers helped her set up the easel and pointed out one or two especially fine flowering shrubs, as well as a collection of plane trees whose branches he was training to meet across the top of one path. 'It's early days but eventually they should create another shady spot,' he said as Daisy admired his patience. 'The garden might seem to transform with the changing seasons but quite a lot of it is about playing the long game.'

Daisy gazed around, wondering where to begin. Everywhere

she looked she saw something beautiful – it all seemed to be vying for her attention. Athers noticed her indecision and smiled. 'I like to take a gentle walk around the path when I first arrive here,' he said. 'Helps me see what needs sorting out first.'

'Thank you,' Daisy said, grateful for the suggestion. When Mary Lennox first discovered the walled garden tucked behind the locked door at Misselthwaite Manor, it wouldn't have looked like this but she could certainly appreciate the way things would have changed as the children worked to restore the garden to its former glory. And perhaps by getting involved with the titanic task of managing all this beauty, she would gain a better understanding of how to bring the secret garden to life in her own illustrations. But first she wanted to drink it all in.

It wasn't until she was almost three-quarters of the way round the perimeter path that she spotted a cluster of roses whose colour she thought she recognized. They were tucked away at the back of what was clearly a dedicated rose bed. Pink and yellow blooms clambered up the bare brick wall and almost spilled over the top, blowsy heads nodding in the heat as they surveyed the garden from their lofty heights. The surrounding roses seemed to be competing to catch Daisy's eye – peach nestled beside yellow, white contrasted with deep crimson red and a more wanton scarlet, but Daisy couldn't drag her gaze away from the vibrant pink and yellow buds at the back. The colour was so distinctive that she was sure they must be the same type as the ones that grew around the door of the farmhouse. Those roses had been planted by her grandmother, long ago. Was it ridiculous to hope that she had planted these roses too?

'She might have done,' Athers said, squinting at the base of the stem for a label. 'It's an older variety, much longer living than the plants we get nowadays, so it could have been around for years. Maybe even decades.'

'The roses at the farmhouse have definitely been around a long time,' Daisy observed. 'I remember my grandmother tending them when I was a child.'

Athers squinted. 'This particular rose is dotted all over the manor house gardens – it's very well established. I can ask my dad if he remembers where it came from, if you like? He worked here all his life, as did his dad before him.'

The thought of connecting a few more dots in Violet's life pleased Daisy. It might even be that Athers' grandfather had known Violet. 'Would you mind?' she asked. 'I'm sure it can't be a coincidence that it's growing here and at Half Moon Farm.'

'It's done well if it's survived all these years,' Athers replied, shaking his head in wonderment. 'Just goes to show you what a bit of TLC and some really good manure can do.'

The sun shifted overhead as Daisy worked, changing the light and shadows across the garden in a way Daisy found fascinating. It was with extreme reluctance that she eventually packed her sketchbook away and closed the lid on her watercolours. 'I have to go and collect my sons now,' she explained to Athers. 'I'm sorry I wasn't more help with the deadheading.'

The younger man smiled. 'Don't be. It was amazing to see you so engrossed in your work. A real privilege.'

'Next time I'll be more hands on,' Daisy promised as he helped her load up the car. That there would be a next time, Daisy had no doubt. She'd fallen under the garden's spell from the moment she'd stepped through the door and the artwork she'd produced reflected that enchantment. The colour and composition sang from the paper, irresistibly inviting, and she knew she'd found her artistic mojo among the peace of the garden. For the first time in weeks, she felt as though she had created something worthy of the special anniversary edition of a much-loved book. Maybe – just maybe – she wasn't going to let everyone down after all.

Chapter Seventeen

984632 FL AJD
75 MTLRV
Royal Air Force

13th October

My Darling Violet

Thank you for your five recent letters, all of which took so long to reach me that I began to fear you had forgotten to write at all. But I shouldn't have doubted – they came and now my heart can cease its anxious wondering. How I wish I could see you now, standing beneath our tree. It is so difficult being apart, dependent on our valiant postal service to stay in touch, but if you ever have cause to doubt my love, run your fingers across the carving we made and know I am ever yours.

Your description of the changing seasons made me ache

for our little corner of England. I can picture the autumn leaves tumbling from the trees, almost taste the smoky October air. You have such a clever way with words, dearest Violet. You paint the scene better than any artist and gladden my soul with every stroke of your pen.

Life here continues much as before. You know that I cannot reveal much of what we are about but I take comfort from the knowledge that we are doing necessary work. My men are an admirable bunch, excellent company and truly brave souls. That said, I long for the day I can return home. On that day, I vow to place a ring upon your finger and nothing – not your family or mine – will separate us ever again. The thought of that is enough to light up the darkness long after my candle has burned away.

Keep smiling, keeper of my heart.

Yours always,

V

Daisy sat still on her bed for several long minutes, the tissue thin letter held loosely in her fingers as tears blurred her vision. She wasn't sure what it was that had prompted such sadness – all the letters she'd read so far were written with the same achingly romantic sentiment that made her want to sigh, both with admiration and the bittersweet realization that she had never inspired such passion. She had no doubt that Stuart had loved her while they'd been together, just as she had loved him and still did, albeit in a different way, but she couldn't imagine him ever declaring her the keeper of his heart. Perhaps such soaring emotion was only ever expressed in desperate times, which only served to make it more touching. But that poignancy wasn't the sole cause of Daisy's tears. The words on the page confirmed her suspicion that the man who had written so adoringly to her grandmother was Valentine Devereaux, who eventually became Ninth Earl of Winterbourne and presumably shattered both their hearts in the process. It was that sense of impending doom that made Daisy well up. She couldn't know what had happened once the war was over but it was plain Valentine had not kept his promise – something *had* separated him from Violet and she'd married someone else – Peter Moon, Daisy's grandfather. It made perfect sense that the break up must be the source of the bad feeling between the Moons and the Devereauxs. But unless Rose knew more than she was telling, Daisy had no idea how she might get to the bottom of anything. Kit had seemed unaware of both the clandestine relationship and the feud that followed. There really was only one course of action open to her. She would have to ask her mother.

Choosing her moment carefully, Daisy waited until Emily's day off on Thursday to raise the thorny subject with Rose. With her sketchpad on her lap, and a pot of tea gently steaming on the coffee table beside them, Daisy and her mother sat in companionable silence, punctured only by the rhythmic click-clack of knitting needles and the occasional muttered oath when Rose dropped a stitch or discovered some other small error. For a time, Daisy allowed herself to be lost in her work – a full spread illustration of Mary's arrival at Misselthwaite Manor – but at length she took a break and saw her mother had poured the tea and was nibbling on a custard cream.

'How's the cardigan coming along?' Daisy asked, reaching for her cup.

Rose sighed. 'Slowly. I can't seem to keep the pattern straight in my head these days. Not like I used to.'

'Looks like you're doing an amazing job to me,' Daisy said. 'The colour is lovely too.'

'It is, isn't it?' Rose replied, stroking the soft lilac wool. 'Drew chose it – he's got a good eye for colour. And he's going to get the roof fixed. That's good of him, isn't it?'

Daisy felt herself frown. 'The roof is already fixed. Don't you remember, I got someone from the village to repair it not long after the boys and I came.'

Now it was her mother's turn to frown. 'Did you? But I could have sworn . . .' She trailed off, staring at her tea in apparent confusion. 'Oh, but I don't suppose it matters who fixed it, as long as the rain can't get in.'

Daisy smiled but inwardly Rose's mistake troubled her. Was it a hangover from the illness or simple old age that had made her forget something that had happened only a few weeks ago? There hadn't been any other signs that her mother was easily confused but it wouldn't hurt to keep an eye on things. She might have a chat with Emily and Magda too, see if they had noticed anything. 'It's fine now,' she reassured Rose, then hesitated. 'But I did find something interesting while I was tidying up. A box of old letters – I think they belonged to Grandma.'

She broke off and took a sip of tea, watching over the rim of her cup for a reaction. 'Probably a lot of her things up there,' Rose said dismissively. 'I could never bring myself to throw anything away, even though Vince called it hoarding.'

As always, the mention of her stepfather's name caused Daisy's stomach to clench. 'So you haven't read them? The letters, I mean.'

Rose shrugged. 'No. Who are they from – anyone I know?'

And now Daisy really hesitated. It wasn't too late to back out, tell another harmless lie and avoid the risk of causing upset. But she would only be postponing the inevitable. Sooner or later, she had to grasp the nettle and hope she didn't get stung. 'They were love letters,' she said, steeling herself. 'But not from Grandpa.'

Instantly, Rose's lips became a thin white line. Her needles began to clack together with ferocious speed. Daisy waited until it became clear her mother wasn't going to speak. 'I haven't read them all yet but they're beautifully written.' She paused, trying to gauge Rose's reaction from the flash of the knitting needles. 'Did you know Grandma was in love with someone else before she married Grandpa?'

'Damn it all to hell!' Rose suddenly stopped knitting, glaring first at her hands and then at Daisy. 'Now look what you made me do.'

'I didn't mean to upset you,' Daisy said, determined to see the conversation through now that she'd started. 'Perhaps you should leave your knitting until after we're finished talking.'

A familiar spark of fury flashed in Rose's eyes. 'And what if I don't want to finish the conversation? Have you considered that?'

Daisy took a breath. 'Yes,' she said simply. 'I know it's going to make you uncomfortable. But I have some questions and I don't know where else to go for answers.'

'Answers you have no right to demand!'

The words whipped out. Daisy felt the sting as they landed. 'I'm not demanding anything,' she said steadily. 'I'm asking. Violet was my grandmother and I loved her and I'm interested in who she was.'

Once again, Rose pursed her lips until they were bloodless and Daisy expected her to maintain a haughty silence until she gave up and left the room. Then her shoulders sagged and she let out a weary sigh. 'I suppose there's no harm in telling you. Although you probably know more than me, if you've read his letters.'

The breath caught in Daisy's throat and she couldn't help leaning forward. 'Whose letters?'

'You've been reading them.' Rose threw her an impatient look. 'Don't you know?'

'They're not signed,' Daisy said, wondering when to voice her suspicions. 'I don't know who they're from. That's what I wanted to ask you.'

'Oh for pity's sake,' Rose snapped, glowering at Daisy. 'If you must know, she was a fool. Fell head over heels for a man who had no intention of marrying her – someone who couldn't marry her, no matter how much he promised he would. And when his family found out, she lost her job and her reputation. His name was Alfred bloody Devereaux.'

She'd been expecting it but hearing her mother say the name still caught Daisy by surprise and not just because she'd grown accustomed to thinking of him by the initial he signed his letters with – V for Valentine. 'She lost her job? The one at the castle gardens?'

'Of course,' Rose replied, as though nothing could be more obvious. 'Where else? They blamed her for tempting him so there was no way they would keep her around to carry on with her wicked seduction.'

Indignation bloomed in Daisy's chest. Anyone who had read Valentine's letters could not fail to believe he had been in love with Violet. But at the same time, she could see why the Devereaux family had done what they had done. Hadn't Kit made it clear that a below-stairs dalliance wouldn't be tolerated, perhaps even today? 'That's awful,' she said, after a few seconds of silence. 'Poor Violet.'

'She took a job here, at the farm, and eventually confided in your grandfather,' Rose went on. 'That was why he hated them – he knew they'd treated her appallingly. But he kept it to himself – I didn't find out until after they refused to let me into their party. That was when I learned to hate them too.'

Daisy flushed guiltily. What would her mother say if she knew Daisy had been to the ball a few weeks earlier and

225

planned to take the twins there for tea tomorrow? 'I don't think Kit knows about any of this,' she said into the loaded silence.

'Perhaps not,' Rose said, eyes narrowing. 'But a leopard doesn't change its spots and apples don't fall far from the tree. A Devereaux is a Devereaux – all of them are bad.'

As much as Daisy wanted to argue, she knew it was pointless – her mother's pronouncement was born from bitter experience that had hardened to granite over many years. 'So Violet met Grandpa here and they fell in love,' she said. 'The story had a happy ending, in spite of all the heart-break.'

Rose sniffed. 'It doesn't change things. That family tried to ruin a young girl's life – the fact that they failed says more about her than them.'

It said more about Valentine's parents, Daisy wanted to correct her, still unable to equate what her mother had described with the impassioned young man in the letters upstairs. Had he fought the demands of his family? After years of fighting in the war, had he come home only to start a battle of a different kind – one he was destined to lose? It was hard to believe he'd given Violet up so readily but once again, it felt as though Daisy only had one side of the story and she had no idea where to go for the rest. There was a guarded air to Rose's expression; if she had anything more to offer, she didn't seem willing to share it now. 'Thank you for telling me,' Daisy said after a few more moments had passed. 'I know it can't have been easy.'

Rose picked up her knitting once more and began to count the stitches. 'You might be right that Kit Devereaux doesn't know what his family did but someone at the castle does,' she said after a lengthy, aggrieved silence. 'They have long memories, just like us, and they won't have forgiven any more than we have.'

Any more than you have, Daisy wanted to say but her mother's mouth had snapped shut and she knew the conversation was over, at least for now. The trouble was her curiosity had only been more inflamed by what she'd heard and she burned to know more. If Rose was to be believed, the only other person who could fill in the blanks was Hugh but Daisy's heart quailed at the thought of approaching him. Perhaps Rose was right and it was better to let sleeping feuds lie, Daisy thought as she sipped her tea. Or perhaps she could use her next visit to the castle to enlist Kit's help – the topic was bound to come up when she told him about the most recent letter she'd read. One thing was certain – she couldn't tell her mother she was on first name terms with a Devereaux. That would only lead to fresh upset between the two families and there had been too much of that already.

Chapter Eighteen

Daisy wasn't sure which of the twins was more excited at the prospect of a VIP visit to Winterbourne Castle. Campbell couldn't wait to go exploring, although Daisy warned him most of the castle itself would probably be off limits. Finn seemed more interested in seeing how the other half lived and Daisy had felt obliged to point out that he was unlikely to encounter a fleet of supercars or floor-to-ceiling televisions. 'You're both going to be guests in Alice's home, please remember to be respectful.'

'I bet they have a butler,' Finn replied, as though she hadn't spoken. 'And silver plates and – and – goblets.'

Campbell let out a snort of derision. 'Alice said she had fishfingers and chips for tea last night. That doesn't sound like something you eat off a silver plate.'

'I reckon they were posh fishfingers, though,' Finn countered. 'And proper chips. Not like the ones Mum feeds us.'

At that, Daisy had felt compelled to defend herself. 'There's

nothing wrong with the fishfingers and chips I give you.'
She recalled Kit's comments about earning his own living.
'I'm sure you're going to have a lovely time, regardless of
what the plates are made of.'

In the event, there was a picnic-style buffet laid out on
an admittedly grand dining table. The plates were perfectly
serviceable, plain white china that Daisy suspected had come
from IKEA and both boys tucked into carrot sticks, cucumber
and salad with considerably more enthusiasm than they would
have at home. 'Cheesestrings!' Finn exclaimed, reaching across
from his elegantly carved seat to pluck a plastic-wrapped
package from a bowl. 'Excellent.'

Kit gave Daisy a pained look. 'We have some genuinely
excellent aged cheddar in the fridge but Alice was adamant
we served those.'

Daisy smiled. 'All the more cheddar for you, I'd say. It
would be wasted on my two.'

'Would you like some?' Kit offered. 'I wasn't sure whether
you'd want to eat – we've never really had children from
school over so I didn't know what to offer you, other than
tea or coffee, but I can easily fetch some cheese and crackers
if you'd like? There's some fig chutney too, I think.'

Daisy shook her head. 'Thank you but we've already put
you to enough trouble.'

Kit pushed back his chair. 'It's no trouble, I assure you. I
wouldn't mind some myself.'

What else could she do but give in? 'In that case, thank
you. It sounds delicious.'

He vanished through an oak-panelled door and Daisy let the chatter of the children wash over her as she took the opportunity to admire the room they were in. It wasn't large, at least in comparison to the rooms she'd visited on the night of the ball. The nearest wall was split by several triple-arched windows, framed with thick brocade curtains and offering an inviting view of the castle, but the other three walls were lined with bookshelves that stretched from floor to ceiling and it gave Daisy a little thrill of delight to see a sliding ladder to reach the upper shelves. A library like this had been the stuff of dreams when she'd been a child and she could only imagine the joy of browsing the leatherbound titles. She had no idea whether Kit and Alice ate in this room every day or whether they'd moved a table in just for this meal but she couldn't think of anything nicer, especially when there was a fire crackling in the currently empty grate.

After a few more minutes of gazing around, Daisy couldn't contain her curiosity any longer. Leaving the children to discuss the merits of Monster Munch over Hula Hoops, she crossed to the nearest bookshelf and ran her finger along the leather, occasionally tipping her head to read the titles and author names that ran vertically along the spines. Many were books she'd never heard of – weighty non-fiction tomes on subjects that would send her to sleep – but she spotted a slender copy of Mary Shelley's *Frankenstein* that might well be a first edition, and several of the Brontë sisters' novels. She was so engrossed in browsing that she missed Kit's return and only realized he'd come back when she heard his voice at her shoulder. 'See anything you like the look of? I recommend the *Journal of the Royal Microscopical Society* if you suffer from insomnia.'

Daisy laughed. 'I'll bear that in mind. But you have so many other wonderful titles to choose from.'

'True,' Kit said, then frowned thoughtfully. 'Actually, I think there might be something you'll find interesting. If I can find it – the shelving is a little haphazard.'

Stepping sideways, he began perusing the books. Daisy waited awkwardly, her concentration broken, wondering whether she should ask which title he was looking for so she could help but then he let out a soft humph of satisfaction. 'Got you,' he said, pulling a slim volume from between its shelf mates. He offered it to Daisy. 'It's not quite a first edition but it might give you some ideas.'

It was a green, clothbound book, a little worn and battered around the corners but otherwise in excellent condition. The title, picked out in faded gilt, was *The Secret Garden* and beneath it there was a golden line image of Mary Lennox kneeling on the grass, a plant cupped in her hands and roses blooming around her head. Daisy felt a small gasp of wonderment escape her as she took the book and reverently eased back the cover. The faintly yellowed endpapers were covered with delicate fronds and flowers. In one corner, someone had pencilled their name – Maude Devereaux. 'My great-grandmother,' Kit explained. 'She was an avid reader.'

Nodding absently, Daisy turned the page to find the publication date. '1912,' she said, her tone hushed. 'Wow.'

'There are some glorious pictures dotted throughout, if I remember rightly,' Kit said. 'Full colour, which must have cost a fortune back then.'

'Illustrated by Charles Robinson,' Daisy read, then looked up at Kit. 'This is a real treasure.'

He smiled. 'I knew you'd like it. You can borrow it, if you like. Take it home and study it properly.'

She gaped at him. 'Oh no, I couldn't. It's a family heirloom.'

'Yes, but it's also a book and books were meant to be read,' he said evenly. 'All it's doing here is gathering dust.'

Her gaze returned to the gently age-spotted pages and she turned a few more pages until she found the first illustration. 'Oh,' she breathed, and any resolve she might have had to refuse Kit's offer evaporated as she took in the intricacy of the work. 'It's beautiful. Can I really borrow it?'

'Of course. In fact, I insist,' he said. 'I know you'll look after it.'

'I will,' Daisy replied fervently. 'Thank you.'

Kit tipped his head. 'You're welcome. But perhaps leave it for now. You don't want to smear the pages with cheese.'

Hurriedly, Daisy closed the book and place it on the shelf, as though she might contaminate the pages with the mere thought of the food she was about to eat. 'Good idea.'

The cheese was every bit as delicious as Kit had suggested and it went perfectly with the chutney, which he said had been made from last year's fig harvest from the tree in the castle gardens. 'I thought we could take a walk after we've eaten,' he said. 'Alice wants to give Finn and Campbell the tour and she's told me in no uncertain terms that we're not invited.'

Daisy couldn't help smiling. 'Sounds good to me.'

The sun was starting to dip towards the horizon as they made their way to the garden. This time, Kit led her past the landscaped hedges to the kitchen gardens, where the air was rich with the scent of herbs. Daisy allowed her fingers to brush the plants, releasing their heady aromas. Rosemary mingled with thyme, sage complimented lemon balm and lavender threatened to overshadow them all. The fig tree Kit had mentioned nodded against a south-facing wall, its branches heavy with ripening fruit. 'Looks like another bumper crop,' she observed.

Kit nodded. 'We'll be up to our eyeballs in chutney again,' he said, then offered her a wry smile. 'First world problems, right?'

It wasn't until they were strolling towards the walled garden that Daisy began to consider how best to raise the delicate matter of her grandmother. But the thought was driven from her mind by a sudden loud screech somewhere nearby. For a heartbeat, she thought it was one of the children but then her common sense intervened. It had sounded more like the wail of a baby and she knew there were none of those roaming the grounds. 'What was that?'

'That would be Woody,' Kit replied. 'Alice's pet peacock.'

Daisy blinked. 'Her pet?'

Beside her, Kit sighed. 'I know. Some children have

hamsters or puppies – she has a peacock. Another weird family tradition, I'm afraid. He's not what you'd call cuddly.'

They rounded a corner and Daisy found herself face to face with Woody himself. Paying no attention to them, the bird raised his turquoise plumed head and let out another shrill cry that was loud enough to make Daisy wince. Then he turned their way and, with a deliberate air, raised his tail feathers and shimmered them into an iridescent fan of blues, greens and blacks. He eyed them expectantly.

'Stop showing off,' Kit told the bird mildly. 'Neither of us have any food.'

Woody took a few steps forwards, his gaze trained beadily upon the humans. When it became clear they were not going to produce treats, he let out a final indignant squawk and stalked past, his beak pointed haughtily to the sky. Daisy turned to watch him go, admiring the beautiful spread of feathers as he sashayed away. 'I wonder what Atticus would make of him,' she said as she and Kit continued along the path.

He glanced at her. 'Atticus?'

'Our cat,' she explained. 'Or wildcat, perhaps. He's definitely got an ego to match Woody's – I wonder if he'd be intimidated.'

Kit nodded. 'I've seen Woody face down one of Hugh's overexcited spaniels. He might have a brain the size of a pea but he's no coward.'

'Whereas Atticus gives the impression he's plotting to take over the world,' Daisy said. 'In fact, they'd make perfect partners in crime – Woody could cause a distraction and Atticus could snatch the snacks.'

He laughed. 'Let's never introduce them.'

A sleepy stillness greeted them as they entered the walled garden.. The fading evening light bathed the beds in gold, turning each petal and leaf into a gilt-edged treasure. Birds harmonized their goodnight melodies as though conducted by a maestro, while bees buzzed lazily from flower to flower, plundering one last haul of pollen before nightfall. Long shadows fell across some of the paths, causing Daisy to wrap her arms around herself. It wasn't chilly yet but it soon would be.

She took a steadying breath as they neared the chestnut tree. 'Do you remember I told you about some letters to my grandmother from an unknown serviceman?' she asked, striving for a casual tone.

'Of course I do,' Kit said with a sideways glance. 'You thought they'd been written by my grandfather – how could I forget?'

'The initials carved on the tree match,' Daisy reminded him. 'And your grandfather did serve in France. But I found a letter that specifically mentions the tree, and the carving. So I asked my mother if she knew anything about Violet's life before she was born.'

'Let me guess,' Kit said. 'She confirmed your suspicions.'

Daisy hesitated. 'Yes. At least she confirmed the letters were written by your grandfather.'

'Then it follows they were lovers,' Kit said.

'Yes,' Daisy said again. 'He wanted to marry her. But we know that didn't happen.'

Kit puffed out his cheeks. 'No. I imagine my family had something to say about it. As I told you the night of the ball, earls don't marry –' He broke off but Daisy was certain he'd been about to say 'servants'. She felt her temper start to rise and perhaps Kit realized because he held up a conciliatory hand. 'Earls don't marry for love,' he went on, his tone more sympathetic. 'Not solely for love, anyway. It's a bonus, if they're lucky.'

It was another glimpse into a world that was so different from her own and it gave Daisy a moment's pause as she considered how it might feel to be told who to marry. 'But at least he was still an earl,' she pointed out. 'Violet lost her job.'

'Yes, I expect she was bundled off quite sharply,' Kit remarked. 'And for what it's worth, I'm sorry – she was probably treated badly. But she met your grandfather and you once told me they were very happy together.'

The sentiment echoed what Daisy had observed to her mother the day before and she had a sudden dizzying flash of what might have been if Valentine and Violet had been allowed their happy ever after. Could they have been happier than Violet and Peter? Daisy had always considered her grandparents to be the perfect couple but perhaps she had only seen what she wanted to see. It was impossible to know. 'Yes, I think they were happy.'

'Then I'm glad.' Kit stopped walking and Daisy realized

with a jolt that they had reached the tree. 'I'm not sure the same can be said of my grandfather.'

Fragments of prose from the letters floated across Daisy's mind. She still believed Valentine meant every impassioned declaration; if Violet had been the love of his life then it seemed eminently possible he had never got over losing her. The thought made her sad, in spite of his privileged existence. 'Then I'm sorry too.'

Kit stared at the tree trunk. 'I'm not suggesting he had a miserable life – far from it. My grandmother was a good match for him, they were well suited and they liked each other enough to produce my father, at least.' His gaze was pensive. 'But I remember he was prone to periods of melancholy. When I was older, I thought it must have been the war made him that way but now I wonder if that was only part of it.'

Once again, Daisy wondered what might have been if Valentine had been allowed to follow his heart.. 'Isn't there anyone you can ask? Maybe Hugh knows more.'

'He might,' Kit said, shrugging. 'I could ask, if you'd like me to.'

Something in the way he said it suggested reluctance and she supposed she couldn't blame him. Was there really anything to be gained by raking over past scandals, especially when your family didn't come out of things looking good? As much as she wanted to uncover the full story, she didn't want to trample over Kit's feelings to get it. 'No, it's okay.'

But Kit didn't seem to have heard. 'Are you familiar with the poem "This be the Verse" by Philip Larkin?'

Daisy couldn't help smiling – the rude words chosen by Larkin had made that particular poem especially popular with her A-Level English classmates. But for her, the sentiment behind the words – that parents inadvertently passed their own issues onto their children – had resonated much more deeply with the teenage Daisy. 'Yes, I know it.'

'I often think of it,' Kit said. 'Mostly when I'm kicking myself for failing at parenting but sometimes when I look back at my own family.' He grimaced. 'I might make mistakes with Alice every now and then but I'm glad I'll never have to tell her who she can love.'

A jumble of complicated emotions surged through Daisy. She'd often contemplated the choices her mother had made in the name of love – choices that had driven Daisy away for years – and wondered whether she would do anything differently. Now that they were slowly rebuilding their relationship she had learned that Rose did have regrets. And since Daisy had never known her father, she couldn't say what his thoughts were on the subject. But she had been determined from the moment she had discovered she was pregnant that she would always put her children's health and happiness first. Even when she and Stuart had fallen out of love and agreed to separate, they had done so in a way that prioritized Finn and Campbell. Just like Kit, she knew she wasn't perfect, but she couldn't imagine ever doing anything to hurt them. 'Maybe that's the subtext of Larkin's poem,' she said at length. 'There's no point telling people not to have children, but at least they can try to avoid the same mistakes their parents made.'

Kit bowed his head in wry acknowledgement. 'Amen to that.'

Daisy glanced at her watch. 'Speaking of children, we should probably find ours. I really hope they haven't fallen off anything.'

'Hugh pushed me off the ramparts once,' Kit said conversationally as they headed for the door in the wall. 'But I haven't heard any screaming. I'm sure they're fine.'

And they were. Finn had a long graze along one shin and Campbell had grass stains on his elbows but neither wanted to leave, forcing Daisy to promise to invite Alice to Half Moon Farm soon, in spite of the complications that might raise. As they stood on the steps at the front of the manor, Kit pressed the copy of *The Secret Garden* into Daisy's hands. 'Don't forget this,' he said, smiling. 'Happy reading.'

Daisy glanced down at the book and a thrill of anticipation ran through her. 'Thank you,' she replied, returning his smile. 'And thanks for having us. We had a wonderful time.'

Kit wrapped his arm around his daughter's shoulders. 'So did we. Sorry about Woody.'

Alice groaned. 'Oh no. He didn't peck you, did he?'

'No,' Daisy said, laughing. 'He just wanted to me to admire him.'

Finn shook his head. 'Wait until you meet Atticus. He'll probably try to eat you.'

'Don't tell her that,' Campbell objected, swatting his brother's arm. 'She won't want to come!'

They began to bicker once more, good-natured but clearly trying to score points in front of Alice. Daisy met Kit's eyes over their heads and they shared another smile, this time with more than a hint of long-suffering comradeship. Then she herded her squabbling sons into the car and drove them home to Half Moon Farm.

Chapter Nineteen

Daisy was washing up the breakfast crockery on Saturday morning when she was startled by a rap on the window. She looked up to see Drew gazing at her through the glass and suddenly her heart was fluttering for an entirely different reason. 'Good morning,' she said, once she'd opened the window. 'Everything okay?'

Drew spread his hands as though giving thanks. 'Everything is wonderful. It's the weekend, the sun is shining and I'm speaking to you. What more could I ask for?'

His enthusiasm was catching – Daisy felt herself smiling in return. 'There speaks someone who didn't wake up to the sound of quarrelling children.'

'That is true,' Drew conceded. 'A wise man once said that the key to enjoying the sound of children playing is to make sure you aren't close enough to hear what they are saying.'

It was a sentiment Daisy could definitely get on board with. She'd been woken by a heated argument between Finn and Campbell over whose turn it was on the PlayStation and things had gone rapidly downhill from there. She wasn't sure how much of it was due to the late night at the castle the day before – by the time she'd got them both showered and ready for bed it had been after ten o'clock – but they currently weren't talking to each other. She was actually quite glad – at least if they were sulking in separate rooms, they weren't arguing. 'Thankfully, things have calmed down now,' she said. 'What are you up to this morning?'

'Checking on the hops,' Drew replied. 'I'm optimistic some will be ripe enough to harvest in a week or so and we can get our first batch of ale on the go.'

For a moment, Daisy was nonplussed then she remembered one of Drew's side hustles was helping Nigel to run his microbrewery, Brew Crew, in one of the modernized barns that lined the courtyard of Half Moon Farm. They used the hops plants that had once been the main business of the farm, although they no longer used the oast house to dry them – that was all done off site, since the oast house had been converted into Nancy's café. Once upon a time hop farming had been big business in Kent, attracting a summer workforce from London to pick the hops. Going hopping was the equivalent of a holiday to some poorer families, and a chance to earn a little extra money on the side, but the practice had eventually died out as automated hop pickers took over. It had been a long time since Half Moon Farm had grown enough hops to supply anyone with enough to turn into beer but Drew's green fingers seemed to have changed that. 'I'll have to try some,' she told him. 'Although I have to admit I'm more of a wine drinker.'

He laughed. 'Ah, but when in Rome, Daisy.'

'When in Rome,' she agreed, although she supposed it depended how long the brewing process took. She and the twins were due to return to Milton Keynes for the start of September, as long as Rose's recovery continued, and that was only seven weeks away – perhaps they would be gone before Drew's beer was ready. The thought caused an unexpected stab of dismay and Daisy knew it had nothing to do with whether the beer would be ready and everything to do with Half Moon Farm. She loved her life with the boys in Milton Keynes but she had to admit she'd come to think of the farmhouse as home. Leaving it, and the friends they'd made, was going to be a bigger wrench than she'd anticipated.

With a slight jolt, she realized Drew was looking at her expectantly but she had no idea why. 'Sorry,' she said. 'I was miles away then. Did you ask me a question?'

If he thought her preoccupation was odd, he didn't say so. 'I wanted to know if you have plans for tomorrow morning. I thought I could take you and the twins out for a walk, show you some hidden treasures you might not have discovered yet.'

Finn and Campbell would both grumble but at least it would give her an excuse to get them out of the house. And she'd enjoyed her last walk with Drew, albeit as much for the kiss they'd shared as his knowledge about nature.

243

Blushing slightly at the memory, she smiled at him. 'That sounds lovely. What time?'

'Around ten o'clock?' he suggested. 'That way we'll get back before the afternoon heat sets in.'

There'd been plenty of heat during their last walk, Daisy recalled, but it'd had nothing to do with the weather. Flustered, she plunged her hands into the sink and began washing the teapot. 'Great. Where shall we meet you – in the courtyard?'

'Sounds like a plan,' Drew said. 'I'm looking forward to it already.'

So was Daisy but she wasn't sure she could trust herself to say so without somehow giving her racing thoughts away. Instead, she summoned up what she hoped was an encouraging but brisk smile. 'Ten o'clock, in the courtyard,' she repeated. 'See you then.'

★ ★ ★

There was plenty of complaining on Sunday morning when Daisy laid out the plans for the morning but Campbell's mood improved a little at the mention of the war relics they might find along the way. 'I suppose there might be pill boxes,' he said, sitting up a little straighter over his cereal. 'We're too far inland for gun towers.'

'I have no idea,' Daisy replied. 'Your grandfather didn't like to talk about the war so I've never seen any of the traces it left around here.'

'Lucky you,' Finn muttered into his bowl.

Daisy fired a meaningful look his way. 'Drew has very kindly offered to show us these things and I'm sure it will be fun. I hope you're going to be polite.'

He scowled resentfully down at his bowl. 'I don't see why I have to come. Campbell is a history nerd – he loves this stuff – but I don't see why I can't stay here with Grandma and Emily.'

'Because Grandma is still not well enough and Emily isn't paid to look after you,' Daisy said. 'It won't kill you to go for a walk, Finn.'

He clearly felt otherwise because his scowl intensified but he didn't argue further. Instead, he settled for silent rebellion: when it was time to leave, he took forever to find his trainers and then couldn't decide whether he needed a jumper. They were almost out of the door when he announced he needed to go to the toilet. Daisy's patience was stretched to breaking point by the time they met Drew in the courtyard, almost ten minutes late, and her mood must have showed in her face because Drew gave her a sympathetic smile. 'Tricky morning?' he asked as she and Campbell reached him, with a clearly mutinous Finn trailing behind.

'Just a bit,' she said, and forced her shoulders to drop. 'But we're here now. Sorry we're late.'

'No trouble at all,' Drew said easily and gestured at the cornflower blue sky. 'I've been admiring this beautiful morning.'

A faintly derisive snort exploded from Finn, causing Daisy to wheel around but Drew reached out to touch her arm. 'Hey, Finn,' he said. 'I hear you're the main man for football intel. Who's your must-buy player for my fantasy team this season?'

Daisy fully expected Finn to ignore this blatant attempt to draw him out but Drew's charm clearly extended further than she'd anticipated because her son looked up from the stone he'd been kicking. 'You want Kellerman-Smith in goal, obviously,' he said, in a tone that suggested no one in their right mind would think otherwise. 'Don't bother with Magellan – he couldn't defend against Campbell – but George Kirby is worth buying.'

Nodding, Drew began to walk. 'Right. But what about up front? Who can't I afford to miss?'

Much to Daisy's astonishment, Finn fell into step beside him. 'Mattheus is a good shout, although Linkman is also worth thinking about.'

Daisy and Campbell followed a little way behind. 'Finn is so gullible,' Campbell observed. 'I bet all my birthday money that Drew couldn't care less about football.'

'Ssshhh,' Daisy murmured, even though she suspected he was right. 'Do you want to see the pill boxes or not?'

The walk took them north of the farm, along the edge of corn fields that rustled in the gentle breeze. Clusters of poppies nodded their heads drowsily, delicate scarlet petals fluttering. The sun was already hot, making Daisy glad she had insisted on suncream before leaving the house, something else Finn had deemed entirely unreasonable. There was no sign of his bad mood now, however. He was animatedly discussing football with Drew and Daisy didn't think he had paused for breath once. Campbell, on the other hand, was engrossed in scanning the horizon for any remains of wartime buildings, which left Daisy free to admire the hedgerows. They seemed to be bursting with dog roses and blackberry blossom, the leaves thick and glossy with the green nubs of berries in evidence already. Daisy made a mental note to return with a basket in August – the blackberries would go very nicely in a crumble with apples from the orchard.

After a mile or so, the path led into the trees and Daisy was grateful for the coolness. Drew was still walking with Finn but he glanced back every now and then, meeting Daisy's eyes with good-humoured resignation. She owed him a drink, she thought as he bowed his head to her son once more. Maybe even more than one.

'Look!' Campbell's voice suddenly vibrated with enthusiasm. 'I can see something.'

He was pointing to a small clearing up ahead, where a squat concrete shape poked up a metre or so above the yellowed, overgrown grass. Horizontal slits served as windows, or gun slots, Daisy guessed. It didn't look very big. Campbell abandoned her without another word and raced past Drew and Finn to reach the structure. Unwilling to be left behind, Finn followed his brother and they reached it at the same time.

Drew paused, waiting for her. 'There are around 6,000 of these pill boxes left in Britain, most around the home counties. Some of them are better looked after than others – sadly, a few have been commandeered by ne'er do wells looking for somewhere to drink or smoke. But the ones round here aren't bad.' He sent a mischievous glance her way. 'You can even go in if you like.'

Daisy shuddered. 'No, thanks. I don't think my back would thank me.'

He grinned. 'They're bigger than you think. The floor is below ground level, so there's room to stand up, and this one has a ladder leading to a room underneath. The idea was that members of the Home Guard could hunker down inside and pick off any invaders but of course, it never came to that.'

Daisy watched Campbell and Finn disappear from view and she guessed they'd gone inside. 'Thank goodness. I'm a bit surprised they haven't been boarded up, especially if they're used for less than savoury purposes.'

'Some have,' he said, shrugging. 'A lot have been demolished – they built around 28,000 of them when the fear of invasion was at its height. But we're lucky around here. The worst that happens is that a family of foxes decides to move in.'

Daisy squinted anxiously at the pill box, hoping it was currently unoccupied. Drew picked up on her concern. 'Don't worry, there's no one living there now. I stopped by yesterday evening to check it was clear for the boys.'

The extra care he'd taken touched Daisy. 'Thank you. That's really good of you.'

He shrugged her thanks away. 'It's a lovely walk, especially at sunset. I'll have to bring you out here again, so you can see how beautiful it is.'

His gaze was warm on hers, sparking a slow burn in the pit of her stomach. A stroll through the trees with him as the sun dipped low and the stars began to appear in the sky would be undeniably romantic and, as good as he had been with the twins, she got the impression that the invitation only extended to her. The thought of being alone with him sent a shiver of anticipation down her spine, lighting a too-familiar ache of desire, and suddenly she knew she was ready to take the next step with him. Nancy had been right, it was inevitable that it would happen and Daisy was tired of fighting it. 'A sunset walk sounds lovely,' she said, her voice low. 'But I'm pretty sure I owe you a drink for putting up with my moody son just now.'

'He's a great kid. I enjoyed chatting to him.' His eyes stayed fixed on her. 'I wouldn't say no to a drink, though. Maybe we could extend it to dinner.'

The breath caught in Daisy's throat as her heart sped up. They were only discussing having dinner but somehow it felt like so much more. Doubt crept into her mind one again – did she really want to do this? But this time she pushed it away. She nodded. 'Dinner. Yes, I'd like that.'

'I'm free on Saturday. Does that work?'

Daisy's pulse quickened again. The twins were with Stuart at the weekend. 'I can do Saturday.'

'Great,' he said, smiling. 'There's a nice place not far from here. I'll see what they have available.'

She nodded. They gazed at each other for a moment, both still and silent as birds sang around them. It would only take a step or two to close the distance between them, Daisy thought, her mouth suddenly dry. She could be in his arms in a second. From the look on his face, Drew was thinking something similar and it was only a shout from the direction of the pill box that prevented Daisy from acting on impulse. 'You need to see this, Mum!' Finn emerged from the side of the concrete box, his expression bursting with excitement. 'There's a room downstairs and someone has drawn a willy on the wall!'

It was the last thing Daisy had expected to hear and she couldn't help a burst of laughter from escaping her. She glanced at Drew, who looked mortified. 'Sorry,' he said. 'I was so busy checking for wildlife that I must have missed that.'

'Don't apologize,' she said, laughter still bubbling up inside her. 'They've probably seen worse.'

Finn was hopping up and down, demanding that she come and look. With a rueful glance at Drew, she gave in and started to make her way towards the pill box. Had there ever been a more effective mood killer, she wondered as her son gestured down the narrow steps into the darkness. Still, at least she had dinner with Drew to look forward to. And she found she was looking forward to it very much indeed.

Chapter Twenty

Magda had arranged to take Rose to a concert in Canterbury on Wednesday evening so Daisy took advantage of the empty farmhouse to return the tea invitation to Kit and Alice. Thankfully, the weather continued to be fine and dry, allowing her to set up a table in the garden and preventing Finn from enacting his plan to challenge Alice to a FIFA marathon on the PlayStation. 'No gaming,' she reminded him, when he suggested it again before school on Wednesday morning. 'You've got plenty of other things to do.'

'Boring things,' Finn replied, rolling his eyes.

Daisy managed to hold out until after they had eaten but Finn had clearly got to Alice during the school day. 'It's not me who wants to play,' he said, when she reinforced the no gaming rule. 'Alice wants to see the new update. Don't you, Alice?'

To her credit, Alice had only hesitated for a fraction of a second. 'Yes please. If you don't mind.'

Daisy glanced at Kit, hoping he might intervene but his expression was studiously polite. She sighed, knowing she was beaten. 'Go on, then. You've got an hour – no longer.'

Finn jumped to his feet, grabbing a Mini Roll, and raced for the door that led into the farmhouse. Alice and Campbell followed, the latter looking considerably less enthusiastic than his brother. Kit smirked at Daisy. 'Outmanoeuvred by a ten-year-old. Welcome to my world.'

'I pick my battles,' Daisy said. 'I'm hoping they'll get bored and find something better to do, although I don't have a castle to distract them.'

Kit glanced around. 'You do have an orchard, though. Young me would be over there scrumping in a heartbeat.'

Daisy could picture him as a child, all blond hair and freckles and scabby knees, his blue eyes always on the lookout for adventure and missing nothing. The image reminded her of Finn, who could find something to fall off in an empty field, and she could certainly envisage him filling his pockets with juicy apples. 'You must have had fruit trees at the castle – was there any need to go scrumping?'

He regarded her solemnly. 'Ah, but you and I both know that a stolen apple tastes a hundred times sweeter than one you're allowed to eat.'

She laughed. 'I'm sure you're right. Maybe I missed out – I only ever ate the ones that grew in the orchard, although I'm sure I ate more than I should have.'

Kit nodded. 'Did you spend a lot of time here? With your grandparents, I mean.'

'Every summer for years,' she replied, and paused. 'Mum had a flat in South London and – well, let's just say it wasn't the steadiest upbringing. I loved the space here, the slower pace of life, the greenness. It's safe to say I never wanted to go back to the concrete at the end of the holidays.'

He was silent for a moment. 'That sounds difficult,' he said quietly. 'I'm glad you had your grandparents.'

'Me too,' Daisy said, although she couldn't help wondering what he could possibly know of grey inner-city estates and missed meals. 'I never expected to be living here, though, even temporarily. It's funny how things turn out.'

'When do you think you'll go home?' he asked.

Again, Daisy felt a tug of disquiet at the thought of leaving. 'At the end of August,' she said. 'The twins are due to go back to their old school for Year 6 and Mum should be well enough to cope on her own by then. With help, of course.'

She'd already negotiated a long-term contract with the agency that supplied Emily and Magda, ensuring Rose would be well looked after once Daisy and the boys had gone back to Milton Keynes. 'But you'll pop back for visits?' Kit said, studying her.

Some of Daisy's unease lift at the suggestion. 'Absolutely,' she said with a smile. 'You're not getting rid of us that easily.'

Kit smiled too. 'Good. Alice is going to miss Finn and Campbell terribly. She'll be glad to know they're not abandoning her.'

Daisy had no doubt it was true – the twins would miss Alice too – but something about the way Kit said it reminded her of Alice's mother, who appeared to be more absent in her daughter's life than present. She became aware that they had once again drifted towards deeper waters and she wasn't sure she wanted to intrude into more of his family history. Kit seemed to spot the warning signs too because he cleared his throat. 'How are you getting on with the book illustrations? Was my old copy of *The Secret Garden* any help?'

Daisy pictured the book where she'd left it, sitting on her bedside table beside a bundle of Violet's letters. She had loved revisiting the story again and had taken great delight in the intricate artwork. It had felt like an enormous privilege to hold a copy that was well over a hundred years old, especially one that had been passed down from one generation to the next, and she had taken care to incorporate little nods to Charles Robinson's drawings in her own work. Very few people would notice, she thought, but she would know. And perhaps Kit would too. 'It's been an enormous help,' she told him, relieved to move the conversation away from choppier subjects. 'Would you like to see?'

His expression lit up. 'Very much so, if you don't mind.'

She hadn't planned to invite anyone inside the room she'd commandeered as a studio and it was untidier than she would have liked. But Kit wasn't there to assess her housekeeping skills, she reminded herself as she pulled out spread after spread of illustration and laid them across the table. 'This is when Mary first discovers the garden,' she said, pointing. 'The door of the garden is just like the one you have in the walled garden at the castle and I added in the fallen down fountain from Robinson's picture.'

Kit said nothing, his focus fixed on the drawings. 'And here's one of Mary and Dickon replanting some roses,' she went on, hoping his silence was a good sign. 'I used the rose beds at the castle as inspiration – these pink and yellow flowers grow there and around the front door of the farmhouse, funnily enough.'

His gaze flickered upward then, to rest briefly on her, but was soon drawn back to the table. 'This one shows the garden in all its glory, when Mary's uncle finds them there. I hope you don't mind but I added the horse chestnut tree. I need to bring them out a bit but if you squint, you can just about see the initials carved in the trunk.'

He bent his head to peer at the image. When he straightened up, his eyes were shining. 'I knew you were good, Daisy, but I had no idea you were this good. They're extraordinary.'

Pleasure washed over her. She hadn't realized how much his opinion mattered to her until he'd started to study her work. 'Thank you,' she said. 'I couldn't have done it without you, or at least it would have taken me a lot longer. Your garden really brought everything to life.'

'I'm sure you could,' he replied. 'You're clearly a brilliant artist. But I'd be lying if I wasn't utterly thrilled that the castle gardens helped, especially since your grandmother worked there.'

So he hadn't missed her oblique reference about the roses, Daisy thought, and the observation pleased her almost as much as his praise. 'I hope the publisher is happy. My agent told me to make the illustrations sing with joy and I've tried my best to make that happen.'

'They do,' Kit said, without hesitation. 'I'm going to order some copies for the castle shop. And it goes without saying that I want a signed copy for the library, plus one for my nephew when he's born.'

'Of course,' Daisy said, slightly bowled over by his enthusiasm. 'Thank you.'

Kit's gaze came to rest on her and she saw sincerity in his eyes. 'No, thank you, Daisy. I hoped you'd immortalize a little bit of the garden in your work but you've done so much more than that and I really can't tell you how much it means. Thank you.'

And now Daisy felt the abrupt swell of unexpected tears against her eyelids. She blinked rapidly before they could spill over and embarrass her. It was strange to think she had disliked Kit for such a long time. Now she was starting to wonder how much she was going to miss him when she left. 'It's my pleasure,' she said, once she was sure her voice wasn't going to crack. 'Never mind apples, I think your garden stole a little bit of my heart.'

'You're not the first person to feel that way,' Kit said, his eyes not leaving hers. 'But at least I can promise it will always be looked after.'

And for a moment, Daisy wasn't sure whether he meant the garden or the piece of her heart she would be leaving behind.

★ ★ ★

By the time Saturday night came around, Daisy was on the verge of backing out of her date with Drew. It wasn't that her attraction to him had diminished – far from it – but the knowledge that there was only six weeks until she had to leave was beginning to weigh heavily on her mind. Nancy had been typically forthright when Daisy had mentioned cancelling. 'So what if you're leaving at the end of August? That's still six weeks of fun – six weeks of steaminess. People have been married for less and had no regrets – take Kim Kardashian, for example.'

Daisy had smiled in spite of herself. 'I'm pretty sure that was only for TV ratings.'

'And you're not even getting married,' Nancy had gone on. 'You're going on a date with someone you already know and like. And if for some reason you're not having a good time, you can make your excuses and leave.'

She had eventually managed to convince Daisy not to cancel but she was still a mass of butterflies as she got ready. The pub Drew had booked was ten miles away and he'd offered to pick her up but she'd declined, wanting to have her own car handy. If Drew thought there was anything strange in that, he didn't say so. He'd simply given her the name of the pub and arranged to meet her there at seven-thirty.

He had chosen well. The Good Hope was a small, thatched pub in a typical Kent village. The table Drew had booked was outside, beneath a fairy-lit marquee, and there was a pleasing hum of conversation from the other diners as Daisy made her way across the grass to where Drew waited. He stood to greet her, planting a barely-there kiss on her cheek that sent sparks racing along her nerve-endings. 'You look amazing,' he said, taking in her peacock blue dress. 'Really beautiful.'

'Thanks,' she said, a little breathily because she had never been any good at returning compliments. 'I like your shirt.'

He'd gone for white with a slender green fern pattern that suited him perfectly and offset his natural tan. The scent he wore was woodsy, with a hint of tar and leather that shouldn't have worked but somehow did. In fact, Daisy spent a little too long breathing it in and had to remind herself to step away from him. 'You found it okay?' he asked once they were both sitting down.

'The sat nav did,' she replied. 'I can't tell you how often I got lost before they were invented.'

'I sometimes miss the days before sat navs and Google maps. There's something quite freeing about not quite knowing where you're going, or where you might end up.' He smiled. 'I think we can be so intent on getting to where we're going that we miss out on adventures along the way. Sometimes the journey is what matters.'

His brown eyes held hers and she got the distinct impression he wasn't just talking about driving. It wasn't the first time he'd sensed how she was feeling without her having to explain and she found his intuition only increased his appeal. Nancy had once told her that he had a reputation for enjoying the thrill of the chase so perhaps it wasn't a surprise that he was so good at the forward and back dance that had led them to this point. And as Nancy had observed, the fact that Drew wasn't truly looking for a relationship made Daisy's life easier. They both wanted the same thing, without any of the ensuing complications, and as long as they were both on the same page, there was nothing wrong with that. 'Journeys are enjoyable,' she said. 'Especially when there's no rush to reach the end.'

A flash of something passed between them and Daisy knew they'd crossed a threshold. The last time Drew had kissed her, she had told him the next time she didn't want him to stop. And since there was a very strong possibility he would kiss her again tonight, she had to wonder what would follow. Part of her was shocked she was even considering such wanton behaviour, but another, the part being encouraged and cheered on by Nancy, was thrilled. It had been a long time since she'd last been intimate with Stuart – that side of their relationship had petered out long before they'd finally agreed to split up – and she had to admit she longed for the sense of connection it brought. But she was getting ahead of herself – there was a whole evening with Drew to enjoy first. Assuming she hadn't forgotten how to flirt, that was.

Without pausing to overthink things, Daisy reached across the table and took Drew's hand. 'I'm glad we're doing this,' she said, lightly traced a swirl on the back of his hand. Much to her satisfaction, she saw his eyes widen a fraction as he swallowed.

'Me too,' he said. 'I've never met anyone quite like you, Daisy.'

Gently flipping her hand, he ran his fingers along the inside of her forehand. A burst of desire lit the already smouldering fire in the pit of her stomach and she had to fight the urge to pull her hand away. Things were moving too fast – at this rate, they wouldn't make it past their starters. Deliberately leaving her hand in his, she picked up the menu. 'What looks good?' she asked, then smiled cheekily across at him. 'And don't say me.'

He laughed and some of the tension between them eased. He let go of her hand and lifted his own menu. 'I can never resist a cheese board but perhaps we can share one later,' he said, a slight frown creasing his forehead. 'So perhaps the mushroom crostini to start and the veggie burger for main.'

Daisy looked up. 'You're vegetarian?'

He nodded. 'I've found it suits me and of course it's better for the planet. But your choices are your own – order whatever you like.'

She had several friends who had made the same leap but Daisy hadn't chosen to do so herself. She admired anyone with the strength of character to give up bacon, however. 'It's looking like the Scotch egg for me,' she said, after a few more minutes' consideration. 'And the tuna niçoise to follow.'

'Perfect timing,' he said, as the waiter approached. They place their orders, with Daisy plumping for a non-alcoholic gin and tonic and Drew deciding on a large glass of red wine. 'I'm not totally clean living,' he said wryly.

'I didn't imagine you were,' she replied, grinning. 'Not when you brew beer for a living.'

He held up a hand. 'Only part time, remember. I'm also a mistletoe farmer and occasional grumpy child wrangler.'

'How could I forget?' Daisy said lightly. 'Did I ever thank you for that, by the way? Finn said it was the best walk ever.'

Drew laughed. 'Did he? I bet it was the graffiti that made it, not me.'

She couldn't totally deny it – Finn had found the drawings hysterical and she'd eventually had to tell him to stop going on about it. But Drew didn't need to know that. 'Well, thank you anyway.'

Once again, his eyes met hers. 'Just being here is thank you enough.'

The conversation moved on as they waited for their starters. Daisy learned that Drew's father had died some years ago and his mother had moved to the Isle of Sheppey. He'd been tempted to follow her but the thought of leaving Mistlethorpe hadn't appealed. 'It's the kind of place that's hard to let go,' he said. 'There's a sort of timelessness about it, even though plenty has changed over the years. It's like those ancient oak trees you read about, the ones that have survived storms and war and outlived empires. Their roots go deep and Mistlethorpe feels a lot like that too. I'm not sure I'll ever leave.'

The sentiment echoed what Daisy had felt the first time she'd driven into the village after decades away. Things were different but the sense of changelessness was the same. It was a world away from modern Milton Keynes but she knew it was something else she was going miss when September came. They continued chatting as their starters came and were consumed. Drew had fond memories of Daisy's grandparents, although he hadn't known them well. He had no good words to say about Rose's husband, Vince. 'I don't think anyone liked him much,' he told Daisy bluntly. 'No one cried when he died, put it that way.'

Daisy nodded but chose not to get drawn down that road. She wanted to remember this evening for all the right reasons and her stepfather had no power over her any longer. Instead, she steered the conversation back towards Drew, asking him if he'd always had green fingers. He made her laugh with sly stories of the outrageous things his gardening clients had demanded over the years. Before she knew it, their main courses had arrived. Her tuna was perfectly cooked, the eggs soft and yellow, the salad beneath warm yet crisp. The sun was setting, painting the sky pink and gold, and Daisy was enjoying herself immensely. The knowledge of what might happen later thrummed beneath her skin, making her tingle with anticipation yet she managed to avoid thinking ahead and stayed in the moment with Drew. They agreed to share a cheese board; Daisy especially liked an oozy soft cheese from Canterbury that she thought Kit would also appreciate. But at last the cheese was finished and she realized the tables around them had emptied. Drew smiled at her expression of surprise. 'I hardly noticed them going either. Would you like a coffee or shall we get the bill?'

Daisy shivered as the cool night air made its presence felt, glad of the jacket she'd brought with her. 'Let's get the bill.'

Drew nodded and caught the eye of their waiter, who came hurrying over. 'I'd better order a taxi. It might take a little while to arrive – there's no Uber round here. We could have another drink in the bar, if you like?'

Daisy waited until the waiter had gone to get the card reader before answering. 'Or I could drive you home. I have to go through the village anyway, it seems silly for you to get a taxi.'

Her tone was casual but her heart thudded in her chest. It made sense for her to give Drew a lift home but there was no doubt it also opened the door to other possibilities. And she might have been contemplating those possibilities from the start of the evening but that didn't mean Drew had. 'Are you sure?' he asked, his gaze questioning.

'Of course,' she said. 'Like I said, it would be silly not to.'

Her senses were heightened as she navigated the dark country lanes. She was hyper aware of Drew in the passenger seat beside her, conscious of his leg so near hers. They spoke little, let music from the radio take the place of conversation, and she wondered whether he felt anything like she did. What would happen when she pulled up outside his cottage, she wondered. Would he kiss her in the car or invite her inside first? And then she had to force both possibilities out of her mind to focus on the road. It wasn't unheard of for a deer to dash out from the trees and she needed to have her wits about her.

It seemed an age and only a few minutes when the sign for Mistlethorpe flashed up. Drew spoke over the music to give her directions. 'Next right,' he said once they reached the High Street. 'And then the second left. Take it slow, it's not much more than a dirt track. There's space to turn around at the end, though.'

A few moments later, the headlights picked out a neat cottage at the end of the lane, Drew's car parked outside. Daisy rolled to a stop and applied the handbrake. Now that the moment was finally here, she felt ridiculously nervous. Surely Drew must be able to hear her heart beating, too loud and way too fast?

'Thank you for bringing me home,' Drew said. 'And for a lovely evening.'

She turned to look at him in the glow of the single streetlamp but his expression gave nothing away. 'You're welcome,' she replied, hoping her voice didn't sound as wobbly as it felt. 'I had a nice time too.'

Drew paused, then reached out to brush her cheek. 'I'd really like to kiss you, Daisy. Is that what you want?'

It was all she could do not to close her eyes at his touch. She bit her bottom lip, more to stay with him than anything, and nodded. 'Yes. I'd like that too.'

For a moment, he didn't move. Then he raised both hands to cup her face and drew her slowly to him. When his lips grazed hers, she thought she might pass out from anticipation but his hands held her, his thumbs caressing her cheeks bones as he pressed his mouth to hers. She heard a soft moan that might have come from either of them, then her lips parted and the kiss deepened. One hand abandoned her face and tangled in her hair; her own hands came to rest on his chest. Before she knew it, they were sliding lower, curving around his back, pulling him closer. She longed to press her body to his but the handbrake was in the way so she settled for sliding her fingers beneath the cotton of his shirt to stroke the skin of his hips. He let out a groan and tightened the embrace, giving up her lips to graze against her neck. Daisy gasped, tipping her head back to give him room, and then gasped again as his head dipped lower to drop a series of feathery kisses along her collar bone. She sank her fingers into his hair, forgetting where they were and never wanting him to stop. But just as she thought he might continue to trail kisses all the way down to the neckline of her dress, Drew took in a ragged breath and lifted his head to stare at her. 'Daisy, I—'

She placed a gentle finger on his mouth. 'Don't say it,' she murmured. 'Just invite me in.'

His eyes widened as he leant forward to kiss her again, hard and urgent. 'You're sure?' he said, when they broke apart. She nodded, reaching for the ignition switch to turn the engine off.

'I've never been more certain of anything,' she said.

Chapter Twenty-One

Daisy woke the following morning in an unfamiliar bed. It took her a moment to process where she was, and then another moment to calm the tsunami of embarrassment and disbelief that washed over her as she remembered the night before. Craning her head, she twisted to see Drew asleep beside her, his hair tousled, and then winced as her muscles protested the unaccustomed workout she'd given them. There hadn't been much sleep, either. A quick glance at her watch told her it was just after seven o'clock. If she'd been at home she might have tried to get back to sleep but that was out of the question now – she felt wide awake. She peered at Drew again – his breathing was deep and even and he appeared to be out for the count, so she took a moment to admire his profile. He had a good nose, perhaps a little too pointed but nobody was perfect and she had plenty of imperfections of her own. Up close, she could see faint white lines amid the tan of his face, suggesting he spent a good deal of his time outside smiling — she liked that. Whether it was a face she wanted to get used to seeing in the morning was another matter but that was a question for another day, she decided as she stifled a yawn. What she really wanted now was a cup of tea. She hadn't been drinking so there was no hangover to contend with but her last glass of water had been hours ago. But it had been so long since she'd woken up in a man's bed that she had forgotten the etiquette. Was it acceptable to get herself a cup of tea in someone else's house? Or was it better manners to wait for Drew to wake up and make her one? Now she came to think of it, the last time she'd found herself in the situation, she'd been more likely to glug down a Diet Coke or a Red Bull than a nice cup of tea. Come to think of it, she would probably have snuck out while her partner for the night was still asleep. That wasn't an option now, however. Lying back, Daisy closed her eyes. It felt too intrusive to go wandering around Drew's cottage. She would just have to wait for him to wake up.

The next time she opened her eyes, Drew was standing beside the bed, clad in shorts and a faded Fleetwood Mac t-shirt with a cup in one hand. 'Morning. You looked so peaceful that I thought about letting you sleep but it occurred to me you'd probably want to get home.'

Daisy's eyes widened. 'What time is it?'

'Just after nine,' he said.

She sat up hurriedly, realized she had no clothes on and dragged the bedsheet over herself. 'I do need to get back. The last thing I want is to come face to face with my mother while I do the walk of shame.'

Drew's mouth quirked. 'Sorry,' he said, clearly trying not to laugh. 'That's really not funny.'

Scrambling to the edge of the bed, Daisy looked around for her clothes. If she wasn't careful, she'd run into Nancy too and while that wasn't quite as horrifying a prospect as her mother, it was still something she'd rather avoid. 'I need to get going.'

'At least drink your tea first,' he said mildly. 'A few more minutes won't make much difference, will they?'

Taking a deep breath, Daisy forced herself to think rationally. She was a grown woman – she could arrive home at whatever time she liked and there was nothing her mother or anyone else could say about it. But it would be nice if the whole village didn't see her driving home from Drew's cottage. It would be nicer still to keep the knowledge of their first night together between themselves for a while. 'Sorry,' she said, and ran a hand through her tangled hair. She took the cup of tea. 'It's just – sorry.'

He sat beside her on the bed and leaned across to plant a kiss on her forehead. 'I get it. Look, why don't I leave you alone to get dressed. Or would you like a shower? It might make you feel less –' he broke off to search for the right word and shrugged. 'Shameful?'

That made her laugh. 'I'd love a quick shower, if that's okay.' She touched her face, felt the crustiness of old mascara, and prayed she didn't have a telltale rash on her chin. 'I don't suppose you've got any micellar water, have you?'

Drew looked confused. 'I don't even know what that is. I've got tap water, if that helps?'

Daisy smiled. 'It'll have to do.' She took a long swig of tea, glad of the heat against her parched throat. 'Now, point me in the direction of the bathroom. Maybe if I reach the farm in fifteen minutes, I might be okay.'

Getting to his feet, Drew opened a nearby drawer and pulled out a towel. 'This way,' he said. 'I reckon you might just about make it if you hurry.'

Seven minutes later, Daisy was dry and dressed and standing on the doorstep of the cottage. She reached up to give Drew an apologetic kiss. 'Sorry to run out on you like this.'

'I'll let you off,' he said, smiling, and ran a hand over his now stubbly chin. 'Thanks for last night. It was amazing, every bit as mind-blowing as I hoped it would be. I hope we can do it again soon.'

Daisy nodded. 'It was good, wasn't it?' She kissed him again. 'And we should definitely do it again but right now I have to go. Sorry!'

There was no sign of Nancy when Daisy crawled around the yard past the Oast House café. Breathing a sigh of relief, she rolled the car slowly across the gravel to park outside the farmhouse and tiptoed inside, shoes in one hand and handbag in the other. Taking care not to disturb the silence, she made her way down the hallway, past the closed kitchen door and reached the stairs without mishap. The fourth stair was treacherous – she avoided that and had just stepped onto the landing when she heard the creak of a door. A querulous voice called out. 'Who's there?'

Daisy stopped. 'Just me, Mum. Nothing to worry about.'

There was a pause. 'Oh, you've decided to come home, have you? We thought you might be dead in a ditch somewhere.'

It was such a Rose thing to say that Daisy had to bite her lip to prevent herself laughing. 'I'm fine. Definitely not dead but I would like to get changed and have some breakfast.'

There was a loud snort from along the landing, followed by the sound of the door closing again. Breathing out, Daisy continued onto her room. No doubt she'd face some sort of inquisition later, both from her mother and from Nancy, but they could both wait until after she'd eaten.

★ ★ ★

It was gone five o'clock on Sunday evening by the time Daisy negotiated the traffic on the M25 and made her way to Milton Keynes to collect Campbell and Finn. Typically, they were not ready and had to fly into a frenzy of gathering their things to take back to Kent. Stuart offered her a cup of tea and she followed him into the kitchen while he made it.

'Good weekend?' she asked, while the kettle boiled. 'What did you get up to?'

He shrugged. 'The usual stuff. We went round to Mike's house, they played football in the garden for an hour or so while we watched the cricket.' He frowned. 'Well, Finn did. Campbell read his book – did you know he's reading something about a serial killer on the loose in London?'

Daisy blinked. 'No. Where did he get that from?'

'The school library, he says,' Stuart replied. 'Maybe keep a closer eye on what he brings home in future.'

His tone was even but Daisy was still in no doubt that he held her responsible for the unsuitable book, not the school. And he might have had a point but Daisy still didn't appreciate being told off. 'I usually do.'

He grunted. 'Maybe you've been distracted.'

'I have,' Daisy said, stung. 'With work. I've got that big commission to finish, it's been taking up a lot of my time.'

Stuart stirred milk into the cups and handed one to her. 'So the boys have said.' He paused and leaned against the worktop. 'Who's this Drew I've been hearing about?'

It was the last thing she'd expected him to say. 'What?'

'Drew,' Stuart said slowly, as though she was a child. 'Who is he?'

Daisy took a slow calming breath. Of all the things to ask her, on all the days . . . But he couldn't know what she'd done the night before. He couldn't. Forcing herself to stay calm she tried to sound casual. 'Someone who lives in the village. He works at one of the units in the farmyard. Why?'

Stuart regarded her steadily. 'The boys mentioned him. Finn says he took the three of you on a walk to see some dodgy wall art.'

Daisy wanted to roll her eyes but instead she folded her

arms and snorted. 'We went to look at an old World War Two building that had some graffiti,' she said. 'I don't think Drew even knew it was there before Finn pointed it out.'

That met with a disapproving silence. 'Campbell says you're very friendly with him,' Stuart went on after a moment had passed. 'He says he saw you cuddling.'

Daisy's mouth dropped open. 'He did not!'

Stuart raised his hands. 'I'm only telling you what Campbell told me, Daisy. And of course it's none of my business who you see and what you do but I thought you had more sense than to parade a new boyfriend in front of the boys, especially without giving me a heads up first.'

She wasn't sure what annoyed her the most – his reasonable, let's-be-grown-ups tone, or the sheer audacity of the accusations. She hadn't paraded Drew in front of the twins, any more than she'd had any physical contact with him where they might see. She had no idea what Campbell thought he'd seen but it definitely hadn't been cuddling. 'I – he –' Daisy broke off and took another deep breath. 'There's nothing to tell. He's not my boyfriend.'

The ice in her voice clearly rattled Stuart. 'There's no need to get defensive. Like I said, it's not my business. Just be a bit careful, that's all. We've worked hard to shield the boys from the effects of the divorce, it would be a shame to upset them now when you're only going to be in Kent for a few more weeks.'

She opened and closed her mouth a couple of times but didn't trust herself to speak. Instead, she placed the cup Stuart had given her on the side and gathered up her handbag. 'We'd better get going. Traffic looked awful over the bridge.'

He sighed. 'You're angry.'

And just like that, Daisy's anger drained away. She ran a weary hand over her face. 'I'm tired. You've made your point, now I just want to go home. Is that okay with you?'

It wasn't until she and the boys were across the Dartford Bridge and racing towards Mistlethorpe that Daisy realized she'd referred to Half Moon Farm as home. The argument with Stuart had run round and round in her head until she'd had to turn the radio up loud to drown it out. It wasn't until they finally pulled into the farmyard, with her grandmother's yellow and pink roses climbing around the door, that she felt the tension of the day drain out of her. Somewhere along the line, she'd begun to think of this place as her home. At some point, it had again become the place she felt safest, just as it had been when she was a child. So perhaps it was no surprise that right then, after all that had happened that day, there was nowhere else she'd rather be.

★ ★ ★

The after-effects of Daisy's run-in with Stuart were still hanging over her on Monday morning after a mixed night's sleep that featured a series of disjointed and unsettling dreams. Finn and Campbell were subdued too, perhaps sensing her mood; neither said much during the school run and went into school without the usual too-loud greeting of their classmates. She watched them go, wondering whether they had also begun to feel the weight of moving back to Milton Keynes, and then decided she was projecting her own feelings onto them. Both boys would be glad to get back to their friends and familiar routines, and nearer to their father. It was only Daisy who'd started to put down roots in Mistlethorpe – roots she was going to have to pull up soon enough. But not today, she reminded herself as she started back to the car. Today she planned to treat herself to a morning in the gardens at Winterbourne and this time she was going to get her hands dirty.

She hadn't paid much attention to the other parents when she been dropping Campbell and Finn off in the playground. Sometimes she would catch the eye of another mum and stop for a brief chat, or at the very least they would exchange smiles. She was even on first name terms with a couple, mostly other football parents. But she'd kept her head down today, keen to get away as soon as possible, and it was only when she began the walk back to the car that she noticed several small clusters of women watching her. It wasn't quite as blatant as whispering behind their hands but Daisy got the uneasy impression that there was a new hot topic on the playground network that morning, and it seemed to involve her. Her scalp prickled and it didn't matter how many times she told herself she was being paranoid, by the time she got to her car she was convinced something was up.

Determined to shrug the feeling off, she was about to set off back to the farm when she saw Kit striding towards her car and looking for all the world as though he had something to say. Her misgivings deepened but Daisy did her best to ignore the foreboding. She waited until he reached her, then opened her window. 'Hello. Fancy seeing you here.'

He didn't smile . . . Instead, he waited stiffly beside the car, as though waiting for her to join him. 'Okay,' Daisy muttered under her breath. 'I'll get out then, shall I?'

When at last she stood beside him, his eyes finally met hers and she saw they were troubled. 'What's wrong?' she asked warily. 'Has something bad happened? It's not Alice, is it?' Another, worse possibility occurred to her. 'Oh god, it's not Cressida, is it?'

His expression changed. 'What? No, it's not Alice, or Cressida – she's fine as far as I know. Besides, who says anything is wrong?'

'I do,' Daisy replied, running out of patience. 'You've got a face like someone just reversed into your Audi. They haven't, have they?'

That raised another flicker but it still wasn't anything resembling a smile. 'No one has hit my car since you.'

'Then what?' Daisy asked again, her bewilderment growing. 'What's going on?'

Kit was silent for a moment longer, as though having some kind of internal debate, then sighed. 'I like to think we've become friends over the past few months. Is that your feeling too?'

Daisy stared at him. First the weird atmosphere in the

playground and now this – what on earth was going on? 'Erm . . . yes? Taking the car thing out of the equation, obviously.'

'Obviously,' he replied flatly. 'What I mean is, we've had some fairly close conversations. Chats I perhaps wouldn't have with many other people.'

She thought back to their exchange in the garden of Half Moon Farm, when she'd admitted to her less than perfect childhood, or their conversation about his family in the walled garden. Both had opened up in a way that might have seemed impossible just a few months earlier but she had no idea why he was raising the matter now. 'I agree,' she said cautiously. 'I think we're friends.'

He nodded, his expression still stiff. 'And would you say that friends warn each other when they judge the other is making a mistake?'

Mystified, Daisy quirked her lips. 'Sure.'

Kit cleared his throat and Daisy realized she'd never seen him so uncomfortable, not even when admitting to some borderline abusive family behaviour. What could he be about to say that made him this ill at ease? 'Rumour has it that you're involved with Drew Entwhistle. Romantically involved, I mean. Is that true?'

And suddenly, Daisy understood everything – the reason for the sideways looks in the playground, the sense that she was the topic of conversation. Someone had seen her with Drew, either arriving or leaving his cottage. Or perhaps they'd been spotted at the pub, even though she hadn't seen anyone else she knew. 'I wouldn't say involved, exactly. We went out for dinner on Saturday.'

He raised an eyebrow, which gave her the hot and cold feeling he knew she and Drew had done much more than that. Daisy stared at him, feeling her flush of mortification slide into irritation. On top of the argument with Stuart, this was all she needed. 'But I'm not sure what business that is of yours, or anyone else, for that matter.'

Kit sighed again. 'I suppose you could say I see a friend making a mistake.'

Another piece of the puzzle dropped into place. Hadn't Drew told her he and Kit didn't see eye to eye? 'Not you as well,' she exclaimed, heat dousing her cheeks. 'Have you been speaking to my ex-husband?'

'No.' His gaze swept abruptly away from her. 'But if he's warning you off Drew then I think you should listen to both of us. I won't go into details but suffice to say he's not a great person and – well, I don't want to see you get hurt.'

Daisy blinked at him, gaping a little. 'We're two consenting adults, Kit. No one is going to get hurt.'

Kit's blue eyes were suddenly fixed on her again and she saw the first flames of anger there. 'You don't know him,' he insisted. 'Listen to me, Daisy. He's not the person you think he is.'

'But how do you know who I think he is?' she said, her voice growing louder with anger and frustration. 'And why is it any of your business?'

He opened his mouth as though about to answer, then

snapped it shut. 'You're right,' he said, 'it isn't any of my business. I'm sorry to have bothered you, forget I spoke.'

Turning away, he took several steps before seeming to remember something. He reached into his coat pocket and withdrew a small bundle, which he thrust towards Daisy. 'I meant to give you these.'

Wrong-footed yet again by another bewildering twist, Daisy stared at the brown paper bundle. 'What is it?'

'Letters,' Kit said, his tone clipped. 'The replies from Violet to Valentine during the war. I spoke to Hugh and it seems you were right – he did know more than me.'

Daisy couldn't help it – she gawped at him. 'What?'

'More to the point, he told me where at Winterbourne to find these letters,' Kit went on. 'I thought you might like to read them.'

Scarcely able to believe what she was hearing, her fingers shaking a little, Daisy took the bundle. 'I – I would. Thank you.'

Kit's gaze didn't meet hers. 'I hope I can rely on your discretion, Daisy. It might have all happened seventy-odd years ago but I wouldn't want any of this to become public. Do I make myself clear?'

'Crystal,' Daisy managed, still reeling at the existence of her grandmother's replies to Valentine's impassioned declarations of love. 'Thank you.'

'Don't thank me yet,' he said, finally producing a smile, although she saw it didn't reach his eyes. 'Wait until you've read them. You might not be so grateful then.'

A moment later he was gone. Daisy stared after him, then transferred her bewildered gaze to the bundle in her hand. Everything else that had happened that morning had been wiped away and all she could think of was the letters and the answers they contained. With shaking hands, she placed them on the passenger seat of the car then started the engine and set off back to Half Moon Farm. Her plans for the day had changed in the blink of an eye. She had some secrets to uncover and she didn't intend to let anything get in her way.

Part Four

Winter Magic

Chapter Twenty-Two

It felt very much like Groundhog Day when Daisy arrived at the school gates to collect Finn and Campbell on Monday afternoon. She kept her head down, hurrying to her usual spot in the playground, determined not to make eye contact with anyone and most especially not with Kit Devereaux. The sea of umbrellas helped, grouped together in multi-coloured clusters to ward off the rain showers as their owners chatted underneath, paying less attention than usual to the comings and goings around them. But rainy weather notwithstanding, it was all too reminiscent of Daisy's first few school runs after moving to Mistlethorpe and she wouldn't be surprised if a deadpan Bill Murray popped up in the crowd. Back then, it had been a careless accident involving Kit's car that made her long for an invisibility cloak – now the mixture of embarrassment and resentment crawling down her spine were the result of entirely different actions. She'd had no evidence that her relationship with Drew Entwistle had become the subject of playground gossip, other than a fleeting impression of sideways looks and poorly disguised whispers, until Kit had declared his disapproval of her spending the night with Drew. And she knew it shouldn't bother her, especially since he'd agreed it was none of his business, but hot on the heels of a lecture from her ex-husband about shielding their sons from her romantic encounters, it had sparked an indignation that had smouldered all day. Right now, she didn't care if she never spoke to Kit again.

Except that wasn't quite true, a nagging voice reminded her. Because just after he'd tried to warn her off Drew, Kit had given Daisy a bundle of wartime letters written by her grandmother to his grandfather. It had been a gift that took the wind from her sails, leaving her to stare open-mouthed as he stalked away, and flipped her perfectly justified umbrage on its head. By the time she had reached Half Moon Farm, surprise had morphed into a grudging gratitude that tempered her irritation. He'd given her something she hadn't dared to dream might still exist – the missing half of the love story between their grandparents. And she hadn't been able to resist diving straight in.

11 Thanet Lane
Mistlethorpe
Kent

8th March

Dear V

Thank you for your letter which came this morning. You say such lovely things, it fair made me blush. You would not be impressed if you had seen me when I got home today, all dusty from work! Mr Athers is making us replant the west side of the walled garden, which will be nice when it is done but looks a terrible sight at the moment. Our tree is as sturdy as ever, though — tiny green buds are appearing on the bare branches. I smile every time I see it, remembering you.

Life in the village goes on much the same, although I expect it sounds ever so boring to you. Mr Barker and his bicycle got waylaid by a squirrel on his way home from church on Sunday and he ended up going over the handle-bars into the pond on the green, which made everyone hoot with laughter except for Mr Barker, who was quite cross even though the duck house broke his fall. I daresay he will get over it but I would lay low if I was that squirrel.

I hope you are keeping well. They say on the wireless that the war will be over soon but the longer it goes on, the more worried I get. Mrs Porter at the baker's got the awful telegram last week and it broke my heart to see her sob. I know we must be brave and do our bit to win the war but I wish ever so much that you were home, Val. I am sending you all my love until then.

Write as soon as you get this.

Your Violet

A sudden cacophony of noise, caused by several classroom doors opening at the same time, snapped Daisy back to the playground. Children streamed out, chattering and laughing, exclaiming at the rain. She kept her head down as she scanned the crowd for the twins – in typical fashion, they were among the last to appear. She expected them to be glued to Alice, Kit's daughter, but she was nowhere to be seen. That was unusual and caused Daisy to risk a more detailed look at the assembled parents, who were flowing towards the gates like the outgoing tide. She could not make out Kit's tall figure among them, even hidden beneath an umbrella – he was not waiting for Alice nor walking with her out of the school grounds. In fact, there was no sign of either.

The mystery was solved as soon as Finn and Campbell reached her. 'Alice vommed all over the carpet,' Finn told her with gruesome relish before she could even ask. 'She had to go home.'

'Oh!' Daisy said with a sudden rush of sympathy. 'I hope she's okay.'

'Probably the norovirus,' Campbell said, with the air of a middle-aged GP. 'Plenty of fluids and rest, she'll be fine in a day or so.'

'Could be the Black Death,' Finn argued. 'We learned about that in history. If she's got boils and pustules then it's definitely the plague.'

'Nah.' Campbell's tone was dismissive. 'You have to try really hard to get the plague nowadays. My money is on some sort of bug, although she did go a funny green colour.'

Finn's eyes widened. 'Ebola. Hundred per cent.'

Daisy looked sternly from one son to the other. 'Can I remind you this is your friend we're talking about? She doesn't have the plague or Ebola, thank goodness, and a bit more sympathy wouldn't go amiss. She probably feels rubbish, poor girl.'

To their credit, both boys appeared slightly shamefaced. 'I didn't say she had either of those things,' Campbell pointed out. 'It was Finn.'

'That's true,' Daisy agreed, herding them towards the gates. 'But you weren't exactly kindness personified. Try putting yourself in her shoes.'

Campbell wrinkled his nose. 'No, thanks. They've got sick in them.'

But it turned out they didn't have to try very hard to empathize; with grim inevitability, both fell victim to the same symptoms just before bedtime. Dabbing their fevered foreheads with cool, damp facecloths long into the night, Daisy could only hope it was a short-lived bug and that she didn't succumb herself. Even if she was lucky enough to avoid becoming ill, it meant an enforced quarantine from Rose and her carers for several days. Her mother was almost fully recovered from her heart surgery a few months earlier but the last thing Daisy wanted was to risk passing anything on. Thankfully, by the early hours of the morning Finn and Campbell's pallor had eased and they slept soundly, the clammy sheen on their skin gone. Daisy brought pillows and the duvet from her room and slept on the floor between their beds.

Their fever was gone the next morning, although both were still noticeably quieter than normal and had no interest in eating. The school secretary told Daisy that a number of children in their class had gone down with similar symptoms. 'Don't bring them back to school until forty-eight hours after the last bout of sickness,' she reminded Daisy. 'I hope they feel better soon.'

They spent the morning playing Uno, sardined in Campbell's bed with Daisy perched on a chair beside them. Around eleven o'clock she managed to tempt them with some toast. While she was in the kitchen, she put aside her prickliness of the previous day and messaged Kit.

I hear Alice has the bug. Hope she's over the worst of it.

It took a few minutes for a reply to pop up on her phone. *Seems to be, thank goodness. Have the twins gone down with it too?*

Yes, along with half the class, she tapped. *Fingers crossed it's just a twenty-four-hour thing.*

His reply didn't arrive until she was back upstairs and coaxing Finn to nibble at the dry toast. *Wishing them a speedy recovery. I'll let Athers know you won't be visiting the gardens for a few days.*

The boys dozed for most of the afternoon. Once Daisy was sure their toast wasn't going to make a reappearance, she retrieved the bundle of letters and settled down at their bedside to read. When she'd first discovered Valentine's letters to Violet, in a cluttered, neglected room at the farmhouse, she'd had no idea who her grandmother's mystery lover had been. It was only when she visited the walled garden at Winterbourne Castle, and Kit revealed two initials carved into a tree, that Daisy had understood why Violet hadn't married the man who had promised nothing would keep them apart. Valentine Devereaux was destined to become the Earl of Winterbourne – marrying a gardener's assistant was utterly out of the question. Even so, Daisy couldn't hold his naivety against him, in the same way she didn't blame her grandmother for being swept along. They were young, their lives overshadowed by war; who could judge them for believing love could conquer all? And they had loved each other, Daisy had never doubted that. But there was no happy ending to come and, as she read, Kit's ominous warning as he'd handed over Violet's replies still rang in Daisy's ears. *Don't thank me yet . . .*

By the time Finn and Campbell awoke, both looking significantly healthier and demanding food, Daisy had arranged both sets of letters in date order. Often, there were several from Violet to only one reply from Valentine but that wasn't a surprise, given the difficulties of operating a postal service in wartime. She'd gone back to the start, scarcely able to believe her luck in having the two sides of the story within her grasp, and it had been a real wrench to drag herself from the past and into the present when her sons needed her.

Being in solitary confinement also meant Daisy hadn't seen Drew since she'd left him on his doorstep on Sunday morning. They'd exchanged messages around lunchtime – him jokingly checking she'd survived the walk of shame and

Daisy thanking him for a very enjoyable evening – but their paths hadn't physically crossed and for that Daisy was slightly relieved. It wasn't that she regretted spending the night with him, more that she wasn't sure what came next. Would there be another date and another night together? What would happen after that? She had no idea. It had been a long time since she'd done anything like this – in fact, she wasn't sure she'd ever been in a situation quite so fraught with complication. Stuart's admonishment about conducting her romantic attachments out of sight of the twins still felt fresh and there was the undeniable fact that she would be leaving Mistlethorpe in less than six weeks' time. On one hand, that made things simpler for both Daisy and Drew – there was no question of forming a relationship – but it also made her feel oddly unsettled, as though the ground had turned to quicksand under her feet. She couldn't help wondering whether she'd made a mistake.

Nancy's response to this suggestion was brisk. *That's THE FEAR. Ignore it.*

Which was easy for her to say, Daisy thought dryly as she stared at her phone. She might have only known Nancy a few months but she was sure her friend had never experienced a moment's self-doubt in her life. Before she could craft a reply, another message popped up. *You had fun – he had fun. Does it need to be any more complicated than that?*

It took Daisy a few minutes of sifting through conflicting emotions to settle on an answer. *I suppose not*, she typed eventually.

Try not to overthink it. See how you feel once the boys are better.

Daisy had to concede that was also good advice – she didn't have to make any decisions now. Perhaps all she needed was time and space to settle into this new incarnation of herself, a woman ready to take a chance on romance again. As Nancy had once observed, Drew might not be Mr Right, but he could be Mr Right Now. He'd certainly done plenty of things right during their night together, she recalled with a sudden flush of warmth, and then had to fan her cheeks. Nancy had been on the money there too: it had been fun. Maybe that was part of the problem.

By Wednesday, Daisy felt confident that the virus was beaten but it was still another day before Finn and Campbell could return to school. Mindful of keeping them away from her mother, Daisy decided a break from the farm was in order and packed them into the car for a trip to take in some bracing sea air. The golden sands of Broadstairs weren't empty – plenty of families with young children were enjoying the July sunshine – but there was room at Viking Bay for paddling in the sea and even a kickabout with a ball. She'd wondered if the boys would still want to slip off their shoes and socks the way they had when they were smaller but it seemed daring the waves to catch them was as irresistible as ever. Finn fell in, as Daisy had known he would, and was drenched from head to toe. He shrugged off his wet clothes beneath the beach towel she held around him and grumbled about the sand sticking to his skin but it wasn't long before he was dry and dressed in the spare shorts and t-shirt she'd brought. Then they'd spent a small fortune playing the penny games in the arcades, and finally made their way up to Morelli's ice cream parlour to watch the tide roll in. Daisy smiled as she watched them plough enthusiastically through sundaes as large as their heads, glad to see the colour back in their cheeks. Their appetites certainly hadn't suffered any after-effects, at least.

She wasn't sure what to expect from Kit on Thursday morning. They hadn't exactly bonded over their children's shared sickness but it had helped to take the sting out of Daisy's irritation. The letters had played their part too, the poignancy reminding her of the folly in holding a grudge. She replayed Kit's words in her head several times, noting that he'd offered his warning about Drew from one friend to another. Reluctantly, she had come to the conclusion he'd meant well and it was quite possible she'd overreacted. But had their friendship been damaged? She wasn't sure.

That question was answered almost as soon as she entered the school grounds. Kit was waiting just inside the gate with Alice, clearly determined not to miss Daisy and the twins. 'Good morning. How are you all feeling?'

'Much better, thanks,' Daisy said. 'How about you?'

Kit patted his daughter's shoulder. 'Glad to be back, I think. Alice was worried she'd miss the school disco to-morrow night.'

Daisy nodded. Finn and Campbell had voiced similar concerns. There was still another week until the end of term but she knew they were looking forward to the disco, even though neither would be doing anything as cringeworthy as dancing. It was a chance to let their hair down with their classmates and part of the ritual of saying goodbye, even though they weren't leaving Mistlethorpe until the end of the summer holidays. 'Thankfully, that shouldn't be a problem.'

They stood together, watching as the children headed for the open classroom door. Kit cleared his throat. 'Have you had time to read any of your grandmother's letters?'

'Some,' she replied. 'I'm trying to take my time and really savour them, but at the same time I want to gobble them all up at once. They're making me see my grandmother in a whole new light.'

He dipped his head thoughtfully. 'I can imagine.'

Daisy wondered if he could. From what little he'd said about his family, it didn't sound as though they were close, nor given to grand passions – hadn't he once told her that earls rarely married for love? Then she gave herself a mental shake, because she really had no idea what the Devereaux family dynamics were like; Valentine had definitely known how to express his feelings, at least on paper. 'Thank you for finding them,' she said, and pulled a wry face. 'In case I forgot to mention that on Monday. I can't tell you how much I appreciate the trouble you took.'

'It was no trouble,' Kit said, but Daisy knew he was playing things down. At the very least, he'd had to raise the subject with his brother, Hugh, which would have involved an explanation of why he was asking. And it was quite likely

Hugh would have been ticklish about the spectre of an old family scandal suddenly raising its head – Kit might well have had to convince him Daisy was entitled to the full story. Then he'd had to find the letters, which she presumed were hidden away somewhere at Winterbourne, and give them to her. He had definitely gone to some trouble. 'Well, I'm grateful anyway. Thank you.'

The tide of parents began to flow towards them. By unspoken agreement, they turned and made their way out of the school grounds. A quick glance along the road told Daisy they had parked at opposite ends and Kit seemed to reach the same realization. He straightened his shoulders. 'I owe you an apology.'

She knew instantly what he meant. 'You don't.'

'I do,' he insisted. 'I stuck my nose in something that was none of my business and it upset you. For that, I apologize.'

Daisy was silent, because she had no argument. Her love life was nothing to do with Kit and his unsolicited advice had upset her. 'Yes,' she admitted after a moment, flicking an uneasy look towards her sons to make sure they weren't listening in. 'But I overreacted. It's never fun to discover you're the subject of village gossip.'

'No,' he conceded, and from his rueful tone she guessed he must have had first-hand experience of that when his marriage had broken up. 'Anyway, I'm sorry. It won't happen again.'

The stiffness in his expression reminded her of the first time they'd met but his blue eyes were soft as they sought hers, as though her good opinion of him mattered. 'Apology accepted.'

'Thank you.' He paused. 'Shall I tell Athers to expect you at all this week or will you be catching up with work?'

Daisy considered the question. On one hand, she did need to focus on delivering her final illustrations for *The Secret Garden* anniversary edition – her deadline was fast approaching – but reading her grandmother's account of working in the castle's walled garden only made Daisy want to walk in her footsteps more and she was all too aware that opportunities to do so were slipping away. The end of term was looming and she couldn't imagine Finn or Campbell showing any interest in admiring the roses or hollyhocks. And above that hung the shadow of their eventual return to Milton Keynes. It wasn't impossible that she could come back to Winterbourne on occasion but it wouldn't be a ten-minute drive. Perhaps she should seize the day, allow the glorious flowers to inspire her creativity. If she tried really hard, she might even convince herself it was work. 'Tomorrow, maybe,' she said. 'In the afternoon, if that's okay?'

'You're welcome whenever suits you,' Kit said without hesitation. 'I'll be at the airfield but you know your way around. Just park up and make your way to the garden – Athers will be somewhere near.'

Just the thought of being at Winterbourne gave Daisy a glow of anticipation. 'I'm looking forward to it already,' she said.

Chapter Twenty-Three

'Here, boy,' Daisy crooned, prowling through the long grass of the orchard and rustling a packet of *Fishy Delishy* cat snacks in what she hoped was an inviting manner. 'I've got some lovely treats for you.'

There was an unexpected chuckle. 'Now that's an offer I don't get every day.'

Daisy straightened up, flustered, as she looked around. It sounded like Drew's voice but there was no sign of him. In fact, she'd thought the orchard was empty apart from her and a throng of chirruping crickets. 'Is that you, Drew?'

The leaves of the trees to her left shuddered and a moment later Drew ducked beneath the greenery, a basket of apples in his arms. Sunlight glinted on the silver strands in his hair as he smiled apologetically. 'Sorry, did I startle you?'

His gaze was warm and she felt her alarm drain away, replaced by a familiar tug of attraction. She felt her frown soften into a smile. 'A bit. I'm looking for Atticus – have you seen him?'

Drew nodded. 'About twenty minutes ago, stalking some poor unfortunate across your garden.'

Daisy groaned. 'Exactly what I didn't want to hear. I don't suppose you know if he caught it?'

'I don't think so. He took off suddenly at speed so I assumed he was in hot pursuit.' He eyed Daisy, who was checking her watch. 'Do you need to be somewhere? I can help coax him out of hiding if you're in a hurry.'

She bit her lip. It wasn't that she was worried about leaving Atticus, more that she was keen to avoid him dragging another tiny corpse into the house while she was out. Neither Rose nor her carer, Emily, had proved robust when faced with the cat's previous spoils of war. But time was ticking by and Daisy wanted to get to Winterbourne in plenty of time before the school run. She couldn't spend all afternoon hunting her cat, who might be in the next field by now. 'Thanks, but I need to get going,' she said. 'I'll just have to hope there's no bloodbath when I get home.'

Drew laughed. 'I can keep an eye out, if you like. Find somewhere to bury the bodies.'

He tried to look sinister, which was so out of character that Daisy couldn't help grinning in spite of her concern. 'You're a man of many talents.'

'I try,' he said. 'Although anything bigger than a field mouse and I'm out.'

'Completely understandable,' Daisy replied, laughing. 'Thank you.'

'No problem,' Drew said, tipping his head. 'And I know you're in a hurry but it's good to see you. Maybe we can grab a coffee or a stroll in the woods soon.'

For a moment, she hesitated, recalling the misgivings that had assailed her while she was nursing the twins through their illness. But now that she was face to face with Drew, none of those doubts had any substance and she found herself wanting to spend time with him again. 'I'd like that,' she said. 'Maybe next week?'

A flash of disappointment clouded his eyes. 'You're not free this weekend?'

'I have Finn and Campbell,' she explained. 'They usually spend every other weekend with Stuart but they're going for two weeks once school breaks up next Friday. I'll have a bit more time then.'

'Of course,' he said. 'Sorry, I should have realized. How about a picnic lunch? There's a shady meadow not too far from the farm, we could take a blanket and make the most of the warm weather.'

It sounded idyllic but Daisy was all too aware of how fast things escalated when she and Drew were alone – a romantic picnic carried a definite risk of getting carried away. 'Let's start with coffee,' she suggested, smiling to offset the downgrade. 'I'm free any day except Wednesday – it's Sports Day and Finn would never let me forget it if I missed that.'

'Monday, then,' Drew said. Shifting the apple-laden basket to one hip, he dipped his head to drop a feather-light kiss on her lips. 'I can't wait.'

The memory of that kiss stayed with Daisy all the way to Winterbourne. It had lasted no more than a second, the briefest brush of soft skin against skin, then he'd stepped back and disappeared into the orchard once more, leaving Daisy rooted to the spot among the long grass, gazing after him. He'd kept his eyes open, she remembered as the moment replayed again in her head, which somehow made the recollection more intense and made her wish they'd had longer, even as she was relieved they hadn't. What was it about Drew that made her behave like a teenager? She wondered as she parked her car on the gravel drive outside the manor house steps. Was it ever going to wear off?

She found Athers in the walled garden, kneeling beside one of the empty flowerbeds with a trowel in his hand. He glanced up as she approached, shading his eyes against the sun. 'Hello. Kit said you'd be coming.'

'Couldn't stay away,' she said, then glanced around, taking in the freshly laid topsoil that covered the ground nearby, and several new raised beds against the end wall. 'You've been busy.'

Athers got to his feet, blond curls bouncing as he nodded. 'Getting things ready for the autumn planting. Won't be long before we need to get things in the ground.' He looked past her. 'No easel today?'

Reaching into her bag, Daisy pulled out a pair of gardening

gloves. 'Nope. I'm here to get my hands dirty. Where do you want me to start?'

If the gardener was surprised, he didn't show it. 'There's plenty of dead-heading to be done, and a jasmine shrub that's trying to take over one of the beds. Have you got your own secateurs or do you need some?'

She flourished the cutters she'd brought from the farm. 'I came prepared. Although I'm not sure these will cope with cutting back a jasmine. Aren't they quite woody?'

Again, Athers nodded. 'You'll need tree loppers for that. But why don't you start with the roses? We can do the jasmine together.'

Daisy did as he suggested and was soon surrounded by the heady scent of mixed roses. Cotton wool clouds had rolled in since lunchtime, offering welcome patches of shade from the mid-July sun, but she was glad to see it didn't deter the bees. More than once she drew back to allow a bumblebee to navigate a blowsy flowerhead, the buzz so much lower than that of the honey bees. They were the double bass of the garden orchestra, she decided as she snipped her way along the rose beds, with the crickets as percussion and birds providing the woodwind. The thought of a tiny insect conductor made her smile – there might even be a picture book in the idea, she mused, and pulled out her phone to write herself a note.

Athers passed by, bearing a wheelbarrow laden with more topsoil. He paused to survey Daisy's work. 'I asked my dad about those roses,' he said, nodding at the glorious pink and yellow blooms that Daisy felt were the jewels in the crown of the display. 'You were right, they were planted by Violet – her pride and joy, by all accounts. It's amazing they're still going strong.'

Not for the first time, Daisy had a sudden image of her grandmother as a young woman. On this occasion she was tending the roses, removing the faded blooms just as Daisy was doing now. The intermingling of past and present was so real that she felt almost as though she was standing alongside Violet, caring for the garden together, and the sense of their two worlds colliding took Daisy's breath away. And then the ghost of her grandmother was gone, and she found herself alone with Athers. 'Daisy?' he said, frowning a little. 'Are you okay?'

She blinked. 'Yes, fine. I was just imagining what the garden was like back then.'

'Much the same, if I've got anything to do with it.' The gardener offered a lopsided smile. 'Dad said the old earl – Kit's grandfather – liked to feel as though time had stood still inside these walls. He wanted to smell the same scents, see the same flowers. I try to honour that, even all these years later.'

The poignancy brought tears to Daisy's eyes. Could it be that Valentine was trying to recapture the moments he'd spent with Violet there? She would never know for sure but it seemed to match what she knew of him through the letters. 'That's a wonderful thing to do.'

Athers glanced at Violet's roses nodding in the breeze. 'I'll take extra special care over those in future. For your grandmother.'

Daisy managed a wobbly smile. 'Thank you.'

Once she reached the end of the rose beds, Daisy and Athers tackled the overgrown jasmine. It had long since finished flowering and was sending tall spikes of green-leafed branches in all directions. Daisy had been right – the stems were hard and woody – but the loppers made short work of them and the shrub was soon considerably less wayward. 'It looks like a sheep shorn of its wool,' Daisy said, surveying the branches they'd cut away with a sudden pang of regret.

'Exactly what it needed,' Athers said pragmatically. 'Shoots will grow at the base of the stems and it'll come back stronger in the spring, mark my words.'

Daisy had no doubt the prediction was accurate – there wasn't much Athers didn't know about gardening. She wiped her sweaty forehead and checked her watch. There was still plenty of time before school pick up. 'What else needs doing?'

He opened his mouth to reply but whatever he'd been about to say was interrupted by the sound of feet crunching along the gravel path. They looked up to see a tall, heavily pregnant woman heading towards them and Daisy realized with a jolt of surprise that it was Hugh's wife, Cressida. Sneaking a glance at Athers, Daisy saw he was unflustered, which suggested he'd known the countess was visiting Winterbourne. Or perhaps he was used to members of the family popping up out of the blue – Daisy had no idea.

'Excellent, I was hoping you'd still be here,' Cressida said when she reached them. She smiled at Daisy. 'Hello, again.'

'Hello – er –' Daisy faltered, desperately trying to

remember how to address the wife of an earl. Had she curtseyed last time? Should she do so now?

Athers came to her rescue, like a mud-encrusted Sir Galahad. He tipped his head respectfully. 'Good afternoon, Lady Winterbourne.'

Cressida flashed her dazzling smile his way. 'Good afternoon, Athers. I hope you haven't been working our guest too hard in this heat.'

The words made Daisy suddenly conscious of just how red-faced and sweaty she must be. She raised a self-conscious hand to flatten her hair, much of which had escaped the neat ponytail she'd tied before arriving at the gardens. She couldn't help comparing herself to Cressida, who was a vision of cool elegance despite carrying a mini central heating system, and the results made her want to sink into the ground. But she didn't want the countess to blame Athers. 'Not at all – it's a real honour to spend time in such a beautiful garden. My grandmother used to work here and I feel a little like I'm following in her footsteps.'

'What a wonderful connection to make,' Cressida said, her gaze warm. 'But I've asked Gladys to lay out some tea in the library – won't you join me for a cup? Kit has told me all about your wonderful new book and I'm keen to hear more about it.'

For a heartbeat, Daisy considered saying no. Cressida might seem charming but she was also glossy and sophisticated and horribly intimidating; Daisy felt very much the grubby yokel in comparison. But the thought of tea in that glorious library was tempting and she suspected it was unforgivably rude to refuse such an invitation. 'I'd love to,' she said. 'As long as Athers doesn't need me.'

He shook his head, as she'd known he would. 'Thank you for your help, Miss Moon. Much appreciated.'

The countess turned towards the door in the wall. 'Shall we, then?' she said to Daisy, who nodded and followed her along the path.

The hallway of the manor house was blissfully cool. Cressida paused to direct Daisy towards a doorway along the corridor that she remembered led to a bathroom. 'I'm sure you're longing to freshen up,' the countess said with a flash of fellow feeling. 'Can you find your way to the library once you're ready?'

Thankfully, the mirror was kinder than Daisy expected. Her face was pink and shiny but nowhere near as tomato red as she'd feared. Cold water removed the sweat and occasional smudge of dirt, soothing her flushed cheeks and cooling her down to the point where she felt less like she'd been dragged through a hedge. There wasn't much she could do about her hair, which the heat had transformed into a frizzy mess, but she did her best to recapture it into a neat-ish ponytail and surveyed her reflection with a frown. She could never hope to achieve the glamour of Cressida but she did at least look more presentable than she had a few minutes earlier.

The countess was sitting beside the open window when Daisy entered the library. She rose, wincing very slightly as she did so. 'It's obviously a great privilege and joy to be a sacred vessel and so forth but I can't help wishing it was a little easier on the back.'

Daisy smiled in commiseration – there had been times she'd feared carrying the twins might finish her off. 'How much longer do you have to go?'

Cressida rested a hand on her bump. 'Another month, would you believe? They might have to roll me into the delivery suite.'

'I felt the same towards the end,' Daisy admitted, hurrying forward to join her at the side table laden with a tea tray. 'But please don't stand on my account. Shall I pour?'

'If you wouldn't mind,' Cressida said, easing back into her seat. Her eyes twinkled as she glanced at an austere oil painting above the fireplace. 'Although I'm sure generations of Devereaux women are rolling in their graves at my appalling dereliction of hostess duties.'

Daisy laughed, surprised at the mischievous observation. 'Would you like milk?'

The other woman pulled a face. 'Can't bear it at the moment, makes me turn green. Could I trouble you for some lemon instead? Gladys usually puts a few slices in a dish.'

Now that Daisy looked, she saw there was a dish of thinly sliced lemon, along with a pair of delicate silver tongs that had probably been specifically made for the purpose of adding lemon to tea. As Daisy bent over the tray, she pondered Cressida's unexpected self-deprecation. Admittedly, prior to becoming friendly with Kit her experience of the aristocracy had been almost entirely formed from watching *Downton Abbey* and *Bridgerton*, but she'd imagined Cressida would be coolly gracious, perhaps even a little condescending – she was a countess, after all. Instead, Daisy was finding her witty and warm, and surprisingly normal, in spite of clearly being someone who was used to turning heads. It was the second time a member of the Devereaux family had confounded her expectations, Daisy thought uncomfortably as she passed a cup and saucer to Cressida. Perhaps it was time to stop judging them before she got to know them.

'Kit tells me you've been inspired by the gardens here,' Cressida said, once Daisy was seated in the chair opposite, a cup and saucer of her own in her hand. 'Is that because of your grandmother?'

'Partly,' Daisy said. 'Although I fell in love with the walled garden as soon as I stepped through the door. I think it would have inspired my drawings even without the family connection.'

Cressida nodded. 'It is a lovely place. We don't spend much time here, as I'm sure you know. Hugh grew up here but he has so many responsibilities elsewhere now.' Her hand curved subconsciously around her bump and Daisy suspected she was thinking about the tragedy that had befallen Hugh's first wife. 'Luckily, Kit is a marvellous help. It's such a weight off Hugh's mind, knowing Winterbourne is in safe hands.'

Her words reminded Daisy of a long-ago conversation with Kit, during which he'd explained that he was merely a tenant at the castle, reliant entirely on his brother's goodwill for a roof over his and Alice's head. She really hoped Cressida didn't view him merely as a help. 'He belongs here,' she said, almost without thinking, and then remembered who she was speaking to. 'I mean, of course he does – he grew up here too. But it's more than that. I suppose what I'm getting at is . . .' She trailed off, trying to pin down her thoughts. 'Do you believe people put down roots, the way trees do?'

The other woman sipped her tea, watching her over the rim of the cup. 'Of course. The Devereauxs have lived here for centuries – their roots are deep.'

Daisy flapped a hand. 'Yes, that's part of it but I'm not talking about the length of time the family has owned the land. When Kit met me in the hall, the night of the Summer Ball, he looked – he seemed – intrinsic somehow.' She paused helplessly, seeking insight. 'As though Winterbourne was an unfinished jigsaw puzzle and he was the piece that completed it.'

She stopped, suddenly aware she had said more than she should. Cressida was still watching her, a slight frown creasing her brow, but Daisy had no idea what she might be thinking. Possibly whether to have her thrown in the castle dungeons.

'You know, I'd never really thought about it but I do know what you mean,' Cressida said slowly. 'Hugh is obviously the earl but I get the sense it's just a title to him, whereas Kit – well, I've always felt Kit *is* Winterbourne. I'm sure Hugh feels the same, although I don't suppose either of us has ever said as much to Kit. I expect he knows . . .'

A thoughtful silence ensued, leaving Daisy to stew in the juice of her own consternation. She still couldn't tell what Cressida truly thought of her observations, in spite of her apparent agreement, and it was making her stomach churn. 'Sometimes it's easier to see things more clearly from the outside,' she offered.

Cressida nodded. 'Perhaps, but you must understand that the law of primogeniture is non-negotiable,' she said, glancing at her rounded belly. 'The firstborn child inherits the title and lands, which then pass to their firstborn. Hugh can't simply give away the earldom, I'm afraid.'

'I don't think Kit cares about that,' Daisy said, and it occurred to her that none of the Devereaux men she knew of seemed to have enjoyed being the earl. 'It's Winterbourne he loves.'

'It doesn't matter. The castle and the title are inextricably linked.' Cressida frowned into her cup. 'I agree it's a rough deal for Kit but I'm really not sure anything can be done. I suppose I could speak to Hugh.'

The words sent a tidal wave of embarrassment crashing over Daisy. 'I didn't mean to suggest —' She stopped as more implications came thundering home. 'Kit didn't ask me to mention this. He doesn't — he's not—'

Cressida raised a hand. 'I know. But it is something that's troubled me, more so since I fell pregnant. Hugh would never ask Kit to leave Winterbourne but that isn't the point.'

Mortification mingled with something approaching horror in Daisy's stomach. Kit would be furious that she'd shared his confidence with Cressida. Why hadn't she kept her stupid mouth shut? 'I didn't mean to interfere. It's absolutely none of my business,' she said wretchedly.

'You haven't interfered,' Cressida reassured her. 'I doubt anything can be done but it won't hurt to look into it.'

Daisy wasn't sure Kit would see it that way but she couldn't take it back now. She was grateful when Cressida changed the subject, and did her best to answer questions about other books she had written and illustrated. Even so, she was aware of a leaden chill that had settled in her gut. It stayed there all the way to the school gates. How was she going to look Kit in the eye, knowing she'd inadvertently stirred up a hornets' nest? And the answer was that she couldn't, not without coming clean. Far better that he was forewarned, she decided as she waited in the playground. She owed him that, at least.

As usual, Kit was a few minutes early, which gave Daisy the opportunity to draw him to one side. She expected him to be angry with her for overstepping their friendship, for hinting at his dislike at being reliant on Hugh's generosity, even though she hadn't meant to do either. She waited, braced, as he silently considered her, while the other parents milled around them. Eventually, he puffed out his cheeks, shaking his head. 'Did you mean what you said to Cressida, about what you thought when I met you at the ball?'

It was the last thing she'd expected him to zoom in on. 'Oh,' she said, wrongfooted. 'Yes, but it was only a half-formed notion – an impression, I suppose. It wasn't until a week or so later, when I was doodling and sketched you in the light, that it properly fell into place.'

He stared at her. 'You drew me?'

Daisy nodded. 'A rough picture. I often start work by sketching random images, it helps my fingers to warm up. But that was when I understood how perfectly you belonged there. Even then, it wasn't a lightning bolt moment – it felt more like something I was remembering, having always known it.' She sighed, wishing once again that she'd kept her thoughts to herself. 'Sorry, I'm not making much sense.'

His gaze remained on her. 'When I was stationed overseas and things were hard, I used to visualize coming home to Winterbourne. I'd imagine driving through the gates, crunching across the gravel, running my hand along the books in the library while a fire crackled and sparked in the grate.' He paused. 'And of course my family were here but it was always the house itself that got me through the darkest times.'

Daisy understood. She'd felt the same way about Half Moon Farm when she was a child. 'Because it was your place.'

'Yes,' he said simply. 'But I don't need to own Winterbourne to feel that. Which is a good thing because it isn't mine and it never will be.'

'But you look after it,' Daisy observed with rising indignation. 'You care. Hugh doesn't even like it there.'

'For a good reason,' Kit reminded her, then sighed. 'Look, being the second son meant I had a lot of freedom – freedom

Hugh never had, because he carried the weight of inheriting the titles and responsibilities and everything that goes with it. Looking after Winterbourne takes some of the load from him, plus Alice and I get to live in the place we both love.' He offered her a crooked smile. 'And it's not so terrible – I spend a lot of my time messing about with planes, which I also love.'

When he put it like that it was hard to argue, Daisy thought. 'But you're not cross with me for blabbering away to Cressida? I really didn't mean to, it just sort of slipped out.'

Now Kit's smile became a grin. 'No, I'm not cross. It was very sweet of you. No one's ever tried to circumvent the laws of inheritance on my behalf before.'

At least he wasn't angry, Daisy thought with a hefty dose of relief. 'Maybe Hugh will find a way,' she said, as the bell rang and they began to move into the playground.

'He won't,' Kit replied firmly. 'But that's okay. I made my peace with it a long time ago, even if I do occasionally grumble.'

She smiled. 'You'll just have to marry a wealthy heiress. Isn't that the done thing in aristocratic circles?'

Kit laughed as he raised a hand to wave at Alice. 'Luckily, I don't think any of them would want me. I'll just have to make my fortune as a flight instructor instead.'

Chapter Twenty-Four

'Going anywhere nice?'

Daisy glanced at her mother, who was hovering in the kitchen doorway, watching her lace up her trainers. 'Coffee with Drew.'

Rose folded her arms. 'A coffee date. Very romantic.'

As usual, Daisy's natural inclination was to shrink away from discussing anything about her love life with Rose. She'd been an expert in deciphering her mother's body language while growing up – the folded arms suggested disapproval but that wasn't reflected in her tone or her expression, Daisy thought. If anything, she looked faintly pleased. And Daisy hadn't been a teenager for quite some time – surely she could talk to her mother as an equal now. 'It's not really a date,' she said. 'We're just friends.'

With benefits, she added silently, but Rose was eyeing her beadily. 'He's a good man. You could do a lot worse.'

'He is a good man,' Daisy agreed. 'Which is why we're friends.'

'Kind and helpful, and good looking. You make a nice couple.'

'We're not a couple,' Daisy insisted, wishing she'd said she was meeting Nancy instead. 'Apart from anything else, I'm going back to Milton Keynes soon, remember?'

Her mother sniffed. 'What's that got to do with anything? It's hardly Timbuktu, is it?'

'But it's not around the corner, either,' Daisy said. She took a deep breath. 'Look, I'll admit Drew and I enjoy each other's company but that's all there is to it.'

'You could do a lot worse,' Rose said again, as though she hadn't heard Daisy. 'He's such a help. Did I tell you he's going to get the roof fixed?'

Daisy frowned, feeling an altogether different type of unease. This wasn't the first time Rose had mentioned repairing the roof. 'I sorted that out months ago, don't you remember?'

Rose waved a hand. 'There's a leak. Drew's going to get someone in to fix it.'

'He hasn't mentioned it to me,' Daisy said, her frown deepening. 'Are you sure?'

'Of course I'm sure,' Rose snapped. 'Why would he mention it to you? It's not your house.'

'No, but—' Daisy stopped. There was an obstinate set to her mother's expression that she recognized all too well. 'It's very kind of Drew to help.'

Instantly, Rose's irritation was smoothed away. She gave a nod of satisfaction. 'He's a good man. You could do worse.'

It was clear there wasn't much to be gained by arguing, Daisy thought, but her mother's conviction that there was an issue with the roof still troubled her. Before she left to meet Drew, she went upstairs to the bedroom that had suffered the worst damage before the hole in the farmhouse roof was repaired. The clutter that had filled the room had long since been cleared; broken furniture had been dumped, ancient magazines had been recycled and the boxes of old papers were now stacked in one corner, waiting for Daisy to sift through them when she had time. The ceiling was smooth, freshly plastered, and the strong smell of damp had gone now that the old, almost threadbare carpet had been replaced. Daisy's eyes scanned the ceiling and walls, alert for evidence of a leak but there was nothing. Her mother must have misunderstood, she decided, closing the door and hurrying to get her bag. Except that it wasn't the first time Rose had been muddled when talking about repairs to the house – had there been other lapses Daisy hadn't noticed? She bit her lip. Perhaps it was time to ask Emily if she'd noticed anything unusual when talking to Rose.

She should have known Drew would pick up on her mood, no matter how hard she tried to push the conversation with Rose to the back of her mind. They'd agreed that the Oast House café was too close to home – much to Nancy's good-natured annoyance – and had arranged to meet in Mistlethorpe instead. Daisy had only been seated opposite Drew for a few minutes before he threw her a concerned look. 'You're quiet today. Is everything okay?'

She didn't answer immediately, fretting that she was over-reacting, that everyone got their wires crossed from time to time. But there was a chance he'd be able to set her mind at rest – perhaps he'd have some idea how the mix up had happened. Daisy cleared her throat. 'I had an odd conversation with my mum this morning. She's got it into her head the roof is leaking.'

Drew frowned. 'It's not that long since the repair. Do you need to get Jonny to take another look? He usually does a thorough job but mistakes happen.'

Daisy shook her head. 'I checked the ceiling this morning and I can't see what she's talking about.' She gave him a helpless look. 'I think she's confused. She said you were going to sort it out, which obviously doesn't make any sense. Unless you mentioned something in passing and she's got the wrong end of the stick.'

He puffed out a long breath. 'Not that I remember. But I'd be more likely to speak to you if I noticed a problem. I certainly wouldn't take it upon myself to sort anything out.'

'No,' Daisy said, sighing. 'That's what I thought. But it's not the first time she's said something like this and I can't help wondering whether she's not quite as well as I thought.'

She closed her mouth quickly, as though doing so would stop any more of her fears from escaping. Drew was silent for several seconds. 'You're worried about dementia.'

'No,' Daisy said. 'Maybe. I don't know. She seems to be herself most of the time but that's often how it starts, isn't it? With little moments of disconnection or confusion. And obviously I'm going back to Milton Keynes soon – how am I going to know if she's getting worse?'

'You'll have Emily,' he offered and took her hand. 'I'd be very happy to keep a closer eye on her too, if it helps. But try not to panic – as you say, it might be nothing.'

The reassurance made her feel a little better. 'Thank you.' She managed a fleeting smile. 'There's always something, isn't there?'

'Always,' Drew agreed. He squeezed her fingers. 'I appreciate we haven't known each other that long but I hope you know I'm here for you, Daisy. You don't have to do everything alone.'

The words caused a sudden lump to form in her throat; she hadn't realized how much her worries about leaving Rose and Half Moon Farm had been weighing on her mind. It was kind of Drew to offer his help and the truth was she would feel better knowing someone beside Emily was watching over things. 'That's good of you. Thanks, Drew.'

'No problem.' His eyes crinkled into the smile that never failed to make her stomach swoop. 'And in the meantime, why don't you let me treat you to a slice of that carrot cake?'

She glanced across to the counter, where a sumptuous, nut-speckled gateau glistened under the glass, and felt the last of the morning's anxiety slip from her shoulders. Her mother had been right about one thing, at least – Drew Entwistle *was* a good man. Daisy smiled back at him. 'How could anyone say no to an offer like that?'

★ ★ ★

What are you doing tomorrow morning?

The message from Kit arrived on Wednesday evening, when Daisy was wrangling a protesting Finn into the shower. A momentary frown crossed her forehead as she mentally reviewed her diary while simultaneously wondering why he was asking. Did Athers want her help in the gardens? Daisy had stood beside Kit for most of the afternoon, watching their children compete at Sports Day, and he hadn't mentioned anything then.

She tapped on the bathroom door. 'Wash your hair, Finn. Use shampoo this time, not bubble bath.'

A muffled howl of outrage told her Finn had heard. Shaking her head, she turned her attention back to her phone. *Taking Mum to an appointment first thing but free after that. Why, what's up?*

The sound of tuneless singing drifted over her as she waited. Finn liked to indulge in the full shower experience once he was in there, despite having to be almost forcibly thrust under the water to begin with. Campbell had always been more fastidious – even as a toddler he'd hated getting dirty and Daisy had never had any trouble getting him to take a shower. He also liked to sing but she could usually recognize the song. Not so with Finn, who valued volume over the right notes or lyrics.

Her phone buzzed just as Finn reached his loudest. Wincing, Daisy stepped away from the door and opened Kit's reply. *I've had a cancellation. How do you fancy a flying lesson?*

The question was so unexpected that Daisy's jaw dropped. A flying lesson? Where had that come from? But at the moment, the sound of running water stopped, along with Finn's singing, and the bathroom door opened. 'I accidentally threw the towel in the toilet,' Finn said plaintively.

By the time Daisy had fetched another towel, retrieved the one in the toilet and dried the wet footprints that criss-crossed the floor, her initial surprise at Kit's message had faded and she was able to consider it more objectively. He'd often waxed lyrical about how beautiful the Kent country-side looked from the skies, and about the sense of freedom he felt in the air. She'd certainly never have a better oppor-tunity to see what he meant.

What time? she typed.

His reply was immediate. *Eleven, at Marston airport. Does that work?*

She did some rough calculations. Her mother's dental appointment was at nine-thirty in nearby Pelby – as long as the dentist was running to time, she could be at Marston by eleven o'clock. If she wanted to be . . .

Okay, she tapped out, before she lost her nerve. *Do I need to bring anything?*

Once again, Kit's response was fast. *Only your spirit of adventure. But make sure you eat breakfast – there's a kettle in my office but not much more. See you tomorrow!*

★ ★ ★

By the time Daisy arrived at Marston, she was seriously regret-ting saying yes to Kit's offer. The airport seemed impossibly small compared to the vastness of Gatwick or Heathrow, just a winding ribbon of concrete nestled in what looked ominously like a field. There was a control tower, she noted, and several hangars. She wasn't sure what she'd been expecting but a sign at the entrance gate reminding drivers to watch out for incoming planes was not on her list.

Kit beamed at her as she got out of her car. 'Good morning,' he called, crossing the tarmac to meet her. 'It's a lovely day for taking to the skies.'

Daisy swallowed, trying not to stare past him at the small blue and white plane just beyond a low building. She'd never been a nervous flyer but the planes had always been re-assuringly large, making it easy to forget how far from the ground she was. There was no chance of forgetting in a two-seater, she suspected. Not even if she closed her eyes. But it was far too late to back out now. She summoned up what she hoped was a breezy smile. 'Hello.'

If Kit noticed her trepidation, he didn't say anything. Instead, he nodded at the brick building off to one side. 'There are lockers in there, if you want to leave anything on the ground.'

The suggestion put Daisy in mind of the rollercoasters she'd been on with the twins, where the risk of losing things was high. She felt a spike of anxiety. 'Do I need to?'

'No,' he said, eyeing her handbag. 'The cockpit is cosy but you'll have room for a bag that small. We don't do loops until your second lesson.'

She thought he was joking but it was hard to tell. 'Great,' she said weakly. 'Is that your plane?'

Kit nodded. 'It is. She's fully fuelled and ready to go. I thought a trip to Dover might be nice, since the weather is good. You'll probably be able to see France and the cliffs are spectacular when it's sunny.'

Daisy hadn't actually considered where they might go but she had to concede that flying over the famous white cliffs sounded appealing. 'Okay,' she said, doing her best to squash the storm of butterflies in her stomach. 'Sounds good.'

He hadn't lied when he said the cockpit was cosy, Daisy observed once she was seated snugly on the left-hand of the plane. She'd had to duck underneath a wing to clamber in and almost banged her head on one of the struts – if she looked out of the side window beside her seat she could see the wheels. How Kit managed to fold his tall frame into the space inside was a mystery. Before her lay a bewildering array of panels and controls inlaid in a walnut dashboard, and beyond the windscreen the nose of the plane was alarmingly close. But even more disconcerting was her proximity to Kit – their bodies almost touched along their entire length once they were both strapped in side by side. His warmth mingled with hers, making her wish the sun wasn't quite so strong.

'As you can see, it's dual control,' Kit said, tapping on the control column that was duplicated on her side of the cockpit. 'I'll take control initially and you can have a go once we're in the air. Happy?'

The thought of actually taking over control made Daisy want to hyperventilate. 'Do I have to?'

He laughed. 'No, but I promise it's easier than you think.' He patted the dash with obvious affection. 'This girl practically flies herself. Now, let me explain what all these dials do.'

Daisy tried to take everything in. There was a compass – that was easy enough to understand – and a speedometer, which also made sense. Another dial told them how high up they were, while what looked like a rolling ball in the middle of a sea of horizontal lines was to ensure the plane stayed level. Numbers swam in front of her eyes as they slid from display to display. And finally, Kit pointed out the radio that sat in the centre of everything; somehow Daisy doubted it was tuned to Heart FM.

'You'll need to wear these,' Kit said, handing her a bulky set of headphones with a microphone attached. 'As we fly, we'll communicate with various air traffic control towers – they need to know we're heading into their airspace. The microphones are voice-activated – all you need to do is speak.'

She slid the headphones on, a little surprised by their weight. 'Will anyone else be able to hear me?'

He shook his head. 'Just me for today. Oh, and when you do speak, there might be times when I don't answer right away. There's usually a lot of radio chatter, sometimes I need to listen so I know who else is in the air around us.'

Daisy hadn't considered that. 'Will there be much traffic?'

'It's not the M25,' he said, grinning. 'Don't worry, I haven't hit anyone yet.'

'Ha ha,' Daisy said weakly.

All signs of flippancy vanished once he started the engine, however. She watched as he methodically checked each screen and dial, his attention suddenly laser focused, and her nerves lessened. Kit was a highly trained RAF pilot, she reminded herself, he'd flown in some of the most difficult conditions possible. An hour-long jaunt to the English Channel and back was nothing, yet he was still intent on making sure everything was as it should be before they took off. Apparently satisfied, he adjusted his headphones and reached for the radio.

A hiss of static filled Daisy's ears, softening the thrum of the engine. 'Marston air traffic control, this is Golf-Bravo-Romeo-Charlie-Delta requesting permission to take off, over.'

A male voice crackled in reply. 'Good afternoon, Golf-Bravo. Where are you heading today, Kit? Over.'

'Due south towards Dover,' Kit replied. 'Return ETA is twelve-thirty, over.'

'Very good, Golf-Bravo,' the voice said. 'Taxi to the runway when ready, over.'

Kit glanced at Daisy and she saw his eyes were dancing as though he were a child on Christmas Eve. 'Ready?' he asked, his voice cutting through the faint buzz of static.

The point when she might have said no was long since past. Bracing herself, she tipped her head. 'Ready.'

There were foot pedals that worked in much the same way as a car, although Kit explained that they also steered left and right. Daisy was glad she didn't have to worry about that – as much as he reassured her it was as easy as driving a car, she didn't believe him. They trundled around the concrete curve, passing the point where Daisy had obeyed a sign to stop and check for landing planes when she'd been driving in, and reached the start of a long, straight stretch that she guessed must be the runway. 'Marston, this is Golf-Bravo-Romeo-Charlie-Delta, ready for take-off,' Kit said.

'Golf-Bravo, you are cleared. Have a good flight. Over.'

The plane began to move forwards, picking up speed. Daisy felt herself jolt in her seat and put one hand against the door on her left to brace. The noise of the engine increased, a dull roar that made her feet vibrate against the floor, and she saw Kit checking the dials once more. Then he eased back on the yoke and it seemed to Daisy that he might have been pulling the nose of the plane itself because suddenly they were off the ground. Her stomach swooped as they rose upwards smoothly. Automatically, she glanced out of the side window and saw the runway falling away. She bit back a gasp and turned to the front, her eyes blurring as the dials swam before them. Everything felt so close. Everything except the ground.

Kit's voice broke through her careening thoughts, calm and matter of fact. 'We'll climb to just over one thousand feet, then level off. If you check the altimeter, it should confirm how high up we are.'

Daisy blinked, trying to remember which dial that had been. Then she saw it. 'Uh, around six hundred feet now, I think.'

'We should be passing over Mistlethorpe in a minute,' he said. 'You'll be able to see the farm.'

'Great,' Daisy managed, fixing her gaze on the nose of the plane while she got her breathing under control. It really wouldn't do to pass out, she thought as the propeller blurred the air. The twins would never let her hear the end of it if she did.

Gradually, she felt the plane's climb start to lessen and she risked another glance out of the side window. The ground was a patchwork quilt of green and yellow, dotted with woodland and sewn together by hedgerows and roads. Houses were sparse at first – they reminded her of Lego bricks – but then she caught a sparkle among a cluster of trees. 'Is that the River Mistle?' she asked Kit, who nodded.

'Yes. You can trace its path by following the lines of trees – they're thickest along the riverbanks.' He eased the controller to one side and the plane banked slightly left. 'Look, there's Winterbourne.'

Sure enough, Daisy saw the castle and the manor house blossoming into view. The moat shimmered like a priceless diamond collar around the castle walls. 'It looks big and small at the same time,' she said, and instantly cringed. 'Sorry, that sounds stupid.'

He glanced at her, smiling. 'I know exactly what you mean. It's bigger than everything else but still tiny from the air. Pocket-sized, in fact.'

The idea made her giggle, although she thought adrenaline might be playing a part too. 'You'd need much bigger trousers. Or a TARDIS.'

They were flying over the village now, the High Street curving alongside the green, with the river flashing in the sunlight. And then Half Moon Farm appeared, nestled between the winding road and woodlands like a toy. Daisy's breath caught in her throat as she stared through the window. It was as though she was Alice gazing down at Wonderland having eaten the cake, except that this was no dream. 'It's magical,' she murmured to herself, forgetting the headphones for a moment. 'Just magical.'

'Isn't it?' Kit said, and she knew without looking that he was smiling. 'So, are you ready to fly yourself?'

In a heartbeat, Daisy's delight vanished. She stared at him in consternation, dread gnawing at her stomach. 'Now? But what if I can't do it? What if we crash?'

'We're not going to crash,' he said patiently. 'All you have to do is keep the nose level with the horizon and fly straight. You can do this, Daisy. Just put your hands on the yoke in front of you and I'll pass control across.'

Her palms were sweaty as she reached reluctantly for the control column. Easier than driving a car, she reminded herself, which might be true but she'd felt sick with nerves the first time she'd driven a car too. 'Ready?' Kit asked.

No, Daisy wanted to say but she knew he wouldn't accept that as an answer. He thought she could do this and she supposed she would simply have to trust his judgement. 'Ready.'

'You have control,' he said coolly and Daisy noticed an instant change in the yoke, a thrum of tension that caused her stress levels to spike. Her fingers tightened instinctively and the plane bounced very slightly in response.

'Oh!' she squeaked, panic coursing through her. The yoke responded to her movement, juddering a little and tilting left.

'Steady,' Kit soothed. 'Don't grip so tightly. The controls are very responsive – loosen your hands and keep an eye on the nose.'

Daisy took a breath and forced her fingers to uncurl. With infinite concentration, she pressed forwards, watching as the nose dropped to align with the horizon. 'Much better,' Kit said, and she thought he sounded pleased, although she didn't dare look at him. 'See? You're flying. Didn't I say you could do it?'

She didn't reply, too busy focusing on keeping the plane level, but she felt her shoulders drop down from around her ears as some of the tension leached out of her. It was odd not having to check her mirrors or consider other vehicles but she had plenty to think about. Occasionally, the plane would tremble, sending fresh spikes of worry through Daisy but Kit explained it was caused by pockets of warm air. The radio crackled as new voices came into range – sometimes Kit answered, with a bewildering range of acronyms that seemed to encompass the whole phonetic alphabet. Then she suddenly became aware that the view beyond the nose was no longer green. A thin line of blue had appeared and was growing thicker with every passing moment. 'The sea!' she exclaimed with a tiny bubble of delighted laughter. 'I've flown us all the way to the seaside.'

'You have,' Kit said, smiling. 'I'll take over now, if you like. Let you enjoy the view.'

Perversely, Daisy felt a small stab of disappointment at the suggestion. 'Oh. Okay.'

He laughed. 'Don't worry, you can fly us home.' Beneath Daisy's fingers, the yoke became unresponsive. 'I have control.'

There was no trace of anxiety in Daisy now when she peered out of the side window. They were passing over a well populated area; houses huddled together and roads twisted like strands of cotton between them. But her attention was caught and held by the ever-expanding swathe of turquoise up ahead, sparkling in the sunshine. It met the forget-me-not sky at the horizon and the contrast seemed to darken the water, turning it an intoxicating emerald green. She wasn't surprised Kit loved flying so much. Right now, Daisy felt as though she never wanted to come down.

'Time to turn around now.' Kit sounded regretful as he banked the plane right. 'I hope you've got some sunglasses – the cliffs will probably be blinding today.'

She thought he was joking, although the white chalk was bright. Birds were circling around the cliff-face, some coming in to land, others whirling away to soar over the white-tipped waves. Gulls of some description, Daisy guessed, but she wasn't much of a twitcher and had no real idea. Campbell would know.

It wasn't until they were back over land and heading for Marston that Daisy became aware of the creeping nausea laying siege to her stomach. Kit had passed control to her again and she'd been concentrating hard on riding the small buffets of wind that occasionally spiralled up to jolt the small plane. At first, she tried to ignore the queasiness, telling herself it would pass, but her mouth grew dry and her tongue felt thick. A throb began in her temples and although she hated to admit it, it was something of a relief when Kit announced it was time for him to take over. She took a swig of water, hoping it was simple dehydration, but the nausea didn't fade. By the time they touched down at Marston – as smoothly as any heavier plane she'd travelled on – she couldn't wait for some fresh air and to feel her feet on the ground again.

Once the plane was at a standstill beside the low building once more, Kit turned to smile at Daisy. 'I hope you're proud of yourself. Well done.'

She did her best to return the smile, although it felt like a poor effort. 'Thank you. I can't believe I flew us all that way.'

'But you did,' he replied. 'Not everyone takes to it that well. You're a natural.'

Daisy's stomach gurgled unpleasantly and she clenched her fingers until the sensation passed. 'I don't feel like a natural,' she admitted, swallowing a groan. 'To be honest, I feel a bit sick.'

Kit studied her more closely. 'You do look a bit peaky, now you mention it,' he said, and patted her arm sympathetically. 'Come on, let's find you some peppermint tea.'

He climbed out of the cockpit and came round to her

side of the plane, ducking beneath the wing to open her door. Daisy swung her feet onto the step, desperate to be back on solid ground, but her legs had other ideas. They buckled when she put her weight on them, sending her heels slithering painfully to the tarmac. She grabbed the door for support – it swung away, knocking her further off balance. With a startled yelp, Daisy let go and stumbled forwards on jelly legs, only to find herself caught by Kit before she could collapse fully into an undignified heap. 'Oh!' she cried as he steadied her. 'I'm sorry.'

He didn't let go immediately. Instead, his fingers slid down her arms to cup her elbows, supporting her. 'Are you okay?'

Daisy swallowed another wave of queasiness. She couldn't decide what was more gut-wrenching – the fear that she might vomit on Kit's feet or the knowledge that she was only standing because he was holding her up. 'Fine,' she said, sounding unconvincing even to herself. 'Just a bit wobbly.'

Still he did not let go and Daisy had a sudden flash of him sweeping her into his arms and carrying her to the nearest bench, like a blond Richard Gere. Buoyed up by an acute desire to avoid that at all costs, she took a step backwards. 'See?'

His hands hovered at her sides until he was apparently satisfied she could indeed stand up, then relaxed. 'Good. Do you want to take my arm?'

Daisy shook her head, then wished she hadn't as wooziness washed over her. The last time Kit had offered his arm had been at the Summer Ball and the occasion had been very different. 'I'll be fine,' she said again. 'I think my legs sort of went to sleep while we were flying – it will do me good to stretch them out.'

'If you're sure?' he said, regarding her intently.

'Positive,' she said, and took a bracing gulp of air. 'Did you mention a cup of tea?'

Inside the squat building was blessedly cool. Daisy excused herself the moment they were through the door. She made for the bathroom, splashing cold water on her face and letting it pour across the pulse point on each wrist, closing her eyes and resting her forehead against the mirror. The nausea was constant, even though she was as sure as she could be that she wouldn't actually throw up. As a child she'd often felt this way after reading in a moving car, but the knowledge that the unpleasantness would eventually pass did nothing to ease her suffering now.

'That's exactly what you're feeling,' Kit said, when she described the sensation to him. 'It's an imbalance between what your eyes can see and what your brain thinks is happening. Quite a lot of people suffer from it when they first go up in a smaller plane.'

She fought the urge to blink hard. The room wasn't quite spinning but she couldn't be sure it was totally still. 'Did you?'

'No,' he said, smiling. 'But flying is in my blood, remember? I've been doing it as long as I remember.'

Daisy took a mouthful of steaming peppermint tea, wondering how many other would-be pilots had sat where she was sitting and felt the way she felt. 'You might have warned me,' she grumbled.

He spread his hands. 'Not everyone suffers – I didn't want to put the idea in your head. I did suggest you ate a good breakfast. A full stomach often helps.'

She shifted in her seat, not quite meeting his gaze. Between the school run and the dentist, she hadn't found time to eat. Something to bear in mind for next time, she thought and then remembered there was unlikely to be a follow up lesson. It was probably a good thing, she decided as she took another gulp of tea. At least she wouldn't have to worry about literally throwing herself at him again. 'I'll bear it in mind,' she said. 'Thanks for taking me up. I really did enjoy it, even if I do look a bit green around the gills now.'

'You're welcome,' he said. 'Let's call it a professional trade. You put Winterbourne's gardens into your book and I let you fly my plane.'

Daisy shook her head carefully. 'Except I'm pretty sure I owe you for that, too,' she replied. 'I heard back from my agent and she said the publisher is thrilled with the illustrations. They're planning a big launch party next year – you should come.'

The invitation popped out before she'd thought it through. By the time the party happened, she would have been back in Milton Keynes for the best part of seven months – there was every chance Kit would have forgotten all about the book by then. But she couldn't take the invitation back, not when she realized how pleased he looked. 'I might just do that,' he said. 'But of course we'll buy some stock for the castle shop. Maybe you could sign them, if it's not too much trouble.'

'No trouble at all,' Daisy said, then winced as her head thudded painfully. 'Sorry to fly and run but I think I need to go home for a lie down.'

She gave an embarrassed laugh but Kit's concern was instant. 'Of course. Are you well enough to drive?' He glanced at his watch. 'I have another lesson in half an hour but I could take you home first.'

Daisy didn't want to imagine the disgust on her mother's face if she was escorted home by a Devereaux. 'Please don't worry. I'll be fine.'

Kit appeared far from convinced. 'Let me collect the boys from school for you, then. I can drop them home – it's no trouble.'

Again, Daisy declined the offer. 'It's very kind of you but, honestly, I'll be fine in a little while.' She got to her feet, on legs that felt so much steadier than they had thirty minutes earlier. 'Thanks again for letting me do this. It really was incredible.'

He rose too. 'I enjoyed the company,' he said, smiling. 'You're welcome to fly with me any time.'

She had almost reached her car when she heard footsteps behind her. Turning, she saw Kit had a black A5 book in his hands. 'I forgot to give you your flying log,' he said, holding it out. 'It contains the records of today's flight, in case you've really got the bug and decide you want to get your pilot's licence.'

It was a nice touch, Daisy thought. 'Thank you,' she said, taking the book and running her fingers over the embossed silver wings on the cover.

'And if not, then it's something to remind you of the day,' he went on. 'Assuming you don't feel so dreadful that you never want to think of it again.'

She laughed. 'I don't feel that bad. Thanks for this, it's a lovely memento.'

It seemed to Daisy as though her smile lasted all the way back to Half Moon Farm, in spite of her thumping head and roiling stomach. She kept stealing looks at the flying log on the passenger seat beside her, wondering what Finn and Campbell would think of it. But regardless of whether she ever flew again, she didn't need a book to remind her of soaring over the white cliffs, almost at one with the gulls. Nor would she forget Kit's calm competence, the patience with which he'd allowed her to learn, or his consummate skill. She'd thought he belonged at Winterbourne but now she realized she'd been mistaken — where he truly belonged was in the sky. The whole exhilarating experience was seared into her soul — she knew she'd never forget a moment. And she had Kit Devereaux to thank for it. How had she ever disliked him?

Chapter Twenty-Five

11 Thanet Lane
Mistlethorpe
Kent

14th April

Dearest Val
*I hardly know what I should write, or if I can write,
after our last meeting. Of course I am only a stupid village
girl, I don't have your fancy words or fine education, but I
don't believe you meant the things you said. How could
you say you don't love me after writing those very words
so many times? After you held me close under our tree and
told me which star to look out for when you were away?
Love like that can't be thrown away because your family
don't think I'm good enough. You said you would fight for
me, Val. You said we were forever. My heart is still yours*

and I beg of you to run away with me tonight. I will wait
by the mill on the High Street until midnight. If you do
not come, I will know nothing you ever said was true.
    Always yours,
    Violet

It was the last letter in the bundle addressed to Kit's grandfather and even now, Daisy could see the dried tear that stained
the paper and smudged the words. Her own tears had flowed
freely, although she'd made sure they didn't join her grandmother's on the letter. Poor Violet, she thought dully. It seemed
as though Val had broken every promise he had made and
even though Daisy had known it was coming, it still felt like
a kick in the ribs. When Kit had first given her the letters,
she'd interlaced the two sets in date order, reading the back
and forth as they would have been written and received. After
Violet's heartbreaking letter to Valentine, there was only one
envelope remaining in the pile addressed to Violet. It was
thicker than the others, which she'd assumed was because it
hadn't been sent on Active Service – the post mark was
November 1946, when she knew Val had long been home
from the war, and the envelope was cream-coloured instead
of blue or grey. Violet's name and address was printed in block
capitals, which was another departure that made Daisy frown.
In the letter she had just read, it sounded as though Val had
at least had the decency to break things off in person but
perhaps he'd risked one final reply. Leaning back against her
pillow, she picked up the envelope and slid the contents out.

At once, she knew she'd been wrong. This wasn't a letter from Val – the handwriting was all wrong, more of a scrawl and considerably less elegant. There was no address at the top, simply the date – 2nd November 1946 – and the salutation below it was equally abrupt.

> *Miss Finch,*
>
> *Kindly stop writing to me. I am sorry for the situation you find yourself in but I cannot help. The accusation you make is entirely wrong – I suspect there are several other hop pickers who might be responsible, if farm gossip is to be believed. Perhaps you will have better luck by writing to one of them.*
>
> *Do not contact me again or I will write to Mr Moon, revealing your shame.*
>
> *Gerry*

Daisy stared at the words, open-mouthed. She read it again, astonished all over again as she took in the coldness of the words. What situation had Violet found herself in? And who the bloody hell was Gerry?

Puffing out her cheeks, she set about examining it line by line. It was clearly not the first time Violet had written to this man – he sounded utterly exasperated with her. Could it be something to do with the loss of her job at the castle? Daisy wondered, then dismissed the idea as ridiculous. The timing was wrong for a start, and Gerry made reference to hop picking and farm gossip, which suggested Violet had started work at Half Moon Farm by then. That she'd taken a job there was something Daisy had always known – it was how Violet had met Daisy's grandfather. Could he be the Mr Moon mentioned at the end? She suspected not – Peter Moon would have been a young man in 1946. Gerry probably meant Peter's father – Daisy's great-grandfather. But what shame was Gerry threatening to reveal? What had Violet done to put herself in such peril? Daisy eyed the date again – November 1946. Her grandparents had got married in December of that year, and Rose had been born the following year. Whatever Violet's supposed shame had been, Gerry's threat had been toothless. Violet Finch had become a Moon and lived happily ever after.

Even so, the incongruity nagged at Daisy. Frowning, she read the letter again. It sounded as though Gerry might be a hop picker, which meant he would have been at the farm for the harvest in August and September, but he had moved on by the time Violet wrote to him in November, some two or three months later. Had he stolen something that belonged to Violet? But why would that result in Violet's shame? Daisy lowered the letter to the duvet in frustration. None of it made any sense.

With a weary sigh, she decided it would have to wait until the morning. Replacing the letter in its envelope, she put it with the others on her bedside table and turned off the light. But the mystery whirled around in Daisy's head and it took a long time for sleep to come. Perhaps she would ask Rose if she knew anything about the enigmatic Gerry, she resolved at last, after what felt like hours of staring into the darkness. Because if Rose couldn't shed light on the secret behind this last letter, it was very likely no one could.

* * *

Nancy's eyes were wide when Daisy finished filling her in on Friday morning. 'It's like a real-life detective novel,' she said breathlessly across one of the tables in the Oast House café. 'Ooh, what if Violet witnessed a murder but she wasn't sure who the murderer was and she accused this Gerry guy, but it wasn't him? So she tracked down the others and eventually the killer was caught but not before he tried to silence Violet.'

Daisy raised her eyebrows. 'This is my grandmother we're talking about. She went on to have a long and happy life – I don't think she was running around trying to catch murderers.'

'But that's the thing,' Nancy said, folding her arms. 'What you're discovering is that there's a lot about your grandmother you didn't know. She had a fling with a Devereaux, for a start. That was probably a big scandal at the time.'

The café owner had been agog when Daisy revealed she had uncovered the reason for the long-running feud between the Moons and the Devereauxs, so much so that Daisy had initially regretted telling her. But she'd needed someone to confide in and she wasn't sure she was comfortable discussing something so personal with Kit, in spite of the fact that he'd read Violet's letters to his grandfather and knew some of the rest from Daisy. Nancy had been the obvious, maybe the only, choice for a confidante. 'Even so, I doubt very much she was Half Moon Farm's answer to Miss Marple,' Daisy objected. 'It must be something else.'

Nancy sat lost in thought for a moment, nibbling on a biscuit. 'Could it have been the affair with the earl, then? I bet that was seen as pretty shameful.'

'I think it was all kept quiet,' Daisy said. 'And how would a hop picker know about it? They didn't stick around for more than six weeks.'

'Farm gossip,' Nancy said, tapping the letter. 'But you're right, it doesn't really fit. All that stuff about not being responsible, and the other hop pickers being to blame for her situation, whatever that means. If I didn't know better I'd think—'

She broke off, staring at the letter with sudden understanding. 'You'd think what?' Daisy demanded.

Nancy shook her head. 'You know what? You should ask your mum about this. I'm not saying another word.'

Now it was Daisy's turn to stare. 'Nancy?'

Her friend pressed her lips together and shook her head again, as though she was afraid her suspicions might sneak out. 'Ask your mum,' she repeated. 'And if she doesn't know then I'll tell you what I reckon happened.'

A frown creased Daisy's forehead. 'Why don't you tell me now?'

'Not my place,' Nancy said, getting to her feet. 'If it's what I think it is then it might change everything.'

Daisy groaned. 'You're not making any sense!'

Nancy patted her arm. 'Go and ask your mum. I bet she knows.'

But there was no opportunity for Daisy to ask Rose – Emily had taken her to her monthly knitting group and the farmhouse was empty. Daisy set about clearing away Finn and Campbell's breakfast dishes, trying to distract herself as she pondered Nancy's words. No matter how hard she tried, she couldn't see what her friend had seen. Clearly she was not destined for a career as a sleuth.

Once the kitchen was clean, Daisy went upstairs to pack the boys' bags. Stuart was arriving that afternoon to take them back to Milton Keynes for the first two weeks of the summer holidays and she knew he would want to beat the Friday evening traffic – it made sense to make sure everything was ready. She stood in the middle of the room Finn and Campbell shared, gazing around and marvelling at how different it was now to when they had first arrived. Children tended to spread out in any case but this was most definitely their room now. It felt strange to think she would be packing it all up soon and transporting it back to their own house in Milton Keynes. She wasn't entirely sure it was going to fit.

The unexpected creak of a floorboard made Daisy stop what she was doing. She frowned, cocking her head to listen. Had Emily and Rose forgotten something or come home early? She wondered, but there was no telltale chatter, no thud of feet in the hall. Daisy was just about to dismiss the sound as her imagination when she heard the unmistakable click of a door closing elsewhere in the house. Galvanized into action, she crossed the room and stared around the landing. 'Who's there? Emily, is that you?'

There was no reply. Hurrying down the stairs, Daisy made for the living room. The door was closed but she pulled it open and peered inside. 'Drew!' she gasped in astonishment. 'What are you doing in here?'

He was frozen in the act of rifling through a drawer in the bureau along the far wall, gaping at her as though she was the intruder. 'Hi, Daisy,' he said, after a momentary pause. 'I didn't know you were home.'

She blinked. 'Clearly. Are you looking for something?'

'I am, yes,' he said with an apologetic smile. 'The key to the old shed at the back of the orchard. I thought I heard Atticus in there, decided I'd better check he hadn't got himself trapped.'

'Oh god, that's all I need,' Daisy said, groaning. 'Mum keeps the key in that drawer, does she?'

Drew looked down, rummaging half-heartedly through the contents again. 'I thought she did. Maybe she's moved it.'

Daisy threw up her hands, imagining Atticus stuck in the shed. She didn't want to think what dangers there might be in there. 'Perhaps it's in the kitchen. There are some keys hanging on the wall in the pantry.'

'Well remembered,' Drew said, and he closed the drawer. 'Shall we take a look?'

They checked all the keys. None bore the label *Shed*. 'Now what?' Daisy asked, gazing around the kitchen fretfully.

Where might Rose have put the key? And then she saw it, a long stretch of ginger tail dangling from one of the kitchen chairs. Bending down, she peered underneath the table and saw Atticus curled up, fast asleep. 'Panic over,' she said, straightening up in relief. 'He's not in the shed.'

'Phew,' Drew agreed, clearly as relieved as Daisy. He cocked his head at her as though something had just occurred to him.

'What?' she asked. 'Don't tell me you've remembered where the key is.'

'No. I was just thinking that we have an empty house and at least an hour before anyone will be back.' He reached out to caress her cheek and she was suddenly in no doubt about what he had in mind.

'Drew, I don't think we can—'

But then he was kissing her and all her objections melted away. His fingers tangled in her hair, tugging it free of the band that held it, sending it cascading down her back. She let out a soft moan as his teeth grazed her neck, running her hands across the muscles of his back. 'Upstairs,' he murmured against her skin. 'Your room.'

They shouldn't, Daisy thought distractedly, her mother might come back early. But now Drew was pulling her t-shirt free and sliding his hands underneath and she suspected if they didn't go upstairs now, they might not make it out of the kitchen. 'Okay,' she gasped, stopping his fingers from wandering any further. 'Let's go.'

It felt all wrong having him in her bedroom but somehow

deliciously right. When it was over and they were curled together, tired but content, Daisy found herself smiling against his chest. She hadn't wanted to start anything with him – had fought against it for a long time – but she had to admit she enjoyed their time together. She was going to miss this when she went back to her old life.

It seemed Drew was having similar thoughts. 'Do you have to leave Mistlethorpe?' he asked, brushing his lips across the top of her head. 'Can't you just stay here? The boys seem happy at school and you said yourself Rose needs you. Surely there's more for you here than in Milton Keynes.'

She stirred restlessly. 'It's not that easy. Finn and Campbell need their dad.'

Drew was silent for several seconds. 'But they see him every other weekend. Would it be any different if you lived nearer?'

'Well, no,' Daisy conceded. 'But neither of us would have to drive for hours to drop them off and pick them up. And then there's school – Finn is keen to get back to his football team and Campbell misses his friends.'

He sighed, his breath ruffling her hair. 'And what about what you want, Daisy? Doesn't that count for anything?'

She didn't answer. Having children frequently meant putting their needs above her own – Daisy didn't know many mothers who would be any different. A fleeting image of Alice Devereaux crossed her mind, with a mother who rarely seemed to put her daughter first but with a father who would move heaven and earth for her, and amended her thinking: she didn't know many *parents* who wouldn't put their children's needs above their own.

'What I'm trying to say is that I'm starting to feel something for you, Daisy,' Drew went on. He wriggled out from under her and propped his head on one hand so he could look into her eyes. 'And I think you feel something for me too. So why not stay and see if we can make a go of things?'

Daisy stared at him, the last of her contentment ebbing away. She'd had no idea this was brewing. 'I can't, Drew. It's not that simple.'

'Isn't it?'

'No,' she said, hearing her voice sharpen. 'I have Finn and Campbell to consider.'

He regarded her patiently. 'I know and they're great kids. The kind I would have liked to have, if I'd met the right woman.' Reaching out, he stroked her cheek. 'It's just that I think I have met the right woman now. And she comes with a ready-made family.'

Daisy's head whirled. Where had this come from? She'd assumed they were on the same page – no strings enjoyment of each other's company. When had he begun to make plans for the future? It was all happening so fast. 'Drew, I don't think we can—'

There was a crunch outside, the sound of wheels on the gravel. Daisy disentangled herself, jumping out of bed to peer through the window. 'It's Mum and Emily,' she said, throwing Drew a panicky look. 'Quick, get dressed! You'll have to sneak out when they're not looking.'

His lips quirked as he reached for his clothes. 'Wow. I feel like a teenager again.'

Daisy didn't smile back as she dragged her t-shirt over her head. 'Hurry up.'

'On one condition,' he countered, snaking an arm around her waist and pulling her close. 'Spend the night with me tonight. Come to the cottage – I want to wake up with you beside me tomorrow.'

In spite of everything, Daisy was tempted. 'I can't.'

Drew stopped in the act of putting on his socks. 'Then I'm not sure I can hurry up.'

It was blackmail, she knew, but the way he was looking at her made Daisy want to give in. 'Maybe,' she said. 'But not if you don't get out without my mother seeing you.'

'Promise me,' he countered, smiling.

'Maybe,' she repeated firmly, and thrust his shoes towards him. 'Now finish getting dressed and wait five minutes. I'll get Mum and Emily chatting in the kitchen so you can sneak out.'

He didn't take the shoes. Instead, he stood up and kissed her, hard and urgent and demanding. 'Eight o'clock,' he murmured. 'You know the address.'

She danced free, throwing him an exasperated look. 'Be as quiet as you can,' she whispered from the doorway. 'Don't get caught.'

Thankfully, Emily and Rose were already in the kitchen, making tea. Emily bent down as Daisy entered, scooping up the hairband Drew had tossed onto the floor. 'I think this is yours,' the carer said, as Daisy did her best not to turn scarlet.

'Thanks,' she said, taking care to shut the door before she took the hairband. 'How was knitting club?'

Rose tutted loudly. 'Elsie Wicks is a show off. She wants to yarn bomb Mistlethorpe High Street but she won't let anyone else submit designs.'

Emily raised her eyebrows but said nothing. Daisy bit back the sudden desire to giggle. 'Oh dear. And do you have a design?'

'No, but that's not the point,' Rose snapped. 'Who died and made Elsie queen, that's what I want to know.' Her eyes flitted to the window and suddenly, her expression changed, like the sun emerging from a cloud. 'Oh, there's Drew.'

Daisy's gaze followed. Sure enough, Drew was passing the window. He raised a hand to wave. 'Such a good man,' Rose said, sighing. 'You could do a lot worse, Daisy.'

Too wrung-out to argue, Daisy simply nodded. 'Yes, Mum. I know.'

Chapter Twenty-Six

Both Finn and Campbell were subdued as Daisy drove them back to Half Moon Farm at the end of their last school day. Campbell sighed, staring out of the window as the trees flashed by. 'It felt weird saying goodbye to everyone. I mean, it was hard when we left our old school but we knew we'd be back. This feels like forever.'

Probably because it was forever, Daisy thought, but she wasn't about to say it: today had been tough. She'd already promised to arrange some play dates with Alice over the summer holidays, although Finn rolled his eyes at her use of the words *play date*. But there was no denying that the clock was counting down on their time in Mistlethorpe. They might come back to visit but it wouldn't be quite the same. 'I know,' she said quietly. 'But Dad will be here to collect you soon. Being back in Milton Keynes will take your mind off saying goodbye.'

Thankfully, Stuart's arrival did seem to have the desired

effect. As usual, both boys went into excitement overdrive when his car pulled up outside the farmhouse and it took Daisy several minutes to calm them enough to gather their bags and last-minute essentials. Once outside, she nodded coolly at Stuart, reminded that things were still strained following their argument a few weeks earlier. 'Hello,' she said. 'How was the journey?'

'Not bad,' he said, stretching his back. 'I'll be glad when I don't have to do it anymore.'

'Mmmm,' Daisy said noncommittally. 'I'll pick them up in a couple of weeks. Don't let Finn buy that horrible, overpriced drink he's obsessed with. I'm sure it's got something bad in it.'

Stuart laughed. 'Noted. Anything else I need to know?'

She lowered her voice. 'Campbell is a bit upset about leaving his classmates here. They both are but Cam might need a few extra cuddles tonight.'

'Of course,' he replied. 'It's hard on them, all this moving around. Things will get easier once they're settled in one place.'

It was probably true but Daisy still felt a pang. 'Don't let them stay up too late.'

'I won't.'

The twins appeared in the doorway of the farmhouse, bags in hand. 'Dad!' Finn bellowed, racing across the gravel. 'Can I get some football cards? The new season is out now.'

'We'll see.' Stuart ruffled his hair, then reached across to pat Campbell on the shoulder. 'Cheer up, mate. It might never happen.'

Campbell didn't reply. Instead, he slung his bag into the boot and slid into the back seat of the car. Stuart's gaze met Daisy's. 'Extra extra hugs, I think.'

She nodded. 'Let me know how they're doing,' she said. 'I don't have any plans this weekend.'

Apart from a possible night of passion with Drew, she added silently, but Stuart definitely didn't need to know about that. She waved them off, feeling the usual stab of loss as the car vanished from view. She still hadn't decided whether she would give in to Drew's demand; on one hand, it would be a good distraction from missing the twins but his words from that afternoon pressed heavily on her mind and she couldn't shake the certainty she was already in too deep. What had started as fun was now in danger of careering into a mess as she prepared to leave Mistlethorpe. And as she'd said all along, the last thing she needed was complications.

★ ★ ★

In the end, she took the line of least resistance and drove to Drew's cottage. Part of her reasoning was purely selfish – the farmhouse felt too empty and two weeks seemed like an eternity, even though she knew she'd be pulling her hair out within an hour of Finn and Campbell's return. She wanted to be distracted from missing them, not moping from room to room, and Drew was undoubtedly very good at distracting her. Besides, there wouldn't be many more opportunities like this – once the twins were back, Daisy would be caught up in the whirl of packing. There would be no nights with Drew then. She would just have to make sure he understood that this was all she could give him, reinforce that she fully intended to leave at the end of August and no amount of persuasion would make her change her mind.

But it seemed Drew had picked up on her reticence that afternoon. During the course of the evening, he didn't raise the spectre of her leaving and focused instead on making her laugh. And later, when they went to bed, he did what he did best, so that she fell asleep spent. In the morning, he made her a late breakfast and made no argument when she said she needed to leave. 'Come back soon,' he whispered as he kissed her goodbye. 'I'm missing you already.'

Sunday was Emily's day off. Daisy spent the day with Rose, taking her out for lunch in Mistlethorpe and watching for any signs of mental deterioration. She'd asked the whereabouts of the key to the shed, had observed Rose's bewildered expression as she tried to think of its location. 'But I don't remember having a key to that shed,' she said, her brow crinkled. 'It's always been left unlocked.'

'Drew said there's a key,' Daisy said and Rose's frown had deepened.

'I suppose if Drew says there's one then there must be,' she allowed. 'But I don't know where it is.'

In the evening, Daisy joined Rose in the living room,

half watching a quiz while her mother knitted. The two bundles of letters were on the coffee table. Daisy was scouring them for any clue to the identity of Gerry, even though she knew she wouldn't find one. After a short while, Rose lowered her knitting and fixed Daisy with an impassive stare. 'Are those Violet's letters?'

'Some of them,' Daisy replied. 'The rest belonged to Valentine.'

She watched her mother from under her lashes, gauging her reaction. Sure enough, Rose stiffened. 'Where did you get those? The ones to him.'

Daisy took a breath. 'From Kit Devereaux. He asked his brother, Hugh, for them.'

Rose's nostrils flared. 'You're on first name terms with them now, are you? Your grandparents will be rolling in their graves.'

Weary after a long day, Daisy felt her temper slip a little. 'Yes, I am, as a matter of fact. They're not monsters, or even especially terrible. I don't see the point in nursing a feud over something that happened more than seventy years ago.'

'They ruined your grandmother's life,' Rose bit back. 'And they tried to ruin mine.'

Daisy shook her head. 'That's not entirely true. I've read these letters over and over – both sides of the story – and I've come to realize that Violet made her own choices.' Rose started to argue but Daisy held up a hand. 'I'm not saying Valentine acted well but she must have known she was playing with fire. And of course I'm sorry she got burned

351

but her life wasn't ruined. She married Grandpa, had you. I think she found happiness in the end.'

Rose glared at her. 'And what about me? What excuses are you going to make for the way that family treated me?'

'None,' Daisy said simply. 'They behaved badly, refusing to allow you into the castle that night, without a thought of how you might get home, but it wasn't Hugh's fault and it certainly had nothing to do with Kit, who wasn't even born. Sooner or later, we have to let go of the past before it consumes us.'

Again, Rose looked ready to argue but something in what Daisy had said seemed to hit home. She deflated back into her chair, suddenly looking old. 'Some of them were monsters. But I suppose you might have a point,' she allowed grudgingly. 'You let go of the past when you came back here to look after me.'

It was the tiniest chink in her mother's bitterness but at least it was a start. 'I did,' she said steadfastly. 'And I would do exactly the same thing again. It's only when we give the past power that it can hurt us.'

Rose grunted. 'Sounds like one of those motivational posters they have in the library.'

Daisy couldn't help it. She laughed. 'Fair point,' she conceded. Her gaze came to rest on the cream envelope containing the letter from Gerry. 'Speaking of the past, there is something I wanted to ask you about.'

'Oh?' Rose said, her gaze suddenly wary once more. 'What's that?'

Unfolding the letter, Daisy held it out. 'This is a letter to Violet, from someone called Gerry. I don't really understand it, or even who he is – do you know anything about it?'

For a moment, she thought her mother would refuse to take the single sheet of paper. Seconds ticked by while she stared at it, her mouth pressed into a hard, thin line. 'Gerry,' she said at last. 'That's a name I haven't heard in a long time.'

'There's no surname, and no address,' Daisy said. 'Just that first name and some pretty confusing assertions.'

Still Rose didn't take the letter but the tension around her mouth lessened. 'I suppose it was inevitable,' she said, shaking her head. 'You'd better let me see it.'

Slowly, she unfolded the paper and gazed down at the words. More seconds ticked by, stretching into minutes now. Eventually, Rose sighed and lowered the letter to her lap. 'What do you want to know?' she asked Daisy, her voice curiously leaden.

Daisy frowned. 'Who Gerry is, for a start. And what Grandma was accusing him of. I can't imagine it was anything too terrible, since nothing ever came of it.'

Her mother let out a low, mirthless laugh. 'Not nothing,' she said in a flat tone. 'Just me.'

Daisy felt the world flip upside down. She stared at Rose, certain she'd misheard. 'What?'

'I said, just me,' Rose repeated. 'I was what came of my mother's relationship with Gerry. Although relationship is too generous, as far as I can tell – it was just one night. Probably not even that.'

The air in the room seemed to have turned to treacle, thick and heavy. Daisy struggled to breathe. 'But Grandpa – they got married that December.'

Rose nodded. 'He knew, of course. She was scared witless, didn't know where to turn. He found her crying in one of the barns, made her tell him everything. The next thing she knew he'd proposed. Said it didn't matter that she didn't love him, he'd take care of her and the baby no matter what.'

And at last, everything fell into place. 'Oh,' Daisy murmured. Tears sprang into her eyes as she thought of the kind and gentle man who had been her grandfather, even more of a gentleman than she'd ever known. 'Oh.'

'She'd have been ruined otherwise,' Rose went on, matter of fact. 'Unmarried mothers went into a home, their babies were taken away. We didn't always see eye to eye, me and him, but I always loved him for that.'

Daisy almost didn't hear – she was too busy revisiting her childhood memories, seeing them through the filter of this new understanding. 'And she loved him,' she said, after a moment. 'Violet, I mean. I saw them with each other – they always seemed so very in love.'

'They were,' Rose acknowledged. 'It might have been a marriage of convenience at first but they were true soulmates. And he never made me feel like I wasn't his.'

'No,' Daisy said, as a memory of Peter Moon presenting her with her first bike floated across her mind, followed by another of him bathing her knee when she'd fallen off. A tear squeezed its way out of the corner of her eye. 'Me either.'

Rose sighed. 'I think he blamed Valentine more than Gerry. He thought Valentine led her on, made promises he couldn't keep and broke her heart, made her vulnerable. So when Gerry appeared the following summer, hops weren't all he picked.'

In the midst of all the revelations, this was the one that gave Daisy a sharp needle of anger. 'He didn't own up, though. He denied you were his, threatened to tell everyone Violet was pregnant.'

'Turned out that was a blessing in disguise,' her mother said in a practical tone. 'It took me a long time to see it but eventually I realized what kind of man he was. Around the same time that I came to see your grandfather for the man he was too.'

It was almost too much for Daisy to take in. The man she'd always known as her grandfather wasn't her blood relative, and yet somehow that made him more her grandfather than ever. But having the final piece of the puzzle only raised another ghost from the past. She gazed at her mother. 'So what made you do the same to me?' she asked quietly. 'Why did you let me grow up without a father?'

Rose met her eyes without flinching. 'Because I was a fool and went looking for love with someone who didn't deserve it,' she said. 'When I realised I was in trouble, I told him what had happened, and just like Gerry, he didn't want to know. So I came back here and confessed everything to the one man I knew I could trust. And he told me I didn't have to worry – that he would be father and grandfather to you, for as long as I needed him to be.'

The dam broke. The tears that had been stinging the back of Daisy's eyes coursed down her cheeks as she realized the true marvel Peter Moon had been. She wished she'd known the truth but at the same time, she was glad she hadn't. Being protected had allowed her to love him exactly as she should. The fact that they didn't share the same blood didn't matter at all.

When Daisy's tears slowed, she saw her mother's cheeks were wet too. Pushing past the table, she knelt at Rose's side. 'Thank you for telling me.'

Rose pursed her lips, then let out a long, shuddering sigh. 'It's about time. I might have done it years ago but Vince always said I shouldn't.' She shook her head. 'It was the biggest mistake of my life, listening to him. I'm sorry, Daisy. You deserved to know the truth long ago.'

Daisy glanced at the letters, laid out on the table, and wondered how her younger self would have reacted. 'I think I found out when I was supposed to.'

'Maybe,' Rose said, blinking as though she might cry again. 'But I'm glad you know now. I've been carrying this secret a long time.'

Daisy wrapped her arms around her mother's shoulders. 'You don't have to carry it anymore, Mum,' she said, her own eyes growing damp. 'Like everything else that went before, it's time to let it go.'

Chapter Twenty-Seven

In the immediate aftermath, Daisy wasn't sure why she thought of Kit first. It should have been Nancy she went to – she was convinced her friend had guessed the truth already – or even Drew, but for reasons she only partly understood, Winterbourne was where she longed to be. She wanted to sit under the tree Violet had loved and sift through everything she'd discovered during her tumultuous conversation with her mother. But perhaps it wasn't so very strange that she felt drawn to the walled garden, since that was where it had all started. Perhaps that was why she trusted Kit with the whole story, that Monday afternoon, as they nursed mugs of hot chocolate under overcast skies. He'd been the one who'd revealed the carved initials in the trunk of the tree, setting Daisy on this journey, and Valentine was his grandfather. She thought he had a right to know how the ripples of that doomed love affair had affected so many lives.

'Wow,' he said, when Daisy finally drew to the end. 'Wow.'

'I know,' she said, taking a long sip of her drink. 'I had no idea when I found those letters that I'd end up unravelling the fabric of my own family.'

'But you didn't. What you found was that the fabric had been stitched differently than you expected. In a way that made it stronger and more likely to endure.' He gave her a pensive look. 'I wish I could say the same about my lot. We've been coming apart at the seams for a long time.'

'I'm sure that's not true,' she objected, although she knew exactly what he meant. 'You've got centuries of tradition holding you together.'

Kit snorted. 'But no actual love. Your grandmother was lucky – she got over my grandfather and found a happiness she would never have had with him. Whereas he chose his title and all this—' He waved an encompassing hand. 'And he never got over losing the love of his life. Then there's me, determined to marry for love, except I had no idea what a healthy relationship looked like and ended up marrying a woman who only wanted my title.'

Daisy frowned. 'But you don't have a title.'

'She didn't know that when she married me,' Kit said, shrugging. 'Back then, Hugh and his wife were struggling to conceive. It seemed quite likely they couldn't have children and Araminta quite naturally assumed everything would come to me. When she realized it wouldn't . . .'

Daisy's mouth dropped a little. 'She left you,' she finished indignantly.

'She left me,' Kit echoed. 'But worse than that, she left

Alice. I took her back a few times, hoping she'd see how much Alice needed her, but it was never enough. *We* were never enough. And now Hugh has Cressida and the baby, so I still have nothing to offer.' He managed a bleak smile. 'It's Alice I feel worst for. She didn't do anything wrong.'

Daisy placed a hand on his arm. 'Nor did you. Except for marrying the wrong person but that happens all the time.'

That elicited a reluctant smile. 'Is that what you did?'

She conjured up a mental picture of Stuart, who had been everything she wanted and needed for years, and who was as devoted to the twins as he'd ever been. 'No, I married the right person,' she said. 'He just wasn't forever.'

'Ah,' Kit said, and hesitated, as though unsure whether to go on. 'And Drew? Is he someone you want to spend forever with?'

Daisy glanced at him, remembering his vehement, eloquently expressed dislike. What was the story there? She wondered, not for the first time. There had to be more to it than a childhood friendship that hadn't lasted. 'Drew is . . .' she trailed off, trying to marshal her thoughts.

'An absolute cad?' Kit put in, then lifted his hands in surrender. 'Sorry. I know it's none of my business. Go on. Drew is . . .'

Excellent in bed, Daisy wanted to say but felt that was probably more information than Kit needed. 'He's what I needed in the short term.' She stopped and considered the words again. 'Or what I thought I needed.'

He was watching her carefully. 'But now you're not so sure?'

Daisy puffed out her cheeks. 'I don't know.' She glanced at Kit, wondering how much she could trust him. 'He wants more than I can give. More than I'm ready to give, maybe.'

Kit sipped his hot chocolate in silence. 'That doesn't sound like a forever match.'

Which was easy for him to say, she thought with a flurry of irritation, given he didn't like Drew. 'What about you?' she challenged. 'Have you thought about giving love a second chance? And don't tell me you're in love with your plane or something lame like that.'

He laughed and she found herself noticing the way his face lit up when he was happy. 'No, I'm not in love with my plane,' he said, throwing her an amused look. 'I suppose I'm just waiting for the right person. One who understands about Alice and accepts we come as a package.'

Her heart ached a little for him, and the scars that clearly still pulled. He was a dedicated father who put his daughter first, as well as a talented pilot and successful businessman who lived in a *bona fide* castle, albeit one he didn't actually own. There would be a queue of women eagerly waiting if he ever joined a dating app. And yet it seemed he couldn't see his own worth. Araminta had a lot to answer for, Daisy thought darkly. 'For what it's worth, I think you're a catch,' she said stoutly. 'Even without a title.'

'Thanks,' he said, his smile widening as he dissected the compliment. 'I think.'

She raised her mug to his. 'Here's to finding our forever person.'

Kit chinked his cup against hers. 'And recognizing them when we do.'

* * *

The two weeks passed more quickly than Daisy would have thought possible. She spent several nights with Drew, who seemed to have realized he'd come on too strong and had reverted to his previous carefree self, allowing Daisy to pretend she wasn't hurtling towards a painful break up. She visited Winterbourne too, and managed to find the peacock mosaic Violet had written about creating from shells in one of her letters to Valentine. One day Daisy hoped she would show her mother the mosaic, and let her breathe in the heady scent of the roses Violet had planted — the blooms she had loved so much that she'd named her only child for them — but for now she enjoyed these small pleasures on her own.

She was washing up in the farmhouse kitchen on Thursday morning when a pair of arms encircled her waist and a voice whispered 'Boo!' in her ear. Yelping, she spun around, finding herself face to face with Drew. He kissed her, a long and thorough effort that left her leaning against the sink, rather weak at the knees. 'Don't do that in here,' she said, although the words lacked any actual rigour.

'Why not?' he said, leaning in to kiss her again.

This time, she wriggled away. 'Because my mother might walk in at any moment.'

'Let her,' he said, shrugging. 'She'll be happy. Rose loves me.'

Daisy couldn't argue with that. 'How did you get in here?' she asked, with a sudden frown.

'The door was open,' he replied. 'I saw my gorgeous girlfriend standing at the sink and couldn't keep my hands off her. There's nothing wrong with that, is there?'

Except that she wasn't his girlfriend, Daisy thought with a little niggle of annoyance. 'Please don't do it again,' she said, and now her tone was much more forbidding.

He sighed. 'But I want people to know about us. Can't we at least tell your mother?'

'Tell me what?' Rose asked from the doorway. She looked from Daisy to Drew. 'Well?'

Daisy opened her mouth to speak but Drew got there first. 'I'm in love with your daughter, Rose. And she's in love with me, although she's not ready to admit it yet.'

'Drew!' Daisy stared at him in consternation.

'Oh, I knew it!' Rose clapped her hands with joy. 'I knew he'd win you over in the end.'

'He hasn't,' Daisy said, glaring at Drew.

'She's not ready,' he said confidingly to Rose. 'But one day soon she'll realize the truth.'

Daisy's simmering temper began to boil. 'I won't.'

Rose rolled her eyes. 'Stubborn. Just like her grandmother.'

'Mum!' Daisy exclaimed. 'Please stop this. Drew is not my boyfriend. We're not— this isn't—' She broke off helplessly because it was clear Rose was only prepared to hear what she wanted to hear. 'Drew, I think you'd better leave.'

He didn't argue but, to her fury, he winked at Rose on

the way out. Daisy ground her teeth and turned back to the sink.

'He'll win you over in the end,' Rose repeated knowingly. 'You're wasting your time fighting it.'

'Not when I'm going back to Milton Keynes in a month,' Daisy said, her tone more clipped than she intended.

She heard Rose sniff. 'A bit of distance never hurt anyone. If you want to make it work, you will.'

'And what if I don't want to make it work?'

'You will,' Rose said confidently. 'Just wait and see.'

It was all Daisy could do not to slam the last plate back into the soap suds. Instead she carefully rinsed it, placed it on the draining board and dried her hands on a tea towel. 'I'm going to the café,' she said, striving to keep her voice light and even. 'See you later.'

She'd been hoping Nancy would be there, ready to lend a sympathetic ear, but her friend had gone to the wholesaler. Daisy ordered a tall latte and a Chelsea bun. When she tried to pay, the card machine merely beeped. 'Been having trouble with this all day,' the girl behind the counter said, her cheeks growing pink. 'I don't suppose you've got cash, have you?'

Daisy nodded and rummaged in her purse for the twenty pound note she'd tucked inside yesterday. It wasn't there. Frowning, she dug deeper, then scoured the inside of her handbag. The money was nowhere to be seen. 'I've done that,' the girl said sympathetically. 'Gone to pay for something and the note has slipped out of my pocket somewhere. Annoying, isn't it?'

'Mmmm,' Daisy said distractedly. Her purse had been zipped closed – surely the money couldn't have slipped out.

'You can pop in and pay later if you like,' the girl said. 'Nancy won't mind – she knows where you live, after all.'

'Thank you,' Daisy said. 'I was sure I had some cash. Never mind.'

She retraced her tracks, keeping her eyes on the ground in case the money had fallen out en route but there was no sign of it. Irritated, Daisy took her coffee up to her room, preferring that to risking another run in with her mother. Drew's behaviour had set her teeth on edge – more than that, had made her angry – and Rose had done nothing to help. But the scene had made Daisy realize she needed to have a serious chat with Drew, and soon. There could be no more nights spent at his cottage, not when he trampled roughshod over her wishes and ignored her protestations. It was time to do what she really should have done weeks ago and end things. She would do it the next day, before she went to collect the twins from Stuart.

By the time Daisy went downstairs again, her bad temper had cooled. She found Emily in the living room looking puzzled. 'Emily? Is everything okay?'

'I suppose so,' the carer said, and let out a shaky laugh. 'I lost my purse for a while but it's turned up.'

Daisy frowned. 'That's odd. Did you put it down somewhere and forget?'

'No,' Emily said, then shook her head. 'It doesn't matter. I expect it was my mistake.'

Daisy felt her frown deepen, sensing there was more to it than the carer was letting on. Emily was usually very sensible and well organized. She always knew where everything was, including Finn's shin pads, which got lost every other day. 'Where did you find it?'

Emily didn't meet her gaze. 'In your mother's knitting bag.'

It was the last thing she'd been expecting to hear. Under the sofa, perhaps, if Atticus had mistaken it for something he could kill, or snagged down the side of a chair. But in Rose's knitting bag was a bit of a head scratcher. It was possible it might have fallen there but Daisy had to admit it seemed unlikely. 'How did it get there?'

'I don't know,' Emily said unhappily. 'It was under all the wool. And there's something else – I'm sure I had a couple of twenty-pound notes in there but it's empty now.'

And now Daisy felt something else settle in the pit of her stomach. It couldn't be a coincidence that she'd also lost money from her purse, could it? But why would Rose steal from them? She had plenty of money of her own. 'I'm so sorry, Emily. I'll replace the missing cash.' Daisy held up a hand as the carer tried to object. 'No, I insist. I've been meaning to talk to you for a while about Mum but this has brought it to a head.' Taking a deep breath, she sought the right phrasing. She didn't want to use the D word. Not yet. 'I've noticed she's said a few odd things recently, maybe even done some strange things. Do you think there's a chance she might have – that there could be something wrong with her?'

Emily looked wretched. 'Not before today,' she said. 'But

stealing is so out of character. It might be a sign that there's something we don't know about.'

'I think so too,' Daisy replied. 'Perhaps it's time for a visit to the GP.'

The theft of the money niggled at Daisy all afternoon. It was so very strange for Rose to suddenly start helping herself – she couldn't understand what had prompted it. Hearing Rose in the living room, Daisy decided to see if she could catch her out. 'Mum, we're out of milk. Have you got any cash so I can nip to the shops?'

She held her breath, watching her mother's face closely. It wasn't something she'd ever asked before, so a moment of confusion would be understandable but that wasn't what Daisy was interested in. She was alert for a sly flash of guilt. But Rose simply nodded. 'Of course,' she said, digging into her battered leather handbag. 'Is ten pounds enough?'

Daisy peered beyond her mother's fingers, trying to see whether a sheaf of notes nestled in the purse, but she couldn't see clearly. Then Rose frowned and looked up, embarrassed. 'Oh, it seems I don't have any money after all. How strange.'

She held up the purse, giving Daisy a bird's eye view of the red-lined pockets, both of which were empty. 'Did you have some earlier?' Daisy asked, taken aback.

Rose offered a helpless shrug. 'I thought I did. Perhaps I spent it, although I'm not sure where.'

She looked so distraught that Daisy wanted to comfort her. There had been no disingenuity in her expression when she'd opened the purse, no guilt when Daisy had first asked.

No sign of anything other than a willingness to help. 'Not to worry, I'll pay by card. Honestly, it's fine.'

She walked into the kitchen as though in a trance. One lot of missing money might be carelessness – three was looking like something else entirely, assuming Rose wasn't simply mistaken. But when had the money been taken? And, more importantly, how? Only three people had been in the house – Daisy, Emily and Rose – and all of them had lost money, albeit relatively small amounts. She'd heard tales of magpies flying in through open windows to steal jewellery but never the kind of money that folded. And Atticus was wily and determined in pursuit of his prey but Daisy doubted he had learned how to open zips or undo a press stud. No, unless they were all mistaken in their belief that they'd lost money, there was only one explanation. Someone else had been in the house.

And then it hit her – the memory of Drew sneaking up behind her that morning. He'd said the door was open – could someone have crept in and rifled through their purses while they were talking in the kitchen? But the farmhouse was hardly on the beaten track. The thief would be taking an enormous risk – if they were caught, they'd need a plausible reason for being there. Her thoughts coalesced. Someone who could reasonably claim they were there to see a member of the family, or trimming the apple trees, or looking for the key to a shed. Daisy's stomach flipped. Someone like Drew.

She sat down heavily at the kitchen table, scarcely able

to believe what she was thinking. A bee buzzed through the open window and she absently waved it back out, her mind whirring. Surely there must be another solution, some other way to explain the missing money. But she knew, even as she considered and dismissed the possibilities again, that Drew was the only answer that made sense. What if he hadn't been rifling through the drawer in search of the key at all, but in search of money? The lie had come fast and easily to him, if so; she'd had no idea he wasn't telling the truth. And doubting his honesty now made Daisy wonder about the times her mother had told her Drew was organizing some work on the house – the windows or the roof. She'd assumed Rose was confused but what if that wasn't the case at all? What if Drew had been taking money from her for work that didn't need to be done?

It was a wild accusation and one Daisy wasn't about to make without proof. But she had no idea how to get it, short of laying a trap for him, and she didn't know how to go about that either. If this was a detective novel, she would have a clever plan that enlisted the help of her trusted associates but she didn't want to share her suspicions with Rose or Emily yet. She wanted to be sure. And she thought she knew someone who could help.

Kit answered immediately. 'Hello, Daisy. Everything okay?'

The enquiry wasn't a surprise – she didn't think she'd ever called him before. 'There's something I need to ask you,' she said, aware her voice sounded tight. 'Have you got a minute?'

'Sure, hold on.' There was a muffled mumbling, a random series of bumps and clicks that suggested he was moving, and then he was back. 'Okay, I'm outside. What's up?'

She took a long breath in and let it out slowly. 'You once told me Drew wasn't the person I thought he was. What made you say that?'

There was a short silence, during which she pictured him gaping in surprise. 'Why are you asking? Has something happened?'

'I'd rather not say right now,' she replied. 'Can you tell me why you don't like him?'

She heard his tone stiffen. 'What's going on, Daisy? If he's hurt you then—'

'He hasn't hurt me,' she cut in reassuringly. 'I just – well, I have a suspicion. Something I can't prove and I wondered if your reason for warning me off him was connected, that's all.'

Another silence. 'I see,' Kit said eventually, and she got the impression he was wrestling with a dilemma. 'But unless Drew has had an affair with your wife, I don't see how it can be.'

The phone almost slipped from Daisy's fingers. She fumbled to catch it, somehow managed to turn it upside down, and then swore as Kit's words replayed in her head. So *that* was the reason they were no longer friends. She let out a low groan. 'Bloody hell, Kit. I wish you'd told me.'

'I tried. That morning outside the school. You told me it was none of my business.'

She had, Daisy remembered as hot and cold shivers chased each other down her spine. She'd been positively rude. Because Drew had laid the groundwork, telling her Kit had come back from the RAF with PTSD, that his wife had left him because of his erratic moods. And instead of comparing the story to what she knew of Kit, she'd taken Drew's explanation at face value. Then again, she'd had no reason to think he might be lying. Until now. 'I did,' she said into the telephone, the words little more than a moan. 'I'm so sorry, Kit. That was unforgivable, especially given you were trying to protect me.'

He grunted. 'Never mind that now, tell me what he's done. Do I need to pull one of my great-grandfather's rapiers off the wall and come round there?'

That image at least made her smile. 'No, it's nothing like that.' She puffed out her cheeks and lowered her voice. 'I think he's been stealing from us. It sounds like Mum has been giving him money for bogus repairs and I caught him going through some drawers the other week, although he explained it away convincingly enough. But I'm starting to suspect he has a key to the house and I'm wondering how many times in the past he's let himself in.'

The silence stretched even longer this time and Daisy didn't like to imagine Kit's stony expression. 'Those are criminal offences. Do you want to involve the police?'

'No!' Daisy said instantly. 'Like I said, I don't have any proof. And the boys will be home tomorrow – I don't want their last few weeks in Mistlethorpe ruined by this.'

'Okay,' Kit said. 'I'll have a think. Just don't confront him, whatever you do. I know from experience that he's a nasty piece of work when he's cornered. Try to keep out of his way, if you can. And double lock the doors.'

'I will,' she said, feeling shaky at the thought of Drew turning on her. He'd never shown the slightest sign of a brutish temperament but she was starting to realize she didn't know much about the real Drew at all. 'And thank you for telling me about Araminta. I'm sorry to drag up more unhappy memories.'

'It just reminds me how much better off I am without her,' he replied. 'Call me if you need me, okay?'

'Okay,' she said, and hung up.

On autopilot, she got up and switched the kettle on. She couldn't remember when she last ate or drank anything – the latte she'd got from the café, she supposed, which felt like days ago now. Without thinking, she started to lay the tea tray but she was distracted by the ping of a message – Stuart, reminding her to bring some trainers for Finn. She put her phone down on the worktop without replying. Another bee, or perhaps the same one, buzzed around the open window. 'Shoo,' she said in exasperation, stepping forward to wave it out again. 'I don't need you in here, I'm trying to think.'

Then a movement caught her eye. She looked up to see Drew standing outside. 'Hello, Daisy,' he said, smiling the same smile that used to make her stomach flip with desire but now only filled her with trepidation. 'I think we need to talk.'

Chapter Twenty-Eight

Forcing herself to breathe, Daisy tried to look unconcerned. She raised her chin and met his gaze with cool indifference. 'So it seems,' she said, stretching out a hand towards her phone, beside the tea tray and, she hoped, just out of Drew's line of sight. 'How long exactly have you been stealing from my mother?'

He ran a hair through his hair. 'I haven't. Look, I can explain everything.'

Daisy's gaze slid carefully sideways as she pressed her fingerprint onto the screen of her phone. Slowly, without appearing to take her attention from Drew, she navigated to the list of recent calls and pressed redial. The screen lit up with a green icon – *Calling Kit* . . . 'It's too late for that,' she said, praying Kit would answer but not wanting to watch the screen in case Drew guessed what she was doing. 'Don't treat me like an idiot. How long have you been stealing from this house?'

He studied her narrowly, as though trying to gauge her conviction, then shrugged. 'A few years. Since your father died.'

'He wasn't my father,' she snapped, causing Drew to raise his eyebrows.

'Okay, since your *stepfather* died,' he corrected. 'I knew better than to try and con him. As a matter of fact, he was the one who gave me the idea – he had his feet nicely under the table here, didn't want for much.' He smiled and she felt a sudden crawl of revulsion that she'd ever allowed his hands to touch her. 'Once he was gone, it was easy. But I only took what I needed – for food and to pay my bills. You have to believe me, Daisy, I'm not proud of myself. But I can change – with your help, I can change.'

She stared at him. 'What do you mean, with my help? Why would I help you?'

He fixed her with a beseeching look. 'Because I love you. And I think you love me.'

Daisy wanted to laugh. 'Don't give me that rubbish. If you loved me, you wouldn't steal from me.'

'I didn't,' he insisted. 'Not at first, anyway.'

Now she did laugh, a harsh incredulous bark that hurt her throat. 'Don't waste your time, Drew. I don't actually care why you took the money. I'm just sickened that you preyed on an old woman.'

He stared at her wide-eyed, as though determined to make her see sense. 'I do love you, Daisy, even if you don't believe me.'

He looked so convincing, so much like the man she'd thought he was, that for a moment Daisy wavered. Then she shook the glamour away. 'I don't think you even know what the word means. But I'm curious, what was your plan – to bleed my mother dry and then move onto the next victim?'

There was a wounded silence. 'How can you say that? I'm not heartless.'

Daisy merely waited, her face cold and implacable. Finally, Drew sighed. 'Okay, I admit there was a plan but it isn't what you think.' He took a deep breath. 'I did it for the farm. When Vince died it started falling down around Rose's ears. I thought if I moved in, I could repair it. But I couldn't move into Half Moon Farm with Rose – too many alarm bells would have rung. And then you came and all my prayers were answered.'

Daisy gawped at him. 'I'm sorry – what? You did it for the *farm*?'

'And for you, Daisy. It would have been so easy and I knew we'd be happy.'

It was all too much for Daisy. 'But—' She shook her head, realizing he was weaving another spell around her. 'I don't believe you. Or maybe I believe half of it. You wanted the farm, the life my stepfather lived, but not me. I was just a bonus.'

Drew studied her, then seemed to realize she was not going to be fooled. 'You were the perfect cover. Like I said, I couldn't move in with Rose, but you? No one would have questioned it if we'd fallen in love and decided to live together.'

The admission was so revolting that Daisy thought she might be sick. 'But why? You've got your own cottage, a decent business with the mistletoe and the brewery.'

He shook his head, still faintly sorrowful. 'The business barely earns enough to cover my rent at the cottage and don't even get me started about that loser, Nigel.' His eyes narrowed. 'By the time I've paid everything, I don't have enough to buy food. I knew Rose had far more money than she needed, so I decided we could help each other – a bit like the mistletoe and the apple trees – symbiosis in action. I did some odd jobs around the farm and she paid me.'

'Except that you didn't actually fix anything,' Daisy pointed out in a scathing voice. 'The roof was falling in when I arrived.'

Drew threw her an injured look. 'I was going to get that done. But everything changed when you turned up – all of a sudden I needed money for dinner and wine. It seemed like a worthwhile risk to cream a bit more cash. I wanted to impress you.'

Daisy's lip curled. 'So you could get the ultimate prize – Half Moon Farm.'

'Not just the farm,' he said, shaking his head with an earnestness she didn't buy for a second. 'You as well. I wasn't faking all that passion, Daisy. I wanted you the moment I saw you, suddenly the farm wasn't enough.' He pursed his lips as though deep in thought. 'The kids I could have done without but I figured I could put up with them.'

It was the first honest thing Daisy thought he'd said and

it filled her with a white-hot rage. 'It's a good thing you screwed up, isn't it? You didn't get the prize – not the farm, not the money and most definitely not me and my sons. So this is what's going to happen next. You're going to leave this place. Leave Mistlethorpe, in fact.'

'Says who?' He sneered, as the last veneer of pretence dropped away like a discarded costume and revealed who he truly was. 'Like you said, you've got no proof. It's your word against mine.'

Adopting what she hoped was an expression of supreme confidence, she waved a hand at her phone. 'That's where you're wrong. I called Kit back when I saw you outside the window. He's heard every word of your confession.'

'You're lying,' he said but she saw from his nervous glance that he was worried.

'I'm not,' she replied, hoping against hope that Kit had picked up her call. 'And I think the testimony of a Devereaux would carry a lot more weight, don't you? If you don't leave Mistlethorpe today and never come back, we'll go straight to the police and tell them everything.'

He shook his head. 'You're lying,' he said again, and this time there was a snarl beneath the words.

'I'm really not,' she said, and crossed her fingers as hard as she could. 'Am I, Kit?'

For a nano-second nothing happened. And then Kit's voice, tinny but unmistakeable, sounded from the handset. 'Sorry to disappoint you, Drew, but Daisy is correct. You'd better do as she says.'

'Oh, please,' Drew said, rolling his eyes. 'What are you going to do, posh boy? Give me a stern talking to?'

'I think we'll leave that to the police,' Daisy said, digging her fingers into the worktop to hide her relief. 'Go away now, Drew. I never want to see you again.'

His scowl contorted into an ugly mask. He stepped forward, raising a clenched fist, and Daisy honestly had no idea what he might have done if Atticus had not chosen that moment to leap at the window ledge and launch himself, hissing and growling, at Drew's head. There was a furious slash of ginger paws, a screech of pain and suddenly Drew was backing away, swiping at the cat in an effort to pull it from his face. Atticus increased his frenzy, yowling like a banshee and digging in with his claws. Daisy saw blood trickle down the side of Drew's face. 'Atticus, leave!'

The cat hissed his disagreement but Daisy, fearful that he might get hurt, steeled her voice. 'Atticus, STOP!' When he showed no sign of obeying, she gazed wildly around the kitchen for something else to tempt him. Her eyes came to rest on an open packet of *Fishy Delishy* and she snatched it up, tipped the treats into her palm and waved the packet so it crackled. The effect was instant. Atticus sheathed his claws and bounced off Drew's head, landing neatly on the ground and prowling towards the window. Leaping lightly up, he bent to delicately swipe one of the treats from her outstretched palm.

'That cat's a menace,' Drew roared, dabbing his wounds with his fingers.

'Luckily, he's not your problem, Drew,' Daisy called, as her hands started to shake. 'Now get off my land before I call the police.'

★ ★ ★

Kit didn't want her to drive alone to Milton Keynes the next day but Daisy insisted she was fine. 'It'll do me good to get out of the village,' she replied. 'And perhaps by the time I get back, Drew will have cleared out too.'

Although there was a decent chance he'd gone already. Kit and Athers had visited his cottage and reported that no one seemed to be home. Kit himself had stayed the night at Half Moon Farm, much to Rose's barely hidden disgust. But by bedtime, he'd managed to charm her, if only a little. Daisy was sure she'd almost seen her mother smile at one point.

She'd rung Stuart from the car on the way up, preferring to explain what had happened without the told-you-so look in his eyes. He hadn't said much, beyond reassuring himself she was unhurt, but had met her on the drive of his house and pulled her into an enormous hug the moment she'd got out of the car. She'd nearly cried then but the sight of Finn and Campbell in the doorway encouraged her to hold things together. And now she was leaning against the counter in Stuart's kitchen, her fingers wrapped around a mug of tea as she tried to avoid meeting his gaze.

'I can't believe you got fooled by a confidence trickster,' Stuart said, shaking his head in wonder. 'You've always been so smart about that kind of thing.'

It wasn't anything Daisy hadn't berated herself for a thousand times. She sighed. 'I know. But everyone seemed to like him – Nancy said he was a good guy, if a bit commitment shy, and Mum absolutely loved him. Only Kit had a bad word to say about him, which makes sense once you know what Drew did with his wife.'

'Kit,' Stuart said, frowning. 'That's the earl, right?'

'No, that's Hugh,' Daisy corrected. 'Kit is his brother but he lives at the castle. Campbell and Finn are friends with his daughter.'

Stuart nodded. 'That would be Alice, yes? They haven't stopped talking about her. I think they've been chatting on the PlayStation or something.'

'Sounds about right,' Daisy said, smiling.

He leaned against the opposite counter and studied her. 'So what are you going to do?'

It was the question she'd been dreading the most. 'I don't know,' she said helplessly. 'Obviously Mum can't be left on her own, not even with Emily or Magda, but I suppose I could look at getting a male carer to stay over at night. Not that I think Drew will come back but you never know.'

'He'd better not,' Stuart growled.

'Anyway,' Daisy went on, 'I think I can get away with going down there every other weekend, as long as you're okay to have the boys, and maybe with more care, Mum will be all right.'

He held up a hand. 'With respect, Daisy, that isn't going to work.'

Her heart sank. He'd always been so good at co-parenting the twins. Was he about to tell her he wasn't prepared to do that anymore? 'What do you mean?'

'You can't live like that,' he said. 'Finn and Campbell can't either. They need a full-time mum, not one who always has an eye on the traffic to Kent.'

'Then what do you suggest?' she asked, suddenly aware that tears were prickling her eyes. 'I can't just pretend Mum doesn't exist – look what happened last time I tried that.'

Stuart's eyes were calm on hers. 'Move down there,' he said as she gaped at him. 'Stay until the twins finish primary school at least, and then we can reassess.'

'But you hate being so far away from them,' she managed. 'You hate the travelling.'

He shrugged. 'I'll cope. It's more important that you're there for your mum. You lost enough years while that menace Vince was getting in between you – don't waste the time you have left now.'

Daisy stopped fighting and let the tears trickle down her cheeks. 'You'd do that for me?'

'Of course,' he said. 'For you and the boys. Like I said, they need you with them, in body and in mind. Another twelve months of Friday night traffic won't kill me.'

She put her cup on the counter and crossed the kitchen to wrap her arms around him. 'You're the best man I ever married.'

He rested his head on the top of hers. 'And you're the best woman I ever let go.'

Chapter Twenty-Nine

Once the decision had been made, the realities of staying on longer in Mistlethorpe dropped into place with an entirely bearable level of grumbling from Campbell and Finn. Daisy's biggest concern had been for their school places but Kit had been helpful there – an informal conversation with the head-teacher reassured Daisy that they would be welcome back for the new term. Both boys trotted happily into their classroom on the first day after the holidays, grinning at Alice and bursting to share stories of their summer adventures. Daisy herself had kept her head down, anticipating a barrage of inquisitive looks following Drew's sudden departure from the village but while some people had to know what had happened, no one seemed to be blaming her. If anything, she was on the receiving end of more nods, smiles and waves than she had been the previous term, which made her wonder whether Drew had been as far above suspicion as he'd believed. And of course Kit was there. His smile had been the most welcome of all.

September slipped by in a flurry of homework, muddy football boots and gently spiralling leaves. Daisy spent much of her time at the farm, undertaking the final adjustments to the page proofs of *The Secret Garden* and starting two new picture book projects that promised to be fun. Her agent, Phoebe, anticipated a flurry of interest in her work once the anniversary edition was published and had told Daisy in no uncertain terms to relax while she still could. 'Autumn is a sign to slow down and winter is a time to hibernate,' she advised Daisy down the phone. 'Then you emerge like a phoenix in the spring, ready for all the plaudits and wonderful jobs that are certain to be coming your way.'

It wasn't the worst advice Daisy had ever been given and she found it suited Half Moon Farm too. It had been a long time since the land had yielded much that needed to be harvested but she was aware that the apples were dropping from the trees in the orchard now that Drew wasn't there to pick them. She gave Nigel from the microbrewery permission to collect as many as he wanted but there were still too many and she didn't want to leave them for the wasps to infest, so she invited the children from Finn and Campbell's class over for an apple picking day. Emily had taken a basketful home to make into chutney and Daisy had even tried her hand at apple crumble, using a recipe of her grandmother's she'd found in an old notebook. It hadn't been bad – both Finn and Campbell had taken seconds, drowned in custard – and Daisy tried not to mind that it hadn't been a patch on Violet's. Perhaps the perfect crumble took practice.

The orchard mistletoe had caused Daisy some sleepless nights at first. For all Drew's faults, he had tended it well and she was loath to leave it to overrun, or worse, bring someone in to chop it all down. But Michaela from *Darling Buds* had stepped in, offering to take over both the management of the plants and Drew's old premises, *Merry Mistletoe*. 'There'll be a big order from the castle in December,' she told Daisy as she signed the contract and took the new set of keys. 'Drew used to say the money was a nice little stocking filler but I reckon I can do better than that.'

'Oh?' Daisy said curiously. 'Do they decorate the castle with it in December?'

'A bit,' Michaela said, 'if you know where to look. But most of the order is for the Winter Ball. It's on the first Saturday in December every year – the whole village is invited. I usually do the floral displays but this year I'll have mistletoe as well.'

'Good for you,' Daisy said, glad all over again that the lush green leaves and white berries would not be going to waste. 'I can't wait to see what you do with it.'

Stuart was as good as his word, navigating the traffic without complaint, even as the nights drew in and the weather took a turn for the miserable. Daisy had finished clearing out the room damaged by the leaking roof and had fitted it with a bed – on more than one occasion, Stuart had been obliged to stay at the farmhouse, thwarted by the vagaries of the Dartford Crossing or M25. Finn and Campbell loved it when that happened, and Daisy found she didn't mind so much cooking for him occasionally when it made their sons so happy.

At the start of November, two gilt-edged envelopes were delivered to the farmhouse. One was addressed to Mrs Rose Bickerstaff, the other to Miss Daisy Moon and Sons. Guessing what it must be, Daisy rescued her envelope from Finn's eager hands and carefully peeled it open. Just as she'd expected, it was their invitation to the Winter Ball at the castle on Saturday 2nd December. Finn wrinkled his nose when he saw it. '*Carriages at Midnight?*' he read. 'What are we, Victorians?'

Campbell gave him the dead-eyed stare he only seemed to use on his brother. 'It's fancy speak – it means cars. Taxis, minibuses . . .' He trailed off, clearly trying to come up with other modern forms of transport. 'Scooters. Not carriages with horses.'

Finn perked up. 'It'd be better if everyone arrived by dragon. Dad let us watch this show about them and they burned an entire city to the ground just by breathing on it.'

His brother pushed his glasses up his nose. 'And then we had to stop watching because that lady took all her clothes off.'

'Good,' Daisy said faintly. 'Why don't you take Granny her envelope? I bet she'll be excited too.'

'I bet she won't,' Campbell observed. 'She said last week that she'd rather die than set foot in Winterbourne Castle.'

Daisy took a deep breath. It was true that her mother had thawed towards Kit while he'd been acting in the role of bodyguard but her antipathy had soon resumed its natural forcefulness. Still, a personal invitation might work wonders, she thought as she watched the twins carry the envelope to the living room. She could only hope.

'Lucky you,' Emily sighed when she saw Daisy's invitation. 'I'd almost consider moving to Mistlethorpe if it meant getting one of those. What are you going to wear?'

'I have absolutely no idea,' Daisy admitted as her stomach went into gloomy freefall. She'd bought a beautiful ball gown for the Summer Ball but she couldn't possibly wear it again. 'I'll have to go shopping, I suppose.'

'You don't need to worry about what I'll be wearing,' Rose said, moving into the kitchen to slap her invitation onto the table. 'I'm not going.'

There was a blob of strawberry jam from breakfast on the table. Hastily, Daisy gathered up the ornate card and reached for the kitchen roll. 'Everyone will be there.'

'Except me,' Emily said mournfully.

'There you are, then,' Rose said with relish. 'Another reason to stay at home. We can have a nice night in watching the telly instead.'

Poor Emily looked as though she lost a pound and found a penny, and Daisy resolved to speak to Kit. Emily spent so much time at Half Moon Farm that she practically lived there. Surely there was room for one more guest at the ball, especially if it persuaded Rose to go too? 'I hear Elsie Wicks is going,' she offered, changing tack slightly.

Rose sniffed. 'Huh, she would. I bet she'll knit a dress, show herself up as usual.'

Daisy hid a smile. Her mother's rivalry with Elsie grew every time they attended knitting club together and she was quietly confident that Elsie's presence at the ball could only encourage Rose to finally make her peace with the Devereaux family. 'It's a month away yet,' she observed. 'See how you feel when we get a bit nearer.'

As the ball approached, Daisy began to grow even more apprehensive about what she might wear. The twins were easy – they'd been fitted for suits to attend a wedding on Stuart's side of the family in October and therefore had ready-made outfits that Daisy knew they would have grown out of by the time summer rolled around. She was glad of another opportunity to get some wear out of them. Daisy herself had nothing in her wardrobe that was remotely ball-worthy and a hopeful expedition to Canterbury had yielded nothing that was not drenched in sequins.

'Not that I have anything against sequins,' she'd confided in Nancy during their monthly cocktail night at the Green Dragon in Mistlethorpe. I just don't feel they'll suit the understated class of a Winter Ball.'

Her friend had nodded wisely. 'There is that. But aren't you going up to London for lunch with your agent next week? Can't you look for something then?'

She could, Daisy thought, and if she was really lucky, Phoebe might take pity on her and tell her where to find a hidden gem. Her agent was always immaculately dressed and never seemed to wear the same outfit twice, despite being snapped at all the most high-profile parties. 'That's a good idea,' she said to Nancy. 'What are you going to wear?'

'Head to toe sequins,' her friend said promptly. 'I don't do understated. In fact, I fully intend to upstage the glitterball.'

Daisy grinned at the image that presented. 'Nice.' She paused, remembering the Summer Ball guest list, which had been an altogether more select affair. 'Do you think Nick Borrowdale will be there this time?'

'I bloody hope so,' Nancy said. 'Michaela's going to give me my own sprig of mistletoe so I'm never knowingly unsnoggable.'

And now Daisy laughed, remembering how charming Nick had been and how lightheaded his gentle flirtation had made her feel. 'Who are you hoping to catch under the mistletoe?' Nancy went on, with a shameless wink. 'A certain pilot, maybe?'

'No one,' Daisy said firmly. 'I'm off men, remember?'

Nancy gave her an old-fashioned look. 'Got to get back on the horse sometime.'

'That's what you said last time,' Daisy pointed out. 'And looked what happened there.'

Her friend had the grace to look shamefaced. 'I didn't know Drew was a wrong 'un. I'd never have encouraged you if I did. But Kit is different. He really is a good man. And he's got a castle.'

She winked again, causing Daisy to frown. 'It's not his castle and I wouldn't be interested even if it was. We're friends and that's how I like it.'

'Keep an open mind, that's all I'm saying,' Nancy suggested. 'If you find yourself under the mistletoe with him – well, it would probably be rude not to.'

'It's not happening,' Daisy said, adopting the voice she used on the twins when they begged for just five more minutes of TV before bed. 'Now can we please change the subject? I don't want to think about kissing Kit, or anyone else for that matter.'

Except that was a lie, she acknowledged as Nancy gave up and launched into a tale about a rude boorish customer she'd thrown out of the café that morning. Because Daisy *had* thought about kissing Kit lately – more than once, in fact, and with or without mistletoe. But she could never get past the thorny issue of who he was. True, he wasn't the earl and never would be, but that didn't make him ordinary. She couldn't imagine planning the supermarket shop with him, or arguing over the recycling or taking the kids shoe shopping, although she assumed he must do that with Alice because she always had shoes, but still. They came from different worlds and while she suspected it would be heaven to kiss him, she couldn't help wondering what would come next. They might manage a fling, in the same way their grandparents had done decades earlier. But ultimately, she was a Moon and he was a Devereaux. Exactly the same barriers faced them that had kept Violet and Valentine apart. And Daisy's heart had taken enough of a bruising from Drew. She wasn't about to subject it to another battering. Besides, she valued Kit far too much as a friend to risk messing everything up over a kiss. She didn't want to go back to dreading the school run every day.

As the week of the ball arrived, Phoebe was only too happy to take her under her wing. 'You want Gigi's, on the King's Road,' her agent declared, stepping out into Charing Cross Road to hail a black cab after their lunch together. 'They have all the best dresses. I'm thinking midnight blue taffeta, perhaps, or sequinned—'

'No sequins,' Daisy interrupted, remembering Nancy's comment about outshining the glitterball. 'Taffeta sounds okay, as long as I don't end up looking like a blueberry.'

But it was a crimson velvet dress that caught her eye, with puff sleeves and a nipped-in waist above a skirt that ballooned ever so slightly to flatter her hips. Admittedly, there were some sequins scattered on the sleeves but she thought she might get away with those. The assistant helped to fasten the buttons at the back, then stood back with Phoebe to assess the effect. 'Gorgeous,' Phoebe declared, as Daisy spun self-consciously round and risked a look in the mirrors. 'You'll steal the show.'

'It is lovely,' the assistant said. 'Would Madam require some shoes to go with the dress? I have some velvet slippers that would be a dream.'

Daisy couldn't help recalling the Summer Ball, where she'd swapped her expensive shoes for a pair of wellies. But that was unlikely to happen this time. She nodded. 'Yes, please.'

Of course the slippers were perfect, as she'd known they

would be. She reviewed her reflection again, imagining this version of herself twirling through the candlelit ballroom. It was the kind of dress she would only wear once but wasn't that a small price to pay to feel like the belle of the ball? Even if she was still very much a Moon underneath. And then she took the dress off and saw the price tag.

'How much?' she gasped, feeling some of the blood drain from her face.

Phoebe waved her objections away. 'You can't put a price on the way it makes you feel,' she insisted. 'And you're making good money. I know – I see your royalty statements.'

There wasn't much Daisy could say to that: Phoebe knew exactly how much she earned and her statements were always healthy. But she'd never spent that amount of money on an item of clothing. She might buy a car for that amount – not a new one, certainly, but a fairly reliable one.

'Do you need another car?' Phoebe asked, when Daisy shared her observation.

'No.'

'Then buy the damn dress,' Phoebe said. 'Put it on eBay afterwards if you have to but wear it to the ball. I promise you won't regret it.'

Daisy returned home to find Kit's red Audi parked outside the farmhouse. Hurrying inside, she came across an incongruous scene: Rose was sitting in the living room with Kit, drinking tea and laughing at something he'd said. They both turned to gaze at her as she opened the door. 'Hello,' she said, glancing from one to the other. 'Is everything okay?'

Rose tipped her head. 'Kit here was just telling me about the guests at the Winter Ball. Do you know that nice man from the television is going to be there? The Irish one with the dancing eyes who plays that smuggler so roguishly.'

'Is he now?' Daisy said, looking at Kit for confirmation. 'What a treat. Shame you're not going.'

Her mother leaned forwards and Daisy swore she looked suddenly ten years younger. 'That's the other thing. Kit tells me he's found a ticket for Emily but she can't go if I stay at home. So it seems very selfish of me to make her miss out.'

Daisy hid a smile. 'I see your dilemma,' she said carefully. 'I'm sure you won't want to deprive Emily. Does that mean you'll be coming?'

'I think it does, yes. Kit is going to send a driver to collect us — won't that be nice?'

'Very,' Daisy said, turning to Kit with a smile of appreciation. 'Thank you.'

Nodding in acknowledgement, he got to his feet. 'I won't take up any more of your time, Mrs Bickerstaff, but I'm very much looking forward to seeing you at the ball.'

Daisy watched in disbelief as her mother actually blushed. 'What lovely manners,' she said, one hand fluttering girlishly. 'If only I remembered how to jive.'

It was all Daisy could do not to grin. 'I'm sure you've still got it, Mum. Why don't I show you out, Kit?'

When they reached the hallway, he noticed the enormous, ribbon-tied box from Gigi's. 'You've been shopping. Is that your dress?'

She nodded. 'Yes.'

His gaze sparkled with curiosity. 'Can I see it?'

'No!'

He sighed in good-natured resignation. 'Fine. I'll just have to wait. Oh, the car will arrive to pick you up at seven-thirty. I hope that's okay?'

'Thank you,' she said. 'And thanks for taking the trouble to visit Mum. I knew she wouldn't be able to resist a personal invitation.'

He nodded. 'That's me – utterly irresistible to elderly ladies.'

'Oh, shush,' she said, batting his arm lightly. 'I've seen you in a dinner jacket, remember? You're utterly irresistible to everyone.'

He glanced at her. 'I assure you I'm not,' he said, then cleared his throat. 'Cressida says she's looking forward to seeing you again.'

The thought of seeing the countess pleased Daisy too. 'Oh, how is she? How's the baby?'

'Both well,' he said. 'Cress is positively glowing and Louis is shamelessly stealing hearts across the London society scene. Hugh is hopelessly proud, so don't expect to get any sense out of him.'

'As he should be,' Daisy observed, smiling at the thought. 'I'm looking forward to seeing them all.'

Kit pulled a face. 'Oh, and Nick Borrowdale asked me to pass on his regards most particularly. He really is the most terrible flirt.'

She threw him a guileless look. 'I thought he was pretty good at it, actually.'

'For goodness' sake, don't tell him that,' he said, then paused. 'So I'll see you on Saturday.'

Daisy nodded. 'See you on Saturday. But also in the playground tomorrow morning.'

His mouth quirked into a grin. 'That too. See you soon, anyway.'

She watched him climb into the Audi, the very same car she'd reversed into all those months ago, and smiled to herself. The Winter Ball was promising to be a night to remember.

Chapter Thirty

Daisy's expectations were high but even she was blown away by the beauty of Winterbourne Castle lit up against the black velvet sky. On the seat beside her, both Finn and Campbell were rendered mute and even Rose had nothing bad to say, although Daisy was sure she must be acutely aware of the last time she'd visited the castle, when the Devereaux family had refused to allow her inside simply because of her name. That wasn't going to happen this time, Daisy wanted to reassure her but it appeared she didn't need to, because Kit was waiting at the top of the stairs, blond hair gleaming amid the golden light. He waited until the car had stopped, then crunched down the gravel towards them and Daisy thought he'd never looked more handsome.

'Mrs Bickerstaff,' he said, helping Rose out of the seat and tucking her hand into the crook of his arm. 'Would you allow me the honour of escorting you inside?'

Rose tutted and for an excruciating moment, Daisy

thought she might refuse. Then her mother spotted Elsie on the steps of the house and she drew herself up to her full height. 'Of course, Kit. Do lead on.'

Turning to glance at Emily, Daisy saw the carer's eyes were wider than dinner plates. 'Come with me,' she said, holding out her own arm. 'It's even grander on the inside.'

It seemed to Daisy that the ballroom was more brilliant than it had been in the summer. Every light glowed, augmented by candlelight that flickered and danced on the exquisite tall vases of evergreen bouquets. Vast globes of mistletoe hung suspended from the ceiling. Daisy knew the green and white had been trained around silver wire cages because she'd watched Michaela making one but she'd had no idea how spectacular they would look once in place. It was the trio of Christmas trees in the centre of the room that really drew the eye, however, lit with tiny twinkling lights and each topped with a sparkling star. The sight made Daisy pause at the entrance of the room, and beside her, Emily gasped. But the twins were made of sterner stuff, they spotted Alice in the crowd and darted away to join her, leaving Daisy in no doubt they would be up to no good very quickly indeed. Emily spotted Rose surrounded by a group of elderly women and hurried over to her, leaving Daisy alone to survey the crowd, which seemed considerably bigger than in the summer. In one corner, she saw Nancy, resplendent in sequins, exactly as she'd promised. The café owner feigned astonishment at Daisy's dress, creating a heart with her hands across the room. 'She's not wrong,' a smooth

Irish brogue cut into Daisy's thoughts. 'That is a banging dress you've got on.'

Daisy turned to find herself face to face with Nick Borrowdale. 'Thank you,' she said as he raised her hand to his lips and kissed it. 'I see you've lost none of your charm.'

He offered her a sorrowful smile. 'It's a blessing and a curse. A blessing because it allows me to talk to the most beautiful woman in the room, but a curse because she won't take me seriously.'

'Oh, stop it,' she said but she was still ridiculously flattered. There were many women here who were more beautiful than her but that didn't seem to matter when she was standing with Nick. 'So how are you?'

'Pining away for the love of a good woman, but otherwise fine,' he said. 'Busy. Too busy. And how are you? Still single, I hope?'

Daisy laughed, because his relentlessness held a charm of its own. 'Still single.'

Nick shook his head. 'I swear, if Kit doesn't do the decent thing soon, I'm going to—'

'You're going to what?' Kit asked smoothly, somehow managing to materialize out of thin air to stand next to them. He paused to place a kiss on Daisy's cheek, just beside her ear. 'You look incredible. Just radiant. And that dress . . .'

Nick gave him a mildly affronted look. 'Hey, don't come over here being all 007 and sweeping my girl off her feet with your poshness. I saw her first.'

Kit smiled. 'I really don't think you did. But I'm not here to quibble. The Earl and Countess Winterbourne request the pleasure of your company, Miss Moon.'

And now Nick rolled his eyes. 'Oh, and now he plays the trump card – the hoity-toity family.' His roguish gaze came to rest on Daisy once more and he smiled. 'I'll see you later, I hope. I'm pretty sure you owe me a dance.'

Daisy couldn't help laughing. 'My speciality is the Macarena, if that helps . . .'

'Sounds perfect,' Nick said, not missing a beat. 'I guarantee James Bond here thinks that's some kind of cocktail.'

'Have you quite finished insulting me?' Kit asked with long-suffering good grace. 'Thank you.'

He offered Daisy his arm and she took it, allowing him to whisk her through the crowd to where Hugh and Cressida waited, surrounded by a small crowd of mostly cooing ladies as they admired the latest addition to the Devereaux family. 'Daisy!' Cressida said, beaming in delight. 'I'm so happy to see you. What a gorgeous dress – I'm terribly jealous of your waist.'

'Don't be,' Daisy said, smiling at the other woman's radiant glow. 'I haven't touched bread for a week.'

At that, Cressida snorted, an unladylike laugh that caused a momentary silence among the assembled ladies. Eyes sparkling, Cressida tilted the baby towards her. 'May I present the Right Honourable Louis Devereaux? I'd offer you a cuddle but I'm afraid he might throw up on you and Kit would never speak to me again.'

'I'm sure he would do no such thing,' Daisy cooed, taking in the baby's chubby cheeks and clear blue-eyed gaze. She smoothed the velvet of her dress and sighed. 'But perhaps I'll wait until I'm slightly less easily stained.'

'Sensible,' Kit said. He turned to his brother, who was hovering at Cressida's elbow. 'Hugh, you remember Daisy, don't you?'

The earl gazed at her blankly for a moment, as though accessing a database of names and faces, then he gave a brisk nod. 'Daisy Moon. The lady of the letters.'

'That's right,' Daisy said. 'I must thank you for sharing them with me. I very much enjoyed reading them. They helped me understand what happened all those years ago.'

Hugh grunted. 'A pleasure.'

Cressida placed a hand on his arm. 'Daisy is a celebrated illustrator, darling. She's been inspired by the gardens here.'

'That's right,' Daisy said. 'They're so beautiful, even in winter when the flowers are all hibernating and the ground is hard with frost.'

'Helps to have a good gardener,' Hugh said. 'And what do you think of my boy, here?'

For one toe-curling moment, Daisy thought he meant Kit. Then the confusion cleared and she realized he meant the baby. Of course he meant the baby. 'Utterly adorable, you must be so proud,' she said, and when it seemed Hugh was waiting for more, she went on, 'Strong. Um, healthy. A good head of hair.'

She saw Cressida's lips twitch but Hugh seemed to appreciate her observations. 'He's a Devereaux. We all have good hair. Good teeth, too.'

Beside her, Kit seemed to be wincing. He tucked Daisy's hand into the crook of his arm once more. 'I must just show Daisy the outdoor lights. Will you excuse us? I promise I'll bring her back soon, Cress.'

The other woman smiled. 'Make sure you do.'

Daisy nodded a goodbye to both Hugh and Cressida, half-wishing she'd managed a little cuddle with the baby in spite of the danger to her dress. But for now Kit was leading her towards the tall doors that opened onto the formal gardens and she was vaguely surprised that he hadn't secured any champagne from one of the passing waiters. 'I did warn you about Hugh,' he said. 'Cress says he dotes on the boy already.'

'Who can blame him? He's clearly an angel,' Daisy replied, and shivered as the night air hit them. 'Ooh, it's chilly out here. Where are we going?'

'To the walled garden, of course,' he said and reached down to produce a pair of wellies.

Daisy couldn't help laughing. 'I see you're prepared this time.'

He nodded. 'I knew you'd be wearing the wrong shoes. But they do go beautifully with the dress.'

She leaned against his arm to remove the slippers and put the wellington boots on. They felt all wrong after the softness of the velvet but she soldiered on, trying not to galumph too inelegantly. 'Is this becoming a tradition?' she asked as they passed through the topiary hedges, lit up by swirling, multi-coloured lights.

'I don't know,' Kit replied. 'Are you going to come to every ball here?'

'Maybe,' she said, even though it was unlikely to happen if she moved back to Milton Keynes. 'Are you going to invite me?'

Kit pushed back the door to the walled garden and ushered her through. 'I think so, yes.'

But Daisy barely heard. Her breath was stolen by the sight before her. The garden should have been dark but instead it was lit with a thousand twinkling lights – some high and strung like fireflies against the night sky, some dotted among the flowerbeds and shrubs, and others wrapped around trees. Brightest of all was the horse chestnut tree, whose bare branches looked as though they were covered in tiny candles. It was a festival of radiance, a roar against the coming of winter. 'Do you like it?' Kit asked when she didn't speak and simply stared in wonder for a full minute.

She turned to him then, her face alight with joy. 'I love it. It's perfect.'

His face seemed to light up then too, as though she'd said exactly what he'd wanted to hear. 'Come on. I've put some seats under the tree.'

As Daisy got nearer, she saw tiny gold baubles hung from the branches of the chestnut tree, reflecting the shimmer and making it seem as though every inch was covered in light. There were two wooden chairs at the base of the trunk, softly lit and inviting. Both were bedecked with cushions and blankets and she saw a small side table to one side, laden with a champagne bucket and two crystal flutes. Once Kit had guided her to a seat, he popped the champagne. 'To you, Daisy,' he said, passing her a fizzing glass. 'For giving me the greatest gift I've ever had, apart from Alice.'

She stared at him, not understanding. 'Sorry?'

He smiled. 'We're celebrating something incredible. I still can't quite believe it but Hugh took me to one side this evening, before the ball began, to tell me he's spoken to the family solicitor. As of January, Winterbourne Manor will no longer be part of the earldom, or automatically passed on following the law of primogeniture.'

Daisy still wasn't sure she followed. Where had she heard that term before? 'Ah. And that's something to celebrate, is it?'

Kit held her gaze, his eyes warm. 'It is, even though it also means baby Louis won't inherit the manor when he's older, even though he keeps the title of earl and the castle itself.' He took a deep breath. 'And that's because Hugh has passed the deed to me. It all needs to be finalized, legally speaking, but as of next year, Winterbourne Manor will belong to me.'

Daisy gasped, almost spilling her drink. Cressida had been so sure nothing could be done that she'd almost forgotten the conversation in the library back in the summer. 'Really? That's incredible – you must be so happy.'

He beamed at her. 'I am. It means security for Alice and

me. It means I can start planning our future. It means—' he hesitated, his smile faltering a little as he regarded her earnestly. 'It means I have something to offer.'

She shook her head. 'You've always had loads to offer, I told you that before. But this is brilliant, I'm so thrilled for you.' She held her champagne flute towards his. 'Congratulations, Kit.'

They chinked glasses and each took a sip. As always, the bubbles fizzed in Daisy's nose, making her want to sneeze. 'It's all thanks to you,' Kit said, his expression growing more serious. 'You and Cressida. I won't forget that.'

'I should hope not,' Daisy said, grinning. 'That's why I expect an invitation to every party you throw, even when I eventually go back to Milton Keynes.'

An odd look crossed his face. 'I think I can promise that. But there's something else I wanted to ask you,' he said, reaching across to gently take the glass from her and put it on the table. He took her hands, eased her carefully to her feet, then cleared his throat. Daisy waited, watching the fairy lights twinkle and dance. Perhaps it was the excitement of his big news but whatever Kit wanted to say must be important, she thought in wonder. She'd never seen him so nervous.

'You might not remember this but when we talked about finding a forever person, months ago, I said that I didn't have anything to offer them,' he began. 'Well, now, thanks mostly to you, I do. No, don't interrupt, I need to say this.' Pausing to collect his thoughts, he fixed her with a quizzical gaze.

'And I've known for some time that the person – the woman
– I wanted to offer everything to was you.'

It wasn't at all what Daisy had been expecting. She felt
her jaw drop. 'But—'

'No, don't say anything yet. Wait until I've finished.' Kit
wrapped his fingers around hers so that his warmth infused
her skin. 'I've thought about telling you this for so long and
now it's finally happening I can't find the bloody words.'
Taking a breath, he tried again. 'The thing is, I love you,
Daisy. You're on my mind all the time, when I wake up, in
my dreams, even when I'm flying. Most especially when I'm
flying, to be honest. I don't think I've met anyone like you
– you're not scared of anything, you see what you want and
you go and get it.' Stopping, he shook his head. 'I can't
imagine my life without you, Daisy. I don't want to imagine
it without you. And I hope – god, I really hope . . . Please
say you'll be my forever person. Please say you love me too.'

The lights around Daisy's head spun and she felt as though
she was whirling through the night on a rollercoaster. Had
she just heard him correctly? Had cool, impassive, maybe
even a tiny bit arrogant Kit Devereaux really said all those
wonderful things? Had he actually just told her he loved
her? And had he begged her to say she loved him too? It
was all too strange, she must be asleep and dreaming. And
yet . . . she could feel the coldness of the ground radiating
into her toes, was aware of goosebumps raised on her skin
where the night air touched it, knew her fingers were shielded
from the chill by Kit's touch. And she could see him in front

of her, anxiously waiting for a reply. All the strangeness fell away as she gazed into his eyes – those blue, blue eyes – and she remembered where she was, beneath the horse chestnut tree that bore the initials of their grandparents, a testament to a love that could never be. The magic vanished and Daisy knew she was going to break both their hearts with her reply. 'I'm sorry, Kit. I can't.'

The words hung in the air, then melted into nothing as though the night itself was disappointed in them. Kit waited to see if she would say more, then shook his head. 'Can I ask why?'

She sighed, for the first time wishing she hadn't found Violet's letters. 'Look around. Here we are in this glorious garden – a garden my grandmother helped to build and your grandfather owned. This is why I can't be your forever person, Kit. I'm a Moon and you're a Devereaux and that is never going to change, no matter how many pretty stories we tell ourselves. We don't fit together. You know that.'

He ran a despairing hand through his hair. 'I don't know that. We're not our grandparents, Daisy.'

'No, but you're still – not quite an earl but a long way from ordinary.' She blinked hard at the glowing garden. 'We don't belong in the same worlds.'

He groaned in frustration. 'Times have changed. I don't give a fig if you're a Moon or a Star or a Smith – no one cares. My family doesn't – Hugh told me years ago to find someone I could love, no matter who they were. And that's you, if you'll only let go of the past and let it be.'

A breeze made the lights shimmer and blur. Daisy stared at Kit, her heart thudding. Every cell in her brain was telling her he was wrong, that it didn't matter what she felt because there was an invisible barrier between them, an insurmountable wall that meant they could never be together. And yet her heart clung onto the line about the past . . . Hadn't she said almost the same thing to her mother in the summer, exhorting her to let go of the past so that it couldn't hurt her anymore? Wasn't Daisy guilty of doing exactly that now, clinging onto the wreckage of an ill-fated love affair when what she wanted to do more than anything was to wrap her arms around Kit and kiss him? So perhaps, she thought dully, shivering slightly as the wind chilled her skin, she should stop trying to think her way out of this and just follow her heart.

Evidently realizing she was cold, Kit draped a blanket across her shoulders. The gesture caught Daisy by surprise but it was so thoughtful, so perfectly him, that it warmed her inside as well as out. He was always looking after her, even though she was capable of looking after herself, there for her without ever once intruding. It was what she missed most about Stuart, even though she no longer loved him the way she once had. And now Kit was watching her, waiting with hope and dread in his eyes and she couldn't bear to see him that way any longer. Without another thought, Daisy stepped towards Kit and stood on tiptoes to press her lips to his.

It was like a glass of water after a week in the desert, she thought afterwards, although right at that moment she was only aware of drinking Kit in, of slaking a thirst that had been troubling her for longer than she could remember. She had no idea when she had fallen in love with him, she only knew that she wanted his lips on hers here, now, in this garden and forever afterwards. She felt his arms slide around her, heard him sigh as she tangled her fingers in his hair, and she wanted the kiss to go on and on. If they could just stay like this, in this perfect moment, nothing could ever go wrong. And then Kit broke away, leaving her mouth swollen and hot even though it had been the gentlest of kisses. He smiled at her, a tentative, uncertain smile that she hardly recognized. 'Is that a yes, Daisy Moon?'

And suddenly, beneath the chestnut tree and bathed in shimmering light, all her fears evaporated. There would be problems – there always were – but if he kissed her like that every day for the rest of their lives, there was nothing they couldn't overcome.

Summoning up a wavering smile of her own, Daisy took a breath in and let it out. 'Yes, Kit Devereaux,' she said, reaching up to caress his cheek with fingers that hardly felt like her own. 'I will be your forever person. But why don't we start with right now?'

The End

Acknowledgements

First thanks go, as always, to Jo Williamson of Antony Harwood Ltd, for almost fifteen years (!!) of support, guidance and excellent lunches. Second in line is my perfect editor, Molly Crawford – patient, encouraging and queen of pom-pom waving editorial comments. I consider myself lucky to have you – thanks for all you do. I am blessed to be published by Simon and Schuster UK – the team go from strength to strength. Many thanks to everyone on the Books and the City team but a special mention to Pip Watkins for her wonderful cover designs, and to SJ Virtue for being an absolute champion of all our books.

There are always people who help me along the way of each book – extremely grudging thanks to the stranger whose car I reversed into, inspiring Kit and Daisy's first meeting. Ha ha. But I am genuinely indebted to artist Claire Henley for talking me through her career in a way that helped me understand how Daisy became an artist – thank you so much for your generosity. Chris Callaghan was kind enough to share his experiences in the RAF, which formed the basis of Kit's career and made me laugh a lot. Hat tip to Clare Watson for her advice on installing fibre link cabling – truly a woman of many talents. Whenever I need a medical condition, I go to Charlotte Dennis, who has never failed to diagnose my characters, as well as dragging me out to run when I need it. Huge thanks to Geoff Crawford and North Weald Flight Training for allowing me to take to the skies – I've used artistic license with the many of the details and any mistakes are absolutely my own but it was an experience I will never forget. The glorious walled garden at Winterbourne is shamelessly stolen from Jenny Williams, of the Laundry Garden on Instagram (@thelaundrygarden). One day, I will go in person but I spent many happy watching Jenny's stories and imagining my characters there. Lastly, I must thank my aunt and uncle, Pauline and Francis Green, with whom I spent so many idyllic summers in the Kentish countryside. It was Pauline who gave me the boxes of wartime letters that inspired Violet and Valentine's story (yes, there really *was* a Valentine!) and I will be forever grateful for the privilege of reading them.

My most heartfelt thanks go, as ever, to my family – T and E, who are the reason for everything, and Luna the Labrador, who wants me to finish this so we can go for a walk. And finally, thank you to my gorgeous readers – I hope you enjoy your time at Half Moon Farm as much as I did. I have a feeling we'll be back there some day . . .

If you enjoyed *Return to Half-Moon Farm*, you'll love...

Escape to Darling Cove

Eve has always lived on Ennisfarne, an idyllic island just off the coast of Northumberland and only accessible when tides are low. There she runs a bar overlooking Darling Cove, a heavenly horseshoe-shaped beach named after her seafaring ancestors, whose links to the Farne Islands stretch back centuries.

Logan is a famous photographer desperate to evade the limelight after a difficult break-up. Renting a cottage from Eve, he chooses Ennisfarne in the hope of anonymity but is immediately spellbound by its natural beauty.

The pair don't get off to the best start, butting heads over Eve's adorable but boisterous Chocolate Labrador. But when Logan's true identity is revealed, Eve realises her new tenant isn't quite the man she thought he was. Is it too late to start again or will Logan's island escape be over almost before it's begun?

AVAILABLE NOW IN PAPERBACK, EBOOK AND AUDIO

**SIMON &
SCHUSTER**

London · New York · Sydney · Toronto · New Delhi